HAUNTED PRINCESS

Poppy Rose Solomon

First published by Poppy's Pages in 2024

www.poppyspagesediting.com

Written by Poppy Rose Solomon

Edited by Pauline Menchavez and Ellyssa Paik

Cover art by Robert Ixer

Cover design by Haylee Buswell (HB Pencil Designs)

Paperback ISBN: 978-0-6456986-4-0

eBook ISBN: 978-0-6456986-5-7

A catalogue record of this book is available from the National Library of Australia

The author acknowledges the Gubbi Gubbi people, the traditional owners of the land this book was written and published on. Respect and gratitude are extended to elders past and present.

MAP

The World of Woken Kingdom

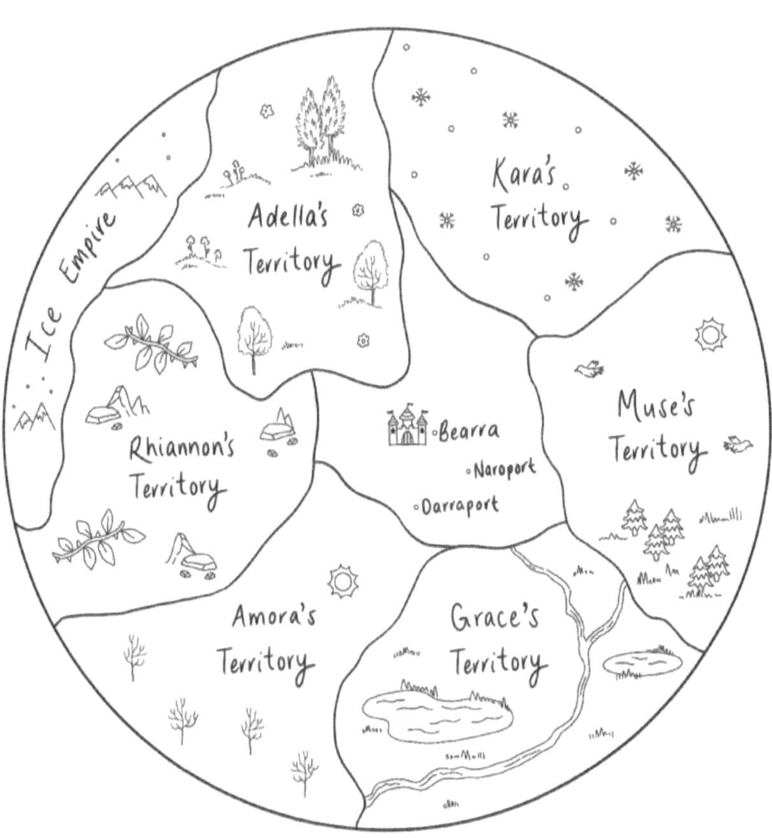

PROLOGUE

SOMEWHERE, SOMETIME . . .

'*Dee*,' Relia choked. She could barely register the shouts of the castle guards or the panicked gasps of the party guests being forced towards the doors. Not when she was being torn from the person she loved most.

Dawn's eyes should have been scanning the ballroom, past the layers of tulle and jewels, searching for Relia. Instead they were fluttering closed. People swarmed around her, maids, doctors, nobles, while Relia was being ushered away.

A guard's voice boomed over the crowd. 'Out of the kingdom! Anyone who is not Bearran must leave *now*!'

No. Not Relia. She couldn't be sent away from her soulmate.

Shouts echoed through the ballroom, piercing the atmosphere with terror. Relia sprinted towards Dawn, wading through the confused party guests, but guards ripped her back, tearing the puffy sleeves of her red dress.

Relia puffed as she mustered all the strength in her small body to force her way through the wall of guards and guests, reaching for her love, but it was no use. She tripped over someone's foot and smacked her knees on the ballroom's stone floor. She yelped, crimson hair fanning as it fell from its elaborate bun. More hands were on her, steering her out of the castle.

She fought for her breath, cradling her bleeding knees. How could this be? They had prepared for this. The entire kingdom knew of the curse. The entire world. But no one saw it as *real*. Dawn was too kind, too powerful, too good, for such evil to even touch her. Yet as the curse unfolded now, the fear of this wickedness Relia had always known would arrive was not only palpable – it engulfed the entirety of the world, the entirety of her being.

The fairies altered the curse; that was the single hope Relia could hold on to. Instead of death on the princess's seventeenth birthday, as the dark fairy Kara had wanted, Dawn would fall asleep. And along with her, the fairies would put the entire kingdom of Bearra to rest, so that she would not be alone when she finally woke – days, months, years, even centuries in the future.

Most Bearrans were utterly unaware of this. Only those in the castle, those invited to Dawn's birthday ball, were told of the sleep that was to consume all of Bearra. While a select few of the attendees were the kingdom's people, most guests were foreign lords and ladies, queens and kings Lire deemed important enough.

While it was one thing for the Bearrans to be trapped, with their homes and families intact, the foreigners had everything to lose if they fell under the fairies' spell. Everyone who was not Bearran needed to evacuate, or they would never know their homes and families again.

Now that the curse was taking effect – now that Dawn was truly falling, dropping in and out of sleep, and it could no longer be denied – the rest of the kingdom had to be forced into slumber. Now, fairies and partygoers hurried to make the necessary arrangements.

They had been told there was a choice, whether to stay or go, but Relia now realised this luxury was only for the Bearran nobles. Shouts of indignation fell on the guards' deaf ears as the foreign guests were rushed out.

She was being rushed out. Swept up in the crowd.

'No. I won't go,' she whispered under her breath, clenching her fists.

Relia always planned to stay, whether or not the curse was real. She and Dawn wished it wasn't – that they could be married one day, and there would never be a prince in the future to take Relia's place. Just like everyone else, they had been naïve.

They were too happy, too careless. Dawn had taken Relia up to her rooms as the guests were distracted by dancing, and in that stolen moment, they shared a kiss. In a fit of giggles, they fell into a pile of half-finished dresses. And Dawn pricked her finger on a needle, just as Kara predicted.

Knowing they made a mistake, Relia and Dawn raced back to the party, pretending nothing happened. But Dawn's eyes began drifting closed, and that was when the castle burst into chaos. That was when

Relia was shoved away and became a face lost in a crowd, no longer Dawn's lover but someone to be removed like a criminal.

Bristling staff now rushed to take Dawn away as the strength left her legs; she had to be held up by maids, who waited for guards to help them take Dawn to a safe place to sleep. Relia cried out again, still unable to free herself from the drowning of bodies as she watched all these people touch her – the once formidable royal turned helpless.

They were on opposite sides of the ballroom, the stars and moon no help in lighting Relia's way as they shone through the large windows. There was so much space between them, a universe holding them apart. Tears escaped her eyes as she realised it was too late for her to hide in the kingdom. But she wouldn't stop trying, not until it was really the end.

Relia tried to shift forward again, her scratched arms and sore knees pinching, but a large, armoured arm swung out, blocking her once again. A number of guards eyed her like predators, as if they wanted to get her out *specifically*. Others shouted at the rest of the partygoers, ushering them to the doors. Relia lifted her eyes and searched for a way around the blockade. The ballroom had emptied enough to make her an easy target; much as she hated crowds, she was discouraged to find she could no longer use the fog of people as a cover.

There were hands all over her, just like there were hands all over Dawn, but these were not gentle and protective; these gripped with a searing, angry strength.

Relia snapped her eyes to the princess, getting as many glimpses of her swaying and stumbling love as she could before she would inevitably be taken away. The golden, tight curls. The bronze skin, stark against a baby-blue gown that was now dragging on the floor. Her round face, her curves, those stunningly full lips partially open in exhausted gasps. Relia knew every speck of emerald and ebony in the princess's half-lidded hazel eyes. Even in this state, everything about Dawn shimmered with her blessings. But Relia loved her for so much more than that. She loved her for what was underneath her beauty.

Dee. My love.

But all that was beneath her beauty was gone: her expressive face, the energy of her body, all frozen as the princess finally collapsed into sleep, sinking fully into the arms of her mother and father, who had appeared behind her.

'Out!' a guard holding Relia by the shoulders screamed in her face, pulling her back to reality. 'Go before I *throw* you out.'

'But I'm with the princess!' she pleaded, her voice cracking. 'I'm not— I'm supposed to stay!'

'Not anymore,' another guard growled, ripping her in the direction of the doors.

'This isn't what she wants – you *know* she wants me here – she'll be furious when she finds out—'

'Well she isn't in charge, is she?' He gestured to the princess, just her curls visible as she was carried out and away. Forever.

Relia trembled, tears threatening to fall as her anger at the guards dissolved into despair; she was defeated, devastated. There was no way she could reach Dawn now. So she did as she was trained to do by the noble family who raised her. She hiked up her scarlet gown and stood tall. She was a lady. Dawn had called her beautiful just hours before. She had gushed about how the gown matched her red hair, how she loved the way it fitted her waist, how it made her skin glow. So even though Relia wanted to tear it off, desperate to breathe in the constricting fabric, she lifted her chin, wiped her eyes, and smoothed out the wrinkles in her dress. The red now shone like blood. That's what it felt like. Blood pouring from her body as her heart broke, knowing she might never see her beloved Dawn ever again.

Feeling as if she were in a dream, she let the guards escort her out of the castle.

Beyond that, she walked . . . and walked . . . not sure where to go. But as soon as she was outside the walls that bordered the kingdom and out of site, her ladylike facade broke – and she vomited in the grass. A carriage was waiting to take her home, but there were so many people, so many tears, so much shouting and rushing . . . Relia would have done anything to be back in the quiet of Dawn's room, barely half an hour earlier. They should have stayed; Dawn should have fallen asleep in *her* arms.

She covered her ears with her hands and sunk to the ground. Yes, Relia had been taught to always be calm, stable, charming, and witty; the perfect lady. But that wasn't her. She was sensitive, easily jarred. So unlike Dawn, so strong and confident. The curse should have hurt someone like Relia, someone the world didn't need, not Dawn, who could change hearts and minds.

Relia fought for her breath. Although it was night, Bearra was always, always too warm. Humid. Like water in her lungs. The shouting of the evacuating guests and the forceful guards provoked her nausea even more, an already angry creature poked and prodded. Was it not bad enough, how she felt on the inside? Why was the world determined to not let her rest? Why did everything have to be so loud, so bright?

Relia stared out with dead eyes, clenching grass as the guests hopped into carriages, dissipating towards the kingdoms they hailed from. It felt like hours as they poured out of the triarue gates. The candlelight and stars turned blurry through her teary eyes. She waited and waited, as if someone could save her, take her hand and bring her back to Dawn, as if Kara herself might return and take back her curse, hold them both and tell them she was sorry.

After some time, the world was almost quiet. Most of Bearra was asleep. Only a select few of the kingdom's people had been invited to the princess's birthday ball – most guests were foreign lords and ladies, queens and kings. Those without such rank slept soundly, or worked into the night, with no knowledge that the fairies were about to send them into magical rest along with their princess.

The castle was silhouetted by the moon, its squarish shape a dark monster that contained Relia's princess.

Relia was drawn out of her daze with a gasp as vines wove along the kingdom's walls, tendrils snaking like a water creature. Unimaginably huge stalks with lethally sharp, thick thorns glowed in the night with scarlet magic. Rhiannon – the fairy of bravery – flew above. She was growing them with her power, building a cage around the kingdom. Her dragon's wings only cemented Relia's horror – a dark fairytale unfolding her greatest nightmares.

Rhiannon's barrier would protect Bearra, but in doing so, it would keep anyone who could save them out as well. It would keep Relia out. A prince was supposed to save Dawn; that was part of the fairies' alterations to the curse. A prince who would be, supposedly, impossibly, her soulmate. But this was the flaw in their plan, because Relia knew that no man would save Dawn. No prince would be Dawn's soulmate, not even in a thousand years.

Bearra was *gone*.

A rainbow of magical colours shone around the kingdom as the fairies' magic took hold, putting the kingdom to sleep. The glow seeped through the cracks of the vines, which were so thick now that Relia could barely see into the kingdom. Purple, pink, red, orange, yellow, and blue, shimmered all around her, encasing the kingdom in rest, shrouding Dawn in layers of magical protection.

Relia tried to tell herself this was good. Bearra needed the safeguard. Many other kingdoms coveted their triarue mines. If all of Bearra's people were vulnerable, anyone would take the opportunity to attack. Dawn might be lost to Relia, but at least she was safe. Maybe she would be blessed with endless, wonderful dreams in her immortal sleep. That was better than death, wasn't it?

Relia wiped away her tears. Her carriage was alone, the driver waiting for her patiently. She couldn't bear to leave, but the pain was getting to be too much. At least if she could be on her way home, she would be back to the comfort of her own bed within a few days. Delaying only hurt her more.

Tearing her eyes from the glowing kingdom, she turned to leave.

But a flash of lilac caught her eye. *Wings.* A purple dress and light hair. Lire, the patron fairy of Bearra, fluttered over the vines. She was coming Relia's way, but Relia shook her head and made for her carriage. The fairy would only be coming to tell her to leave, if she had even noticed her there at all.

But the fairy caught her gaze, and Relia knew that the fairy wished to speak with her. They were both close with Dawn, after all. When Lire's feet touched the ground in front of her, Relia bowed respectfully, her shoulders still shaking.

'My dear,' the fairy said, her voice so lovely, so calming and wise, it instantly put Relia at ease.

She remembered the times Lire showed her and Dawn magic and wonder. When she took them to a quiet canal and enchanted the fish to glow as they flitted upstream. When she brought glittering lights, like stars she pulled from the sky, into the castle air the time she caught Relia crying. When she let Dawn and Relia stay in a suite in her estate, showed them around the beautiful grounds she had cultivated. No, the fairy never approved of Dawn and Relia being romantic, but she always showed them both care. She was a mother figure Relia could trust when she needed space from her adoptive parents. Someone who could bring her wonder in times of depression. And Relia knew that was special, because few people had that privilege.

So now, how was she to know that the world was full of liars, when she'd never been given a reason not to have trust?

'You poor, sweet thing,' Lire said. 'I understand the pain you're in, seeing your friend lost. I too grieve the princess. I've come to make sure you are . . . alright.'

Relia almost laughed. *Friend. Alright.* She couldn't have been more inaccurate.

Dawn and Relia had been friends for a long time, of course. As girls of high status, although they lived far apart, they saw each other often. They fell in love slowly, hidden in corners of parties and balls, playing in gardens as their parents had meetings. But any romance between them could only happen if Dawn's parents approved, and any overstepping, any mistakes, risked their entire friendship. As they grew older, they began to love each other quietly, kissing each other's cheeks, talking into the night, knowing they might never really be able to be together – and not caring a single bit.

Now the nightmare they always dreaded but never quite believed had come true. They would never see each other again.

Lire tilted her head, awaiting Relia's response.

'I wanted to be in there with her,' she whispered to the fairy, breaking into tears again. She should care about her image in front of Lire, how this reflected on her family, but she could barely think over the pain of her aching chest. So she let herself sob, let her makeup run. 'I should have been allowed to stay.'

The fairy shook her head. 'The terms of the spell were clear. Only Bearra was to sleep. Everyone else had to leave. It would not be fair to do it any other way.'

But Lire wasn't the fairy of fairness. She may have been wise, but that didn't mean she knew everything. Relia hated her for a moment, then immediately felt guilty about it. None of this was Lire's fault. She'd never been anything but kind.

'You loved her, didn't you?' Lire said, curiously but gently. 'You loved the princess, and that's why you wanted to stay. You were prepared to leave behind your entire life to be with her.'

Relia nodded, biting her bottom lip. She felt like such a child, so small and weak in front of this immortal being who looked down at her, whose wings towered above. How could she stand there, sobbing, in front of a deity?

'Then I'm sorry to you,' Lire said. 'Heartbreak is such a terrible thing.'

'You don't understand.' Relia looked at Lire pleadingly. 'No one does. This . . . It isn't fair. Why can't I be with her? Why— Why would Kara do this?'

'Because some people are so spiteful that they do not care who is caught up in their revenge.' Lire sighed. 'I blame myself, partially. If I had made sure Kara was never left out of our world, if I had been kinder to her, asked her to come to Dawn's blessing ceremony . . .'

'It wasn't your fault,' Relia said automatically. Everyone knew this. Kara was the darkness to Lire's light. She met the fairy's eyes. 'Please, tell me, how am I supposed to live, knowing I will never see her again?'

Lire gazed at her for a long while, a hand on her shoulder, touching her skin where her sleeve had torn. 'My darling Relia,' she said softly. 'I have an idea that might help you, but I see how pained you are, and . . .'

'What is it?' Relia pulled her hands together as if begging. 'I'll do anything. *Anything.*'

Everyone knew to trust the fairies. They were magic, they were power, they were kindness and all things blessed. So, when Lire said, 'You have to die,' Relia believed her.

'Are you saying Dawn is never coming back?' Relia's brows arched up in the middle, her bottom lip wobbling. 'Because if she's not, then maybe you're right. A world without her, maybe it's best that I simply—'

Lire held up a hand. 'No, that isn't what I'm suggesting. Relia, all hope is not lost. You know of Muse's Forest, yes? For hundreds of years, Muse has chosen women who die there to live on as spirits. Women who had been shunned by society, hurt by men, or worse. Haunting the forest forever, leading an undead existence, but knowing peace far from the cruel lives they led.'

Relia did not understand. Wasn't it better to be . . . *gone*? If Dawn was lost forever, she would be too, just as Lire suggested.

'The princess will one day wake, along with her kingdom,' Lire continued. Her eyes sparkled in the rainbow of the fairies' magic, now dimming as Bearra fell to sleep. The light created streaks through Relia's wet eyes. 'It could be ten years, or a hundred, or a thousand, but one day a prince will find his way into Bearra and wake the entire kingdom with a kiss. The only way you can see your love again is if you can find a way to live forever. And the only way for you to do that . . . is to die.'

Relia let out a sob. 'But— But if you're so sure someone can wake her, why can't I be the one? I may not be a prince, but I'm from a noble family, and I *know* that Dawn and I are soulmates. I should be the one to break the curse. *Now*. Why should I wait a hundred years for a man to do something I could do tonight?' Her brashness surprised her, but she knew she was right.

Lire's expression hardened. 'You are not Dawn's soulmate, and you are not royalty. I will not have you bring shame to her and her kingdom by pretending you are any match to her. The princess will marry the prince who wakes her. Bearra will be saved by him, and he will become their new king. It is destined.'

'B-But—'

Lire exhaled and softened. 'What I am offering you is your best option, my dear. You may never be with the princess in the way you want – it was never an option and never will be – but by immortalising yourself, you can see her again one day. Is death not a small price to pay for what you long for?'

Relia trembled with frustration and grief. Lire's words bore into her soul. The fairy was right. Relia never truly had a chance with Dawn, no matter how much they cared for each other. Even if Dawn woke within Relia's lifetime, their love was doomed. But this, a way to see her again, to just talk to her . . .

'I would pay the price,' Relia said.

'Good girl.' Lire smiled kindly, as if everything were coming together perfectly, as if everyone was happy, despite how awful every aspect of this night had been. 'I'll help you with this, but I would ask you to do me a favour, for Dawn's sake. Relia, I need you – Bearra needs you – to use your time as a spirit to scout for me. Find out what you can about Muse, listen to the wanderers and whisperers of the forest.'

'I'm not sure I—'

'You do this, and when Dawn wakes, I promise I will come back for you. I will bring you back from the forest, back from the dead, and back to Dawn. You can never be with her, but I can give you a life in Bearra. I can give you everything you want. You swear your loyalty to me, and it's all yours.'

Relia blanched, clutching her stomach. So much had happened in the last few hours, she wasn't sure she knew what was real anymore. How could she be here? How could this be happening? Had anyone, in all the world, ever felt such deep horror? But, Lire's proposition, did it not make sense to agree?

'What about my family?' Relia asked. 'Can they know? Can they visit me?'

Lire shook her head sadly. Her wings lowered. 'Anyone's knowledge would compromise our goals, Relia. I'll tell your driver to return home and tell your family that you were stuck in Bearra when it was closed off. They cannot come looking for you. Your anonymity in Muse's Forest, and once you return, is vital. Otherwise, how can you be a good spy for Dawn?'

'I suppose . . .' Relia began to cry. Again. Although she was willing to do anything to see Dawn once more, the thought of her family not knowing the truth sent a fresh sting through her gut. No, they were not her real parents – they were long dead – but she did love them. She hated the idea of lying to them. Of being in Muse's Forest, not far from where they lived, but unable to ever talk to them again. And although she felt right now that she had nothing left to live for, she was terrified of dying. But it wouldn't be *dying,* would it? 'Are you sure,' Relia said, 'that if I die there, I will become a spirit? And not simply *die?*'

'My sister Muse has pity for women in pain,' Lire said. 'I have no doubt that she will choose you to join her forest. And if not, I will find a way. You will invent a new story. That you loved a boy who became stuck in Bearra, tearing you apart. You will reinvent yourself with a false name, construct a new persona. Same story, different characters. Can you do it? Will you do it for the princess, if you claim to love her so much?'

Relia swallowed, wiped her tears once more, and raised her head. 'I will.'

CHAPTER 1

The girl tosses the dishcloth at me and I screech as I jump back, the dirty sink water drenching my apron. '*Elsie!*' I'm not one to get angered easily, but frustration boils beneath my ribcage. She can *never* let me rest.

Elsie rolls her eyes, picking up the cloth from where it splatted on the floor. She drops it in the sink with ceremonious irony. 'Oh, who cares! You do know we aren't really servants, don't you? Have some fun.'

I bite my lip, silently begging her to keep her voice down. The kitchens of Bearra's castle are bustling as always; a double-edged sword. More people to blend in with. More people to discover we shouldn't be here. 'We mustn't be caught, and we mustn't lose our jobs.'

'And if they catch us?' Lilac magic dances around her hand. Elsie appears fifteen at most, wide-eyed and bright, but I know the truth, and she knows I know. She's older than me and just as powerful. 'What can they do?'

'They aren't weak.' I place a hand over hers as if smothering a fire. 'And if they don't kill you, Lire will.'

'Blah, blah,' she sulks, getting back to work.

She's lucky. When Lire brought us back to join her army, she got a second chance at a life she thought she lost long, long ago. Lire gave her an even *better* life. A job in a castle. A role as a spy. Elsie got her body back, and new magic. She would never be hungry, she would never be weak. She would take back the power she'd always longed for; she was *excited* to serve Lire, no matter what Lire's plan was.

The other girls, the other spirits, they're not like me. Lire selected spirits she thought might wish to join her. But she chose me when I was still alive.

Most spirits were driven mad over their time in Muse's Forest. So many had been killed by men, tortured by men, that they craved revenge after death. They loved drawing in unsuspecting male travellers to the lake, haunting them, taunting them into senselessness before letting them drown.

Those other girls faced too much to care for the world – they lost their hearts, so why not take this opportunity Lire was giving them to help destroy everything? And Muse was happy to give Lire her spirits – not that her consent would matter much now. Not when she's . . .

I shake my head. I still can't believe a fairy is *dead*, let alone murdered by a mortal.

But that's the least of my concerns. I never had any love for Muse, and I don't want to help Lire. I *must*. She's been using me as her eyes and ears for a century. No one else knows the princess, knows Bearra, like me. Who else could spy on Dawn, learn her secrets, gain her trust?

I get to be with her again, that's the deal. Lire told me that one day I could come back to Bearra. That I could never be with Dawn, but I could at least be near her. She didn't tell me I couldn't be *Relia*. She didn't tell me Dawn could never know I was with her again. She didn't tell me I'd have to betray her.

I trusted the fairy, and I thought she loved Dawn. I didn't know, not until it was too late, that Lire was not on Dawn's side. And that consequently, neither was I.

Lire used magic to modify my appearance beyond recognition. My red hair became brown. My long nose became small. My skin became pale and freckled, and my body became smaller, everything slighter and slimmer. I was masked; plain, tiny, and easy to blend in. Even my voice had to be altered.

Lire made it clear that if I gave Dawn any indication of who I might really be, my time here would be over. And, *fairies*, it hasn't been easy.

Carlotta, the princess's maid that I have become, is quiet. She is loyal. She's mild-mannered but kind. She stays in her place and listens. Carlotta is a person I can tolerate hiding within, but every day I watch Dawn through eyes that aren't my own, and she watches back with such a foreign gaze – the way a princess looks at her staff, not her lover. And every day, my heart breaks.

But I wouldn't change a thing. Because finally, after a hundred years of waiting, a hundred years of torment, I am with her again. Betraying her and lying to her is such a small price to pay.

At night I cry, curled up in a ball as the guilt makes me nauseous. Then, when I see the princess's face each morning . . . I remember why I'm here.

'You are an awful maid, you know,' Elsie says, splashing me from the sink. I groan. She knows she's pulling me out of a daydream. 'I don't know why you're pretending as if you really care.'

'Hush,' I whisper, busying myself with polishing Dawn's – *Her Royal Highness's* – favourite glass.

Though she isn't entirely wrong. Before I became Carlotta, I'd never worked a day in my life. I was the girl who *had* maids. How I've gotten this far in one of the castle's most coveted roles is a miracle. Or, I should say, is the work of Lire's power.

Despite being a maid I do love being in the castle. As the world rapidly changed around me, Bearra stayed exactly the same. It still hasn't opened up to the world. It's comforting, being in a place that feels like home, unchanged by time.

Still, these days I understand things much better. I see the cracks in a kingdom that was once so powerful. The queen and king never show their faces, unable to rule without Lire's wisdom. And of course there's people like Maya, Dawn's new friend, whose families nearly starved because of the curse.

I hadn't known, when the kingdom was put to sleep, the dangers the people would be in. Neither had Dawn. We thought we could see everything from our castles, yet we existed in such small worlds.

✦ ◦ ✦ ☾ ☀ ☽ ✦ ◦ ✦

When I reach Dawn's rooms, my small feet already aching from the hard, steep servant's passages, her voice floats through the air, along the rays of sunlight that stream through the curtains. I knock quickly, then hurry inside and place her breakfast and tea on her desk.

Even before I see her, the aura of her presence alone makes my chest fill with warmth.

Then, the waterfall of golden curls over a pink nightgown, and I have to blink to stop my eyes from glazing over. She's facing away from me, speaking with Maya.

Maya's eyes find me, and Dawn follows her gaze. The princess beams like sunshine, most likely at seeing her breakfast, not at seeing me, but for a moment I pretend. I pretend we're Bearra's queens, married, sharing this room. We're seeing each other for the first time today after a long night, and our hearts fill with fireworks and honey. I pretend she sees me – the real me – and is as mystified as I am seeing her.

'Carlotta,' Dawn says, unknowingly ruining my fantasy. Her two white cats snooze on her plush bed and she pats them lovingly. To me, she smiles – politely. 'Thank you.'

I return her smile and nod, my heart aching so deeply I want to tear it out. 'Anything else I can do for you this morning, Your Highness?'

Maya snickers, her short, mousy hair falling over her eyes. She tucks it back. '*Your Highness*,' she teases.

Dawn raises her brows impatiently. 'I may be your friend, Maya, but I am also the princess. *Some* people actually like to treat me as such.'

'Well,' Maya says, 'it's hard to see you as *Her Highness* since I've seen how you act after a few glasses of wine.'

Dawn's cheeks turn rosy. 'Out, Maya. Go waste your time with Teddy. I have a lot to do.'

I fight back a grin. Not many people can get Dawn to blush. Since arriving here, I quickly accustomed to their squabbling. Though they constantly disagree, their love for each other is strong. I only wish I could be friends with them as well.

Maya waves a hand dismissively and leaves, chuckling to herself.

'My apologies you had to witness that,' Dawn says, making her way over to her breakfast. Her eyes light up when she notices the fresh croissants.

I skip out of her way and make myself useful, straightening the curtains she already opened herself. 'It's alright,' I say. 'It's never a bad thing to have someone to challenge you. And I, of course, am only honoured to be serving *Her Royal Highness.*'

Dawn laughs. Most people treat their maids more like animals or tools. But I've always known Dawn for her kindness. She's always been the one person I'm never afraid to speak to.

'Maya is right.' Dawn sighs, wiping her fingers on a napkin after already inhaling half a croissant. 'You must stop calling me that. It's embarrassing. I would expect it of most people. But you, Carlotta . . .' She says my name slowly, drawing it out, enjoying the way it rolls on her tongue. Like she did when I was Relia. 'You are my friend too. I value you too much to act as if I'm better than you only by my birth.'

I nearly tell her, *You* are *better than me,* but I hold my tongue. 'Dawn,' I say, unused to saying the name out loud. Unused to saying it with these lips. 'Thank you for saying that.' A good maid would refuse. She would argue, tell the princess she was flattered, but couldn't possibly refer to her so disrespectfully. But the part of me that's still Relia lights up. 'I also consider you a friend.'

Dawn takes another croissant and stands by a south-facing window, taking in her kingdom, but her shoulders are hunched and her hands run along the silk of her nightgown. In front of anyone else, she wouldn't dare let her body language betray her like that. 'Do you know why I love having you as my maid?' she asks.

'I always make sure the croissants are warm?' *Even if I have to use magic to do it.*

Dawn lets a small laugh escape her. 'That is *one* reason, but in the short time you've been here, you have always made me feel comfortable. You listen, but you also always know exactly what to say. I have friends – good ones – but no one can calm me the way you do.'

My chest almost bursts. If only she knew. If only she knew why, and how. 'It's my job,' I say, bowing my head ever-so slightly.

She turns to me, her lips downturned as if she's disappointed by my response. 'Then I should start paying you more.'

Dawn has me follow her to the throne room. I often wait near her when I don't have chores, in case she needs anything. Well, that's the excuse we both use. Truly, neither of us wants to be alone.

'Amora's bringing us more magic,' Teddy says, tapping his heavy shoes against the floor.

'Which will only be of use if we can train our soldiers on how to use it,' Dawn replies.

Teddy cocks his head, his freshly cut hair shifting in waves of red. 'We will.'

Their voices echo through the long hall, and the morning sun berates us through its stained-glass windows. The doors are closed to visitors as Dawn's inner circle schemes. Maya, Teddy, and a couple of high-up guards and advisors. The queen and king, as usual, are nowhere to be seen. So Dawn sits on the throne, the others lounging around her in a circle on lovely chairs of their own.

I wring my calloused hands, my back pressed against the wall in the corner. Though it still never feels quite right, existing as I do now, movement and touch help with the dissociation from my body. My heart and lungs are still my own, I'm still Relia on the inside, and if I breathe, I can usually feel okay.

But when one has not existed in a physical body for a hundred years, and then one becomes real again, it's . . . jarring. Lire's magic didn't just disguise me; it ate up my spirit and spat me back out, newly whole, and yet not quite. I don't know when – or if – I'll ever be myself again.

In fact, I don't know if I can survive at all without Lire.

'We need more than magical soldiers,' says General Largon. Old enough to be Dawn's mother, the Bearran warrior draws the eyes of the younger leaders – though everyone respects the princess's authority most. 'Our magical fighters will be important, yes, but if they can't stand iron, they'll only slow us down. We need soldiers who can fight with weapons that will hurt the enemy. We cannot simply fight fire with fire.'

If only she knew that Lire's most monstrous soldiers – myself, Elsie, and the other girls scattered across the world – are impervious to iron's effects. That's what makes us so special to the fairy. We aren't simply ghosts. Something about being undead makes us able to both use magic *and* not be cut down by the rare metal. A thought that disturbs more than comforts me, as I have so little understanding of what exactly I am.

'Then we'll create two groups,' Dawn says, her hands folded over a sleek, golden dress. 'One will be trained with magic, and one will be trained with iron weapons. Any able-bodied Bearrans who don't want to join the army must offer time in the mines, getting us as much triarue as they can for our magic users. When Sierra and her crew come back with the iron—'

'If she comes back.' General Largon narrows her weathered eyes. 'And if the Reed even finds it. Remind me why we're placing our trust in *pirates?*'

'Because they'll get the job done,' Maya argues through gritted teeth. The young woman tugs at the collar of her lacy, dark-grey dress as if it's strangling her. 'Believe me, nothing will stop Sierra. The *Reed* will get us our iron. Unless you're offering to go out and find it yourself?'

Before Largon can yell at Maya – something she's done before, and likely would do again – Dawn raises a hand to signal her to calm down. 'Well,' says the general, seething but quiet, 'they'll have to get their job done *promptly*. As we wait, we must focus on gaining more triarue – the one guarantee Bearra does have.'

'Is that wise?' Teddy says, toying with a piece of fabric he's torn from his own blazer – a very nice, expensive one. Most people still believe he's a prince, and he certainly looks the part when he wants to. The way Dawn and Maya gaze at him with such admiration, they must think he looks princely too. But the way *he* looks at *Maya*? Oh, it's so romantic I could cry. 'If triarue strengthens the magic around it,' he continues, 'arming our people with it will make the enemy stronger too.'

The Bearran citizens are beginning to realise the truth about Lire and that Jacob was never their saviour. But they don't know Jacob and Teddy are the fairy's sons. And although Teddy helped save Bearra once and is still fighting for them now, I'm not sure they would still trust him if they knew the entire truth – especially not with him sitting right by Dawn's throne.

People would fear his power; the same power that runs through me. And Lire doesn't give her magic to just anyone. We're rare. Notorious.

Dawn glances at me, and I give her a reassuring smile. Her face relaxes so slightly I'm sure I'm the only one who would be able to tell. Our perfect princess. Blessed by every fairy except the fairy of darkness. Sometimes she's so flawless, so bright, that she's almost difficult to look at. But I do. We all do.

Everyone knows not to look directly at the sun, but how could we not gaze in awe at the star that gives us life?

And I'm under her spell most of all. It didn't wane in a hundred years, and it's only stronger now. I've never been able to stop loving her. She's the sun, the stars, the moon, the earth.

She is life, and I am death.

How could I not adore her?

'We have the strengths we have,' Dawn says with finality. 'For now, we do what we can, and we work tirelessly. We wait for Sierra. We wait for Amora. We plan, we work, and we rest before the war truly begins.' She observes her team cautiously. 'I would also like you all to think about reopening our kingdom. We still need the protection of keeping our borders closed – at least until the threat of war is over – but we also need to consider our future once the war is over. When we win, I want to let our people out, and bring the future in.'

Maya claps. 'It would be about ti—'

A crack like lighting crashes from the castle's east. I gasp as distant screams sing through the walls, making me cover my ears with my hands. Streaks of yellow magic soar past the wide windows. I squeeze my eyes closed.

War.

'Not yet!' shouts Largon.

I press myself against the wall harder, cower behind my arms.

'Carlotta,' says Dawn, her voice cutting through the air. I open my eyes, and she's in front of me, and I breathe. 'It's going to be alright. Please take Maya and anyone else who can't protect themselves to safety.' She pulls my hands down and waits for me to respond.

Trembling, I nod. The screams are dying down, but the crashing grows more intense – people must be evacuating, but whoever is attacking the castle hasn't stopped.

Shh. I remind myself I don't need to be afraid. I'm already dead. But the noise, the glow of magic, the chaos— I'm frozen in place.

Dawn turns to the others. 'Be ready to fight for the lives of every Bearran. And if we don't all make it . . .' she says, standing up, brushing her golden curls behind her shoulders, 'all I can say is thank you.'

I'm supposed to be on Lire's side, I'm supposed to be helping tear the princess down from her seat of power – but how can I? I want to protect her, run to her, cradle her. I'm the one with magic. She shouldn't be calming me. I should be taking control.

But I am not Dawn.

'I won't hide,' Maya says. 'I can take care of myself. And what about you? You're going to fight, *Your Highness?*'

'You expect I'd cower and let my citizens die for me? I'm blessed with Strength, just as you are.'

Boom.

'*F—*'

Boom!

Bricks scatter and we drop to the ground. Someone screams as the roof on the far side of the throne room caves in entirely with a final crash; dust chokes and blinds me as it raises through the air. I can't see anyone, but they shuffle along the ground with heavy breaths. People reach for each other; my arms are scratched. Only once the debris has settled can I see the others clinging to each other, Dawn looking me all

over as if checking for injury. Thank the fairies it seems we're all okay
– but my sight is still blurry.

We move as one, following the princess into a sheltered servant's hall. More booms resound through the castle, amplified by the
acoustics of the wide stone halls. I'm nearly knocked over by the shock
of each one. How much has already been destroyed? How many have
been killed?

My heart sinks. I'm supposed to be on the same side as the attackers.
I'm part of this devastation.

'General Largon.' Dawn points down the hallway with a steady
hand. But there are tears in her eyes, tears I can't wipe away. 'Go. Now.
Get our fighters ready. If this is Lire, we may not survive it. But we
will *not* let Bearra go down without a fight.'

The general nods. 'Your Highness.' She breaks into a sprint, her
closest soldiers trailing her.

The advisors who were with us glance around wide-eyed, so when
a guard walks past, Dawn orders for them to be led to a safe place. She
must have forgotten she already asked me to take them – but I can't
force myself to leave her side. Maybe she knows that.

But Dawn stares between Maya and me. 'What did I say to you
two? Go!'

'No!' Maya growls, and Teddy covers his face with his hands. It's
only the four of us now. But I don't balk at Maya's outburst. We're
all used to her never agreeing with anyone.

I simply shake my head, and reply to Dawn, 'It's our job to take
care of you.' Because Lire be damned, I'll die before abandoning my
princess. My resolve is returning, the adrenaline bursting through my

fear. I'm no longer frozen. Dawn may not know I have the power to protect myself, but I do, and I can. I will.

'Fine,' she says through gritted teeth. She readjusts her tiara and hikes up her skirts. 'Then let's go and see what we're dealing with.'

CHAPTER 2

We hurry through a back exit of the castle and out onto the hilltop. Bearra spreads out in a perfect circle, its walls of stone and thick vines enclosing us. Everything is in its place: the white walls and terracotta roofs, the sparkling canals, the market stalls in the town square, and the outer farms.

But the air is filled with smoke and canary-yellow Musan magic, making me sputter and gasp. The light soars past us in offensive flares. I duck and cover my head with my hands, but the blasts are like sunlight, unable to be entirely avoided. The castle is hit with another wave – I can't see where it comes from. Dawn, Teddy, Maya and I stumble for cover, nearly rolling down the cliffside as another section of the castle caves in.

Across the kingdom, fires pour through houses and trees, along the canals and through the farmland. Whoever is doing this, we need to find them and stop them before . . . before . . .

Crash.

I cower. I shake. I try to catch my breath. It's no use. My lungs aren't working, my heart has run away. I clench the grass between my fingers and dig my nails into the dirt, so unused to the loudness.

Before I died, I was so sensitive, so fearful. And then a hundred years of death, of a quiet, dark, dream-like existence, numbed everything. Now, every day, every *feeling* comes back with a searing, screaming vengeance.

As I watch the magic destroy Bearra, my insides twist and knot and my mind goes foggy. I can feel the fear emanating off everyone else, crawling over and under my skin. An entire kingdom's worth of horror is inside *me.*

And I have to save them. I *have* to save them. I have to save Dawn.

But I'm not supposed to. I'm not allowed to. I could lose everything.

Then Dawn reaches out to help me up, and I manage to take a deep but shaky breath. Her hair is haloed by the fire and magic behind her, her hand so warm in mine. She's scared underneath, I know, but if she can be strong, so can I. I have to be brave for her, just as she's being brave for us.

I stand, my heart rate decreasing. Drop her hand and tear myself away from her gaze only when another *boom* pulls me from her.

Dawn glances between the three of us; her circle. 'Our soldiers will be on their way to the attackers. Our citizens will have to protect themselves and their homes from the assault as best they can. As for us, we'll do what we can to lead them.'

Lilac magic twists around Teddy's tapping hands. When Maya notices it, she pales. From what I've gathered, either she's still afraid of it, or she's afraid he's revealing his secret to Bearra.

Teddy hardens his jaw. 'None of us die today. Promise?'

'Promise.' Maya haphazardly swings a mace she found on the way out, likely one that was mounted as decoration. She can barely hold it up, but she grips it with determination. 'Lire will *not* be responsible for my death. I'm going to live to become an old, miserable monster. Just like her.'

'As am I,' says Dawn. She's glowing in the yellow light of magic that arcs over us. There isn't a colour in the world that wouldn't make her shine.

I attempt to smile, despite the anxiety wracking my body. 'And me.'

Dawn nods. 'Don't play hero, any of you. Let the soldiers do their job. Remember the kingdom needs us alive.'

'But *you're* going to fight?' Teddy asks Dawn.

'Whoever this is, surely they wouldn't dare to hurt a princess. I'm here to set an example. If I can find their leader and talk to them . . . Even if Lire has come—'

'They're going to kill you,' Maya says.

'If they do, they'll regret it.'

Maya groans.

Cautiously rounding a corner of the castle, towards the road that leads up the hill to the entrance, we finally get a view of the magic-wielding attackers, who are focused mostly on destroying the castle.

Bearran soldiers, led by General Largon, shoot arrows at them from a distance as they take cover from the projectile magic.

Our enemies are yet to notice us hiding behind castle walls – though it won't be long, because with every fiery blast of power, more bricks crumble around us.

As I scan the battle, my muscles itching to run screaming, I notice there aren't many attackers – only five or six. 'Dawn.' I nudge the princess. She leans close to me, her ear by my mouth. I swallow, heat rising in my cheeks. 'There's only a few of them. Why?'

Teddy must hear, because he says, relaxing into a smirk, 'They've overestimated themselves. Or underestimated us. I can handle five Musans with a bit of magic *easily*.'

Another flare of magic sets alight a school building below the hill. No – not just 'a bit of magic'. But he knows that.

'They aren't Lire's?' Maya says, tearing a layer of fine lace off her dress – ecstatic to finally have a chance to ruin it. 'I guess they could be anyone who knows we're weak, breaking in just to steal triarue.'

'No,' Dawn says. 'They're too organised to not be Lire's, and they broke past the vines. Anyone who has managed to get that much magic couldn't be stupid enough to try to attack us with no backup.' She sighs through her nose, then proceeds to walk around to the other side of the hill – where the attackers are facing off with General Largon and a few dozen of her soldiers.

'Dawn!' we all yell at once and rush to follow, but she's already halfway there.

She clears her throat. 'Excuse me,' she calls, stepping carefully over upturned grass that was, minutes ago, perfectly flat and green. '*Excuse me!*'

They ignore her at first, and I almost take the opportunity to grab her and pull her back to safety. But the princess, blessed to be seen and heard, magnetises their attention above all the noise.

Our enemies stop – all five of them, their magic dulling as if eclipsed – and turn to her.

Dawn raises a hand to her soldiers and they stand at ease. 'If you would kindly discontinue destroying my castle and instead talk to me,' she scolds the attackers, 'I'm sure we can come to a peaceful conclusion before any of you should have to lose your life.'

One of them saunters over to us – their leader, it seems – but her appearance doesn't match her magic. Rather than the sun-kissed colouring of a Musan, she has the dark complexion and height of someone from the west: Rhiannon's Territory. I know it's an outdated thought, to assume someone's home territory from their appearance. The world is different now. But it sends shivers down my spine to imagine just how far Lire's influence has spread.

'We aren't looking for peace, Princess,' she says, her voice gravelly. 'We're here on behalf of our fairy, Lire. This has merely been a taste, a test, an experiment. She wanted to see how you might fight us – and you've barely been able to do so much as tire us. Honestly, we only came to have some *fun*. I don't know if the fairy will be pleased or disappointed at your utter failure.'

Dawn looks her up and down, then straightens her skirts. 'I would be careful not to jump to conclusions. Your fairy knows me better than almost anyone – so she knows I *don't* fail. And I know she doesn't play, so you can tell me now why she's sent you.'

The leader laughs humourlessly. 'Certainly, Princess. I'm not here to argue. Lire does have a message for you.'

'Go on.'

I inwardly wince – Lire told me nothing of this. Why not at least warn me?

The woman grins, baring her teeth excitedly. 'You have one month until Lire's *real* attack. Until the war officially begins. Next time, she's bringing her army.' She snickers. 'Based on today, it's clear that surrender is your best – *only* – option, and you're lucky Lire has been gracious to offer you an entire month to make your decision.' She runs her eyes over the kingdom below us, still smoking and burning. There is only disdain in her expression. 'Do not pretend to be brave, Princess Dawn. If you don't surrender to Lire, we will kill every last Bearran and burn this kingdom to ashes.' She turns to leave, gesturing for her four companions to follow.

'Well, thank you for your message,' says Dawn, waving a hand. 'Though you'll find that I do not dignify such discourteous, cowardly threats. If Lire wishes to discuss surrender, she can beg me herself.'

The leader spins around, glaring at the princess with yellow magic steaming like fire from her black eyes. 'Lire won't let me kill you today, but you and your kingdom will fall. Back down now and we will leave peacefully. Keep arguing, and I'll make sure we leave as much destruction as we can before we go.' She gives Dawn a sinister grin. 'We'll only be back in a few weeks anyway.'

'Surrender! Please, princess!' a Bearran soldier shrieks. 'Surrender to Lire and save us! We can't wi—' Another thumps him over the head.

'We'd never!' shouts the thumper.

'No,' Dawn agrees, 'we won't. Not today, and not in a month. We're not afraid to fight, and not only for Bearra. We will save the world from Lire's destruction.'

And it will all be futile, I think with a shiver. How easy it is to forget that I'm not on her side. That *I* am part of Bearra's downfall. Even so, with or without me, how could anyone stand up to Lire? The attackers, with their snickers and eye rolls, seem to think the same.

'Go home,' Maya says to them boredly. 'We'll see you in a month.'

All eyes go to her: *Who does this girl in the torn dress think she is?*

But while they're watching Maya as she's stood straight, her jaw tense, I find myself drawn to one of the attackers. His yellow magic glows faintly in the sunlight, almost hidden. I barely catch it in the shadows of his palm.

The arguments pick back up around me, but I can barely hear them – Dawn, maintaining eye contact with the leader, doesn't notice the oncoming attack.

Lire's soldier raises his hand.

And I don't think—

I *jump.* Towards Dawn, tackling her to the ground. A wave of magic flies over our heads and smashes through the castle walls, just missing us. Chaos explodes in screams and magic and clanging weapons and thudding footsteps. Dawn pants in shock, and I pull her up. She tries to go back into the fray, but I pull her hard, and together we scramble towards the safety of the castle's fragile walls, kicking up dirt behind us.

We get behind a layer of singed brick and I force the princess into a dark corner, pushing her back against the wall as I protect her with my body. She's looking all over my face, and I'm looking all over hers, both of us heaving, shaking, my heart racing.

For a second I see my Dawn. My *Dee*. Not just the princess, but my love, my friend. She's almost gazing at me with those same, adoring eyes, those eyes that I never understood, because how could someone as brilliant as her adore someone as ordinary as me?

'You . . .' she breathes. 'Carlotta, you saved me. *Carlotta!* You could've hurt yourself!'

Hearing that name snaps me out of my daze. I swallow and control myself, turning back into the maid I'm supposed to be. Back into the person who was certainly not supposed to save the princess I should be helping an evil fairy defeat. 'I was doing my job,' I whisper.

The ceiling creaks above us. 'Like I told you,' Dawn says, 'I need to pay you more.' She yanks my hand and we scurry back out of the shadows just before the brick caves in, smashing fatally behind us.

Soldiers outside scream for the princess – '*Where is she?*' – but I've got her. *I've got her.*

Our lone moment over, we sprint back to the fighting, into the bright sun. Soldiers drop around us, roaring in agony. There's barely any magic in Bearra, and their weapons are outdated – a hundred soldiers would struggle to hurt one expert magic-user.

Dawn fumbles, gripping my hand, and she lets out a defeated gasp as another section of the castle collapses. My insides seem to go empty

– if even Dawn has lost hope, then I can't even pretend to *try* to have any.

With no meaningful help from Teddy either, we're struggling. He has immense magic that the Bearran soldiers balk at, but he's clearly holding back. He could kill our enemies with ease – he knows that. He said it himself. So why isn't he?

I can only watch, trying to press Dawn behind my body. I can't help – not without exposing myself. I can't save them without Lire punishing me. Without losing Dawn.

But if this is it, anyway, if I become the last resort . . . 'Dawn—' I start.

Maya lets out an incredulous laugh, her light-brown hair a wave thrown back as she gazes at the clouds.

What? I stumble over my own feet, grasping Dawn's arm.

Over our heads, a carriage is *flying* through the air on wings of navy Gracian magic. Two young women hang out the windows firing arrows, while the boy wielding the magic fires offensive waves of blue at our enemies from the skylight.

My stomach almost flips. *What on earth is happening? Is this the end?*

Maya cries with joy, jumping from foot to foot, and draws out every syllable as she shouts, 'Si – err - a!' The attackers have all but stopped, shocked as the rest of us, and they gape at the laughing Bearran. Maya points at the carriage. 'That's my best friend! And she's insane! You'll wish you ran home now!'

The raven-haired Reed waves back with a wicked grin as she shoots another arrow from the carriage – right into the wrist of an attacker, who screams as their magic is snuffed out.

Relief settles over Teddy and Dawn's faces while the rest of us look on in confusion. Largon shifts her sword defensively. Dawn gives her a nod, and the general orders her soldiers not to attack the newcomers.

I shake my head, blinking away a memory. I've met Sierra – in another life – and know her *vaguely*. I know the mission she was sent on, know the connection she has to Dawn, and I know, although no one else does yet, that she killed Muse.

A battle of magic ignites around us in blue and yellow. Teddy joins with his rare lilac magic, and the colours streak across the sky, alighting the clouds, the smoke, the world, the screaming faces.

A wave of yellow smacks into the flying carriage. With a *crack* it's sent hurtling into the castle. But the women leaning out of the windows aren't screaming. They're *laughing*. The boy with the blue magic holds the carriage up just enough to have it soar over our heads and land on a flat part of the castle's roof, knocking even more bricks from the structure.

Lire's soldiers try to attack the group on the roof as six pirates jump out of the carriage at once, weapons ready. The one Sierra shot through the wrist has gotten back up with animalistic vengeance, sending back fiery yellow, but the attackers are confused and now truly outnumbered. Bearran arrows resume their fire from every angle.

Dawn watches on with a stern but sure look of victory. Her tiara is pressed gently back into place atop her head, and I try to relax and observe the pirates, trying to remember them. My memories of my spirit life are vague and faded. I spoke to Sierra, and the others, but can't quite picture exactly what they looked like, how they sounded.

The small girl with the red hair and the tanned young woman with the long, crooked nose. The three men: a red-haired boy who looks just like the small girl, a man twice anyone else's size, and the dark-haired one with the magic.

But Sierra, with her long limbs, shocking agility, and fiery demeanour, stands out. The Reeds were a powerful family in my time – I must have met Sierra's grandparents or great-grandparents. She is a testament to them, in her beauty, her skill, and the pure power she radiates despite not having any magic.

Realising there's no need for us to be standing slack-jawed in the line of danger, I take Dawn's hand and pull her towards a shaded inlet of the castle, a set of near-hidden stairs that lead into the servant's basement rooms. Dawn seems determined but dubious – a rare look for her – but allows me to take her out of the fight. Bearran soldiers part as we fall behind them; the arrows they send at the attackers barely make it, but at least it's some protection for us.

The princess stares on, her fingers squeezing mine, sending heat up my arm. The enemy has forgotten about her now, too busy fighting the pirates and Teddy. Even Maya finally retreats, knowing there's no more she can do to help, especially not with just her heavy mace. Thank goodness.

Sierra's pirates – the fairy killers – are *experts*. They take two of the attackers on the rooftop while Teddy takes the other half on the grass. Teddy relies on his power alone to push back the enemies, but the pirates work in a flawless dance of slashing, gleaming metal, and bodies whirling through the air as they fight like a pack of wolves, in perfect harmony. Despite Lire's soldier's magic, the fight has become easy.

On the rooftop, an attacker's magic cuts out and he stumbles to his knees. He stares at his hands, trembling – I can sense his fear even from our hideaway – and when he tries to relight his Musan power, the crooked-nosed pirate flashes her sword against him and he retches backwards in agony. 'Iron!' he yells. 'They have iron!'

Dawn gasps in my ear. 'They— They found it,' she whispers, though I barely hear her over the commotion. We kneel in the grass, green stains pressing into our skirts. Dawn is recovering from the shock, awed by the sight of the iron, but as my adrenaline wears away, I'm losing myself. It's as if the scene in front of me isn't real, like I'm looking at a painting or reading a novel. My vision swims and my arms feel light. *We were attacked. We were attacked. Lire is merciless.*

The girl with the iron sword takes one final swing, slashing across her foe's chest before he's sent flailing over the edge of the castle. He screams and lands with a thump, unconscious and bleeding heavily.

I can now clearly see why Maya and Teddy were so relieved to see Sierra here. Even the ones who mocked Dawn earlier are starting to panic, though they don't show any signs of giving up. And of course they won't – they can't face Lire after losing.

Teddy glances up at the pirates, struggling as the three attackers on him send a triangle of sun-like power at once. 'Sierra!' he calls to the rooftop, the pirates distracted as they enjoy their victory – and while the magical one still fights another of Lire's soldiers. 'Come down here and help?'

The black-haired Gracian calls back, 'I can't get down! Just fight them!'

'Fly!' Teddy responds, sending up a wave of lilac to block the three-way attack.

Fly? I wonder, still struggling to ground myself, looking on as if I'm not a part of the story at all, as if I'm simply a spirit again. My heart rate slows as I leave reality and retreat into my mind. The peace cuts through the noise, the flashing light, as my consciousness protects itself from everything around me. There's a numb silence.

Maya races over to Teddy and pushes him aside just in time to stop a block of grey brick from the castle landing on his head. He gapes at her, but she seems to have an idea and pushes him towards the three enemies, who, in their surprise, let them pass through.

Suddenly they're on the far side of us, trapping the enemies in between themselves and the soldiers – giving the Bearrans a better opening with their arrows by forcing the enemy to face the other direction.

'Sierra!' Teddy calls again. 'Are you coming down or not?'

One of the attackers copies the pirates' carriage idea and flies themself up to the rooftop to take down the Reed – but she kicks them in the face right before they can send a wave of yellow magic at her. 'I can't fly down!' she yells back to Teddy, a wince in her voice.

'Uh, *swan!*' Teddy shouts, sending a gust of wind-like magic under the enemies' feet to trip them over. Lilac magic glows around them, and suddenly their shoes are glowing, sticking together. He's holding them together to stop their movement. I almost laugh as they struggle to get up.

Clever. And, I realise, that's why we're winning. Lire's soldiers aren't good at using their magic. They're relying on strength alone without any strategy to back up their attacks. As long as we can outsmart them, we can win this fight.

'Teddy, I really can't!' Sierra presses.

While the attackers are confused, flailing around on the bruised grass between arrows and lilac, Teddy looks up to Sierra. 'You can't transform? Wait, you broke the curse?' His eyes light up and his magic cuts out for a split second as he waves excitedly. 'You broke the curse!'

'Uh huh!' She kicks her attacker in the face again. They try and fail to use their magic to heal their bleeding and cracked nose.

'How? When?'

'Teddy!' Maya shouts as their opponents on the ground – who realise they can still use magic, despite their feet being stuck – fire another wave of magic at him.

The auburn-haired boy turns just in time to use another gust of power to send the attack away. He spins back to Sierra just as quickly. 'What about your sisters?'

'I don't know!' she shouts impatiently, her black hair flying. 'I haven't checked! We came straight here!'

The Amoran girl with the iron sword slashes at another of the enemies – the one the blue-magic boy was fighting – throwing them off the roof beside their ally. The girl is a brilliant fighter, possibly even better than Sierra, but she's hesitant to kill. Sierra wouldn't think twice about gutting these assailants, but the Amoran barely knocks them out.

Meanwhile, a Bearran soldier manages to land an arrow into the shoulder of one of Teddy's trapped enemies on the ground – they faint before they've even started to bleed.

'Lire is coming for you!' the last conscious one says. 'She's coming, and you're all dead! It doesn't matter if you kill us!'

The blue-magic boy, finally with an opening, flies the six pirates down from the roof, leaving their enchanted carriage burning and abandoned. Sierra saunters straight up to the final attacker and gives him a punch to the face which knocks him out with a fracture that leaves most of us cringing.

All the yellow magic that blinded us just seconds ago blinks out. We're left only with the sunshine.

And we've won – *we*, if I have any right to say that – but even as the panic dies down and I return to my body, the feeling in my arms returning, my heart won't stop racing once again. There's a wave of nausea at seeing the bodies of the enemies on the floor, and though I'm sure most are still alive, I don't know what to do or think.

Should that be me, lying unconscious and bleeding in the grass?

Those people were on my side, weren't they? Should I have protected them, instead of protecting only the princess?

But I didn't even protect her. I stood here, useless. I didn't help anyone. Not even myself. What's wrong with me?

Dawn stands, brushing her hands on her dress. I scramble up beside her. The soldiers turn to her at once, awaiting her orders. 'Take the living attackers to the cells,' she orders, 'and remove their magic. I don't care if you have to force it out of them. Any dead can be left outside

Bearra's borders for Lire to find. We have heard her message, and now she will see our response. Bearra will never surrender.'

'That's right! You tell them!' Maya shouts, which after a moment of awkward silence riles up the soldiers. Suddenly they're all shouting and whooping with relief. Some of them even put their pride aside to thank Teddy and the pirates. But there's certainly a wave of doubt crossing the people on the hill. *Why does the prince have our enemy's magic? Why are we trusting strangers from the outside world?*

Dawn clears her throat. She doesn't need to be loud to get their attention back; all eyes snap to her. 'There has been a lot of damage done today,' she says. 'Do what you can to rebuild. This isn't going to be the last attack, and we must find a way to better defend ourselves. Thicker walls, more bunkers for those who can't fight. I want teams out in the streets checking on our citizens and putting out fires. I want teams in the castle checking the destruction.' A hint of sadness plays on her expression. 'But first let our people see what has been done today. Make sure they know that if they want what is left of their home to survive, it is now time to fight. Whether they want to join our army, donate their time to mining, farming, anything that can help . . . They must. We need to work together to save Bearra. Understood?'

Nods travel through the crowd as Sierra and her friends watch on in silence, and that's when I finally sense it: an emotion amongst them, dark and physical, roiling through the pirates like mud. *Grief.*

CHAPTER 3

Maids hand out glasses of water and steaming cups of tea as we recover in one of the castle's few undamaged sitting rooms. I watch as the others talk: Dawn's inner circle, plus the new crew of pirates and their leader, Sierra Reed. Back to business just like that, as Bearra licks its wounds outside the castle, the smoke clearing as fires are put out. Ebony's iron sword is hidden out of sight to save Teddy and Arden the illness it forces upon anyone with magic. *Except for me*

Dawn insisted I stay right by her side, despite my protests to hurry back to the kitchens to help prepare her lunch – and get away from everyone for a moment to gather my thoughts and finally let myself calm down. 'You saved me today,' she'd said earnestly. 'Now you must rest.' Her hand sits between us on the plush sofa we're seated on together, and it takes every ounce of strength I have left not to hold it.

Her cats – Sunny and Summer – sit in our laps. Summer purrs contentedly as I scratch behind her ears. Between her soft white fur and the even rumbling of her vibrations, my shoulders begin to untense.

I'm glad to be with Dawn right now, and I know Lire would want me here, overhearing this conversation, but now that the chaos of Lire's attack is over, my mind is stuck on Elsie. The girl could be in trouble – who knows what she was up to throughout all of that commotion? Also, she was there when I met Sierra and her crew in Muse's Forest. They'll recognise Elsie if they see her. She isn't disguised like me. So if she appears in this room . . .

Everyone introduces themselves, and Maya and Teddy are especially excited when they realise that Sierra is *with* the blue-magic boy. Arden is a handsome dark-haired man with a face that's equally stern as it is sweet. The way he looks at Sierra, and she at him, isn't something beautiful and soft like Maya and Teddy's love. It's fiercely protective, all fire.

They have four friends who make up the crew. The red-haired siblings, Lark and Wren; and Ebony and Levi, the Amoran fighter and her burly partner.

But a vague memory of my spirit life resurfaces. An Adellan girl with both bows in her dark ringlets and a bow as her chosen weapon. She's no longer with them, which must mean she's the source of the grief I felt so strongly from them.

At a certain point in the introductions, they turn to me, as if not realising I'm only a maid. I try to sink into the shadows behind Dawn's radiance, seen and not heard, but Dawn places a hand on my shoulder and looks at me proudly. Which sends my heart racing.

'This is Carlotta,' she says to the pirates. 'She's my best maid, and today she stayed by my side through the battle. She saved my life.'

My mind fogs up as turn by turn they offer smiles and little waves, muttering *hellos.* I shrink at the attention, but I do my best to smile politely.

Ebony looks at me with an unreadable expression, tilting her head. '*Carlotta.* We met a Carlotta in Muse's Forest just recently.'

'That's right,' Sierra says, narrowing her eyes, and I feel my heart drop out of my chest. 'A ghost. But you don't look anything like her. I suppose she died long before any of us were even born.'

I swallow and choke out, 'A g-ghost? Oh my. I was named after my grandmother. She died long ago.' Which would only make sense if I weren't Bearran, but I can only hope they don't question the timelines that would *easily* give me away. *Fairies,* I'm awful at thinking on my feet.

'Oh!' Ebony says, and for a second I think I'm done for. 'Sierra, remember what the other Carlotta told you?'

'To pass on a message to the princess . . .' Sierra starts, tapping Arden's knee as she thinks, and I exhale. 'With everything else we have to tell you, I'd almost forgotten the encounter entirely. But there was something strange going on with those spirits.'

'I'm still stuck on ghosts,' mumbles Maya. 'What ghosts?'

'I'll explain later,' Sierra dismisses her, then turns to Dawn – but not before glancing back at Maya with a quick wink and mouthing *later* again. 'Carlotta told us the only way to defeat the fairies is to turn them against each other. Only they are powerful enough to destroy each other. She said you have to play their game.'

I sense myself paling. My encounter with the pirates is so blurry, but they're saying I told them something that could help Dawn stop Lire? How could I be so reckless?

But, of course, how could I not?

'That's a nice idea,' says Dawn, 'though I'm not sure where we would even start.'

Kara, I want to say, *obviously*.

But every agonising second, I have to remind myself why I'm here. How I'm here. And how easily I could lose my place with Dawn by giving her advice. Lire can tear me away from her the moment I step out of line. *Let the world fall*, I remind myself. *Nothing is more important than her.*

'That isn't the worst of it,' Sierra says. 'What we've come to tell you is actually linked to what that ghost said to us in Muse's Forest. I . . . I don't even know where to start.'

Arden wraps his arm around her waist, and she softens. 'I think it's best if we start at the beginning,' he says.

And they begin, a cacophony of loud voices speaking over the top of each other and explaining one, two, five stories at a time as each pirate explains their side of the story.

At a certain point, I wonder if my head might in fact combust, but what I gather is this much: Sierra found the pirates and demanded they help her break her cygnus curse, since it was Arden himself who placed the curse upon her; Sierra visited Bearra to ask Teddy for advice – and Dawn requested she look for iron; the pirates spent two months following both goals, leading them to Muse's Territory, where they met me; they were told to pass on a message to Teddy and Dawn, to 'stop holding back, and step into their power if they want to win'; after realising Arden's father might be the key to all their problems, they visited him only to find he was working for Lire – but he gave them the location of Lire's iron stores; and they made haste to reach the iron, but Muse was already there to fight them, and they—

'You *killed* a *fairy?*' Maya gasps.

Sierra nods excitedly. 'Yes. We. Did.'

'And you survived? That's . . .' Maya drifts off, catching the shift in Sierra's demeanour.

There's a silence until Wren whispers, 'She killed our friend,' and there are tears in their eyes as they explain *that* part. I nearly get choked up just hearing about it.

They end with this: before killing Muse, the fairy told them Lire's plan to bring back the dead as her army.

A bead of sweat runs down my neck as I do my best to look shocked.

'But that isn't possible,' Maya says, almost green at the thought. Very little sunlight reaches this section of the castle at this hour, making her grey eyes more serious in the shadows of the sitting room. 'No magic is able to resurrect someone.'

'No,' Sierra replies, 'unless you're in the one place in the world where the dead are somewhat alive.'

'Muse's Forest.' Teddy pales.

Sierra nods. 'That's what Muse was boasting about right before we put her down. They're undead, which means their magic works differently. We think they could be impervious to iron, or even worse, unkillable.'

Dawn's fingers twitch. 'So we're going to be facing an army we can't stop, even with the one weapon we've found.'

'Oh, it's worse than that,' says Sierra. 'Lire has already done it. She's using them as spies. Apparently they're already within Bearra's walls, and there's no way to detect them.'

My eyes widen. I feel so exposed, I could be naked in midday-sun in the middle of a crowd, everyone staring at me. Thankfully, they're all too focused on their own anxiety to even remember I'm here.

'This fight was a week or two ago,' says Arden. 'We came as quickly as we could, but with all that's happened . . .'

'We were slow to travel,' Sierra finishes. 'The *Neptune* had some of the iron on it, which slowed down its magic, and with us all grieving and exhausted, the ship had trouble following our intended route.'

'As soon as we arrived, we saw you were being attacked,' says Ebony. 'I had the idea for Arden to fly us in with a carriage. It was insane, but—'

'It worked,' finishes Levi. 'Who needs physics when you have a shipload of magic?'

'Hm,' says Dawn, brushing her golden hair behind her shoulders as she leans to pick up her tea. 'I'm not sure relying on magic to such an extent is wise. But, truly, thank you. I never would have expected a Reed and her band of pirates to save us, but here we are, indebted to you.'

Sierra straightens. 'There is a way for you to pay us back.'

'Anything that's in my power, Lady Reed.'

'Our friend, Opal.' She sucks in her lips and swallows. 'We still need to bury her. And we want the most extravagant, beautiful grave.

Maybe not Maya's-Grandmother gaudy, but something that will be a testament to her memory, and her sacrifice. A sacrifice that means we might yet save your kingdom.'

'Consider it done,' says Dawn. 'And we can hold a memorial service in the castle.'

I look to Dawn and let myself smile. Her grace never fails to amaze me, her ability to show kindness to these people she barely knows, to criminals, even though she's a future queen.

Something in Arden relaxes at her agreement. The poor man seems to be in a constant state of stress. But a sense of peace settles over the room with the promise of giving their friend a proper burial.

So when Elsie wanders in, a tray of sandwiches in her hands, I nearly scream. She holds it flippantly; already a couple of sandwiches are falling apart. She's chewing. Has she already eaten one? She halts when she sees Sierra and the pirates.

Fairies, does she remember them?

Get out, I try to tell her using only my eyes. But she sees me sitting beside Dawn, and smirks. *Elsie!* No one has noticed her yet. But if they recognise her, they'll kill her. Or worse, she'll kill them. I lock eyes with her and give the slightest shake of my head, which is surely signal enough to show my pleading. *Go. Before they see you. Go!*

Elsie tenses, seeming to sense my urgency. Another *perk* of being undead – we feel other people's emotions, sometimes even sense things before they happen. This empathetic ability has saved me more times than I like to admit . . . and it makes me a better spy.

Elsie ignores me most of the time, but for once she sees sense. The girl presses her lips together, drops the sandwiches on a table in the doorway, then hurries out of the room. A few people watch the back of her with confused expressions, shocked at her impolite behaviour.

Then the small pirate, Wren, simply fetches the plate herself and brings it to the middle of the sitting room, tucking in.

I breathe a sigh of relief, and Dawn instantly turns to me. 'Everything okay, Carlotta?'

'Hm? Oh, of course. I was just— I'm hungry, that's all.'

Dawn giggles. 'Then eat as much as you like.'

I couldn't be less hungry, but I lean forward and take one of the sandwiches. The bread is dark and crisp, filled with ripe cucumber and a soft cheese. Nothing like the food I would have eaten at home; there, we had fewer delicacies, even in my position as a lady. I often forget how different the cuisine is around the world – though at least in Bearra it hasn't changed over the past hundred years. I take a bite, and I actually do feel better.

Dawn watches me eat with an amused smile. She must think I've never tried food fit for royalty before. We lock eyes, and looking at that wonderful, blessed smile, I almost beg her, *remember me*, but of course she can't. She never can.

So I avert my eyes, pretending to close them in pleasure as I eat.

'One more thing,' Sierra says to Teddy. 'You need to bring back my curse. If we want to win this war, I'll be a better fighter because of it. Being able to transform and heal will make this much easier.'

Teddy nearly spasms. 'Sierra—' he shakes his head violently '—you know I don't use risky magic unless I absolutely have to. Besides, you only just broke the curse! If I went around turning everyone into shapeshifters, there'd be chaos.'

'But it's *me*, Teddy.' She looks to Maya. 'Tell him.'

Maya shrugs. 'I don't know anything about curses, except that they aren't good. But, then, you're the expert.'

Teddy's leg bounces. 'Not today. But if you let me think about it, find a way that isn't so dangerous—'

'*Fine.*' Sierra blows air out of her mouth impatiently. 'I *suppose* that's good enough for now.'

Dawn stands, her pristine dress falling around her bronze ankles. Earlier, helping her out of her torn outfit from today's attack and into this newer one – more formal with the arrival of the pirates – was an indescribable torture. Those lovely, freckled shoulders, her smooth back as I tightened her corset—

'We have a lot to do,' she says. I sense the muscles in her face straining to remain poised despite her exhaustion. 'If there really are undefeatable spies in our midst, we must find a way to seek them out and stop them. Perhaps our attackers can give us a lead, if any of them survive the night in our dungeons. For now, I want you all to rest. Our guests will be given quarters, but please forgive us if the rooms are less than perfect. Half the castle happens to be caved in.' She looks to me. 'Carlotta, if you would escort me to my room?'

I rise quickly and curtsy to the others, recalling that once, I was above them; a noblewoman who would have stared down her nose at pirates. *None of this is real.* With fresh shame, I lead Dawn out of the sitting room.

'Elsie,' I breathe as soon as I find her in the kitchens. She's usually down here, listening to gossip as countless people pass through.

'What was that earlier?' She puts down the unnecessarily large knife she was using to chop carrots. 'You were afraid. And why were you sitting with the princess? What happened to just being a good maid?'

I keep my voice low, and motion for her to continue chopping. People think we must be close friends. We began working here at the same time and share a room in the maids' quarters. They only see us as gossipers, so they would never suspect anything, but I'm still always afraid someone might suspect us.

In reality, we're not so much friends as reluctant allies. Babysitting Elsie – with her reckless and violent tendencies – has only ever made my job here harder. I don't hold any love for this emotionless soldier of Lire's, despite our many years spent together in the forest and her deceptively innocent exterior.

'In the forest,' I explain to her, 'not long before Lire came to resurrect us, do you recall a group of young people finding us and asking questions about the war?'

Elsie frowns. She remembers even less than I do. She's too happy with her new life to dwell on the past. 'I'm not sure.'

'Well *that* was *them*. Sierra Reed and her friends. Elsie, if they'd have seen you—'

She pales. 'Lire said no one would recognise me. I'm too old. She said—'

'We couldn't have anticipated this. But you have to be careful. While they're here, keep to the kitchens as much as you can. For both our sakes, be good and stay hidden.'

'I will,' she says, her voice high and quiet. 'I know Lire would want us to kill them for what they did to Muse, but if the Reed can kill a fairy, I'm not taking any risks.' She seems almost fearful, something I rarely see in her. But the girl is quick to change the subject. 'But you didn't answer my other question, Relia.' I glare at her for using my name, even though no one is within earshot. 'Oh, stop looking at me like that, and tell me – why were you seated with the princess?'

She doesn't know about my connection to Dawn. No one does except Lire. But it must be obvious how much I care for the princess, even to those who don't know my love for her is more than a maid's adoration.

'In the attack, I . . . saved her life,' I say disbelievingly. 'I pulled her out of harm's way. For that, she rewarded me.'

'Perfect,' says Elsie. 'I never would have thought of that. I'd have let her die. But now she'll trust you even more. Lire is going to be very pleased.'

'Yes,' I say, hoping my unenthusiasm doesn't show too clearly. 'Precisely.'

✦ ❖ ☽ ☀ ☾ ❖ ✦

Elsie sits beside me, her nose freckling in the dream sun, though it gives off only a numb heat. We're on a lone mountain overlooking a vast and curiously endless body of water, with strong waves that lap at the white sand by the edge.

'It's called an ocean,' Lire says, striding towards us, bare feet on fluffy grass. She doesn't have wings here. She never does in her dreams. 'We don't have any in our world, there is no seaside, but elsewhere you can stand at the edge of land and watch as water stretches infinitely into the horizon.'

We remain silent. Lire says things like that sometimes, things we don't understand, things I think only people as ancient as the fairies could know.

This is yet another of our strange abilities. We can invade and influence dreams and nightmares. While the dream may not be 'real', we can speak with Lire this way, giving her information.

The magic carried through from our time as spirits. The hundred years I spent dead are hazy, but I recall whiling away time checking on the people I cared about. I appeared in their dreams as they slept, and sent them stories and places they could feel safe in as they rested. Mostly sweet dreams to my adoptive parents and sisters; they dreamt of me a lot, never knowing if I'd gone missing, ran away, or was dead. And, of course, I always visited Dawn.

I'm not quite sure how we do it. This was all much clearer when I was a spirit, and those memories and feelings are so hard to reach. I do know that now I can only do it when I'm asleep myself; I didn't sleep as a spirit, so that certainly feels different.

I simply lay in bed and visualise the lilac fairy. When I next open my eyes, I'm in another realm – in the dream of whomever I chose to visit. In Lire's mind I have my own body again, red hair falling blurrily over my broader frame – not the spindly maid, but a woman who is stronger, taller, more regal. A woman who was raised to take up space.

'I'm so pleased to see you, my girls,' Lire says, with an expression of genuine warmth. 'What can you tell me of today's attack? My soldiers never returned to me. It seems like it was a terrible waste of magic.'

'Sierra Reed,' I tell her. Although there's a detachment, a darkness in the dream world, I can almost taste bile in the back of my non-existent throat. I don't want Lire to become angry, and really, I don't want to tell her anything at all – especially when she never warned us about the attack. 'It seems that after ki—' The words get caught in my throat. 'After their fight with Muse, they came directly to Bearra, and arrived just in time to help defeat your attackers.'

Lire frowns, and the dream turns red at the edges. The anger festers within me, piercing into my own heart, growing and gnawing. 'And I suppose the Reed girl told Dawn that I have spies in Bearra? Muse was idiotic enough to boast about my plans right before she was murdered, according to the soldiers who made it back that day.' She pauses. 'Bless her soul.'

'Yes, Dawn knows,' I say. 'But we aren't suspected. After standing by the princess's side today in the battle, she only trusts me more. I continue to get closer to her.'

'We're *both* doing very well,' Elsie is quick to add. 'They must have known there would be spies. As long as they don't find out it's us, we shouldn't worry.'

'*I'll* decide what we worry about,' Lire snaps, and Elsie's eyes flash with fear. 'The Reeds have been Grace's protectors for generations. They have always caused me trouble. If you can find a way to kill Sierra Reed, do it. The only thing worse than a Reed is a Reed loyal to Bearra. As I unfortunately had to learn.'

'They also had an iron sword,' offers Elsie, an attempt to make up for her blunder. Her dark hair floats slightly in the dream world, and she wears grey here, always, which unironically shows her true colours. 'About half the attackers were killed, and half have been detained. But Bearra's real advantage was the pirates' iron.'

Lire grinds her teeth. 'The two of you cannot be hurt by iron. Prove to me that you're worth my while, my girls. Use that advantage. Destroy the sword if you're able, but do not expose yourselves for it. I still need you where you are.'

'It wouldn't be any use,' I say to Lire before thinking. *Why* do I *talk*? She gives me a stern look, but waits for me to elaborate. 'The effort to destroy their sword would be wasted when they can simply get more iron.'

'Fine,' Lire says. 'Keep an eye on Bearra's new guests, then. Report anything interesting back to me. Do you have anything else to tell me, or may I rest?'

Elsie and I shake our heads.

'Then sleep well, my dears,' she says, suddenly softening. She reaches out and cups our cheeks. It feels so strange, not quite right in this dream world. But her hand is warm and caring. She truly does love us in some strange way. She sees us like her children, perhaps, despite the cruel games she plays using us.

My heart warms, so twistedly grateful for the affection. I know it's wrong, but it feels so good to have someone who really knows me look into my eyes with care. It feels so good to have a mother again, after so long. I smile up at her, and leave the dream, drifting back to my own body as I drop into a deep sleep.

CHAPTER 4

SOMEWHERE, SOMETIME...

Dawn, beloved princess of Bearra, had countless problems that could not be solved.

As she had done each morning since Lire's betrayal, she visited her parents' rooms to wake them. They lay side by side, the queen and king, groaning in half-sleep.

'Mum,' the princess whispered. 'Dad?'

Only yesterday, the castle had been attacked by Lire's soldiers, and the kingdom might have fallen if not for Sierra and her friends. Dawn had to give them credit. She hadn't trusted them before, not really. Now she owed them everything.

The pirates, Teddy, Maya . . . All people who owed Bearra nothing. Carlotta, too. They all could have run away, but instead they fought for her kingdom. They stood by Dawn's side.

And yet, the queen and king wouldn't even leave their bed. Not even to go to the bunkers within the hill for safety. The attack passed them by, with no damage done to their part of the castle. Luckily. Even the thunders of destruction weren't enough to rouse them.

As usual, the princess was left to deal with the entire situation on her own.

Dawn had many allies and friends, without whom she would have fallen apart. Yet while she could have a million friends, they could never erase the fact that she, in the end, bore the lonely burden of responsibility. She was the only princess, Bearra's future queen – if it was even still a kingdom when the time came for her coronation.

Dawn was at her wit's end. She was finally ready to confront her parents. They would abandon her no longer. Bearra was in desperate need of its leaders, especially after Lire's attack. Dawn would *make* them get up. No more excuses.

She stepped closer to her parents' bed. Two middle-aged women, one maid and one guard, stood by the door, always waiting to attend to the royals' needs, but otherwise the room always remained silent and dark.

Dawn reached out to pull back the blankets and reveal the sleeping faces of her mother and father. But . . .

Where were they? Their places were filled with cushions. The groaning and snoring she thought she heard was merely coming from the open window as it creaked back and forth in the breeze.

Panic gripped Dawn, a thousand attackers squeezing the air from her chest. What had happened? Dawn spun to the guard and maid. 'Where are they?'

They shook their heads, as shocked as she was. 'Princess, no one has been in or out, we're certain—' the guard stopped, voice shaking. If Dawn were not blessed with Kindness, she might punish the staff that let her parents disappear. But she would be patient. She would calm herself and look.

Dawn steadied her breathing, her lungs screaming and making her nauseous. 'Have the castle searched immediately,' she rasped, clinging to the blankets. They were cold; her parents had been gone a while.

If they'd merely gotten up for a walk, or fairies-forbid to do their jobs, there would be no reason for secrecy. Whatever this was, they were in trouble.

The maid rushed away while the guard stayed to watch Dawn.

The princess didn't know what to do.

'I'm sure they're just downstairs enjoying breakfast, Your Highness,' said the guard.

Dawn shot her an exasperated look. 'We both know that isn't the case.'

The princess was already run down. Not just due to the attack and her new guests, but the iron they brought. Dawn did not have any magic of her own, but the blessings she had been given as a baby were intwined in her very being. Iron did not affect her as badly as it would someone with real magic, someone like Teddy, but it still added another layer of tiredness.

Their only weapon was, most ironically, a double-edged sword.

All Dawn had, really – the only thing in the world that made her feel better – was Carlotta. And Carlotta was someone she *paid*. But having someone who was all hers, who could answer to her every need, listen as she talked, tell her what she needed to hear . . . Carlotta was invaluable. She was the one light in Dawn's endless darkness. The princess had been falling apart before her new maid made her way into the castle, barely a month or two ago – a replacement to her long-time maid Kelina, yet another person Dawn had lost because of Lire.

Now Dawn might not even have her parents, though one could argue that she had lost them a long time ago. But the princess knew this time was different. It had all gotten too much, and now they were *gone*. Where, she did not know. How long they would survive, she did not know. But they were wasting away in here, barely able to function. They must have seen no escaping their pain other than, well . . . escaping. Dawn was familiar with the feeling. But while running away from their responsibility was one thing, it was now apparent that even she, their only daughter, was not enough of a reason to stay.

'Your Highness, what's that?' The guard pointed to a lone envelope sitting on the dark wood of the desk. It sat under the window, unused since the queen and king stopped doing . . . everything. This letter was new.

Dawn forced herself to walk over, to pick it up and open it with her thumb. It was folded over in a way that kept the small note in; they hadn't bothered to use the royal seal. Outside Bearra, they had presses and glues for these things now, but Dawn thought her parents likely wouldn't have even bothered with that. The paper was almost grey; not like the pure white they had outside, either.

For Dawn was written on the front in her mother's script.

She sighed and unfolded it, her eyes prickling with tears. She stayed facing the wall so the guard wouldn't see her face. She knew what it would say.

My darling, the note read. *You were always meant for this. Blessed since birth to be the greatest queen the world ever had. Since you were a child, you have proven wiser than us, a better leader than us. We command a room with our crowns – you command a room with your presence alone.*

We are mere burdens to you, and we cannot live this way anymore. We do not want to leave you, but it is better that we do. Know that we love you. We hope we can find new lives somewhere, and we will see you again one day, when the war is over. Until then, sweet princess, do what you were born to: lead.

Seven Blessings,

Mother and Father.

Dawn gripped the desk to stop herself falling to her knees.

'Your Highness,' said a different voice, not the guard or the maid. She couldn't turn around, not yet. 'We've searched the castle, and we cannot find the queen and king anywhere. Would you like us to extend the search throughout the kingdom?'

'They—' Dawn's voice was squeaky and cracked. She sniffed. 'They aren't in Bearra anymore.'

'Dawn?' another voice called. *Carlotta.*

This made the princess turn. As soon as Carlotta noticed Dawn crying, tears began to shine in her eyes too. *That* was the final straw. Dawn broke down just as her friend gathered her in her arms, wrapping the princess in a tight embrace as they lowered to the floor in a suffocating flurry of skirts.

Carlotta must have gestured for the others to leave, because footsteps sounded, the door shutting behind them.

Dawn rose slowly, Carlotta not letting go, and climbed into her parents' bed. She pulled the covers over herself and curled up into a ball. The same as when she was a child after she had nightmares, although then her parents were there to comfort her. Now all she had was their scent.

And she had Carlotta, running a hand softly over her back, waiting with her for an unknowable amount of time as Dawn wept into the pillows.

When Dawn woke, the covers were no longer over her head. At some point Carlotta must have moved them, and instead the princess's head was in her maid's lap as Carlotta stroked her hair. The sun was no longer streaming through the windows, so a few hours had passed. Had Carlotta been there the entire time?

Dawn knew it wasn't fair, but she pretended to be asleep a while longer, relishing in Carlotta's gentle touch. *When you only have one person in the world . . .*

She thought of Relia, and for a few minutes, could almost pretend it was her hands in her hair instead of Carlotta's.

'You're safe,' Carlotta said gently. 'It's okay, Dawn.'

The spell was broken with Carlotta's raspier voice. Dawn sat up groggily, her eyes crusty, completely unlike the princess she was supposed to be. She leaned against the pillows and Carlotta shuffled back politely.

'You . . .' Dawn started, a hesitant question on her lips. She felt terrible asking what she was about to ask; she knew it wasn't polite. Still, she needed something, anything at all, to give her some hope. 'You're an orphan, aren't you? How . . . How do you cope?'

'I am,' said Carlotta, reaching for the hem of her dress and running it between two fingers. 'I can't lie to you and pretend it's easy. But Dawn, you find ways through it. Family may be your first support system, but not everyone who cares for you has to be related to you by blood. Just when you start to think you have nothing left, you begin to realise how much is out there.' She breathed slowly. 'When my parents passed away, I spent a lot of time wallowing in a darkness that I thought would never lift, and then one day I decided to take a job here. *This* job. It was a distraction from my grief, a reason to leave my house . . . And it ended up saving me. Knowing you, and being here, is how I cope. This castle and the people within it are my comfort.'

Dawn nodded, lacking the energy to reply.

She felt as if she'd dreamed of both Carlotta and Relia as she'd slept, as well as her parents, and the seven fairies, though she couldn't quite remember. She dreamed of Relia and Carlotta most nights, sweet dreams, the two of them morphing into each other, but the visions shattered each morning as she woke.

Dawn knew she should have sent Carlotta away with the other maids to hide during the attack the day before, but in the moment, she was selfish. She wanted Carlotta by her side, because having her there made her stronger. In fact, she'd almost insisted that the maid move up into her quarters after the attack. She'd wanted that even before yesterday, longing for the comfort of the other girl by her side.

There was no way around it, no more pretending the pull wasn't there. Dawn had feelings for Carlotta, and that was a dangerous, dangerous thing.

CHAPTER 5

I stay with Dawn the night, but by the next morning she's already able to wake herself up, eat, and make her way to the ballroom – our current makeshift throne room – for meetings. The glittering space is one of the few wings undamaged by the attack.

I follow her there, feeling strange after spending the night on pillows on the floor of her parents' room, with an ache in my neck. I help some other maids arrange seats beneath one of the large bay windows, and suddenly it's business as usual: we're sitting around with most of the inner circle, assisting Dawn with her daily meetings, supporting her as she deals with the most irritating of her subjects, and discussing the war in any spare moments.

Finally, a middle-aged woman complaining about potato prices totters out the doors, and my relief is tamped by a prickle down my spine. I look to Dawn, wringing my hands together as a cloaked figure enters the ballroom, their head tilted.

The princess keeps a straight face, her tiara gleaming. 'What can we help you with?'

But it's Teddy who stands and shuffles towards the anonymous person. A flash of pink appears between them – *magic.*

'Wait!' I shout, standing up, placing a hand in front of Dawn.

My heart thumps as eyes glance around the room, everyone wondering what to do as Teddy turns to me, shaking his head. 'It's okay,' he reassures us, palms out. His red hair shines in the sunlight. He gives Dawn a meaningful stare, and a knowing expression passes between them. 'We need the room.'

Dawn nods, tapping my arm to gesture that I should sit back down; I do, my cheeks flushing. The guards and maids slip out of the room without fuss. When I first became Dawn's maid, I would have followed them, but her trust in me now demands the respect of her inner circle as well; no one expects me to leave.

The doors are pulled closed, and the cloaked person pulls back their hood.

It's as if the room lights up with the pink magic radiating around her. The cloak hits the floor, and she shakes herself free. Once my eyes have adjusted to her aura, the first thing I notice is her wings, glittering in every colour of the rainbow. Pure light. She has tan skin and a long nose, brown hair tied into two braids either side of her head, and pink, *everywhere.*

Amora.

Almost all of us gape in shock and fascination, but Dawn, Teddy and Maya appear . . . relieved?

But of course. The fairy is supposed to be on our side now.

I haven't told Lire about this. I wasn't supposed to know – very few do, which made it easy for me to keep it secret. Because if Lire finds out what Amora is doing, all of her people will be in trouble. It's a secret worth keeping, at least for now.

The fairy hugs Teddy and Maya. 'I'm sorry it's taken me so long to see you. Things are . . . They aren't going well in my territory. Or anywhere, for that matter. People are scared.'

'Then why did you come?' Dawn asks, her fierce royal eyes narrowed.

'Good question,' says Sierra, seated with her crew, all of them leaning forward, hands on their weapons, observant and ready to strike. 'Is someone going to tell us why there's a *fairy* here?'

Amora looks Sierra up and down. 'And is someone going to tell me why the fairy *killer* is here?'

'Sierra?' Maya says, a snicker on her lips. 'She's fine.'

'Amora,' Dawn presses. She has no excitement at seeing her ally, and I'm not sure whether it's because she thinks Amora has brought bad news, or because she can't muster any joy after losing her parents. 'Why are you here?'

The fairy moves to the semi-circle of seats, her footsteps light as a feather, and Teddy pulls up a chair for her. When she sits, her wings relax slightly. 'I didn't want to make a scene coming here, and I apologise for the disguise. You know how delicate this situation is. But

I told you I would help, and I will. I heard of the attack that occurred here. It's time I give you my magic so you can begin arming yourselves.'

'Please.' Teddy smiles at her gratefully. 'But first, we need to update you on what's been happening on our end.'

Amora's face scrunches. 'I can feel it. You have iron now.'

'Yes,' Dawn says. 'The team we sent to scout for the metal was successful.' She gestures to Sierra and her crew. 'They reached Lire's iron stores, and killed Muse while they were at it. We now have something to defend ourselves with, and one less enemy to worry about.'

'But there's bad news too,' says Teddy. 'Lire brought back spirits from Muse's Forest to join her army and work as spies. We don't know how powerful they are, but we know they're among us, and they can't be detected.'

'I'm aware,' says Amora, and the circle breaks into distrusting whispers.

I, meanwhile, loose a long breath and clutch the arms of my chair.

Maya gives her a stern look. 'Excuse me?'

Dawn raises a hand to hush the room. 'Fairy, tell us what you can.'

'We all have our spies,' Amora says indifferently. 'When I was alerted to Lire's plan, I remembered something and had an idea. It isn't necessarily a fantastic idea, but I thought, if you were desperate . . . Well, now, you have spies in your midst that you can't identify, and who have magic we know nothing about. You aren't going to last long.'

I sit back. Swallow. Stare at the hem of Dawn's dress.

'Well, tell us then.' Sierra watches the fairy blankly. 'We love a bad idea around here.'

Amora's wings flutter with irritation, though I wonder if she's also a little scared of the Reed. Who isn't? 'There's an enchanted mirror, one of a kind, which could expose these spies,' Amora explains, gazing out the window. 'When Dawn was born, Grace and I wanted to create a magical object for her. To be honest, it was a bribe more than anything. It was why we fairies all showed up to bestow our blessings on her – why Kara was so furious she didn't get the chance. We wanted the princess's favour, because whoever ruled Bearra ruled the triarue mines.

'So Grace and I hatched a plan. We experimented to create something we thought could be useful, something no one else would have. This was before magic became so accessible, of course. There weren't enchanted objects and people didn't just *have* magic.'

She looks at her hands, glowing pink, as if remembering how it felt to hold the object. 'We enchanted a mirror, giving it the ability to show where magic has been used. It reflects power. It would be a way for the princess to protect herself.'

'We could use it to find the spirits?' Dawn asks. 'Where is it? I don't remember having such a thing.'

'That's the problem,' Amora says. 'We made it so only you can use it, Dawn. Lire was furious when she found out what we did. At first she tried to steal it for herself, then when she realised she couldn't use it, she threw it away. I don't know where. But if you can find the mirror, it could be the tool you need to protect Bearra.'

My chest goes cold. *Fairies. Fairies. Fairies.* There was supposed to be nothing that could expose me. My greatest threat was myself. Why didn't Lire warn me about this?

Dawn takes a moment, her eyes wandering back and forth as she thinks. 'We'll send out Sierra's crew, then.' She turns to them. 'You succeeded in finding the iron. You've already done the impossible. I believe I can entrust you with this. That is, if you're up for it?'

'No.' Amora gives the princess a cautious expression. 'The magic of the mirror is clear. Only you can use it, so only you can find it. To anyone else it will look like any other handheld mirror. You alone will see the magic within it and be able to use its power.'

Dawn rubs her temples, but Maya answers for her. 'Then it's useless. Dawn can't leave Bearra on a wild goose chase. Even before the war, the princess couldn't do such a thing.'

'We'll make a new mirror,' says Ebony, and Levi, as expected, nods along. 'We have plenty of magic.'

'I wish it were as simple as that,' says Amora.

She meets Ebony's eyes in an almost maternal fashion. Ebony certainly appears to be from Amora's Territory, though the world is so diverse these days it's impossible to tell. Could the two have met, or is it simply a respect formed between a human and their patron fairy?

Amora explains, 'Similar objects could certainly be made, but they wouldn't have the power of the original mirror. Lire's spies were made with pure magic, combining two fairies' power. Just like the mirror Grace and I made, combining our power in a way never done before and never done since. If you want to achieve something as complex as outing these spies, you need the mirror's ability.'

Sierra stands, her black hair falling down her back in glossy, straight strands. She points at the fairy. 'I don't trust you,' she says. She responds to the glares from people around the room with a shrug. 'You come here just in time, tell the princess she has to go after some object we have no proof exists . . . Isn't it convenient? Wouldn't that make Bearra all the more easy to invade, with the princess gone?'

Teddy stands to argue, but Arden is first, stepping in front of Sierra. 'She's right,' he says. 'We've been warned enough times not to trust anyone. Especially a fairy. Teddy, clearly you have an – an *attachment* – to Amora. But that isn't enough. We can't take the words of a fairy, and the *son of our enemy*, without any questioning.'

'That's ridiculous,' says Maya, gripping the sides of her chair. 'Sierra, tell him that's—'

'We trust you pirates without any questioning,' Teddy almost barks. 'Sierra's tried to kill nearly everyone in this room, but now you and her want to tell us who we can't trust? Amora has only ever helped us.'

'Helped you,' mumbles Sierra.

'She has nothing to gain!' Maya argues back.

'A kingdom full of triarue that will be left leaderless?' says Arden, his ears turning red. 'And, let me guess, with Teddy left in charge. No, there's nothing for them to gain.'

'I've never trusted him,' Sierra affirms. Maya glares at her. 'What? I still think you could do better.'

Amora crosses her arms. 'Will you all stop with your childish arguing for one moment so we can discuss this seriously? When Lire's spies take you down, you'll be wishing you listened to me. You already have enemies coming from every angle. Have you even considered the Ice Empire and their motives? Have you thought of the other fairies? You can't win this war. I'm giving you a lifeline.'

Sierra seethes. 'You're taking the perfect chance to manipulate and take advantage of this kingdom!'

They begin to argue over the top of each other, and I find it difficult not to cover my ears. My breaths come faster, uncontrollable, as the room grows louder and louder. Unable to take it, I squeeze my eyes shut.

'Quiet!' Dawn growls, her voice carrying above all the others in the room, calling me back. She doesn't have to stand, or scream, or wave her arms. The attention snaps back to her in an instant.

Suddenly there's silence again, and I hear birds chirping distantly outside, footsteps in the halls. It's like cool water being poured through my brain. I exhale and open my eyes to see everyone sitting once more, tense with irritation and anticipation.

Dawn brushes her tight golden curls back from her face. 'Lire gave us one month to surrender before her final attack. We have no time to argue. We have no time for questioning. If there is an object that can give us even a small advantage, I will go and find it.'

Before the room can ignite again – before even my own mind can ignite with questions – she raises her hand. 'I will not be gone long, and I will leave the kingdom protected. Bearra will be fine, because you will all be here to lead it in my absence.' I give her a wide-eyed look, urging her change her mind. She can't *leave*. She's been so afraid since her parents left; is this just her excuse to follow them, to run away? This is a hasty, dangerous plan. But she goes on. 'No one outside this room needs to know I'm away. If outside forces don't know of my absence, they won't see it as a vulnerability and attack. Amora.' She turns to the fairy, as if none of the arguing ever happened. 'Tell me any leads you may have on where this mirror may be.'

Amora smiles sweetly, her pink lips triumphant as she glances at the pirates. 'It isn't something Lire will have guarded. She was more than happy to toss it away, thinking it useless. In fact, I wouldn't be surprised if Lire forgot about it altogether. I imagine it will be hidden away in one of her properties, or one of her iron hoards. You'll have to search them all.'

'*Fairies*,' says Teddy. His eyes are darting around, and he's squeezing Maya's arm. 'I think I know this mirror. My brother . . . Lire gave him one when we were young. I remember she told him something about it being . . . I don't know . . . She said it was old, very, very old, and she wanted Jacob to have it, to remind him of what was meant to be his. We didn't even know about Dawn back then, except for the stories everyone knew about Bearra. But my mother took the mirror from somewhere and made a real show of giving it to Jacob.'

Dawn tenses at the mention of Teddy's brother. The one she was supposed to marry before he was killed. Even for Teddy to bring up Lire and his brother is shocking. He barely acknowledges his past, and remembering he's the son of the fairy I'm working for, remembering that this entire conversation is about a mirror to expose me—

Fairies. I. Am. Doomed.

I've thought for a while that Teddy might be my greatest threat. Now I'm sure. His connection to Lire, her magic within him just like it's within me . . . if fire fights fire, it could burn us both.

'So do you know where it is now?' Maya asks him.

Teddy's face falls. 'No. Not long after that, I began to travel and stay away from home as much as I could. I spent most of my time with Amora and didn't see my brother for years. If he had the mirror when he—' He throws his arms up. 'I'm sorry, I don't know. But you could check our old apartment in Naroport. Our childhood things might still be there.'

The pirates glance between themselves with disgusted looks. 'Naroport?' moans Sierra. 'You don't want to go there.'

'No, that's a great lead,' Dawn says, but her face is harder than usual. 'Thank you, Teddy. I'm sure Sierra and her friends will be happy to take me to Naroport before returning promptly back to Bearra as its guards. I'll make my own way home once I've secured the mirror.'

Maya scoffs. 'Dawn, I understand you have to go on this mission, but you can't be suggesting you'll go *alone*?'

'Of course I am,' says the princess. 'I need everyone here, protecting the kingdom. I won't risk more lives by bringing people along. And if the mirror is still in Lire's old apartment, I won't be gone long.'

'At least let me come,' Maya says. 'I'm not a magical fairy pirate princess warrior whatever. Bearra doesn't need me, but someone has to be with you.'

'No,' I say, but I hear my voice as an echo. The room turns to me and sweat builds in my palms, but it's as if they aren't my palms, which of course they're not. Panicking, I explain, 'Sorry, but you can't go, Maya. I'll go with the princess. That's *my* job.'

Dawn turns to me, hazel eyes wide. 'Carlotta,' she whispers. 'I cannot and will not ask you to do such a thing.'

'You don't have to ask,' I say. 'Taking care of you is what I'm paid for. Accept the help. Otherwise I'm certain no one in this room will hesitate to chain you up to stop you from leaving.'

Sierra clears her throat. '*No.* The princess doesn't need a maid. She needs a guard. Guards. An army! This is all ridiculous.'

'Thank you for your opinion, Lady Reed,' says Dawn. 'But I'll make my own decisions. I know what's best for Bearra, and I won't hesitate to do it.'

'Thank you for your decision-making skills, Your Highness,' Sierra says venomously. 'But you're not my princess. I'm here because the world needs saving. I'm not happy to stand by and watch one of the few people holding things together sacrifice herself for nothing.'

'Sierra,' Maya warns. 'Please don't cause a scene.'

She rolls her eyes and sits back down. 'Fine. But we can't allow this without a backup plan. With the queen and king gone, who's going to rule when the princess never returns?'

'Teddy and Maya will,' says Dawn, with a finality I'm not sure anyone expected. She doesn't seem to be joking. 'I've spent months with them as my advisors. I trust them enough to leave my kingdom to them. For now, and if I don't return.'

Maya cringes and shuffles back in her seat. '*Dawn.*'

The thought is almost too terrible to bear. Dawn gone, ripped from the world once again, and knowing it would be my fault. I want to race behind one of the huge, draping curtains hanging over the ballroom windows, wrap myself up, and disappear.

Am I really going to go on this mission? What am I going to tell Lire? What *can* I tell her? I can only keep so much from her, and if

Elsie finds out the things I've kept from the fairy, the things only I know from my closeness to Dawn—

I can't breathe.

If I help Dawn too much, my time here will be over. But if I do what Lire wants, Dawn won't make it through the war. Lire will let Dawn live, she told me she would, but that won't matter if Dawn lets herself die. How am I supposed to keep us together and alive?

'Yes, Maya,' Dawn continues. 'In fact, I have the perfect idea, inspired by Lire herself. No one has to know I'm gone if there's someone disguised as me, taking my place . . .'

'*Dawn*,' Maya presses.

'Teddy will use magic to make Maya look and sound just like me, and together you'll rule Bearra while I'm gone.'

Chaos breaks out again, and I barely catch a single word in the resounding shouts.

All I know is that this is a bad idea – and I can't do anything to stop it.

CHAPTER 6

She thinks she has everyone fooled, but she doesn't just want to go to find the mirror. I'm certain Dawn is reacting so recklessly because of her parents leaving. This is an opportunity to search for the queen and king.

Thank the fairies she's allowing me to come, even if it means Lire will know *more*.

But I've spent weeks learning to lie to the fairy of wisdom. Anything I can keep from her, I do.

It began with white lies – tiny things like the colour of a dress or a barely-noticeable word choice – as I tested my limits, but it kept growing. I learned that in our dream worlds, I am more in control than she is. Lire may be scarily powerful, but she doesn't have my undead abilities. That's how I've kept Amora's alliance with Bearra from her.

How I'll keep the truth about the mirror from her. And how I plan to keep Dawn alive and Bearra safe for as long as possible.

Until the inevitable. Until either Lire defeats Bearra in one month's time, or Dawn finds out I'm a spy and has me banished, imprisoned, or whatever awful punishment she'll deal to me for betraying her so terribly.

The closer we get to this mirror, the closer Dawn is to discovering the truth. What will she do when she looks at the reflection and sees Relia instead of Carlotta?

Dawn is scared that she has only weeks to save her kingdom. I'm terrified that I have only weeks before we lose each other again.

Maya's family is at the castle again tonight; she has to explain to them what Dawn is having her do. There's her mother and father, a sweet couple in late middle age whose parental instincts seem to extend to everyone they meet. Prima, the oldest sister, who Maya seems to clash with the most, and her husband Matthew. Finally there's Briar, the middle sister, who loves everything romantic and luxurious. When they're here, the rest of us watch the five of them in curiosity and, well, jealousy. Because none of us have what they have, or if we ever did, it's long gone.

Once, Sierra would have let that family die to save her own – I know the story of the crown – but now she looks at them with a deep sadness. The pirates are a tight-knit family of their own, but I know that despite how many families one might create or be welcomed into, it's never the same as the first.

Some of us are over a hundred years old, and yet we are all too young for this, all left without anyone to guide us.

Dawn, at the head of the table, smiles politely at Maya's mother and father. 'I'm sorry we'll be taking Maya away from you for a while.'

I'm seated beside her, once again within the inner circle. No other maids have ever been afforded such privilege – to sleep in the princess's rooms, to dine with her, sit by her side at all times. To talk without being prompted, to eat without asking. Is it only delusion to believe that Dawn sees me as more than a maid? That part of her knows it's really me under this disguise?

A week ago, I would have been serving food at this dining table. Now I'm an equal.

But at what cost?

'Our daughter *loves* Bearra,' Maya's mother replies with a laugh.

Briar nearly chokes beside her. 'Since she got a fairy prince for a boyfriend.'

'Hey!' Maya shouts, but when people start to snicker, she slumps back with a small smile.

Teddy places an arm around her. 'As long as I get to be her fairy prince boyfriend,' he says, 'she can love or not love wherever or whatever she likes.'

Maya smirks. 'Thank you, my sweet darling lover.'

Dawn leans over to me and whispers in my ear, 'There are too many couples in this room. It's unbearable.'

'You're the princess,' I say, loosing a nervous giggle. 'Make coupling up illegal.'

She smiles, and for a moment it seems as if she's looking at *me* again. Relia.. A dozen dances and dinner parties with whispered conversations just like this flash through my mind – do they flash through hers, too? Then her eyes snap back to the dinner table. 'I couldn't possibly.'

Wren bursts into laughter, sharing a private joke with Ebony. They're watching Lark. He's across the table seated next to Briar, and they're tasting each other's food.

'I'm a better chef,' Lark says, though I have to concentrate to hear him above the chatter of the room. 'I can make better food on a moving ship with half a kitchen and half the ingredients.'

Briar smiles, her face so incredibly similar to Maya's, though her expressions are much softer. 'Then you must visit me sometime and show me your favourite recipes.'

The Musan boy, with his flaming red hair and wide smile, has more charm than I would've expected when he says, 'Do you prefer sweet or savoury?'

I can sense the butterflies flying through them, unless that's just my own. Dawn is still leaning closer to me than necessary.

'Sweet, always,' Briar says, eyes twinkling as she places a hand over his to take back her fork. He lets her take it, then swipes a piece of food off her plate with his fingers. She gasps, but after a moment they laugh wildly together.

'So you understand the situation,' Dawn says to Maya's parents, drawing my and their attention back to her. 'While Maya is acting as *me*, she cannot visit you. She cannot speak to you as herself unless you are in private. She'll be guarded at all hours, every moment of every day.'

Maya's father nods solemnly. 'And how will Maya's absence be explained?'

'Oh, don't worry yourself,' Sierra says with a smirk. 'No one will miss her.'

Maya grimaces. '*Thanks.* But you're right. People barely notice me. I'm just the peasant who trails around behind the princess and prince.'

'They still think you're a prince?' Sierra asks Teddy.

He replies, 'Not for much longer, now they know I have magic. We've been avoiding having to explain it.'

'They should just be grateful you have power,' says Maya's mother. 'And used it to fight for them.'

'We can only hope,' he says, giving her a shy smile.

I sit back for a while, listening to the conversations until the night turns late and the exhaustion of the crowded room begins to overcome me. I glance at Dawn, hoping she too will want to retire soon, because I'm not sure I can leave without her.

Then, when the talking has finally begun to die down into yawns, Maya's sister Prima clears her throat. Her husband, beside her, taps his glass with his fork to garner attention. It works; the yawns and sighs cease as everyone's eyes meet the couple. 'I have something I'd like to say,' says Prima.

Maya glances at her sister's stomach. 'Oh no. Are you . . .'

'Maya,' Prima hisses. 'Don't ruin it!'

'I didn't say anything!'

'Yes, you did!'

'Hush!' their mother says. 'Prima, you have the floor.'

Prima settles back in her chair, taking her husband's hand. 'Well, Maya's worst nightmare has come true. I am, in fact, pregnant.'

Maya nearly spits out her drink as her family gasps delightedly.

A solemn feeling, however, fills the rest of the room. I know what some of us are thinking: there couldn't possibly be a worse time to bring a child into the world. How do Prima and her husband hope to take care of a baby while a war is happening around them?

But Maya's family are all hugging, and the room uplifts. The tiredness is shaken with surprise and hope, and everyone eventually stands to congratulate the couple. Still, at the other end of the table, Maya's face is hardened once more. She glances at Dawn, sending a non-verbal message. *We're winning this war. We're protecting this child.*

How could I expect any less from the girl who travelled the world and fought a fairy to save her family?

In my dreams, I meet with Lire alone. I plan to speak with Elsie later – I still haven't seen her, since I've barely been back to our room, and I must tell her about my new mission. But for now I have to give the fairy some explanation of what I'll be doing without telling her enough to use against Dawn.

'The Reed girl and her friends,' Lire says, as always wingless and glowing in her dream world, 'are they still in Bearra?'

'They plan to officially join Bearra's army and train them in using iron weapons,' I explain. I don't tell her that they'll also be helping the soldiers learn to use the magic Amora gave them. She can wait for Elsie to give her that information – at least, with the story that the magic was stolen, so we don't implicate Amora – and I want to buy Dawn some time.

Lire sneers. 'These children and their audacity. I know you loved the princess, Relia, maybe you still do. But I'm not sure how you can stand to be around that group of brats. When we win this war, there will be plenty of people to fight for your love. Nice young women – or men, if you like – who don't act like animals. I wouldn't have anything less for my sweet girl. I'll give you everything you could ever want.'

I sigh and nod politely, because what can I say to someone offering me everything, yet nothing that I want? I never know how to respond to the fondness she shows me when every day, in the real world, I and everyone around me hate her.

'Tell me how you feel,' Lire says gently. 'It's only you and I. We can speak honestly.'

I stammer, 'It can be difficult, living in the castle.' *But not for the reasons you think.* 'That's what I needed to speak with you about, in fact. The princess wishes to send me away on a mission. I could be gone for a few weeks. I tried to get out of it, but she was determined. I'm to travel alone and search for the queen and king. Dawn doesn't trust anyone else to do this. She's convinced I could bring them home.'

Lire grits her teeth.

'I can try again,' I reassure the fairy. 'I'll feign illness so she doesn't make me leave.'

'No,' Lire says. 'I have spies in the furthest reaches of this world, as far as you can travel before the ice consumes you. But *you* are my favourite.' She cups my cheek with her palm. 'Relia, if you can bring

Dawn's parents home, that will solidify your place at the princess's side permanently. You are my chosen one because no one can get close to her as you can, even when you're in disguise. I know she already trusts you immensely. Elsie has told me how you've been sleeping in her rooms and eating at her table.' Her hand moves to rest on my shoulder. 'Although I warn you to be careful. Do not get *too* close; this is the best possible place you could be. For me. For us. So seek out the royals and bring them home, and report back to me what you find along the way.'

'Of course, Lire,' I say. 'I'll do all I can to bring you the information you need.' Lying in dreams is so simple – it isn't so much about what I do and say as it is about altering the way the dreamer perceives me. Here, I am in control. Outside, I never know how to do or say the right thing.

'Good girl,' she replies, giving my cheek a pat before letting her hand fall back to her side. 'I'll have Elsie keep a closer eye on the princess and her inner circle while you're gone. And I'll make sure to warn her to behave. You should try to enjoy your time away, my dear. I will reward you for all your hard work.'

'Thank you,' I say. 'I'll report again soon.'

'Don't leave it too long.' She turns, her back bare where her wings should be, her body in a simple purple wrap that dips down her spine.

The dream becomes fuzzy as she walks away, and I drift into dreams of my own. Dreams about Dawn, about balls and palaces, about my mother and father, about the family who took me in when they were gone. The past haunts me still, but I never want it to leave. It is too precious.

The next night, after a day of scheming how we're going to do this, Dawn places a bag of triarue into her luggage as Teddy secures an opal bracelet around her wrist. She gazes at it excitedly. 'I've never had to pay for things before,' she muses.

'It isn't *fun*,' replies Maya.

We're in Dawn's room, the four of us and Sierra, preparing to leave early tomorrow. Sierra and Arden will sail us to Naroport, then it'll be up to us to make our way from there. The rest of Sierra's crew will stay in Bearra as protection, and, possibly, insurance. By the time we leave, before the sun rises, Maya will be sleeping in Dawn's bed, ready to wake up and be the princess until the real Dawn returns.

'Well, you're about to see just how much fun being *me* is, Maya,' Dawn says, gesturing to her wardrobe, overflowing with crowns and gowns. Maya nearly crashes to the floor as she fake-cries.

'I still think this is a terrible idea,' Sierra says. 'Just so you know that I was against it when everything falls apart.'

'This isn't just about the mirror,' Dawn says. 'We can look for allies as we go, like the woman who gave Ebony her iron sword, and see if we can meet with any more fairies – see if we can stir up tension between them. It's like the spirit told Sierra, we have to turn the fairies against each other if we want a chance to win. And I need to get out of here, now. I need space, I need air, I need—'

'To look for your parents,' Maya finishes. 'We understand. We really do. But Dawn, we're all worried about you.'

'I'm flattered that you all fear for me so much,' Dawn says, 'but I'll be fine. You forget that I'm *Strong*. I have six blessings. What can't I handle? Besides, I'll have Carlotta to look out for me.'

Maya begins wrestling one of the rings from her fingers – the blessed rings that match Teddy's. Between them they have magic from every fairy except Grace, whose blessing belongs to Sierra. 'You would be surprised,' Maya says, yanking the ring off, 'just how helpful Darkness can be, as well.' She hands it to the princess. 'Now you have all seven.'

Dawn blanches. 'I appreciate the offer, but I don't particularly want magic from the one fairy who hates me enough to have cursed me to die.'

'I wouldn't worry,' says Sierra, kicking her feet up on the bed. 'Someone cursed me once, and I simply ended up falling in love with him.'

'We aren't all so lucky.' Dawn throws some more clothes in her bag. 'I don't think Kara sees me that way.'

'You never know.' Maya winks. 'Just take the ring, Dawn. Having all the blessings might be exactly what you need.'

When Dawn still doesn't budge, I take the ring from Maya myself, then pick up Dawn's hand gently and place it on her finger. She doesn't fight me, and it fits perfectly. Does her skin feel the same as mine does as we touch, crawling with a lightning-like magic?

My fingers linger a moment too long.

'Thank you,' Dawn says, quickly moving back from me.

I swallow, embarrassed.

'Carlotta,' Maya says, turning to me. Except for Dawn, the inner circle address me so rarely that sometimes I forget I'm not invisible.

'Yes?' I answer, my voice small.

'If things aren't going well out there . . . You bring the princess back home, okay? I'm not just saying this because I want to be her for the least amount of time physically possible. We can't let anything happen to her. I don't care if you have to tie her up and drag her all the way back here.'

I smile. 'That was already my plan.'

'Carlotta!' Dawn says. 'Don't start agreeing with Maya. She'll only lead you down a dark path.'

'Certainly, Your Highness,' I reply, a hint of humour in my tone. 'I could never disobey you. Then how would I get paid?'

They snicker, and something, a warmth, begins to fill in my torso. There's so much joy in making others laugh. Making other people momentarily happy. Will I ever fall into that category of *other people*? Will I feel like I'm truly one of them someday, or will I always feel invisible, hidden in the wings, drowning alone?

'We're going to be okay,' Teddy says after a while, quietly, tapping the glass of the window. If the presence of the pirate's iron has affected him, he hasn't let it show. Though it wouldn't be like him to let anyone know when he's in pain. 'We've always won so far. No matter what happens after tonight . . . We just have to believe we'll be okay.'

Maya slips her arm around his waist, so small against him. Sierra perches on the edge of Dawn's bed, yawning. Dawn hums as she places a hairbrush in her travel bag.

I watch, as a good maid does, and fight the tears pricking in my eyes. Because I know we won't be. There is no version of our future where any of us are left *okay*. There is no one, even in the furthest reaches of the world, that this war won't touch.

CHAPTER 7

SOMEWHERE, SOMETIME...

Prince Zeus of the Ice Empire, despite being almost unnaturally hand-some, despite being the only prince left in the world, and despite his many attempts, was unlucky in love.

His first lover left him for a poor, young pauper. The next accused him of loving himself more than he could ever love another.

Then there was Sierra, who turned him into a bird.

One woman, however, always had a part of his heart: his childhood best friend – or more accurately *rival* – Isla. Well, she was General Isla now, a favourite of Candace and the empire, a warrior who would *not stop turning him down*.

But why? Everyone else adored him.

He stalked out of his room sulkily, his shoulders hunched, hoping for someone to come and compliment him or delight him with a gift.

His loyal followers always made him feel better. But they were growing fewer and fewer, since Candace.

Candace.

Just thinking her name put a bad taste in his mouth. The woman – about the same age as his parents, the *actual* rulers of the Ice Empire, if a little younger – had been usurping the queen and king for years. Stealing away those who were loyal to them, attracting them with her magic. Never calling herself a fairy, but certainly perpetuating the rumours.

Zeus grunted as he stepped onto one of the castle's many balconies that overlooked the mountains and city. The Ice Empire's castle was made of blinding, all-white marble, blending right into the ever-snowy edge-of-the-world landscape. Built into the strength of a mountain, battered by blizzards but always standing tall over its empire, the castle was a clear symbol of unwavering might. And it was beautiful. The perfect backdrop for the perfect man – both the empire and Zeus were ultimate displays of masculine excellence.

From here, he could see down into the town, where his subjects wandered about, probably thinking about how they wished they were him. It was difficult to see well from the castle – it was so tall and broad, separated from the town at the mountain's base – but he chanced a wave at what looked like three women.

He could see their bodies shaking with giggles as they stared back at him in their colourful dresses. Sheepishly, they waved back.

A bloom of pride entered Zeus's core. This was exactly what he needed. He could imagine the flushes in their cheeks, the flutters in their hearts.

He ran a hand through his perfectly combed hair, straightened his perfectly tailored suit, and licked the perfect curvature of his lips. After turning his idyllic bright eyes up to the sun for a moment, letting the light catch in his white hair and pale skin, highlighting his strong angles, he moved, satisfied, back into the castle.

Candace may have magic. She may have a lot of support. But there was one thing she did not have: the magnetisation and adoration that came with alluringly handsome looks and a dashing personality. And Zeus knew that sometimes, that was all one needed.

He reluctantly made his way through his morning responsibilities, just waiting for the moment he could go to the courtyard and meet with his favourite general. *Isla. Gorgeous Isla.*

Sure, she was Candace's protégé, and he was the prince in a royal line *losing* their power to said Candace, but how could they deny the tension between them?

Still, it was only now that Zeus was serious about Isla. He'd always tried to find someone else – even let Sierra Reed kidnap him and turn him into *a swan* – but that absolute failure put things into perspective. After spending the better part of a year moping around the world, hiding and shameful, Isla was the one who found him and brought him home. But everything had changed. Candace had swayed the royals. Their army had grown twice in size – almost as much as their newly acquired land. Isla and her best friend Elm – though Zeus liked to think of Elm as his best friend as well – had grown in their power and barely seemed to miss him at all.

Then, just weeks ago, Zeus snuck out the window – in swan form, of course, having so far successfully hidden his curse – for a night-time soar, before he *fell directly out of the sky.*

His stomach dropped; stars twirled around him as he flailed for some balance. And that was when he noticed his wings were gone, and he was no longer a beautiful bird in flight, but a hulking, gorgeous prince plummeting to the ground.

He hit the soft snow with a heavy *crack*, the sound being his left arm, which had since been in a sling. Before, it was as if his body reset each morning. Anything from a bleeding wound to a slight scratch would be healed as soon as he was human again. But suddenly the curse was lifted – had Sierra found a soulmate's kiss to break it? He hoped so, but also . . . he did not. Because part of him would always love her.

Now, though, Zeus was better. He was fully human – he had his nights available again, after a year! Which meant wooing Isla had gone from a distant dream, a slight flirtation, to a real possibility.

Zeus hopped into princely action. First he went to the nurse, who insisted once more that his arm was healing perfectly – though he checked in constantly to make sure. He said good morning to his parents, who were busy going over plans for the next winter. He had tea with the senator of architecture, who wanted to speak to him about erecting a new statue – one of *Candace,* for her work in the war. Ugh! He stopped for lunch at noon, and then, ready for his duties as an honorary army leader, finally hurried to the courtyard to see Isla.

The young woman turned around and groaned as soon as she saw him. Isla's dark-blonde hair and hazel eyes were almost of the same exact hue, complementing her white-pink, windswept Ice Empire skin. She wore the uniform of an empire soldier: ice-blue leather jacket, white pants and undershirt. Some chose to wear another thick coat over the top, which was often necessary, but it was so difficult to move and fight in a coat that most soldiers forced themselves to adjust to the cold instead. Though for most people the uniform made them look standard, made them blend in, on her . . .

When it came to Isla, the pants and jacket hugged her curves perfectly, the light colours made her look like a fire beneath, and her medals made her stand out against the soldiers she led. She gestured for them to train amongst themselves – about a hundred of them lined up in the courtyard – and stepped over to the prince. Isla could not have looked more annoyed to see him.

No one else looked at him like that. She was a dream. 'What do you want?' she demanded, eyebrows raised. She wasn't tall, but her straight back and serious attitude hid that well.

Zeus pursed his lips. 'I'm here to ask you to join me for dinner.'

'Every day,' she replied, 'you ask me to join you for a meal. And every day, I tell you: *no.*' Her voice had a raspy quality to it that drove him crazy. 'I have a job to do, Your Highness. It would be best for both of us if you left me alone.'

He sighed. 'You know, you only get away with talking to me with so much disrespect,' he said, 'because of *your mummy.*'

Isla glanced up at the castle, looming over them like the dark clouds setting in. They didn't have long until the next set of snow came rushing down to cut their training short. 'Candace is not my mother,

Zeus, and the only reason I'm not allowed to *murder* you is because of *your* mummy and daddy.'

He flushed. *Fairies*, this tension between them! 'Well,' he replied with a shrug, 'neither of us can help who raised us, I suppose. We can just help what we do with our future. And you and me, Isla – we're a perfect match.'

'Which I'm certain you think of every woman who catches your eye,' she says, 'until they ultimately leave you.'

'I'm *cursed*,' Zeus whined. 'Everyone wants me – and who wouldn't? – yet I can only seem to find affection for those who don't.'

'What was it Wendy said? Your ego is bigger than the castle . . .'

He frowned. 'This is the problem. You know me too well. If you met me now, you'd be desperate for me.'

She smiled, pushing loose strands of hair behind her ears. 'And yet that isn't the case,' she said sweetly, 'and all I'm desperate for is for you to leave. Go and bother Elm.'

'Yet last time I disappeared,' he leaned in and whispered, 'you weren't as happy as you act as if you would be now.'

'Last time you disappeared,' she hissed back, 'you were kidnapped and turned into a bird. I should've let the Reed girl eat you alive.'

If *only* one of them would eat him alive. It would make all the torture worth it.

Because that was the other problem with Isla – she alone knew about his curse, and his kidnapping situation. She was the one who, in the end, had found him. Which is likely why he'd been able to get over Sierra so quickly. Isla had him wrapped around her finger, but she could blackmail him with this information at any time, or worse still, tell *Candace.*

On cue, the false fairy wandered into the courtyard wearing all pine-green – the colour she always wore, because she was trying to copy the real fairies and their monochromatic costumes. Honestly, was there a shortage of dyes? Did they all want to look poor?

'Hello, sugar,' she said endearingly to Isla. The two of them had risen through the ranks of the Ice Empire together – two orphans who had somehow found their place in a world that didn't want them. Candace gained magic slowly over time, becoming powerful enough that the empire had to listen to her. And Isla, her adopted daughter, was pulled into power along with her and became their youngest general.

Isla nodded. 'Candace.'

Both Isla and Zeus had learned early on to never show affection for their parents in public – it only perpetuated the idea that their power and influence came from the luck of their birth, and not because they deserved it. Of course, Zeus would always be a prince, but Isla could lose her position at any time. Unless, and everyday this seemed more and more likely, Candace usurped the crown entirely and made herself the new leader of the empire.

Would Isla have any pity for him then, or would she allow him to be cast out and forgotten?

But Zeus was beginning to form a new plan to deal with just that. If it was between Candace conquering the world for the Ice Empire, or getting back his family's power, he knew he wanted his power. The empire didn't need the world, but he needed the empire.

So Zeus was going to find Sierra again – one of the most powerful people he knew – and convince her to help him kill Candace. And if that didn't work . . . Well, if Sierra couldn't be counted on, his backup plan was Bearra. Zeus's family needed saving, and who better to ally with than the kingdom with the most magic in the world? A kingdom whose princess was his age, freshly woken and unengaged, needing a prince to marry?

Zeus was done lazing around – he was taking back his power no matter what it took. *Then* Isla might love him.

'Good afternoon, Candace,' he said. It was difficult, with the magic and power she exuded, not to imagine wings on her back. Big, green ones, maybe feathery. No, they would be scaled like a tree snake's, slithery and venomous, just like her.

She looked him up and down. 'Bothering my daughter again are you, Prince?'

'I like to think we bother each other,' he replied.

'If I bothered you as much as you bother me,' said Isla, 'I would consider it a successful day.'

Zeus shrugged and glanced at Candace. 'How can we help you?'

The woman's agenda was clear – she wanted world domination, and she had made the Ice Empire the world's strongest army, and herself the world's most magical human, to do so.

Why, exactly, did she want to rule the world?

Well, who wouldn't? Some people were just better at making it happen than others. That's what made the Imperials – the empire's people – love her, and made Zeus and his parents fear her. The Ice Empire had been fine on its own for centuries without a fairy, but as soon as power had presented itself, the people followed it blindly. They would follow Candace off a cliff, but while she would fly, they would fall.

Candace seemed to be fighting the urge to roll her eyes, but she retained her decorum, as any good fairy would. She brushed a few flecks of snow from her dress. 'I only came to tell you about dinner tonight,' she told Isla, all but ignoring Zeus's presence. 'We have much to discuss, if you'll make sure you're home.'

Isla put on a mockingly devastated expression. 'How awful,' she whined. 'Zeus, I really won't be able to join you tonight.'

He scrunched his face in reply, peeking at the soldiers and hoping they were too busy in their sparring to notice the embarrassing rejection. Although, they'd watched Isla reject him dozens of times now, so he really shouldn't let it get to him.

'Actually,' said Candace, watching Zeus thoughtfully. 'Come to dinner with us. Our discussions involve the war, and it could *potentially* be beneficial to have your opinion.'

Zeus's entire face widened, his mouth opening in a grin and his eyebrows raising in surprised excitement. 'Oh, Candace.' He knew it must be something of a trap, but he couldn't make himself care. 'I would not miss it. Have your staff send my staff the details.' He turned to Isla. 'I'll be wearing my finest suit, just for you, sugar.'

And with that, he was off.

Maybe Candace wasn't so terrible after all.

CHAPTER 8

General Largon guides us to an old underground passage out of the kingdom, the opening now blocked by thick vines and cobwebs. Teddy and Arden take the lead, using their magic to create a path for us to squeeze through. Maya and Sierra follow close, Dawn and myself trailing a bit behind them. Largon holds a torch behind us.

'I don't like leaving the others,' Arden says, whispering over his shoulder to Sierra, falling into step with her. He obviously doesn't think I can hear, or doesn't care. I'm no one important, of course. 'What if something happens to us? The ship?'

'They'll be fine,' Sierra responds. Her eyes have a rare softness to them that appears only when she looks at him. He's the opposite. When he looks at her, his gaze is filled with a protectiveness, a hardness, a blaze. They're oil and water, and yet . . . 'You worry too much, *captain.*'

'We're in the middle of a war, Sierra. I think the rest of you don't worry enough. This isn't meant to be fun.'

'The rest of us,' she replies, 'have come to terms with how chaotic our lives are, and accept that all we can control is how we respond to that chaos. Stay worried and all you'll feel is fear. Try to have fun, and at least the pain will be worth it.'

'We're leaving them alone for two days in a kingdom they don't know,' he presses, eyeing Dawn, who seems too lost in her own thoughts to notice.

'Exactly. Only two days,' Sierra reassures him, 'And Maya will be there. She owes me, remember. Bearra owes *us.*'

He takes a deep breath, his head tilting down. 'I know. Only, since . . . You know. I can't let anything else happen to any of you.'

Opal. Her name doesn't need to be said aloud for Arden's meaning to be obvious. Their grief still fills every crevice of every room they walk into. All the pirates seem hard on the outside, but it isn't their truth. It's something they've crafted, an armour to protect themselves. But they feel pain as much as anyone else. Seeing Arden's reaction almost puts a lump in my throat, despite me never knowing the girl they lost.

This empathy I feel . . . Sometimes the emotions around me are so strong they *hurt.*

'You're right,' Sierra tells him softly. 'But she would want you to be happy, don't you think? You can grieve her as long as you need to – maybe forever – but you can't let that grief infiltrate every part of your being.'

Arden's jaw hardens and he grips Sierra's hand like a lifeline. She leans into him and rests her head on his shoulder. I look away, giving them their privacy. It's beautiful, seeing their persevering love even through such deep grief. And yet I can't help the jealousy boiling within me – jealousy that they have the privilege to know each other and be with each other fully and entirely. Something I'll never have.

Our footsteps echo through the tunnels, and I do my best not to memorise each turn. The less I remember, the less Lire can learn. She knows I'm leaving today. Just me. Elsie only knows what everyone in the castle knows, the same lie I told Lire: I'm going alone, sent by Dawn, to look for her parents.

The thought of leaving Elsie makes my skin prickle. I don't trust her not to cause trouble. But at least while Dawn is with me, away from the kingdom, she's safe. And we'll be alone. *Together.*

I pull at my silky sleeves. We're attempting to fit in out there by wearing modern clothes – which are just awful, in my opinion. Why replace luxury and beauty, well-made materials, and perfect hand-done stitches, with mass-produced simplicity? And, put simply, it is not my style. Sierra and Arden have on what they arrived in, patched up from the fight. Meanwhile, Maya is grumpily wearing one of Dawn's dresses – a stunning baby-blue gown that looks nice on Maya, but mesmerising on Dawn.

Suddenly we're at the end of the tunnel, and it's time for four of us to leave and follow the river towards the *Neptune* – and for the other three to turn back. The sun is yet to rise, so there's no light at the end of the tunnel. I bristle at the idea of what might be awaiting us.

'It's time,' says Largon.

Teddy lowers his hand, still encircled with faint lilac. 'Let's do this, then.'

Maya scratches her arms in the dress she so clearly despises. It's no wonder she ran away from Bearra – she's as modern as they come. 'Remind me again why I'm being subjected to this?'

Sierra offers, 'To win a war that threatens the lives of everyone in the world?'

'Don't remind me,' Arden whispers on a deep exhale. I like him. He's a little bit like me – on the inside, at least. Filled with nerves, though he's much better at hiding them. He worries incessantly about his friends. I sense the way fear can build in his chest, tightening his ribcage and constricting his lungs. The way he looks down because his head is becoming cloudy.

Sometimes all it takes is a joke, even by someone who means nothing by it, to activate a fear so intense I'm not sure my mind is quite sound. Other people don't seem to understand – they can go, and go, and go, feel and feel, hurt, run, face anything, and still have a strength in them I can only dream of.

Arden watches his crew like a hawk, fiercely protective and always anxious about keeping them safe and happy. Losing Opal must have broken him, but I feel as if there was a great loss even before her, one that triggered these instincts in the first place.

I just hope Sierra and their crew know how much he cares for them.

'No, I'm really serious,' says Maya. 'Can't we find another way? *I'll* go on this quest. So what if only Dawn can know which mirror is the right one? I'll bring back every mirror in the world. Just don't make me be a princess.'

Teddy doesn't appear to be listening. 'I'm not sure how well this will work. We may need to experiment as we go, depending how long— I mean, I'm certain Dawn will only be gone for a few days, but . . .' He scratches the back of his neck. 'I don't know how my mother did it with her spies, disguising them. I don't know if it's just a mask, or if she fully changes their bodies with magic. We'll just have to figure it out.'

Maya gags. 'Do not even think about changing my body.'

'You don't want to look like someone blessed with beauty?' Sierra teases, and Dawn nods appreciatively. It might be the first time the two have ever been on the same side about something.

'I don't want her to change at all,' says Teddy. 'This magic is experimental. I'm going to be very careful. And yes, we'll start with just a disguise. If we need to take more intensive measures later on, then we'll cross that bridge when we come to it.'

Maya groans, but she doesn't know how lucky she is, to be turned into a stunning princess. Unlike me, who was turned into a plain, small servant. And she'll only be masked. I can barely remember my old body.

Then again, I wouldn't ever want to be Dawn. Many people wish to be the people they admire, wish they were rich and esteemed and beautiful. But if we are those people, we don't get to love and adore them. And oh, how I love to love her.

'Do you want my help?' Arden offers. Quick to focus on the task ahead, the pirate captain seems to have forgotten his argument with Teddy over Amora. 'With the magic, I mean. I'm not very good at using it, but I do have plenty.'

Teddy shakes his head, his hands already alight with lilac. 'Thank you. But I've got this.'

We all watch on as the magic passes over Maya, glittering around her in the dark tunnel. It highlights her wincing face as her features shift. Teddy glances between Dawn and Maya, perfecting the disguise, like a painter copying a posing model. The magic settles upon her face and creates an uncanny mask. At first, Maya's shifting appearance makes my eyes ache, but the magic soon settles into a smooth image. Instead of a grey-eyed girl in a dress that doesn't fit her, a second Princess Dawn stands in front of us, golden curls cascading over the baby-blue that is shocking against her bronze skin.

Maya stretches her hands out in front of herself, watching them curiously. 'It's so strange, I feel exactly the same, but . . .'

'You'll need to work on your princess impression,' I say, surprising everyone by speaking. I'm met with frowns and slight amused smiles. But I'm not ashamed to say this; Dawn is perfect, and to see someone distort her image *deeply* offends me. 'Dawn stands straighter, and she keeps her face softer and more expressionless. And she isn't all stiff, and she doesn't move her hands around in such a way.'

The real Dawn raises her eyebrows at me, and I wonder if I've overstepped. She must see the panic in my eyes, because she says, 'No, Carlotta, go on.'

'I didn't mean to be rude,' I stutter. 'It's just . . . Well, it's my job to know the princess.'

'Then maybe *you* should stay,' Maya says. Her voice still sounds the same, and I can't make my head wrap itself around watching that voice, those mannerisms, come from Dawn's image. 'Stay to help me be like Dawn, or even better – *you* just be the princess, and *I'll* go with Dawn!'

'No,' Dawn says. 'The plan is settled. I need to leave now, because looking at myself like this is incredibly disturbing. We'll be back as soon as possible. Suddenly I don't like the idea of someone stealing my life.'

'It isn't stealing,' Maya says, 'if I didn't want it in the first place.'

'More positive,' I tell her, and when she frowns at me I realise I've spoken without thinking again. *Fairies.* 'You're going to give yourself away with the way you talk. Teddy needs to disguise your voice, but more than that, you need to speak like a princess.'

'Of course,' Teddy says before Maya can protest. 'I'll do that. Carlotta, you're very clever. Why on earth do you work for the castle when you could be out doing . . . something more interesting?'

My heart stops, then starts again. I'm not sure what to say.

Dawn unknowingly saves me. 'I forbid it. Carlotta is stuck with me for life. And working in the castle is a very distinguished role, Teddy. One needs to be clever to handle me.'

I let out a shaky laugh, and when Dawn and I meet eyes, I feel something so powerful, so confronting. The experience of being seen. Of desperately wanting to know what another person is thinking when they look at you. Of a thousand things being said in one moment of eye contact.

Sierra reaches out to touch Maya, stunned by the disguise. Maya flinches back, but not before Sierra's fingers feather through her hair. 'Oh, no,' Sierra says.

'What? Am I having a bad hair day?' Maya asks bitterly, with an irritation I've never seen on Dawn's face.

'In fact,' Teddy says, 'you are.' He passes a hand through the curls falling from Maya's head. The disguise shimmers, revealing the light-brown hair beneath. It's like peeling back a painting to find another beneath it.

'It's okay,' Dawn says quickly. 'Just don't let anyone touch her.'

'I already wasn't planning to let anyone touch me,' Maya says, waving off the hands following her. 'That is not a problem.'

'Are you all quite finished?' asks General Largon, watching us from where she's propped up against the tunnel wall. I think half of us forgot she was even here. 'I have meetings to attend.'

We say our goodbyes quickly, a mixture of anxiety and sadness and hope and a million other things, and suddenly we're out of the tunnel and into fresh air. It's a short walk to the nearest river large enough for the *Neptune* to have anchored, left unprotected in the middle of nowhere. I find myself – me, a former lady, who never would have imagined it – on a *real pirate ship*. And not just any pirate ship. A magical one.

✦ ⬦ ✦ ☾ ☀ ☽ ✦ ⬦ ✦

Dawn allows Sierra and Arden to take her on a quick tour of the ship before insisting on staying on the deck. The wind rustles through her hair, and her hazel eyes are turned up to the sun. It's as if she's floating – outside her kingdom for the first time in a hundred years. Like she's breathing again.

It makes me realise how badly she needed this. The mirror is only a small part of this adventure. An excuse. It isn't even only about her parents. Dawn so desperately needs rest.

And I secretly hope it takes us forever to find the mirror – so long that we don't make it back to Bearra in time for Lire's attack. So long we're forced into hiding somewhere quiet, forced to create new lives, to live together in peace, away from anything and anyone else.

I picture us in a little cottage in Adella's Territory, the sun always shining, surrounded by blooming flowers and ripe apple trees. She'd have distant family there on her father's side; maybe we could befriend them, share our crops, make them strawberry jam and laugh with the children. We would sleep in a bed harder than we're both used to, softened by the way we hold each other as we dream.

If only I were anyone but myself.

Arden announces that we're close to Naroport by the afternoon. Of course, it's one of the nearest cities to Bearra, and being a port city, the waterways lead us in with ease.

Arden and Sierra are thrilled to be back on the ship, playful and at ease. They're free here, comfortable in their territory. Their grief can blow away in the wind, rather than growing stuffy within them, within the darkness and the thick walls of the castle.

'We'll wait a day for you to return, in case we're lucky and Teddy's lead is correct,' says Arden. 'If you don't meet us by then, we'll assume you haven't found it, and we'll head back to Bearra alone.'

Dawn swishes her skirts, lighter and duller than usual so she can hide in plain sight. 'I would still prefer you didn't wait at all and went directly back to Bearra. They need you more than I do. But yes, you can give us a day, if that's what will appease you.'

Sierra groans and unsubtly rolls her eyes.

We're sitting around the table, in the cabin area under the deck. I've only been on ships a handful of times, and certainly not one like this. It's dark, but not as dark as one might think. Instead of being the damp, mouldy, sweaty underneath of a regular pirate ship, this is more like a house – a home. Its inhabitants have things lying around everywhere, and there are several private rooms down here as well. The ship feels much bigger inside than it looks from the outside, and easily has enough room for six. June – their black cat – is accustomed to finding hidden spots in the cabins until she wants food, in which case she's happy to bother any and all of us by purring at our feet.

The kitchen is behind us in the common space, and Arden and I made a simple pasta dish for dinner. He mentioned that he isn't accustomed to cooking, since Lark usually does it, and I smile remembering the way Lark flirted with Briar, boasting about his cooking just days ago.

It has actually been a very nice evening, just the four of us on the water sailing smoothly towards Naroport, but Sierra suddenly picks up an attitude, groaning and kicking at the walls.

'Is there an issue?' Dawn asks diplomatically, though I can sense her frustration.

'You want to do your mission alone, I get it,' Sierra says. 'But I don't want to be holed up in Bearra waiting for an attack. I want to be out here *fighting*. It's what I'm supposed to do!'

'I understand how you feel,' Dawn says. 'But it isn't a matter of what we want to do. Bearra needs your protection. It's critical. You were the only reason we survived Lire's last attack, and that was barely a nudge compared to what she could do next. Imagine if next time it's a fairy, or another army, or, *fairies-forbid*, the Ice Empire. I'm sorry, I know it isn't what you want, and I know how beneficial it would be to have you out here on missions, Sierra, but where I need you is protecting my people.'

Sierra's eyes fill with an impatient rage that makes me flinch. 'You have soldiers for that, and I'm not one of them. You don't give me orders.'

'But those soldiers need training *from you* if they're going to be any help.'

'We all have to make sacrifices in this war,' I tell Sierra. My words are empty – how hypocritical can I be? – but I can't help defending Dawn. 'To save the world, not just ourselves. I'm certain that Her Highness will reward you when this is all over.'

'You mean *if*,' says Sierra. She's still standing, raised to her full height as if to intimidate us at the table. 'If this is ever over. We can't just sit around behind Bearra's walls and wait for an attack. We need to get out there and show people we are not weak. I know hiding has worked for you for a long time, but it won't last forever.'

Dawn raises her chin. 'Then go, Sierra. If it's what you want.'

'Excuse me?'

'Your decisions are your own. But your friends stay with me.'

Sierra's eyes narrow. 'Is that a threat?'

'Certainly not,' the princess says calmly. 'As you have repeatedly made clear, I am not in charge of you or your friends. In fact, you have the most bargaining power, considering what I owe you, and how badly I need you. But as Carlotta said, we're all making sacrifices. I'm sure your friends, if given the choice, would prefer to do the *right* thing, rather than follow you into chaos. We need you, Lady Reed, and your crew helps our numbers, but we need Ebony and Arden most. So choose to go if you wish, but you'll be leaving your friends behind.'

Sierra leans back in her seat. 'If I ask, they'll come with me.'

'No, we won't,' Arden says quietly. Sierra whips her head around, glaring at him, and he raises his hands in surrender. 'I agree with you, of course I do. I hate feeling stuck and useless. But we've come to help Bearra. That doesn't just mean doing what we think is best. Dawn is the princess for a reason – she knows what Bearra needs. Maybe once their soldiers are trained better, and armed with magic, they'll be strong enough to take care of themselves. Then we can go and do what we do best. But right now—'

'Right now we're supposed to babysit a kingdom while its princess is running around the world looking for her mummy and daddy?' Sierra spits.

I push myself to my feet, my chair groaning as its legs scratch across the floor. 'Do *not* speak to Dawn like that.' My chest rises and falls with deep, hot breaths of anger. For a moment I forget myself – or, more accurately, remember myself – and lose my façade of quiet weakness. I am Relia again, ready to protect the woman I love.

Then I grab the back of my chair, blink slowly, coming to my senses, and sit down as if I've only had a bout of motion sickness. 'My apologies,' I mutter. 'I shouldn't have lost my temper.'

Dawn places a hand on my arm, and the blaze within me only intensifies, rushing to the spot where our skin touches. 'I appreciate your support,' she says. 'But believe me, I have heard worse, and I can handle the criticism myself.'

Sierra rolls her eyes. 'I'm starting to see why Maya always hated you, *Dawn*.'

'Well,' Dawn says, 'Maya has a habit of coming to care about those she once hated, doesn't she? And I didn't try to murder her. I just happened to represent something she resented. But I can't help who I am and what I was born into. Rulers don't need to be loved by all, Reed. They need to rule. If I let everyone do what they wanted, I wouldn't have a kingdom. I appreciate that you have come to aid Bearra, but you must at least pretend to follow my rules.'

Arden tries to place an arm around Sierra, but she shrugs him off.

'I do not want any ill will between us,' Dawn says after a long moment. 'So let's come to a compromise, shall we? What can I do for you, to ensure you're happy to do what I need?'

Sierra's purses her lips, then her eyes dart around as she considers Dawn's offer. She demands, with no lack of ferocity, 'You'll let us patrol the river systems around Bearra for several hours a day. Everyone except Ebony and Arden – they stay back. And we'll only go far enough that if there is trouble, we can get back quickly, or better yet, can intercept it first.'

'Wonderful,' Dawn says. 'We have a deal.'

Arden cringes at Sierra. 'You're going to leave me and Eb stuck behind while you get to have all the fun?'

Sierra raises her brows without emotion. 'Absolutely. You were against me before, so why complain now? It's like Dawn said, she needs you. Only for the magic you have, which *anyone* could have, really, but it happens to be you who needs to stay behind.'

'This is my ship! You can't just play with the *Neptune* all day while I work.'

Sierra pats him on the leg. 'You can have it back when we win the war.'

She glances at me, winks, and I snicker. If Dawn dislikes her, so do I. But it doesn't mean I can't love her a *little* bit.

CHAPTER 9

We've stopped in a marina within the city, hopefully not too far from Teddy's old apartment. *Lire's* old apartment. Once again, I'm completely unsure of what I'm doing, but I'm all too aware of how much danger I'm in. I wring my hands and watch the ships sailing smoothly across the water to calm my nerves.

There are awkward goodbyes with Sierra and Arden, who still make it clear they protest what we're doing. But once we're alone, Dawn lets her guard down.

I teach her to hunch her shoulders and loosen her gait, just as I had to learn to become Carlotta. I place a hat over her beautiful but conspicuous golden hair, and it's like she's a different person. No longer the princess, but simply Dawn. The real Dawn – the girl I know, not the girl Bearra sees as their leader. *Dee.*

I watch as her eyes roam the streets, scanning intensely. Is she looking for her parents, trying to find them in the anonymous faces of the crowds? Neither of us has ever been part of this kind of community – the regular, the average, the workers – and although I'm pretending to be one of them now, there's still a clear disconnect. I'm not sure how to . . . interact. That said, I'm not particularly adept at interacting with anyone.

And as if I don't have enough to worry about, I also have to be careful not to show that I know anything about the world, since Dawn thinks I was stuck in Bearra the last hundred years. Even though my time in Muse's Forest is hazy, I could easily mention things by mistake.

This city is all new to me, though, and I don't have to feign my wonder and apprehension. Bearra has been such a haven because it's stuck in *my* time. Okay, *and* because it's home to the princess I've spent my entire existence, alive and dead, detrimentally in love with.

Despite being used to long hours on my feet from working in the castle, I quickly tire from walking. The streets are hard and uneven, and the tall buildings offer little respite from the elements. The greys of the road and the sky melt into the jarring colours of the street signs. People shuffle all around us as vendors and sellers shout for attention. Everything is so loud, I can't make out anything I actually want to hear. How are we supposed to find a mirror in a place like this?

But even shoulder-to-shoulder with strangers in the humid air, Dawn looks more alive than I've seen her since becoming Carlotta. So I continue without complaint, following a mesmerised and excited Dawn, and a light rain begins to fall. She drags me under the awning of a shop, and I laugh at the playfulness in her expression. Pressed against a wall like this, I'm reminded of saving her in the recent attack. That memory should fill me with fear, but I can only recall the joy at holding her and meeting her gaze.

Oh, these moments between us. In them, I'm almost certain she knows who I am.

'This place is incredible,' she says, her eyes glimmering even in the overcast weather. 'I mean, I don't like it. It's as disgusting as the pirates said. But *look*.'

'I agree.' If she's happy, so am I – despite how much I hate it here.

'You could be anyone here, couldn't you? No wonder this is where Lire chose to hide her children.' Even the mention of the fairy doesn't seem to darken her spirit. 'This is the world a hundred years later . . . I don't know why I was so afraid of it. Although it only shows me how far Bearra has to come.'

Someone bumps into her as we squeeze our way back through a crowd, and Dawn almost laughs with delight. She pulls off her hat and shakes out her hair, raindrops flying as it bounces. The sun peeks through the clouds, as if summoned back by her joy.

'And they just rule themselves here,' Dawn muses. 'Choosing their own leaders, making their own decisions without the need for royalty. I can't even imagine it.'

I shuffle so I don't walk into a child barely attached to its parents as they're lost in conversation, even standing in the middle of the pathway.

'Would you want something like that?' I ask. 'Would you give up your power and let the people choose someone else to lead them?'

'It seems fair, doesn't it? I'd like to think that I'd earned my right to rule, not just inherited it. And I wouldn't mind a break. An elected leader has no obligation to do their job forever; a princess doesn't get to stop being a princess.'

'But even then, it wouldn't be a fair fight. How could someone else compete with *you*?'

Her face falls. 'Of course, because there is no one in the world like me. Everyone expects me to lead and use the power I've been given. Doesn't anyone realise how crushing it is to have all that responsibility? To have *no one who can compete*. I thought Teddy understood – maybe he's the only one who does – but no one grasps that I don't *want* to be seen in that way.'

My stomach twists with jealousy, and a surprising note of irritation. 'Dawn, not everyone else is incapable just because they aren't powerful like you and Teddy. Do you truly think that a farmer, or – or, a maid – isn't as intelligent and complex as you, just because they're normal? I know I said no one can compete, but you surely can't think that those without your blessings can't possibly know what you go through. Everyone knows what it's like to be afraid of making mistakes. I don't have to be royal or powerful to know how you feel.'

I don't know why I speak to her this way – because we're alone, and away from her kingdom? Because I need her to know that I'm just as good to her as Teddy? Better? I missed a year of her life, and in some ways it's like he replaced me. But it isn't only jealousy. She may not know the thin ice I walk upon, but I can't stand her suggesting that I don't understand her hardship when I risk everything, every day, to stay by her side.

Dawn's mouth opens in a perfect circle – I've found the princess in a rare moment. She's stumped. 'Carlotta, I'm so sorry, that is not what I meant at all. I suppose it can be difficult for me to empathise with all of my subjects, being in such different realms of life, but that does not mean I don't see them as equals.'

I step back; her apology catches me off guard. She really does care what I think of her. Of course she didn't mean to offend me. How could I let my anger take over so easily? 'I know,' I tell her, honestly. 'Of course I know. I just . . . Sometimes, maybe, I forget who you really are. I forget that you aren't just my friend. You're the princess, and if I didn't work for you, you wouldn't have anything to do with me.'

Her skin shines in the sun-shower, and she surprises me by taking my hand. *My hand.* The effort it takes not to explode then and there is almost lethal. But Dawn only seems concerned, as if she can't feel that I'm burning up under my skin.

'You mean the world to me,' she says. 'I know you stay quiet in front of the others. I know you prefer to be invisible. But believe me when I say I see you. Always. Haven't I told you enough times that you're more than just my maid? I don't only care about you because you do your job so well. If you quit right now, I would still invite you to stay by my side. I need you.'

I turn away. What am I supposed to say? That I feel the same? That I would stay by her side no matter what? If this were another time, if I was another person, that would be true. I would die for her. I still would, but with Lire over me, controlling everything, have I let myself get too close?

'Maybe I *will* quit,' I say with a laugh, trying to lighten the mood. 'I quite like the idea of simply being by your side, without having to do any of the work.'

She smiles, though there's still worry in her eyes. 'When we win the war, if that's what you want, then that is what you shall have.'

We arrive at the apartment building an hour later – the city is so frustratingly, horrifically large, and walking through it is like wading through mud with how congested the streets are.

The building blends seamlessly into its street: not too short or tall, not too wide or slim, the same brown brick as everything else. The occupants wandering in and out of the wooden doors are perfectly middle-class. We almost didn't find it amongst the labyrinth of similar architecture, even though Teddy's directions were clear.

We don't have a key, but I'm sure we can find a way in. If I must, I'll use my magic to unlock the door when Dawn isn't looking. The power wants to be used, after stirring within me, held back for so long. I feel jittery, as if I'm waiting for a fight, for a reason to let loose. And yet, I know Lire only gave me the magic for emergencies. I know the consequences of being seen with it.

Dawn leads as we take steep stairs up to the fifth floor and walk across a raggedy carpet to the apartment number Teddy gave us. The doors are all painted blood red, and a single window at the end of the hallway gives us light. Dawn reaches out to the door handle experimentally, turning it slightly.

And gasps as it gives way with ease.

'This doesn't feel right,' I whisper. 'Maybe we shouldn't go in. What if it's warded? What if—'

'Hush,' Dawn says. 'We just have to see— Oh.'

The door opens fully, revealing a well-lit apartment that seems small, though I'm not sure what to compare it to. This is my first time seeing one. The windows have a lovely view of the city, and there is space for a kitchen and sitting area.

I wonder, would it be nicer to live here, or in a castle? This is certainly better than the maid's quarters, and half of Bearra.

But the apartment is entirely empty, ice cold in its lack of occupants.

My shoulders drop, though out of disappointment or relief, I'm not sure. Of course I wanted Dawn to find something, to be able to feel some hope. I don't want her finding the mirror and exposing me, but couldn't there have been *something* here?

'What an awful turn of events,' mumbles Dawn. I'm not surprised that she feels equally at odds about our adventure needing to continue, but her sarcasm does surprise me. 'Well, we had best go and tell Sierra and Arden.' Her eyes are expressionless as she takes in the apartment. She slumps against a wall and yawns – an uncommon sight for the princess – then places her hands in the pockets of her skirts.

I leave her for a moment to check the three small bedrooms down the hallway, but they're as empty as the main living space. When I return to Dawn, I shrug and say, 'Lire must have had everything moved out when she brought Teddy and his brother to Bearra. Could she have taken it to her estate? Or could Ja— Teddy's brother have kept it, left it somewhere else?'

Dawn stares out the window. Both our reflections are faint in the glare of the glass. A ruler and a peasant. A sun and a moon. Everything bright, and everything invisible.

'You can say his name,' she says. 'Jacob. I was engaged to him. And I know I have a bad history with the man, but I am not afraid of him. Not anymore.'

It's easy to forget that someone as lovely as Dawn has blood on her hands.

'Of course,' I say. My voice is small, raspy after speaking so much during our walk and talking loud over the crowd. And it's weak from disuse – a strange thing for a Musan, which is what I would be considered today. 'Well, you knew Jacob well.' His name tastes bitter on my tongue. 'Can you remember anything that might lead us to a clue?'

Someone clears their throat behind us, and while Dawn stays leaned against the wall, I jump in fright. I catch my breath, realising it's only an old man standing in the doorway. How long has he been there?

'If you're looking for the boys,' he says, tugging on his faded blazer, 'you'll find no one has lived here for a while.'

Dawn's brows raise. 'You knew them?'

The old man glances around the empty apartment, its whitewashed walls and dusty floor. 'The brothers grew up here with their nannies. Though they were always here and gone. They travelled a lot; to see their parents, I assume. They must have been rich. It happens. People of high standing find themselves with some scandalous pregnancy, and hire nannies to keep things hush-hush. But the boys have been grown up for years, and they don't live here anymore. This place was cleared out over a year ago.' He cocks his head. 'Though it isn't any of my business, nor yours.'

'You'll find it is our business,' Dawn says, of course unable to take the princess out of her tone. 'Jacob is a close friend of mine, and he has gone missing. We heard he once lived here and thought he may have returned.'

A woman in a simple, beige working dress with a basket of fresh vegetables in one hand and a small dog in the other shuffles beside the old man, moving him out of her way so she can peek into the apartment. 'You're looking for Jacob?' she says. 'He moved out some time ago. Nightmare, that boy. But his sweet little brother . . .'

Dawn smiles politely, but her tone is impatient. 'So we hear.'

I step in. 'Do you have any idea where he may have gone, or where the boys' things were moved to?' Even these strangers startle at my words, as if they hadn't noticed my presence until now.

'I shouldn't tell you this,' the woman says, with a glance to the old man, 'but I do know where their things were moved. Strange people came to take everything – and I asked – of course I did – because I was being neighbourly and didn't want to see their things being taken. But they told me *nothing.* So I eavesdropped – as any good person would do – and heard them saying everything was to be taken to a storage location in Kara's Territory. The place it would be least expected, they said, to cover their boss's tracks. I've no idea what any of it meant.'

'That's right!' the old man says, squinting at the ceiling as if trying to remember. 'They cleared out the entire place, no questions asked, and scrubbed it top to bottom. No one's been in or out since. It's just sat unlocked and unused, though someone must own it.'

Dawn and I share a glance. A small smile.

'Can you remember anything else?' Dawn asks. 'Anything about them, or the things that were taken?'

They're quiet for a moment, pondering, before the woman says, 'They were secretive. You could tell the family were hiding something – as soon as the boys were old enough to take care of themselves, they were rarely home. Although a woman did come to visit them once in a while – but she'd always be all covered up and anonymous. When the apartment was cleared, she wasn't there, but she must have been the *boss* those movers were talking about. Someone who has trouble in Kara's Territory – if that's the last place anyone would look to find their things.'

'Do you have any idea *where* in Kara's Territory it might be?'

'Big place,' says the old man, his initial caution thrown to the wind as he's caught up in the thrill of neighbourly gossip. 'The things may have been moved somewhere in the city, easy to access, or out in the tundra, impossible to find. Anyway, I thought you were after the boy? What do his things have to do with it?'

'Sure,' Dawn says distractedly. 'This is very helpful, thank you.' Her voice again becomes diplomatic, automatic. Then she takes my hand and leads me out of the apartment, and I only have time to say a quick 'thank you' to the man and woman before we're racing back down the stairs.

CHAPTER 10

Sierra's sharp eyes dagger Dawn when we get back. We explain what we found. We explain where we're going. And she just glares even more furiously.

'It'll take you a week at least to get there,' Arden argues with us, leaning against the bench in the kitchen area of the ship.

A single candle burns, bouncing off his soft features. Despite having similar Gracian looks to Sierra, he's darker and rounder, while Sierra is a knife's edge. Still, he's lean in a way that one finds one's eyes drifting, occasionally, to the muscles in his arms. I don't have any interest in him in that way, but I can appreciate art when I see it.

'And then,' he says, 'how long will it take you to look for wherever Lire's things are being stored? If you even find anything there. Then another week back to Bearra. You're unlikely to be home before Lire attacks, if she even gives us the month she promised, and you may not even end up getting the mirror. You're not seriously thinking of going?'

Sierra nods. Furiously.

He's right, of course, but Dawn has blinders on. The princess is often adaptable and flexible, but when she really makes her mind up about something . . . Well, I am not going to be the one to argue with her.

'Bearra doesn't need me, it needs the mirror,' she insists. 'We need a weapon to counteract Lire's. If we can identify her spies, we can find a way to stop them. If we keep flailing as we are, we might as well hand the world to her. I have to go. No one else can. And I *want* to.'

'We could stop you,' Sierra says quietly. She's leaning beside Arden, their bodies close, one of her arms behind his back. Her legs are so impossibly long – all of her is. 'It isn't personal, Princess. I don't care about you. But I know there's a kingdom that needs you to lead it, and that kingdom's fate is very important to the fate of the rest of the world. If Lire attacks and you aren't there to guide your kingdom, they have no hope. Do you understand that? I've seen the way they look up to you. It's sickening. Everyone was already against this mission, and now you're going to the most dangerous territory, and won't make it back before our month is up. It isn't reasonable.'

'And yet,' Dawn says, waving a hand, 'I'm going to do it.'

'Then— Then we *will* stop you,' says Arden, but there's a slight shake in his voice.

'You won't,' I tell him, trying to convey peace with my eyes. 'We're going to get our things, and we're going to go find horses, and we're going to Kara's Territory. We're more than capable, and we can be back before Lire attacks.'

'Can you two even *ride* horses?' Sierra says. 'And through deep snow, of all things! You think you can leave on this big quest because Maya did it, right? But she had Teddy. You're just—'

Dawn stalks past her, towards Ebony and Levi's room, where our luggage is.

Sierra grunts, and Arden and I share a knowing, pained look. Which is nice. At least someone understands me.

'Carlotta!' Dawn calls, with an unusual tone of impatience. 'Would you help me?' After a moment she adds, 'Please?'

'I suppose I'm going,' I mumble, then follow the princess. She's on the floor trying to pick up her bags. There are too many to carry, too many even for horses. 'Dawn, we don't have any winter clothes.' No longer defending her in front of the others, I let some of my doubt show. I lean down to help her, resting my hands over hers as she grips a heavy satchel.

When she glances at me, her eyes are glassy. 'Are you saying you don't want to come with me?'

I take a breath. 'Of course not, I'd go with you anywhere. You know that. But it feels as if you're making this decision out of desperation, rather than truly thinking it through.'

She shakes her head. 'No. No. Well, maybe. And if I am? Today has been the happiest I've felt since— Since the night before the curse. Why am I the one stuck with this responsibility? Why does it have to be me to lead? Why? *Why?*' Her hands shake. 'I have to go. I don't even have my parents at home anymore, I-I need this. If I don't go on this quest, Carlotta—' she lowers her voice '—I am going to lose my mind.'

I help her put down the satchel and move my hand to her forehead, pressing my fingers against her skin. She frowns at me, but doesn't stop me, so I bring my other hand up and begin tracing calming circles around the crown of her head. The franticness is pouring off her, infecting the air around her, driving her to mania. I would do anything to take that pain away.

'Dawn,' I whisper. 'I know how you're feeling, and I know what you think you have to do. If it's what you need, then we'll do it. But the others are right, too. We're putting ourselves – and the world – in a very dangerous situation. We need to be absolutely certain that this is the right move, and not just something we want.'

Her eyes are wide, wet with tears when they reach mine. She pulls my hands down from her head and holds them. 'I am certain. Completely. Entirely. I know this is what I have to do, and I know I need you there with me.'

I nod. 'Then I have an idea.' She gives me a pleading expression. 'Trust me. Arden?' I call.

He's here in a second, looking down at where we're perched on the floor. 'Yes?'

'Did you enchant this ship?'

'No. The *Neptune* was like this when I got it. Why?'

'It can't be so hard to do, can it? People have enchanted carriages now. A lot of them. They just don't have enough magic to last very long. Like the carriage you flew into Bearra.'

'Yes . . .'

'But you have so much magic, you could do *more*. You could enchant a carriage for us – one that'll be resistant to snow and get us all the way to Kara's Territory and back. One that's fast, and safe.'

He winces. 'I really don't know. This is something you should ask Teddy, not me.'

'You only have to try,' I say. 'You get us transport, and I can guarantee our mission will be much faster, and safer.'

Dawn lights up. 'Yes. Yes! Arden, I don't want this one to fly, please, but— Carlotta, that's an amazing idea.'

Arden crosses his arms with a painted expression. 'Okay. We'll try.'

And I smile, and smile, and wonder if I'll ever stop, because I *helped*. Oh, no.

✦ ◦ ✦ ☾ ☼ ☽ ✦ ◦ ✦

When we asked Arden to make the carriage speedy, I had no idea just how fast that might be.

We sail along the roads like a ship through water, the carriage somehow knowing when to stop, when to turn, and how to avoid danger. After the first few hours of constant, sickening fear, we relax in our seats. We sleep through much of the journey, and talk through more of it.

With the amount of magic Arden has saved up, the enchantment was far easier than we could've imagined. Besides, even if the magic *does* happen to run out, I can just boost the carriage when Dawn isn't looking.

Our goodbyes were brief, but I giddily remember Sierra and Arden whispering to each other as we stepped into the carriage.

'They're in love, aren't they?'

'Of course. Just look at them.'

My head's been spinning for the two days we've been traveling, but suddenly we're in the crisp, deep snow of Kara's Territory, much faster than the week Arden initially anticipated.

Truly, those days may be the nicest either of us has ever had, watching the landscape change through the windows, not needing to do anything but *be*. The snow thickens around us until all we can see is white through the steamy windows. By the time we reach Kara's Capital, leaving the carriage outside the city's magical bubble, the tension in Dawn's body has relieved so much that she's almost unrecognisable.

We step into the city, grateful for its warmth, covered in all the flimsy winter clothes we purchased in Naroport and could fit on ourselves to keep out the cold. Dawn smiles at me, which is enough warmth in itself, and we find ourselves lost in conversation as we wander this new kingdom without much care of which direction we're going.

'Let's find a place to stay,' Dawn says after a while, her breath pearly in the icy air. 'We should plan to be here at least a few days.'

'Certainly.' I keep my hands hidden within my cloak to avoid the urge to hold hers as we walk. 'We should take our time. We'll have to scout storage facilities first, then if none of those are any good, start thinking of other places the mirror may be hidden. It's unlikely to be easy.'

Dawn shrugs. 'Sounds like the perfect holiday.'

And we walk, and we laugh, and we eat and relish the sun, and we could be anyone – two normal girls out for a day, enjoying their normal lives.

Then we see them: Ice Empire soldiers, rallying the citizens of Kara's Territory. The dark fairy herself is seated on a throne in the centre of the town square. Shaking hands with them.

Fairies.

A soldier steps into our path. 'What are you ladies doing here?'

CHAPTER 11

In the days since Maya Nova began living her double life, she had existed in a state of constant confusion – and fear.

Maya's resentment towards Princess Dawn had mostly faded since they became friends. But now that Maya had to *be* the princess, she wasn't so forgiving. Yes, she empathised with Dawn's struggles more: she had to attend meeting after meeting, always looking her best, always communicating in that flat but kind royal tone, always keeping the small smile on her face. If this weren't torture enough, it was the weight of a kingdom on her shoulders that hurt most of all.

And yet, she could not ignore the luxuries of being royal.

She slept in the most comfortable bed in the castle – maybe the world – and was delivered breakfast whilst still snuggled within it every morning. She was always covered in the smoothest silks and shiniest jewels. She could read any book of her choosing in the royal library, and she could have her pick of infinite foods. Dozens of staff eagerly met her every need.

Maya was a far cry from the near-starving girl she'd been less than a year ago, and if she had to choose between power or hunger, she knew what her fate would be. Dawn had a difficult life – but in so many ways, a perfect one.

This knowledge brought back much of Maya's previous resentment, because she was *right*. While Maya was starving, Dawn was getting everything she could ever want up here in the castle. Even so, the royals had the citizens of Bearra fooled: the people doted over Dawn to distract themselves from their aching stomachs. Maya had always felt like the only one to see the disparity between the rich and the poor, and now things were even clearer.

It was so easy to forget your people were starving when you had everything at your fingertips. And when you were starving, it was so easy to forget that the people you wished you were, the people at the top that you idolised, were the ones hoarding the food.

Today, Maya rolled over in bed, lost in the dreamy world of Dawn's cloud-like cushions, and nearly hit Teddy in the face. She pulled her arm back as she slowly woke. She felt so safe seeing him there, on his side, facing her. Maya smiled.

It had taken her a long time to trust Teddy. She knew she loved him, but only recently had she begun to let herself be truly vulnerable. As the war grew more serious, she just couldn't keep holding onto her feelings of betrayal – his lies about his mother, about the crown, all of it. It seemed like nothing now, looking at the bigger picture of their lives. She just wanted him, she wanted love, and those old inhibitions were gone.

Now, when she looked at the sleeping young man, she didn't sense a threat. She just felt . . . affection. Deep in her gut lay a true love. A soft love. A sweet love. A love untainted by the past. They were building their future together, even if it wasn't going to last long.

Since many people expected Dawn and Teddy to eventually marry, it wasn't a huge scandal that they were, apparently, suddenly very close. Teddy had already been caught in Dawn's bed with Maya, to little surprise from the castle. Maya and Teddy wanted to be together desperately – although Teddy refused to offer Maya more than a friendly hug while she looked like Dawn. He was right; it was the respectable thing to do. That didn't mean the distance wasn't driving her insane.

After dropping off Dawn and her maid Carlotta, Sierra and Arden swiftly returned to Bearra. They explained that the princess demanded to leave, as if she were giving up on Bearra entirely. '*It was as if she was hysterical,*' Sierra said.

Maya feared she might be stuck in this new role forever. The idea that she would be caught in the prison of this mask any longer than a few weeks sent nausea roiling through her stomach.

She tapped Teddy gently as she heard a knock at the door. *Breakfast.* It always came slightly too early for Maya's tastes, but this was the time Dawn ate, so this was the time Maya would.

As the door opened, the scent of pancakes wafted into the room. Maya was halfway through a grateful sigh when she realised who was carrying the tray: the group of pirates she was only now starting to tell apart.

'Oh,' said Maya, rubbing her eyes. Did they have to bother her this early? Truly? At least it wasn't maids. A few days ago, they'd come in before Teddy and Maya had woken, snuggled together in a way that Maya's true appearance shone through her mask. They'd had barely seconds to whip away from each other before the soft knocking turned into a flurry of people who could have discovered their secret. Since then, they'd made clear rules not to be disturbed until they were up and about already.

The pirates did not follow rules.

If Maya *had* to have visitors, she only wished it could be her family. She wanted to be there for Prima's pregnancy, especially. But she was barely allowed to see them as the princess – it was too dangerous, since Dawn would have no reason to constantly meet with them. If anyone was to ask, Maya was living with her family again, down with a terrible flu keeping her locked in her room. Well, the excuse worked last time.

Yet nothing stopped Lark from constantly visiting her parents' house to take Briar out for walks. Maya wasn't certain about her sister being courted by a pirate, but *she* was dating a half-fairy boy, so she couldn't exactly judge her.

Sierra strode right in and lay herself across the bed; Maya had to pull up her nightdress. The disguise spell worked in strange ways – she could wear clothes, and the spell worked with them, and she could touch most physical objects, but if a person tried to touch her, their skin would fall right through hers, breaking past it to Maya's real body beneath the veneer of Dawn's.

Maya struggled to explain it. She still felt like herself. There was just another layer on top, one that felt like a cool breath of air. Unfortunately, it still felt like her skin touching the itchy hems of Dawn's dresses. Couldn't Teddy have at least figured out that part in her favour?

'Why are you here so *early*,' Maya groaned, sitting up to take in the group of six in front of her. She still couldn't quite believe she was friends with Sierra Reed and a crew of pirates.

'I'm leaving to patrol soon,' Sierra explained. 'Arden and Ebony will stay back to guard you, as agreed with the princess.'

Maya raised her eyebrows. 'Thank you for coming in and letting me know?'

Teddy stirred next to her, grunting in his half-awake state, his soft red hair plastered over his forehead.

Wren, holding the breakfast, placed the tray down on the bed. But before stepping back, she stole three orange slices, handing one to her brother. *Pirates.*

'We thought we should all meet before we're separated for the day,' said Arden, his pitch-black eyes broody and deep. Maya certainly understood what Sierra saw in him. He was very much, undeniably, attractive. Yet, she still wasn't sure how they'd become a couple after he cursed her. Sierra wasn't particularly forgiving or communicative.

'We need to discuss what to do about Dawn,' Sierra added.

Maya sat up, trying and failing to drag Teddy up with her. 'What about her?'

Arden looked pained. 'She's . . . Well . . .'

'She's probably not coming back,' finished Sierra. 'Like I told you a few days ago, she wasn't in her right mind. Even if she does return, I'm not sure we can trust her to lead.'

Maya blanched. '*Shh*. Why can't we just ignore that?'

'I did have an idea,' Ebony said cautiously, as if holding back her excitement. She was like that – she loved thinking of things, sharing things, even if they weren't the most positive. She could say nothing all day then spend ten straight minutes talking at once. 'We don't need to use it yet, but in the event that we need to do something drastic, the two of you could marry. You would effectively become queen and king of Bearra. Then we'll stage Dawn's untimely death, leaving Teddy as a widowed king. Then, Maya, you can be yourself again, and marry Teddy and become queen – as yourself. Well, if you wanted to.'

Teddy began to laugh, nearly choking on the water he was trying to swallow. 'You want to take the crown from Dawn and give it to *us*? She was born to lead Bearra. *Made* to lead Bearra. I don't know what it is about her that you don't like, but believe me, she is the best person for the job.'

'You didn't see her on the ship,' Arden replied quietly. 'She was—'

'She wouldn't listen to reason,' said Sierra. 'We've all told her we didn't want her to go on this mission, but she did anyway, even when it would take her all the way to Kara's Territory. And she took her poor maid with her. The princess left us because she can't handle her job anymore. We can wait and hope she returns, or begin planning in case she doesn't.'

Teddy shook his head. 'No. Dawn is coming back. I know she is. I . . .'

'I know she's your friend,' Ebony said, 'but this kingdom is at stake. The *world* is at stake. If Dawn can't lead us in this war, someone has to.'

Maya felt as if her brain had turned into a cloud; foggy and without substance, unable to grasp any thoughts. 'But we couldn't . . .' she mumbled. 'We can't—'

Shouts rang outside like clanging bells and Maya's chest tightened. *Another attack? So soon?* An attack where she, surely, would be the target. *Fairies.* And again, why this early in the morning?

They hurried out to the balcony to see what the commotion was. But it was not an attack.

It was a protest.

Bearrans stormed around the castle, shouting, screaming, holding up signs. Dozens of them. They threw eggs at the castle walls, and Maya ducked below the balcony railing so they wouldn't see her. One word was amplified above all others:

Surrender.

Maya looked to Teddy for answers. How could this be? The people wanted to surrender . . . to Lire? But Teddy had gone perfectly still, confused, maybe even hurt.

Did they think that if Bearra surrendered, the fairy would have mercy? Yes, if they gave in to her before their month was up, they could stop the war. But these people did not know the *true* Lire. They would not be saved – they would be doomed. And if they'd be doomed either way, shouldn't they try to fight?

Maya had thought all of Bearra was on the same page about that.

Teddy took her hand and led her back inside. She was shivering. If the people wouldn't follow Dawn, how could they expect *Maya* to lead? Was all this trouble even worth it?

'It's only a few people,' Sierra was telling her, though to Maya, her voice seemed distant. 'We'll hear them out, try to reason with them. Maya – you're in charge now. You'll be able to convince them they're wrong.'

But they aren't wrong, are they? Because a year ago, she would have been one of them. One of the suffering and scared, angry at the leaders sitting in their safe castle with their food and cushions and jewels, while those outside were facing the brunt of the war. She would have been there screaming, holding up a sign, throwing rocks at the castle and all those within it.

'Most people are still on our side,' said Teddy. 'I'm sure of it. They . . . They have to be.'

But Maya could only wonder: *Am I really helping to create the world I want Prima's baby to grow up in?*

CHAPTER 12

Dawn makes her first mistake by looking the soldier dead in the eye. 'We're on a walk,' she declares. 'Why, sir? What are *you* doing here?'

Ice Empire soldiers are everywhere, some a part of the rally while others guard it. How can there be so many? Surely this is only a piece of their army and most remain in the empire. *Fairies.*

The fairy of darkness and death, Kara, is seated on a throne of deep brown wood at the front of the rally in a blocked off crossroad, wearing all black. Her moth-like wings, with their eerily realistic eyes, send a shiver down my spine. This only confirms the rumours: Kara is indeed allying with the Ice Empire, the forces of the world's edges working together to choke the rest of us.

I'll have to tell Lire all of this tonight, though I'm sure she already has spies here. But this is still fantastic information to give her. Even if it isn't *new*, it'll show her my loyalty.

'Don't be snarky with me, little girl,' grunts the soldier. 'This rally is not a place for ladies like yourselves. Ladies who, based on your clothes and accents, are not from around here.'

'We're sorry,' I stutter before Dawn retaliates. She gives me a funny look, but I glare at her, hoping she'll understand. *You aren't the princess here.* The last thing we want is to get in trouble with Kara or the Ice Empire 'We really were just going for a walk. We didn't realise what was happening here. We'll be on our way, sir.'

He grumbles, his white uniform shifting around his shoulders. 'I believe you, but your friend here could use a lesson in respect. The streets could get rowdy.' He softens slightly, and I realise he isn't angry with us; he's just doing his job. 'I am happy to escort you home, or wherever it is you're lodging. Although I haven't been here long myself, I'll make sure you get there safely.' He looks us up and down. 'And, *fairies*, get yourselves some thicker coats before you freeze to death.'

'Your kindness is much appreciated,' I say with a shy smile, nudging Dawn when she opens her mouth to reply. 'But we will make our way home alone just fine.'

He tips his head. 'Ladies.'

Dawn's face remains in an unusual expression of confusion, but once the soldier has walked away, she gestures with her chin and I follow her behind a building. 'He was *horrible*,' she says. 'Of course, the Ice Empire are bad, but goodness . . .'

'He's not *your* soldier,' I reply, pulling my cloak around my shoulders. 'I understand it can't be easy, but you can't speak to people like that.' I quieten my voice even more than usual. 'You can't treat people like you're in charge while we're here.'

She mulls that over for a while. Then a mad glint enters her eyes – the same one she's had before every absurd idea she's come up with since her parents left. 'Actually,' she says, 'being the princess is exactly what I plan to do.'

I stop myself from sighing out loud. It's as if she hasn't heard everyone's arguments a hundred times: stay safe, don't take risks, protect yourself and therefore your people. There's no stopping her from throwing her life away if she chooses, and yet I keep following her, tying my life to hers. How long can I keep putting up with her impulsive behaviour?

Forever, of course. Forever, or until Lire demands otherwise.

'I have a plan,' Dawn says, pulling me further into the warm shadows of an alley beside a bakery. She isn't looking at me; her eyes scan the ground as she schemes. All her golds are dulled in this territory – the only one that never blessed her. It doesn't feel right, seeing her in a place with so little sun. But maybe if she had a little more darkness, she would be able to slow down. 'Just hush and let me think.'

'I said nothing.' Should I have? It hurts me too much to disagree with her. I already fear she's secretly furious with me for hushing her in front of the soldier.

'Well—' she starts. 'Don't look so concerned, Carlotta. Now we've seen this, we *know* Kara has allied with the Ice Empire. We're here now, and we should try to find out what we can. I'm going to reveal myself to Kara and speak with her.'

I nearly faint. 'She hates you! She'll kill you, and if she doesn't, the empire soldiers will.'

'They won't. This war isn't *that* dirty yet. There are rules to these things, and killing a princess doesn't look good for anyone. Okay, our side has killed a fairy of course, but that's beside the point. Speaking peacefully with Kara is sophisticated and wise. If I can find out what it is the fairy wants most, I could make some sort of alliance with her. Imagine if we had Kara and the Ice Empire's army on our side! We'd have a real chance of defeating Lire.'

'Why would they ally with us? They want to take Bearra as much as anyone else.'

'Which is why we'll make them a compelling offer.'

'*Dawn.*' I place my hands on her arms as if to hold her down. 'We came here for a mirror. Please don't let yourself be sidetracked by idealism. I do love your positivity, but today we have a mission to complete – for Bearra and the world. Haven't we risked enough?'

My heart races, but if it's life or death, I have to try to stop her, don't I? *Fairies*, what would Lire want? What do *I* want?

It doesn't matter, apparently – she's already strutting back to the rally, her curls bouncing off her layers of clothes as she speeds away. I nearly scream in frustration and fear, but I hurry to walk by her side.

Because that's who I am. And this is who she is.

The same soldier who first stopped us has his huge body blocking our way before we can even get *close* to Kara. Already the soldiers in the crowd are jeering and pushing each other around playfully. Our soldier looks down his nose and shakes his head. 'I told you two. This isn't *safe.*'

Dawn wastes no time. 'I am Princess Dawn of Bearra, and I would like to speak with the fairy, Kara. Immediately.'

The soldier's laugh is booming and guttural. 'What is this, some sort of joke? You want to get close to her for what, to beg for magic to mend your clothes? You're pretty, sure, but your story is particularly lazy.'

'Give the fairy my message,' Dawn says, 'and let her see for herself.'

'Good try.'

I groan, reaching into my pocket for my bag of money. We have no currency they'd accept here, and I refuse to give him any of our triarue, but gold is gold. 'Get us an audience with Kara,' I say, handing him some coins.

His eyes widen. Maybe soldiers aren't paid so well, or he's already thinking about how he'll use this gold to warm himself in this cold place. Growing up rich, I learned quickly that almost anyone can be bought. 'I'll be right back,' he tells me.

Dawn smirks at me proudly, and I nearly faint again. 'You're good at this,' she says. 'I had never thought my princess skills would fail me so embarrassingly.'

The corners of my mouth quirk. 'It was only a bribe. When one is not Princess Dawn of Bearra, one must find their own way about life.'

'Is that so,' she says, tilting her head.

When the soldier returns, he has another two soldiers either side of him. They're dressed differently, in black – Kara's guards. As if she needs them. 'She claims to be the princess?' one says, looking Dawn up and down.

'I think it could be her,' the soldier says. 'She has the look, doesn't she?'

'That she does.' He meets the princess's strong gaze. 'If you are who you claim to be, why would you wish to have an audience with our fairy? You may not recall this, since you were an infant, but she cursed you to die. None of us expected you to wake in our lifetimes, but *here you are.*'

'Kara was manipulated,' Dawn says matter-of-factly. 'Myself – and Bearra – are no longer sided with Lire. Your fairy and I have more in common than she expects, and I'm sure she is more reasonable than she's given credit for.' Dawn holds up the single ring on her hand – the plain, grey one Maya gave her, blessed by Kara. I'd entirely forgotten she had it. 'This blessing should be proof enough that Kara can trust me. And if not that, she might at least listen.'

The guard thinks for a minute, working his jaw. 'Fine,' he finally decides. He reaches out to touch the ring, but stays a small width away. It's as if he can sense his fairy's power within. 'But know that if you try anything—'

'Yes, I know.'

We're led through the crowd amidst stares – some puzzled, some curious, and some ogling – and up to the makeshift throne with the fairy atop it. A guard whispers to her, and she nods for us to approach.

Kara is a sight to behold. Not colourful and beautiful and deific like the other fairies, but a shadowy and mirthless force. In her looks, she's quite plain, but it's the power that radiates from her that's the true essence of the fairy. I can sense it from afar, and it's even more terrifying – and yet somewhat comforting – up close. There's something peaceful in death, as well as in the deep cold. I'd know. In the dark, the world may feel scarier, but really it's just quieter. That's what Kara represents, and that kind of raw power is why Lire hates her so much.

The other fairies are active, always moving, always talking in some capacity. Kara barely seems to breathe. 'Princess,' she says, her voice deep and soft. The eyes on her wings glare at us, and I itch to shrink away from them. 'I must admit, I am surprised to see you. And curious as to why you've brought my blessing back to me, after so much hardship was undertaken for it to be obtained.'

Dawn stands straight, her stare unwavering. 'The blessing came from my friend, Maya Nova. You may not remember her, but you trusted her once. Can you trust me, now?'

Her face stays flat. 'Princess Dawn,' she says, 'I would be more concerned that you cannot trust me.'

'Well, I am running out of things to lose.' Soldiers gather around us, listening to the fairy and the princess. A patch of sunlight peeks out of the clouds, as if Dawn's very presence can bring light to this cold, dark city. Even her understated clothes look royal as she's touched by the sun. 'I see you have joined forces with the Ice Empire, and that's an intelligent decision. I currently have few allies. We both hate Lire and want to see her gone. Does it not make sense that we're on the same side? That we could work with each other, rather than against?'

The fairy's face still barely moves. The other fairies are frightening, sure, but Kara is the opposite of Lire. I've learned to deal with Lire's whims, with her hatred, with her intellect – but this is an entirely new power I have no familiarity with. Does Kara have any empathy, or is everything to her as black and white as she is?

Yet, there is an opportunity for me here. Lire hates Kara; they have been rivals since the beginning of the world. I can be more useful to Lire if I not only spy on Dawn, but on Kara and the Ice Empire – Lire's only serious enemies. If I can feed her enough information about them, it might distract her from Dawn and Bearra.

'I understand your reasoning,' says Kara, 'but I don't see what Bearra has to offer that I cannot simply take for myself.'

'Because you cannot simply take Bearra. No one can. I created a contingency plan for just that reason,' Dawn says. She pauses, as if cautious to share it. 'A failsafe for Bearra. If we can't be left safe, if the war becomes so hopeless that there is no point in our continuing existence – Bearra will be destroyed.' My stomach flips. *Fairies,* what? She explains, 'Magic has been settled all throughout the kingdom to create the perfect self-destructing system. The entire kingdom is enchanted, so that if it falls, it *falls.* There will be nothing left for anyone. That way, even if Lire does beat us, she'll never get her hands on the triarue we have – the one thing she really wants.'

I can sense that she's lying, but even I was fooled for a moment – and afraid. Because even if it's a lie now, is this something she's been really considering? Dawn would never kill her own people. But Dawn hasn't been herself lately.

Kara's eyes narrow. It's the first expression I've seen from her, which must mean she's buying Dawn's claim.

Dawn folds her hands neatly in front of her. 'If you work with us, I'll make sure you're given what you deserve. If not, you'll get nothing from Bearra. It will all be gone. Triarue is *not* indestructible.'

The fairy is quick to change the subject. 'Why are you really here, Princess? I know you didn't travel all this way without guards to only speak with me about an alliance.'

Dawn breathes, taking a moment to consider her words. 'There's no point in keeping it secret, I suppose, if we're going to be allies. I've been told of an enchanted mirror that can reveal hidden magic. Lire has spies in Bearra – woken spirits from Muse's Forest – and the only way for me to identify them is by using said mirror. Grace and Amora made it for me as a gift, but in jealousy, Lire took it away and hid it. In my search for this enchanted object, I have been led to your territory. Where better to hide it than the last place anyone would suspect?' Dawn glances at me. 'That is why we've come. Only I can use the mirror, and only I can find it. It is of the utmost importance that we bring it home. When I saw you were working with the Ice Empire, that was when I realised we might be able to strike a deal while I'm here.'

Kara says, disinterestedly, 'Your mirror *is* here. I know of it. Lire's hideaway was discovered in the mountains years ago and I had it raided. Everything was brought back into the city. The mirror now sits in our best blacksmith's workshop. They have been attempting for years to understand what its exact purpose is.' Her eyes fall on us, half-lidded. 'If we choose to make an alliance with Bearra, I will present it to you as a gesture of good faith.'

Dawn brightens from the inside out – I feel it before I see it. 'That is wonderful news, Kara.'

I want to feel happy for Dawn that we've discovered her mirror, but instead my core fills with dread, my fingers icing over and my spine stiffening. *No no no.* It can't be over so soon. She can't find out who I am – not yet. I don't want to be discovered, nor do I want us to return to Bearra. I love us out here – together, friends, equals, more. Because it's almost as if we are *us* again.

'You'll stay with us for a few days,' Kara says, 'as I ponder my decision and speak with the leaders of the Ice Empire. Once our decision is made, you can either go home with your mirror, or I will find something else to do with you.' Her face is expressionless once again, impossible to read. I'm unable to gauge her emotions even with my magic. Maybe she has none.

Whatever *something else* is, it's bound to be even worse than risking my identity with the mirror, and I am not going to let it happen. Knowing that much is enough for me to go with Dawn, following the soldiers up to Kara's Citadel – the dark-stone structure at the edge of the city.

Looming above us, and around us, and beneath us are a thousand fears. Can we possibly trust Kara and the Ice Empire? Do we have only weeks until Lire destroys our world as we know it? What happens when all my secrets come out, to both Dawn and Lire? And will that even matter, if we have barely any time left?

I look at Dawn. She's striding forward, confident. I breathe in the frigid air, trying to remind myself there is still hope. We are together, and I have not lost my princess yet.

CHAPTER 13

Kara tries to put me in the depths of her cold castle with the maids for the night, but Dawn won't have it. Instead I find myself sleeping in the next room over from her, in a bed befitting royalty. For the first time in a long time, I'm reminded of home – of my old life. Noble, rich, respected. How did I become . . . whatever it is I am now?

When I rouse myself the next morning and go to wake Dawn, my answer is right in front of me. All I need is a glimpse of her face, her hair, and I know I would sacrifice *anything* for her, change my life a thousand times. I never know which moment is the last I'll get to see her. But I was with her a hundred years ago as well, and I know to be more careful this time. To drink in every second.

Last night, I visited Dawn in her dreams. First, I appeared as myself – as Relia – in a long navy-blue dress, my hair piled up in crimson braids. She was having a nightmare. Her parents were back in Bearra, but they were screaming at her, telling her how terribly she'd done as a ruler in their stead, that it would have been better to leave Bearra to Lire. Their faces were wrong, distorted. They began ordering around their people – terrible demands that would only destroy the kingdom. Forced Largon and dozens of her soldiers to walk off the edge of the castle's rooftop. Dawn's voice wouldn't work. She couldn't argue against them.

I changed the dream. I stepped up behind her; she was wearing the crown Maya destroyed, which I'd only seen in paintings. I took her hand. She turned, smiled with relief, pressing her forehead to my shoulder.

'It's okay,' I whispered. 'I'm here. I'm always with you.'

My haunted princess. She had dreams like this often, and I had learned the best ways to comfort her, the right things to change.

When she stepped back from me, the scene was different. She was still holding my hand, but I was Carlotta now, in a simple pale-blue shirt. Her subconscious often saw the two sides of me as one, in some sick irony. Her parents were no longer yelling, but seated eating dinner, smiling and laughing. We were in the dining room, across the table from them.

Dawn relaxed – I could sense her mind slowing. The crown was gone from her head, her hair let down. She leaned over to me, smiling peacefully, and whispered, 'I love y—'

I ended the dream abruptly, waking with a gasp.

She'd never said anything like that before – not in dreams, and certainly not real life. Not to Carlotta. For the first time I wondered if I was overstepping. Was I seeing things I wasn't supposed to when I visited her dreams? I thought I was helping. But was I putting ideas in her head, making her feel things she wouldn't without my influence in her subconscious?

Were those words the result of a dream-state, or did she truly mean them?

Days ago, when I overheard Sierra and Arden say that Dawn and I are in love, I was elated. But mostly, I was afraid. Love was never part of the plan. It was inevitable for me, but Lire was clear – Dawn and I will never be together.

If Dawn is beginning to love me, I can't imagine anything better, and I can't imagine anything worse. The last time she loved me, our kiss alone set off a curse that began this entire situation – from Bearra's sleep, to my death, to the war. What's next?

No, I won't keep visiting her dreams, at least for a while.

Now, in an ornately carved, dark wooden bed, in a dim room in Kara's Citadel, Dawn stirs, beautiful even in these moments of half-consciousness. Her eyes rarely become puffy, her skin never sullen. Her hair could be windswept by the worst summer storm and still remain in those perfect curls. She doesn't need the sun shining on her to glow.

I place a hand on her shoulder to gently nudge her awake.

She smiles up at me before she seems to remember where she is, then she sighs. Yet there's a determination in her that was beginning to fade before we left Bearra, and I'm glad to see it returned.

'I'm not sure what we're to do today,' I tell her. 'Kara asked us to wait, but are we prisoners? Should we go out into the city and be . . . searching, for something? Or do we wait in here?' I shouldn't bombard her with questions like this first thing in the morning, but I need to know before I panic.

She hops out of bed and pulls the curtains open. In rushes the brightness of a city covered in a sheet of sparkling white snow. 'I think we should explore, unless Kara decides we're prisoners. Don't you?'

Usually the idea of exploring a foreign city would frighten me, but a day out with Dawn, a day of *fun* as we wait for whatever is next, is too enticing for me to refuse. Standing with my hands behind my back, I say, 'I've heard this city has hot springs, not far east from here. That is, if they didn't disappear in the last century.'

Dawn grins and does an adorable jump. 'I've always wanted to visit those! We must go.'

Of course, I've known about her wish to visit the hot springs for more than a century. She was the one who gave me the idea. To me, the idea of dipping myself in hot water in a place as cold as this makes my skin crawl; as Relia, I might have had the strength to refuse and offer an idea of my own.

But Carlotta does what Dawn likes, because I only wish for her happiness.

Once we're ready and we've eaten the breakfast delivered to us, we attempt to leave. But a guard situated just outside Dawn's door stops us. 'You're not to leave your rooms until Kara permits it,' she says, her muscular body looming over us. A black tendril of magic snakes around her thumb. I'd always heard that Kara was very hesitant to share her magic, so if she's arming her guards with it, that can only mean trouble.

I bet I have more magic than you, I think, wishing I could use my power just once. How much easier it would make things. *You have no idea what I'm capable of.* Though of course my magic isn't trained. Hers surely is.

'Then I would ask that you pass on our request for *permission,*' says Dawn. 'We don't wish to leave the city or get ourselves into any trouble. We just want to explore. Kara surely doesn't expect us to stay in our rooms all day. That is no way to treat your guests.'

'Kara's expectations,' says the guard, 'are not my business. I've been told not to let you leave, so I will not until I hear otherwise. You're not a princess here, Bearran.'

'Is that so?' Dawn actually looks taken aback for a moment. 'Very well. But know this behaviour does not reflect well on your fairy or territory, and I am very much reconsidering my offer of alliance.'

'I'll certainly pass that on,' says the guard, and we're ushered back into the room.

The door shuts behind us and I shudder. 'We *are* prisoners,' I breathe, my hands turning clammy.

'Disastrous,' Dawn says, though she sounds more impatient than upset or afraid.

'Do we— Should we try to escape? Or wait for Kara to decide what to do with us?'

Dawn raises a brow teasingly. 'Escape?'

'She wouldn't be keeping us here, imprisoned, if she were seriously considering your offer.'

'I won't lose hope for our alliance yet,' she says. 'But I have a lot of experience with sneaking around a castle and not being caught. I suggest we at least do some spying while we're here.' She hurries to the bed and arranges the pillows and blankets to look as if she's still asleep within them.

I swallow. 'If we're caught, Dawn . . .'

'It was your idea, and in case you haven't noticed, we're already caught.'

'Okay, if we're caught *worse*.' But unfortunately, her ridiculous smile is enough to encourage me to follow her off the edge of a cliff. 'What's your suggestion, then? Are we leaving through the window?'

'If we use any servant's passages, we're sure to be seen,' she says. Her eyes examine the small balcony attached to her room. 'But I'm certain there'll be a way to climb down outside, and they haven't locked that door.'

'Because who would expect a princess to be foolish enough to try to escape that way?'

'Precisely, it's perfect.'

'And where exactly will we be going?'

'Around!'

'*Around?*'

'We'll search for the mirror. I'm sure Kara has already had it brought to the castle. Even if something does go wrong – if she doesn't accept my offer – I don't plan to leave empty-handed.'

And suddenly I'm on the small, flimsy balcony buffeted by wind, trying to stop myself from freezing up entirely – from the cold or from the fear of plummeting to my death, I'm not sure. *When I said I'd follow her off a cliff. . .*

The citadel is smooth black marble – barely any grip to the stone even if it weren't covered in sleet. And we're in one of the tallest turrets. The balcony isn't far from the edge of Kara's dome of warmth. Nothing but white snow and grey rocks lay below us.

'There's a balcony directly under ours,' Dawn says, peering over the edge. She's wearing a thick white coat with furry lining; a gift from Kara. 'All we have to do is manoeuvre down to it. Hopefully it's just an empty guest room with no guards around, and we can sneak through the palace from there.'

'Oh, easy,' I mutter.

'I'll lower you down first,' she says, her eyes calculating, 'then you can help me down.'

'I have to go first?'

'Well, I'm the one who has to trust you to catch me.'

'*Catch you.*'

She pulls me over to the edge of the balcony, feeling around the stone to test its grip – which is not encouraging. The fall looks even further now, the rocks at the bottom merciless.

'I'm not sure I can do this,' I tell her, my voice barely a squeak. My hair batters my face in the bitter and freezing wind. My arms and fingers are stiff.

'Hush, Carlotta,' she says. She taps my thigh, making me gasp. 'Put your leg over the barrier.'

I force myself to do it, and end up straddling the marble. Dawn keeps tight hold of my arm. I remind myself it isn't *so* scary. I have magic; I can soften my fall if I must. And I've already died once before. It isn't such a terrifying thing. Not really.

Dawn helps me shift around so I'm sitting on the barrier with my feet hanging over the edge. Tears prick at my eyes, both from the wind and the fear, but I let Dawn lower me down, inch by inch.

'I'm stronger than I seem, see?' she says. Our faces are close together, warm breath on each other's skin, and she kneels to lower me more easily. 'You're okay.'

My feet are dangling and I'm trying to steady myself but I can't stop rocking back and forth. All that's keeping me from plummeting into the abyss is Dawn's grip. Who was I kidding? *Of course death is terrifying!*

I take deep breaths, fighting the urge to close my eyes. I think I'm about to be sick when my feet suddenly touch something solid.

I sigh with relief. 'I'm almost there!'

'Of course you are,' Dawn says. 'I'm not letting go. Tell me when you're steady.'

I wait until my feet are planted firmly on the barrier below, then allow her to release her grip. The tension in my shoulders loosens at once, and I want to slump to the marble floor. But Dawn still has to come down.

It's difficult to see her properly from below, but she's already swinging her legs over. Fearlessly, recklessly. 'I need you to find something to hold on to, then grab my waist!'

I'm not sure what she expects me to do – it seems impossible – but I manage to find a strong enough foothold by the edge of the barrier and hook an arm around a pillar. 'Okay,' I breathe. I reach for her as she lowers herself down, somehow gripping the marble. 'I've got you.' I try to sound reassuring, but it comes out closer to a question.

And yet my instinct to protect her kicks in as I watch her, and my fear is overtaken by adrenaline. It feels easier to touch her, to hold her, grip her, and pull her towards me. To safety.

'Can I let go?' she asks.

'Just a minute.' I shift her a little so I can bring her down.

'Oka—'

She slips from the barrier, screeching.

'Dawn!'

Time slows as her dress twists in the wind and her hair streams around her, a puff of sunset-cloud plummeting towards the ice and rock below. Without thinking I use magic to push her towards me, to steady us. The smallest bit. Not enough to notice – *fairies, don't let her notice* – but enough to save us.

We tumble onto the lower balcony, her body pressed against mine. I'm about to burst into tears, but Dawn isn't upset or afraid. She's *laughing*. I can feel the adrenaline lighting her up inside. Joy. Something I haven't seen in her in a long time. 'Thanks, Rel—' She almost chokes. My heart stops. I nearly gasp aloud. Her cheeks flush with embarrassment as she collects herself. 'Carlotta. Thank you, Carlotta. Sorry. I was – confused – for a moment.'

I try to smile warmly, but the hope blooming inside me makes it difficult to not beam. We're gazing into each other's eyes, breathing heavily, and I whisper, 'Dee, it's okay.'

Then she looks at me with a serious frown, pressing herself up from the floor. 'What did you just call me?'

I balk. Only I ever called her that. Only *Relia*. 'I'm so sorry, Your Highness.' I rub at my sore elbows, only now realising how hard I landed on them. 'I— I think I heard Maya say it once.'

She looks lost for a moment. 'Oh. I'm sorry for reacting that way. It's okay,' she stammers. 'Of course you didn't mean anything by it. It's just . . . Someone else once called me that. Someone you remind me of.'

'Someone I remind you of?' I try to keep the delusional delight off my face. Try to keep the Relia off my face. 'Who was she?'

'Someone special.' Dawn turns wistful. 'Someone who, despite our love for each other, I was never allowed to be with. She would have passed while we were sleeping. You would have loved her; it's a shame you never got to meet.'

My chest goes warm. I could kiss her, right now, touch her. Why can't I? Why can't Lire just let me be happy? 'I'm sorry you lost her,' I say.

'It's okay. Well, it isn't, but she was never truly mine to begin with. We both knew our fate. And now . . . Not to say you replaced her, Carlotta, because no one could, and I don't only love you because of that, but, well, you fill some of the gaps she left. You make me laugh like she did. You have the same smile. It's a nice reminder that not everything lost is always gone forever.'

She must still be bursting with adrenaline to say all of this so freely. Can she possibly mean it? Is she saying it without saying it? *I love* you. I'm not sure what to respond, what to think. Being this close to her again is all I ever wanted, and all I was supposed to avoid. Could it be that she truly cares about me? That she loves *both* versions of me?

But that's the danger, isn't it? Lire warned me against just this. If she found out . . .

'Thank you for saying that, Your Highness,' I say carefully, looking away. I try to seem impassive, as if her words have little effect, as if I'm not bursting inside. As if this doesn't hurt me too. 'It is an honour to work for you.'

She blinks. 'Carlotta, I thought that maybe—'

'Let's start moving.'

The castle is grim and creepy and cold. We spend hours stalking through halls and peering through cracks. But we could spend weeks in a castle like this and find barely a small amount of its mysteries.

We don't talk much. My mind just keeps going over our conversation again and again. I can't stop thinking that Dawn might love me. So the hallways stretch on and on, endlessly.

'We've found nothing,' I whisper to Dawn as the sun begins to set. 'We need to return to our rooms before they discover we're gone.'

'So what if they do?' Dawn says. 'They shouldn't have kept us locked up. It's highly disrespectful. It isn't as if we'll be punished for this.'

'Isn't it?'

Dawn shrugs and moves on. 'We'll go back when we find something. The month Lire has promised is rapidly passing, and I can't waste time here being imprisoned when I could be doing something.'

'And what if Kara is no longer interested in an alliance when she realises we disobeyed her? Is that not also important?'

'She wouldn't have been a good ally if she expects to order us around.'

You need her, I want to say. *She's the only person who might have a chance against Lire.* How many times have I tried to tell Dawn to turn the fairies against each other? Why won't she listen?

'Daw—'

She freezes, spinning and placing a finger to my lips. I gulp. She steps lightly, pushing me back into the darkness of a corner. 'I hear her.'

'Ma'am,' a voice says from somewhere down the hallway. Distant enough I have to strain to hear. 'We need to know what to do with the Bearran princess. Candace is waiting for your decision to be made, and if you don't make one soon, she'll take an action that you won't like.'

'Don't threaten me,' Kara snaps. 'I know what your *fairy* is capable of, but she does not want me as an enemy. I have a plan for the princess. At least, I *will* have a plan. I'll ransom her to Lire, or just kill her, I don't know. You tell your superiors they'll know my decision when I choose for them to. Candace had best keep her hands off my prisoner.'

'She will, as long as she doesn't see a better use for her.'

'Like what? Candace knows nothing of Bearra. She's a child like the rest of you mortals. I've been studying the piece of Lire's magic that her son gave to me, and it's no different to mine. Fairy of wisdom this, darkness that – it's all just part of Lire's stories. We come from the same source. I can use that against her.' She takes a long pause, hushing the other woman when she tries to speak. 'Yes . . . I have a plan. I know how this girl works, and her connection to Lire. This mirror she's looking for? She'll do anything for it. Which means we have to find it first to make sure it never gets to Bearra. Then we can keep the princess and the mirror, since surely Lire has spies within our midst as well. Or we can destroy them both.'

Dawn releases a breath, and I grip her arm. I try to turn to go, but Dawn shakes her head, planted in place. What more could she need to hear? We need to run.

'What about Bearra's king and queen?' the guard asks. 'They'll want their daughter back, too.'

'I have that kingdom in the palm of my hand, and you know what? If Candace wants a piece of it, she had better make me a good offer.'

CHAPTER 14

We left most of our things in the carriage when we arrived, so we didn't bother to go back to our rooms before sneaking out of the castle. No one seems to realise anything is amiss, and we aren't stopped as we race out into the city. We're still in our 'regular people' clothes, so we don't look like runaway princesses – just very cold tourists.

'Where will we go?' I ask Dawn, huffing breaths of icy air and hefting up my heavy skirts to walk faster. 'We have no clue where the mirror could be. And as soon as Kara realises we're gone, there'll be a bounty on us throughout her territory.'

She waves for me to follow faster, not turning back as she staunches towards where we left the carriage. 'We'll have to check for storage facilities outside the city. We'll find this mirror. I know we will. It's here somewhere.'

'Dawn,' I breathe. 'I think we have to go home.'

She stops. Spins to face me. 'Don't tell me to give up, Carlotta. Not after all we've been through.'

I bite my lip, wanting to hold back my thoughts, but then remember that right now, pushing Dawn away is the best thing I can do for both of us. If she loves me in the way I suspect, I must make her doubt those feelings. 'Your parents aren't going to be here either,' I say flatly, and as guilty as I feel, it's also empowering to push back for once. 'I've come this far with you, Your Highness, and I've done everything you've said, even when it's put me in danger. But it's time to give up.'

Her eyebrows turn up in the middle. 'Carlotta? But you can't mean that,' she says weakly. 'Out of everyone, you were the only person . . . I thought . . .'

'You have to see that the reason everyone is disagreeing with you is because we care about you. Bearra needs its princess. I am sorry that this hurts your feelings, but—'

'You've never told me this before— I didn't know you felt—'

I wait for her to finish.

'I'm not just a princess,' she says, turning around and continuing to walk so I'm forced to shuffle behind. 'I'm a person. I have *flaws*. Why can't anyone accept that? Everyone else is allowed to make mistakes! No one else would be blamed for leaving! My parents weren't, because no one ever expected anything of them! But when I need something for myself, when I make a decision that isn't to everyone's liking, the world turns against me?' Her voice wobbles, as if she's trying not to cry. 'I'll have the carriage take you home, Carlotta. I won't force you to stay with me a second longer if that's really what you want. But I'm not returning until I have the mirror. And fine, I'll admit it, I plan to find my mother and father as well. Hate me for it if you must. I'll get used to it.' She shakes her hands like she's trying to rid herself of something. 'I am *done* being the perfect princess.'

'I . . .' I begin, but I'm not sure where to start. 'Dawn, I'm not trying to leave you. I'm telling you we should go home. Please just listen to me!'

'I don't have to listen to anyone! I thought you were my friend, Carlotta. I thought—' She cuts herself off, shakes her head, and continues speeding through the ancient, cobbled streets.

When we finally reach the carriage, we're both out of breath and frustrated. Dawn and I rush inside, now out of the city's bubble of warmth, and hurry to cover ourselves in clothes. The carriage heats itself up slowly, using its powerful magic – okay, yes, and some of my own magic, because I really am freezing. I want to curl up beside Dawn so badly, but instead I seat myself on the opposite side of the carriage.

'Well?' I ask after a while of sitting in tense silence. 'Where are we going?'

'Anywhere but Bearra,' she says, pouting like a child. 'I don't care.'

'Lire is going to attack within weeks,' I say, and *fairies*, it feels good to be so harsh with her. Now that I've broken past the initial guilt and fear that she's going to hate me, I'm glowing with the strength of standing up for myself for the first time. 'We can't keep wandering the world. Not when we have no clues for where to go next.'

'Let her attack,' Dawn says, her arms crossed, her gaze dark. 'Let her have Bearra. The world. As far as I can see, there's nothing I can do anyway. I might as well enjoy my last days travelling.'

'You don't mean that.'

'And what if I did?'

'Then you wouldn't be *you.*'

She rolls her eyes. 'Everyone thinks they know me so well.'

I do know you. More than anyone.

She stares out the window, but I know she isn't mad at me – she's mad at the universe. 'I am so sorry, Carlotta. I'm sorry I ever got it into my head that you were any more than my maid. That I was anything more than a princess. I'm sorry I abused my power and dragged you along with me through all of this, and put you in danger only because of my own selfishness, just because . . . Because I hate to be apart from you. I thought you felt the same. That this was what you wanted. But I understand now. You're not my friend, or anything more or less than that. You're my subject and my servant, you fear me and I rule you, and I am responsible for you only in those ways. I'm going to take you home, and then I'll leave Bearra in disgrace. I won't return ever again unless I have something to show for it.'

I want to scream at her, tell her who I am, for surely it would wake her from this depression. Everything is going wrong. I wanted to push her away just a little, not make her lose all hope.

Why, why do we have to love each other from so far apart?

'*Dawn,*' I begin, but before I can continue, something catches my eye. I stand abruptly, reaching to the window over her head. Tucked into it is a piece of paper, pink and pressed with flowers. As I get closer, I smell that it's scented with rose. Dawn follows my gaze as I pluck the note, opening the textured paper with my stiffened, cold hands. 'Dawn!'

'What is it?' She pulls herself over to look.

'A note! Someone must have put this here while we were in the city, someone who knows who we are.' I squint, trying to read it, but it's dark outside now and we have no candles. If she weren't here, I could use magic to form some light, but of course, that isn't possible. 'Can you make out what it says?'

'*Princess,*' Dawn reads. '*Remember you have more friends than you know. Do not trust Kara. Go to Amora's Territory. There you will find your mirror.*' She gasps. 'There's an address at the end, I think, but I can't read it. Carlotta, this is how the pirates were led to their iron sword! A friend of Bearra is trying to reach us!'

'It's a trap,' I say immediately, heart already hammering. 'This can't be real. They couldn't . . . Why would they just give us the address? What if someone else found it? And how did they know this is our carriage? What if Kara put it here in case we ran away?'

Something in Dawn changes instantly, her anger and anguish turned to excitement as her eyes crease and a grin puffs out her cheeks. Oh, no. She's really gone mad, hasn't she? 'Who cares!' she says. 'We must go. It's like Sierra said. We have allies everywhere, they're just operating in secret. There are more people than just the Bearrans who want to save the world.'

'Yes, on the other side of the world!' The usual Dawn would never take such a risk – at least, she'd send someone else to chase it. But I can see by this new gleam in her eyes that her mind is already made up. She has found an excuse to escape, and it has stolen her away. As much as I want that escape as well, her attitude terrifies me. I argue, 'It'll take us so long to get to Amora's Territory, search there, then get back to

Bearra, we'll miss Lire's deadline! Using the mirror won't matter when it's too late.'

The only way to save Dawn and keep us together is to let Bearra fall, to never let Dawn find her mirror, yet I can't help but defend her kingdom and its people. I began this nightmare with selfish intentions, manipulated into being a villain I never wanted to be – but the Bearrans and their kingdom have trapped my heart. I want to help them *and* I want what I've spent all these years fighting for.

I've never had the guts to say what I want, do what I want, take what I want. And now that I really am stuck between two worlds, I can't choose either – but I know I'm not choosing myself.

So why do I keep protecting others and never myself? How long can I keep playing both sides and hope that I'll find a happy ending somewhere?

One wrong move, and everything will fall apart.

'Carlotta,' Dawn says excitedly. 'It doesn't matter if it's the other side of the world. We happen to have the world's fastest carriage.'

'But Dawn—' As if obeying her sentiment, the carriage lurches forward, throwing us to the floor in our heap of clothes. '*Dawn!*'

'I'm sorry!' She shuffles back to her seat before lifting me up by my waist and patting my head to fix my hair. I nearly crumble inside, gasping. The carriage hasn't stopped racing, and we shake as we try to catch some balance. 'Okay, I got carried away,' she says, blushing and staring at my skirts, which have hiked up around my thighs. 'Oh, I forgot for a moment . . . I'll have the carriage drop you off at home before I continue to Amora's Territory.'

My cheeks heat as the satisfaction of her looking at me like that mixes with the jealousy that she's staring at someone else – Carlotta, even though that *is* me, but *yet* – which swirls with the anxiety reminding me I can't get too close to her.

I drop my head in my hands for only a short moment before collecting myself. 'No. Absolutely not, Your Highness.' She must know I have no interest in leaving her, because if I did, the carriage would not still be travelling so fast. 'Just because I have fears, and opinions of my own, does not mean that I won't follow you anywhere. You aren't only a princess, Dawn.' I take a breath, wondering if I'll regret my next words. 'I'm sorry. We *are* friends. You matter to me and I won't let you do this alone. But, if we're going to do this . . .' I falter, take another breath, then say as firmly as I can, 'If we do this, you must promise to begin listening to me.'

'I— Yes, Carlotta. Anything—'

'You weren't wrong when you said I fear you.' Tears sting my eyes – *fairies*, I really hate this – but I force myself to speak frankly. 'It isn't your fault, but I struggle to speak my mind to others, and it puts me in danger. It always has. From now on, we must be *true* friends. Friends who can be honest with each other, and listen to each other, and respect each other.'

She swallows, eyes wide, and fidgets with her hands. I have *never* seen her like this. 'Of course,' she says. The rocking of the carriage makes it difficult for me to focus on her wounded gaze. 'If it means I don't lose you, I'll make all the compromises you need. I am so sorry. I don't know how to be equals with you, and I've made mistakes, but

I'm going to try. With all my talk of caring for you, I've never truly shown it through my actions. From now on, I promise I will.'

My heart swells even as it aches. If I cannot be her lover, I will be her friend. Her *equal*. Could I ask for anything better, or am I treading on such thin ice that I'm risking us both? And wouldn't Lire benefit from this partnership as well?

I hate that the fairy and her schemes can ruin such a moment, a moment in which I should feel relieved, happy. But becoming closer to Dawn is no help to either of us. I have to believe I can keep us both from harm. I have to believe I can keep balancing, treading carefully enough I'll get us to safety.

'Thank you,' I tell Dawn. 'Truly, thank you.'

✦·◦✦ ☾ ☀ ☽ ✦◦·✦

As the carriage races through the night, I visit Lire to update her. I must keep telling myself, over and over, the story I am trying to weave. But all these lies are becoming knotted.

We're back on the cliff, and the wingless fairy walks with heavy footsteps to where I'm seated in the grass. I watch my hands in the dream for a while. *My hands.* Not calloused and sullen like Carlotta's, but pale and freckled and soft.

'I'm glad to see you,' Lire says, her light hair in weightless loose waves. 'Elsie is a better warrior than she is a spy. I also don't like to see the princess in Kara's Territory without you.'

I swallow. Surely she isn't aware we were there *together*. I can only hope the news of Dawn's presence in another territory doesn't reach Bearra, or there'll be trouble for everyone – especially Maya. If only I could warn Dawn about what Lire knows.

'The princess left the kingdom?' I enquire softly, creating an air of confusion over myself. 'I was just in Kara's Territory; if I'd known, I would have met with her. I'd thought that the queen and king would hide in the last place anyone expected – Kara's Capital. That's why I was there. I can't imagine why the princess was.'

Lire watches her ocean, its grey waves rolling towards us below the cliff's edge. 'Dawn wishes to ally with Kara, but she will have no such luck. Oh, her territory is an awful place, Relia. If it is too late for you to attempt meeting with the princess, I would like for you to return to Bearra. I should never have encouraged you to leave. I need my best spy where she can do her best spying, and that is in the castle, with the princess. She should be there soon. The kingdom has only three weeks to surrender or prepare for my attack, and I need you there to find out what Dawn is planning. None of my other spies can get close enough to her. I do not want to have to attack, but if my hand is forced, knowing their plan will ensure as little damage as possible.'

I recall what Dawn said to Kara – her lie about Bearra self-destructing should they lose the war. Has Lire already heard? And if Lire does know, what does that mean for the war?

She also hasn't said anything about the mirror, so I can hope that's stayed quiet – unless Lire doesn't want me to know about it.

'I'll do what I can to find the princess,' I say. 'Is she staying in Kara's Citadel? I've come all this way – I don't think returning so soon is best.' I try to change the dream, to change her emotions, to make her listen and agree with me.

Lire nods, her eyes glassy. 'Dawn escaped from Kara's hold. She could be anywhere, but she can't have gotten far.' She kneels in front of me and places her hand on my shoulder, giving me an achingly motherly gaze. 'I trust you'll be able to find her, Relia. Bring her home. You do know her better than anyone.'

I do – and it's my greatest weakness.

I squint as I wake, sunlight beaming through the carriage's windows. Dawn is asleep on the seat opposite me, also covered in blankets and clothes. Thank goodness she insisted on bringing so many dresses.

When I pull the skirt from over my head and peer outside, however, we're already out of the snow. It's still cold, certainly, but not half as bad as last night. How I slept while we were moving so fast is beyond my understanding. But I know I needed the rest. I snuggle back into my makeshift bed again, smiling into the sunlight, catching glimpses of Dawn's peaceful, sleeping face.

Then all the motion sickness catches up to me, and my stomach howls and tenses, my head spinning as the blood within drops. Oh, *fairies.* My conversation with Lire returns with a fresh wave of anxious nausea.

I need my best spy where she can do her best spying.

My thoughts race as I hold my stomach, throwing blankets off me, and—

Dawn wakes with a bright smile, and it all goes quiet. 'Morning, Carlotta.'

My muscles relax as my heart warms. *What was I so worried about, again?* 'Morning,' I reply, my voice croaky. I tilt my head to the window. 'We're already out of Kara's Territory. We'll be in Amora's within days.'

Dawn breathes a near-silent, 'Impossible.' She glances at the warming landscape. 'Just how much magic did Arden put in this carriage?'

And . . . just how much magic have I added while she's been asleep? The answer is too much. It's best, isn't it, to get us back to Bearra as fast as possible? Best for everyone except me, it seems.

'Isn't it something,' I say. 'At least Kara has little chance of catching us unless she flies here herself.'

'Precisely,' says Dawn. She shakes out her curls and straightens her dress. Her eyelashes are thick over her hazel eyes, curled and long and perfectly-framing. Sleep makes me look a wreck, but nothing could make Dawn even slightly imperfect. 'I know you think this is a trap, but I'm highly optimistic this morning.'

Her hope seeps into me and makes me question my own troubles – how bad can things possibly be? She's happy, so I am too.

She opens a bag of our food and takes out some bread and oranges. Oh, no. 'Let me put together breakfast,' I blurt. I know where this is going. Am I not already ill enough? *Fairies.*

'Absolutely not. It's time I show you my favourite meal.' She peels the oranges and separates the sections, placing them individually on the slices of bread – getting juice everywhere in the process. My stomach turns over and over and over until I'm not sure I'll survive the next hour. When she's satisfied with her orange-to-bread ratio, she places another slice of bread on top of each. 'Orange sandwiches!'

'Oh,' is all I'm able to say. I can't tell her, of course, that she's made me eat this once before and it is *sickening*. She loves it. She knows Relia hates it. But she doesn't know Carlotta does.

'See, it's just like marmalade,' she explains, licking her lips. She hands me a sandwich and I take it warily, the juice dripping down my fingers. 'This should be a delicacy. It's the only meal I can make. And I'm an important person, so that must mean . . . something, in the cooking world.'

'*Cooking.*' I take a bite, juice oozing out of the soggy bread. The orange sections burst as I bite. My face scrunches up as Dawn watches me closely. 'So nice,' I say over a gag. I try to take another bite but it's as if my body won't let me. Why can't I chew? 'No. I'm sorry,' I say, swallowing with difficulty. 'But this is awful.'

Dawn gasps. '*No.* You can't really think that!' She's already finished hers, by some miracle.

'I'm not sure what exactly makes you think this is good,' I say, my voice shaking as I fight a nervous giggle through my words, which turns into a full laugh. We told each other we would be honest now, did we not? 'But it is quite foul. It's the worst thing I've ever had the misfortune to taste. You had best stay being a princess, because you will *never* be a chef.'

'Incorrect. Everyone else who has tried this loved it.'

'You really believe someone would tell a princess that her favourite food is disgusting?'

She purses her lips. 'Well, fine, *one* person has tried it – someone I know wouldn't lie – and she loved it!'

I raise my brows. 'Liar.'

'Well, you weren't there, so you can't really say that, can you?' She still seems offended, but she's giggling now.

Little does she know. 'I can say what I like now, as we agreed. And I say you're a liar.'

She smirks, a conniving look coming over her face. 'Then I don't have to treat you as a respected member of my staff.' She takes a section of orange and flings it at me.

It bursts on impact with my cheek, and I gasp. I jump up, handling the sandwich still in my hand and shaking my head warningly. She's laughing wildly, watching me like a teasing child. I inch closer to her, sandwich ready, and squish it right into her perfect face.

The juice drips down her neck and chest and down my hands. Now I'm the one laughing.

'Carlotta!' She howls, orange in her mouth. 'I didn't know you had it in you!' She takes my hands, steals what's left of my sandwich and clenches it over my head so the juice covers my hair.

'Yuck, Dawn!'

And it becomes *war.*

We trip over dresses to throw food at each other, to wrestle each other, ruining our clothes, our hair, the carriage, heaving for breath, laughing so hard our stomachs clench painfully, dripping with juice, sticky all over.

An absolute wildness overtakes me, a confidence and sense of fun I haven't felt in a hundred years. Her hands are clenched around my wrists. We're staring right at each other. My heart is racing. Her emotions are so vivid I can feel them more than ever – or are they just my own? I feel as if I'm an earthquake devastating my own mind and body. Or a volcano about to erupt. A snowstorm meeting a forest fire. *Fairies.*

I drop, panting. She grins, knowing she's won. And of course I let her, because I know nothing will make her happier.

She breathes over me, her face flushed, and I melt from within, ice to her sunshine.

What happened to pushing her away?

CHAPTER 15

Sierra Reed always loved a fight, but nothing could compare to the thrill of fighting alongside her friends – it was more exhilarating than she ever could have wished for.

This battle, however, felt different. As she jumped on one of Rhiannon's soldiers – this lot were scouts looking for ways into Bearra, no doubt – something was missing. She punched him in the chest and all she felt was a sore hand. She threw him over the side of the ship, and the splash sounded more tiring than exciting.

Sierra sighed, wiping her brow. Why was Bearra always so fairy-forsaken *hot*?

She didn't want to admit why she was really feeling this way, because she was *not* that kind of person. But it was difficult to ignore that fighting without Arden by her side simply wasn't the same.

Levi, too, was faltering without his beloved Ebony to watch his back.

But Wren battled alongside them – the girl became a fiercer warrior by the day – without a care in the world as she slashed and carved and beat her enemies. Sierra watched her with an inner warmth – pride?

But their usual crew of seven – Sierra's head spun – *six* – was cut cleanly down the middle. Lark had also stayed behind in Bearra to walk with his new sweetheart: Maya's sister, Briar, which left another gaping hole in their crew.

Even the *Neptune* wasn't running as well as usual, feeling the loss. As if it weren't hard enough after already losing—

Sierra sprang back and geared up for a powerful kick to a soldier's side before Levi called her name. It gave her enemy just enough time to scramble away. '*Fairies,*' she grumbled, telling herself she'd kick someone else later to make up for it. She sprinted towards the back of the ship, where Levi was pushing back two soldiers – neither of them magical, to Sierra's disappointment – in the silhouette of the lowering sun. They'd been out all afternoon.

'Can you get this one?' Levi called, tilting his head to the soldier on his left.

Sierra started towards him, then jumped in surprise as an arrow went through the soldier's shoulder. They immediately fell, giving Levi the opening to send a knock-out swing to the other soldier's head.

Huh?

Sierra squinted in the direction of the arrow, to find Wren howling at the helm of the ship. Opal's bow in hand. Sierra swallowed her grief;

Wren had adored Opal, and she'd been practising with the bow since they lost her.

'That all of them?' Wren shouted down. Her red hair gleamed in waves as the choppy layers flew around her face. She was made for this – for the water, for the battle, for fierceness.

As if in answer, the ship began turning back towards the kingdom. *Oh.*

What. A. Day.

'Suppose so,' Levi called back, tossing the remaining unconscious and bleeding soldiers overboard. They'd float somewhere and survive – possibly.

Wren hopped down to them and Levi pulled her to his side, tussling her hair with a laugh.

Sierra flopped unceremoniously onto the deck with a sigh. 'When are we going to get a real fight? I thought there was supposed to be a war happening.'

'Me . . . Too . . .' Wren droned with boredom. 'They say we have three weeks until it becomes real. But hopefully Lire comes sooner so we don't have to keep dealing with this *monotony*.'

Sierra smiled at Wren. 'You so understand me.'

'Personally,' Levi said, sitting with them, 'I'm happy to have survived another day.' He dropped his voice. 'Don't forget we have to be back by dusk for the funeral.'

Sierra sighed again. She wasn't looking forward to Opal's funeral. Yes, it would be good for Arden, but to her it was an emotional event she did not have the energy for. She was accustomed to death – she'd been the reason plenty of people died. And it wasn't as if she and Opal had been close, so why did she need to mourn? It was a waste of her time. If anything, the loss affected Sierra mostly because it affected Arden.

'It still feels wrong,' Wren said. 'Just being on the ship without her.'

'Because she was here before any of us,' Levi said. 'We all had our reasons for finding the *Neptune,* and this family, but after Arden, she was the first. We've never known any of this without her. It's . . . It's never going to be the same.'

It was certainly more peaceful, but Sierra was not going to say that out loud. She'd come to realise peace wasn't such a great thing. At least if Opal were with them, she would have caused enough chaos to keep their time under Princess Dawn's thumb interesting.

Wren ran her fingers along the curved wood of Opal's bow. 'I just hope Arden's okay. He's been so jittery and nervy – more than usual. He's been . . . weaker. He's always had a sadness within him, I think, but usually he could keep it under control. Usually he's strong.'

They both looked to Sierra as if she knew more. 'I don't know what to tell you.' She couldn't explain that part of the reason Arden was so shaken was that he'd lost a sister before. She wanted to. She wanted him to share that burden with his friends. She didn't want to carry it for him alone. But she would. 'I haven't known him as long as you. I like to *think* I know him, but . . .'

But since she lost her curse. Since they lost Opal. Since Sierra had renounced her family for good and joined Arden's crew. Since she and Arden realised they were in love, and everything was different.

What *hadn't* changed? How was she supposed to know anyone, anything, for certain?

Did she and Arden really know each other? His kiss had broken her curse, yes, but it felt as if they still had so much to uncover. They were soulmates, she knew that. She loved him desperately. Maybe he was all she truly did love. Had ever loved. But it was all so *confusing*.

Sierra Reed did not *love* people. She did not make people *happy*. She made people hurt, she made them fear, she strove for power and she always, always won.

Fairies. If only she could still become the swan, she could fly far from here, clear her head high in the clouds. But that part of her was gone. She was raw and empty. A dried-up well.

Several versions of Sierra Reed had existed. The hopeful but hated child. The vengeful young woman. The swan. The one who realised her true family weren't the Reeds. And now . . . Now she was new again.

'Don't worry,' Wren said. 'You make him better. That I do know.'

Sierra's shoulders untensed. Marginally.

✦ ◦ ✦ ☾ ☀ ☽ ✦ ◦ ✦

At the edge of Bearra sat a graveyard. A special one, owned by the royal family themselves, to honour those who had given more than most to Bearra. Soldiers, leaders, those who died to save another. A secret garden, it was surrounded by fading red brick and hidden away in the castle's grounds, and still not entirely repaired from Bearra's sleep.

This was where they finally lowered Opal's body into the ground, in a coffin lined with triarue and filled with her favourite jewels –

which she had stolen over her years as a pirate. Someone had put her in a puffy yellow dress that had once made her look radiant but now highlighted her cold, grey skin.

None of the six left behind could bear to look at the girl for long, so the coffin was closed and buried quickly.

Sierra held Arden's hand as they stood over the fresh grave. No one else was there, no other graveyard visitors. The world was unusually quiet, as if even the birds, the insects, knew not to disturb the dead. Only the six people who truly knew her attended the funeral.

Ebony was curled up under Levi's shoulder, and Lark and Wren were perched opposite the others, crying silently. Sierra was sure Lark still carried guilt for lying to them all about the magic; she wondered if he blamed himself in part for Opal's demise. They all did, in their own ways. But the young man was good at being quiet, remaining unnoticed. Wren glanced up at him, wide-eyed, and he placed a gentle arm around her shoulders.

Arden stepped to the centre of their circle – the edge of the grave – treading as if he were walking on slippery ice or a crumbling cliff face. 'We haven't— We haven't had to do this before,' he said, his voice croaky. 'I don't think we ever expected, despite all the danger we got ourselves into—' His eyes were glued to the ground. 'She was just so bright. She was the most alive of us. The most unapologetically *present*. I couldn't imagine her growing old. Opal always seemed immortal to me. She was my first friend. My sister. And I never could have imagined a life without—' He wept with deep sobs, crouching in the dirt.

Sierra went down with him, arms around him, and the others followed. She'd only seen him cry a handful of times. The pain he was in was unimaginable to her. Her arms shook with him; his tears dripped to her hands, warm and wet.

After a while, Ebony stood slowly. 'She was one of the most frustrating people I have ever met. We were so different. And because of that, she was my best friend.' She sniffled. 'Opal pushed me out of my comfort zone and constantly challenged me. I'm a better person because of it. I'll miss her every day. But I won't miss the constant jangling of her jewellery and the clanking of her heels as she walks around the ship.' She smirked at that, and it earned a small laugh from Wren and Levi. 'We'll miss our sister forever, but I'll always remember her. I'll always remember to push myself out of my comfort zone, out of my own stubbornness, in her honour.'

'And me,' said Lark. 'I'll carry her with me everywhere I go. She isn't gone until we all are.'

Arden almost smiled, sitting back, cross-legged. Sierra moved around him, never not touching him, not even for a second. He wiped his eyes. 'You're right,' he said. 'If she can't live, we'll live for her. We'll immortalise her. And we'll start by winning the war.'

Something burned within Sierra. With the princess locking the pirates down in Bearra, they could not honour their friend. Still, Sierra swore that she would kill Lire for what she'd done. She and her friends would together hold the knife as they drove it into the fairy's heart.

How hard could it be? They had one fairy's death on their hands already. Lire was less a deity than a fly to be swatted.

'Trust me,' she said. 'We'll win. Our enemies had better know that losing Opal has only made us stronger. Because she lives in us all now, and she never held back.'

Arden squeezed her hand.

'Well, I loved her dresses,' Levi said with a distant smile. 'I loved how she always made our days brighter, more colourful. I miss that.'

'That's a beautiful sentiment,' said Wren. 'But I don't think Opal's dresses will fit you.'

Ebony snorted. 'We can work something out.'

Arden exhaled, the corners of his lips turned down. 'We still need to go through her things.'

'Not today,' said Sierra. She leaned her head on his shoulder.

He nodded. 'Not today.'

'But we'll get through this,' said Ebony. 'We will. We've all known grief in our own ways. We can carry this too.'

⁕ ⁕ ᎒ ☼ ᎒ ⁕ ⁕

When the pirates returned to the castle, the protestors were back – they'd been there nearly all week, showing up each day without fail. Shouts filled Sierra's ears, and she wished she could become the swan and fly high above them, pretending they didn't exist. Unfortunately, their protests could often be heard from every room in the castle.

Nightmare. Why couldn't people just . . . follow quietly?

While some in the castle sympathised with these protestors, Sierra had been tired of them from the beginning. How weak did a person need to be to *want* to give up their kingdom to an evil fairy? Even if Lire let the people of Bearra live, what kind of place would Bearra become?

Sierra already didn't see the appeal of living in the ancient kingdom. But if Lire was dictating over it? *Fairies.*

The pirates wiped their tears as they stalked up to the castle, the noise of the protestors almost enough to drown out their grief. The Bearrans circled the castle, held back by soldiers who were, in Sierra's opinion, being far too soft.

'Someone needs to put a stop to these people,' Sierra said as they shouldered their way past the crowd to go up the steps into the castle. Arden was gripping her hand tightly, letting her lead the way. 'Bearra is vulnerable enough as it is without . . . *this.*'

'She refuses to do anything,' Lark replied, referring to their fabricated princess, Maya. They so often referred to her as *she* now, in case anyone overheard them and caught onto the deception. 'And I agree with her. Doing anything to upset her people further, make them feel as if they aren't being heard, will only make them more agitated.'

Sierra rolled her eyes. Of course Lark would say something like that. But Maya was usually stronger than this. 'Then she needs to give them something they want to satiate them,' Sierra said. 'Rather than sit on her little throne and be the princess of absolutely nothing.'

No, Maya was not *really* Dawn, but she was acting like her. Surely if the real princess was gone, they could run things more . . . their way. But Maya was determined to follow Dawn's instructions, even though she hated her role.

Sierra couldn't help but think that Opal, at least, would have agreed with her that Maya needed to take control. Opal would probably distract the protestors with whatever bright dress she was wearing, knock them over the head to shut them up, then take everything in their pockets. The thought made Sierra tear up a little – was *now* to be the moment that the grief would finally hit her?

Sierra took a deep breath. *No.* There wasn't time, and she had to be there for Arden.

'But she didn't want this,' said Wren, running the tip of a knife against the stone wall with a steady *shriek*. Guards glared at her, but half the castle was crumbling anyway, and what were they going to do, throw a fourteen-year-old – and one of their best warriors at that – in jail? 'She tried to refuse it and no one let her. How's she supposed to know what to do with the protestors? Maybe biding time, until *the other she* is back, is the best thing to do.'

'She'll be biding for a long time.' Sierra turned in time to catch Ebony and Levi share a look she couldn't quite read. Did they disagree?

They entered the castle's eastern sitting room: Maya's favourite place to spend her time as Dawn, and one of the few places not damaged by Lire's last attack. The *princess* sat with her *prince* in a corner lit with the day's last touches of sun. In this room, the furniture was dark and the carpet was nearly black, always smelling musty, but the walls were bright white and covered in paintings, the ceilings high and the windows wide.

It wasn't the most decrepit place for them to make their base.

Sierra squinted at her friend. Although she knew that it was Maya there, not Dawn, Teddy's illusion was mind-bendingly uncanny. Illusion magic was new, and extremely difficult; a testament to Teddy's power.

Admittedly, he still frightened her – a little. He was one of the few people in the world she wasn't certain she could defeat. At least the iron here weakened him when it was close by. She hated that it hurt Arden, but she was glad it could be a backup plan if Teddy ever turned on them.

Dawn – *Maya* – moved her gaze to the pirates, looking them up and down through wide hazel eyes that showed far more expression than the real Maya's ever did. Teddy had tweaked her mask well enough now that touch couldn't reveal the truth beneath. It was convenient, but even more befuddling for Maya. She nodded at the servants and guards lining the walls, and they scuttled out quickly, leaving the eight of them in the room alone. Luckily General Largon was out training – she was such a bore, either standing quietly and listening or talking to them patronisingly just because she was older and more experienced. Like she'd won half the amount of fights Sierra had.

Teddy stood, letting go of Maya's hand. He was never anything close to small, but he looked particularly muscular at the moment – he'd been training, it seemed. His red hair looked lighter, his face sun-kissed. Maya's eyes were like magnets to him, following him at the slightest of his movements. 'I hope the funeral went well,' Teddy said. 'Well, as well as one *can* go.'

'We appreciate the princess's kindness,' said Ebony, with a smirk at Maya.

'The princess,' said Maya, rubbing her eyes – who could've imagined that Dawn could ever appear tired? – 'is happy to help.'

'The princess seems to need a nap,' observed Sierra.

Maya rose from her chair, Dawn's dress falling in waves of luxurious baby-blue silk. 'It's the protestors. The sound. Constantly. It's exhausting.' She yawned. 'I just want *her* back so I don't have to think anymore. Thinking just for myself was always difficult. All these people . . . I understand why she was going mad.'

'If you like,' Lark said, 'Levi would love to play the princess for a while. We were just talking earlier about how much he loves beautiful dresses.'

The group all seemed too sombre to laugh, but Levi added earnestly, with the hint of a smirk, 'I'm not going to say no to being a princess.'

Teddy grinned, and even Maya brightened. She gestured for everyone to take seats, and they scattered around the sitting room. Tea was already brewing on a table in the centre, and the pirates helped themselves to the sweets laid out in porcelain bowls.

Sierra sat beside Maya and Teddy. She decided to get straight to the point. 'We must do something about the protests. Maya – *Your Highness* – I know you're afraid to make any decisions, but—'

'It isn't that,' Maya replied. 'I just don't think it's fair to punish or silence these people.' Even her voice sounded like Dawn's. Sierra couldn't believe how much she missed Maya's grey eyes and light-brown hair – practically greyscale compared to Dawn, who was sometimes as stifling to gaze at as the sun.

Maya continued, 'They are making things difficult, yes, but their concerns are valid. I know Bearra is a monarchy, but in the rest of the world, all people are given a voice. I just think . . . If I weren't in this castle, if I were living my old life, I would be one of those protestors.' She wrung her hands, then gave Sierra a sincere look. 'I would be angry. I've always been angry at the royals. It seems I was never as alone in that sentiment as I thought. How can I silence those I empathise with?'

Sierra cringed, sitting back and nearly hitting Arden. 'You think they're right in saying we should surrender to Lire?'

'Never.' Maya lost herself gazing at a painting of Bearra's canals for a moment, then said, 'But how could anyone convince them they're wrong? Bearra is hanging on by a thread – that thread apparently being *me* – and if we don't surrender, everyone will be doomed. They want a chance at survival, and we are choosing to take that chance away. We're all willing to die to stop Lire from winning, but who are we to make that choice for the people of Bearra?'

'If they aren't willing to die for their kingdom,' said Sierra, 'they should just leave. Bearra is the centre of the world and the centre of the oncoming war. If they want safety, they can go somewhere safe.'

Maya shook her head, making Dawn's curls bounce. Sierra watched them, mesmerised. 'They have nowhere to go. And this is their home. They have a right to be here and to have an opinion. They just think that surrendering is their only option, and for the most part, it does truly look like it. We haven't inspired much confidence.'

'Ebony is out training soldiers all day every day,' Teddy said. 'We're rallying the people to help however they can. What more can we do? We're clearly trying.'

'If Dawn isn't back soon,' Maya whispered, 'we'll *have* to do something drastic. That, or we'll have to listen to the people. Because if it comes down to us all dying or letting Lire win . . . I think I know what we have to do.'

Sierra recoiled. What happened to Maya? Was she slowly turning into Dawn, the disguise more than a mask? Anger rose in Sierra like piercing steam. Anger at Maya. At Dawn. Lire. The world. Opal was dead. Opal. And they were doing nothing.

They were going to give up?

No.

She stomped out of the room, Arden trailing her quickly. She wanted to be alone, but she couldn't turn him away. Still, she waited until she was back in their room to let herself fold, crouching in the corner of the room and letting the tears finally come.

Sierra Reed rarely felt hopeless. She rarely let herself be vulnerable. But today, she was weakened. Thoughts of Opal battered her soul, thoughts that none of this was worth it in the end. All this pain . . . How could anyone cope? How did people go about their lives and not destroy the world when they felt this agony?

She let Arden hold her, and they gripped each other in their shared pain, neither able to help the other, but doing all they could. At least if they were together, one whole between the two of them, it would not be so bad that they were each falling apart.

CHAPTER 16

When we finally hop out of the carriage in Amora's Capital, I run to the nearest hedge and vomit right into it.

Nerves. As always. But right *now*?

This could be the most important moment of my life – finding this mirror at last and potentially having my secret revealed – and instead of feeling alert and ready to deal with any outcome, I feel physically ill. My mind is so foggy, it's as if I'm barely here.

Even worse, the wonderful and sickening haze of the air in Amora's Territory makes me feel . . . looser. This is my first time experiencing it, and under other circumstances it might be lovely. But for this moment, it's the last thing I need.

Dawn's enjoying it, though. Her eyes are half-lidded in relaxation, but she's as steady as ever. She hands me water and pats my back. 'I didn't know you had such bad motion sickness.'

She's glowing, excited. And I. Am. Withering.

'Not motion sick,' I mumble, trying to straighten and sip the water, just to curl over again. 'Anxious.'

'Well, I'm sorry I can't empathise more, Carlotta.' We sit on the side of the road, halfway into Amora's Capital, the note with the address clutched in Dawn's hand. The sun is painfully bright, and here, the trees and houses are sparse. 'But, I had a friend once who suffered from nerves. When she felt as if she were losing control, it helped when I held her hands. I would . . .' She swallows, and I sense some nerves of her own. 'I'd run my fingers over her skin, or she'd squeeze my palms to release tension. We— If you wanted, we could do that.'

I shut my eyes tightly and cover them with my hands. *Me.* It always comes back to Relia. That innocent, romantic girl with the red hair and the pink dresses and the impossibly huge love that consumed her. Why am I so jealous of . . . of *myself?*

And how could I possibly accept Dawn's kindness right now, knowing I don't deserve it? Knowing I only feel so anxious because of what I'm doing to *her?*

Relia would. Relia would accept the help. But I am a ghost of her. A demon pretending to be a friend. I am nothing.

I swallow the lump in my throat. It's almost painful to say it, because it's so far from the truth. 'I'm okay.' The magic in the air, which makes my head spin with lust, also makes my refusal near-impossible. Still, as I push myself to my feet, I say, 'Don't worry. Let's go to the address and get this done. I'll feel better then.'

In fact, there is nothing that would make me feel worse.

The last couple of days of travelling were like a different world. One where I let myself be vulnerable, and so did she. We talked for hours, laughed until our cheeks hurt, and in the silence between conversations, I experienced just as much joy. I let myself get close to her – so close one could almost call it, well—

No. Anything romantic must be put to a stop. I've had my fun. Now I must lie in the bed I've made for us.

Dawn peers down, crunching the note. 'Okay,' she mumbles. Her disappointment is palpable. But if I hurt her a little now, it could save us both from a mountain of pain later.

✦ ◈ ⟨ ☀ ⟩ ◈ ✦

We walk in a torturous silence as the towns of the territory appear around us. I can just make out the sparkling pink palace in the distance, though where we're going is far from it. The address we've been given isn't close to the inner city, and out here, the towns – and the people within them – are less friendly and relaxed.

This, I imagine, is a poorer part of Amora's Territory. A place where the workers live, not the partiers. People don't wave to us as we pass their workshops, their farms. Their clothes are dulled from long days in the sun, their faces more weathered.

The sun sits high, highlighting thin roofs and faded-red roads. The foliage is bare and dehydrated. Like Bearra, it's warm here, but this is a dry heat. Dawn wipes a layer of sweat from her forehead.

I try to spot the palace again, but its sparkle doesn't reach here. I wonder if Amora is there, hidden and scheming how to help herself and Bearra. And I doubt the fairy has ever seen this *boring* part of her territory. Not decrepit, but with a distinct lack of the joy held elsewhere.

'There,' Dawn says, pointing across the road to a building that appears abandoned, with pieces of wood rotting and half-falling. Okay, this town is a *little* decrepit. The only indicator that this is the place we're looking for is a small, silver '17' above what was once a front door. 'My mirror is in there.'

'Let's be pa—' I start, but she cuts me off.

'If you want to wait out here, you're free to do so.'

If only I had the capability to be apart from her. 'I've told you I won't leave you to do this alone.' Because, regardless of whether this is a trap, I am very much walking into my inevitable doom. So I may as well go with her and do all I can to keep her safe before I'm ruined.

She takes my hand without asking for permission, gripping it hard so I can't shake her off. My skin is clammy under her royally-soft fingers. Her hair is tied back in a ribbon the same bronze as her skin, and as she tilts her head to take in the building, I find myself staring at her bare neck.

Then Dawn starts walking, pulling me out of my trance. 'We're saving my kingdom today,' she says. 'You and I.'

The decaying structure has a thick scent of mould that immediately makes my nose itch. The wooden floors creak and crack beneath our steps as we tiptoe inside. I'm about to ask where we're going when I notice a staircase going belowground.

'Basement,' we say at the same time. We glance at each other and nod. I grip Dawn's hand as strongly as she grips mine.

The sun streams through the tears in the roof just enough to bring a dim glow to the basement. Except, when we take the final step and land on a dirt floor, there's nothing to see anyway. Just dirt walls, bare and stretched a few metres each direction from us.

My heart thunders. This *is* a trap. Someone's going to be up there, ready to cage us down here to die. We're about to be buried alive.

You have magic, Relia. You won't die.

The thought doesn't help.

Dawn must hear my quickened breaths, because she moves her arm around me and pulls me to the left, to the back of the stairs. 'Whoever is helping us wouldn't want just anyone to find the mirror. I think there's more to this place. Just . . .' She hits the dirt wall under the stairs with her palm, making dust fly through the few rays of light. Again and again she hits at it, in different spots.

'Dawn, what are you doing?' I ask, shaken each time her hand makes contact with the soil, since she's still gripping me.

'I grew up in a castle, learning everywhere you can hide something within inconspicuous architecture.'

'Dawn . . .'

She hits one more spot, at this point the dirt and dust almost choking me, but this time it's different. This time, the sound is hollow, as if— 'There's a secret door.'

My breath catches. '*Oh.*' I push my hair behind my ears to look closer, and help her clear away the packed dirt. Within seconds my fingernails are filled with it, my hands scratched. The feeling of dry dirt on my skin is so irritating I have to take more deep breaths.

Then Dawn takes my hand back, and the irritation subsides. She's glowing from within – I can feel it, like her light is shining from me as well. 'We did it, Carlotta,' she whispers, as if she can't quite believe it. 'We've found the thing that could save us. They'll all see now. This was worth it.'

Beneath the dirt is a tiny door, a safe cut into the packed earth, with a wooden handle that only needs to be turned to reveal whatever is within. Dawn stares at it hungrily.

I can't breathe. My heart is about to fly out of my chest. My head is spinning. 'I still can't believe this isn't a trap,' I breathe. 'Why would someone leave it here? Why would they lead us to it? How did they have it in the first place? Know what it was? That we were even searching?'

'It doesn't matter!' says Dawn, fingering the safe's handle. 'Allies. We have allies. Someone must have known someone who knew something about something . . . People want to help us, and they have to stay anonymous to protect themselves. But if we get the mirror, and we have this proof that people out there are on our side . . . We could win this war.'

I force my breathing to turn gentle, force myself to hide in the shadows, become invisible, unfeeling. I want to argue, I want her to hold me, I want to put a stop to this, but I can't ruin her good spirits. Maybe it's selfish. But if this is the last time I'll see her smile, I won't waste it. Her hope is infectious. Even though I know Bearra will never have a chance, I almost wonder, as I have a thousand times, if maybe, just maybe . . .

Her hand drops mine as she opens the door, fingers closing over the handle one at a time as if time has slowed. The anticipation makes me sick to my stomach again, but there's no more food to come back up. Is my life flashing before my eyes? My parents, the nobles who adopted me, my sisters, the music, the dancing, the balls, the girl, the *end*, the feeling of death.

I inch closer to her so I can see past the door as it swings open.

Neither of us reacts to what lies before us. Frozen. I don't know why I thought I had more time. I don't know why I thought it would all happen painfully slowly, stretched out as I avoided the mirror's gaze, as I discovered whether or not it worked. I don't know why I thought I would have time to hide, time to run.

I suppose I didn't really believe, ever, that it would actually be in there.

But the mirror sits upright in the small safe, white-gold and shimmering. It is carved with patterns of roses around its oval shape, about as big as my handspan, with a handle engraved with delicate ripples that reflect water. It's as beautiful as anyone would expect – fit for a princess, created specially by two fairies. I'm not sure if it's just my particular magic that allows me to sense it, but the object is undoubtedly enchanted – *very* enchanted.

The reflection is as dim as the basement, but in it are two young women. Dawn and Carlotta. I always forget how much shorter I am until I see us like this. I blend into the background beside her, the princess radiant as the sun, but not casting any light on me as if I were the moon.

Dawn's emotional state is pure shock, and at first I think it's just from seeing the mirror. She really has done it. Found the impossible. Discovered the object that can help Bearra win the war.

It's here, I think excitedly. And somehow it hasn't revealed me. A foolish smile tugs at my lips. Everything appears normal. I have more time. I'm safe. *We can remain together.*

Dawn steps back slowly, watching my reflection, and I *then* remember that I can't use the mirror's magic. Only she can. And she's seeing—

'Relia,' she chokes out, looking between the mirror and me, her eyebrows pinched up in the middle. Her hands are trembling, and they reach up to clutch her chest. I've never seen her look like this. Not even at her worst. Her distress stabs at me, cinching my lungs. 'R-R—'

I snatch the mirror from the safe and close the door, stepping towards her. It's cool against my skin, the magic rippling up my arm. 'Dawn?' I adjust my expression, feigning confusion. If there's a way out of this, I must try. 'What's wrong, Your Highness?'

She keeps staggering back, staring frightenedly at the mirror in my hand. Tears pour over her cheeks. 'I saw—'

'This *is* a trick,' I say. 'Someone planted this mirror here, it's a fake, and it showed something that would scare you. That's what happened, isn't it?' I try to reach for her, touch her arm gently to calm her, but she rips herself away. We keep dancing like that until she's backed against the dirt wall. 'Dawn, speak to me.'

'Not you,' she stammers. 'No. Not *you*. Not the only person I thought . . .'

'What are you talking about? What did you see?'

Her body is shaking now. Seeing her this way, experiencing her emotions – I'd end my life to see her suffering stop. '*Relia*,' she whimpers.

I shake my head. Try to keep a calm composure despite the way my skin prickles all over. 'What's that? What's Relia? Dawn, are you alright?'

I try to imagine myself as she just saw me. What did I look like when I was last *her*? The same night I died, the same night Dawn slept? A sixteen-year-old girl in a ruffly pink dress, a tight corset, her hair half up in intricate braids, red curls falling down her back, pale skin, cheeks always flushed. Alive, in love, *me*.

Her voice goes dark. 'Hand me the mirror,' she commands. 'Now.'

'Not if it's going to frighten you again,' I say strongly, but inside, I am a whirlpool, I am weak, so weak – can she see?

'Give it to me!' she screams, eyes wild, and this time I have no choice but to oblige.

I grip the handle until the last second, keeping it faced away from me. But she takes it in her stammering hands and turns her back to me, holding the mirror to the wall so she can see us both.

I bite my lip and step back, shoulders hunched, shame and heartbreak and guilt and an ocean of emotions – yes, an ocean, Lire's word, the only concept I can imagine to describe the depth of my agony – making me small, making me feel as if I'm so deep inside my own head that I'm not physically in this basement at all.

Her jaw drops, and several emotions cross her face at once. Confusion. Anger. Shock. Disbelief. *Relief?* 'Relia,' she whispers. 'Relia . . .'

I want to keep lying to her, telling her that whatever is in the mirror is a trick. That I'm Carlotta, her maid, her best friend, who has been through so much with her. How could she believe this *object* over me?

But I can't find it in me to do it.

'It's me,' I whisper, voice cracking. I gasp out a sob as tears blur my eyes, my face scrunching up in pain. I can't meet her eyes. 'It's me.' I stop trying to look, instead crouching on the dirt, burying my face in my hands. *Doomed.* If Dawn doesn't abandon me for this, Lire will kill me.

'No,' Dawn says. 'You couldn't have— You didn't . . . Carlotta? Please. *Fairies,* please tell me there is an explanation to this that won't break me.'

I shake my head, still not looking up.

'*Relia,*' she says wistfully, and she keeps repeating it. 'It's her. Exactly as I remember. But she's in so much pain.'

I let myself fall to the floor, staring at the ground. *Just bury me.* Why can't I hide? Why can't I run?

'Carlotta,' Dawn says. 'I don't know what's happening, but I need you to explain this right now. Tell me what you know. Tell me why I'm seeing *her.*'

'I told you,' I cry. 'It's *me.*' I take a few heaving breaths. 'Carlotta isn't real. I'm not . . . I *am* Relia. It's me.'

Saying it out loud is like a weight lifting from my body. But the shame wracking me is still unbearable. I finally force myself to look at

Dawn again, my princess, and wipe the tears from my eyes so I can see.

She crouches in front of me, eyes darting up and down my body 'But Relia is dead. Relia grew old and died. She can't be . . . This mirror shows the truth, but— But there is no world in which that is the truth.' She clenches her fists. 'It *is* a trick. It must be. Lire's army – they're spirits – Relia can't have become – she would never. She was supposed to live a long, happy life without me. She was supposed to . . .'

'But I couldn't live without you,' I sob. My voice is whining and high, stretching through the cave in its infinite pain. 'I wasn't strong enough. I couldn't survive a day after the curse took you. I had to give us another chance, I . . .'

She searches my face as if looking for Relia beneath the illusion. '*You're* one of Muse's spirits,' she says, her tone devastated. She looks at me with such pity, even after all I've done to her. 'You took your own life in the forest, and became one of them, and ended up as one of Lire's spies.'

I want to reach out to her, somehow explain through touch that I love her, because I have no words. I have to tell her I love her so much, and I am so sorry. Yet I can't. She hates me now. I can't ever be near her again.

I strangle out, 'It was the only way to see you again. I didn't know if you would be gone two weeks or two thousand years. There's only one way in the world to survive time.'

Her lip twitches. 'So you lied to me. You couldn't have me the first time around, so you became someone new, a hundred years later, and made me fall in love with you all over again, broke my heart all over again.'

I bury my face in my hands. 'I tried to push you away, Dee. I told you. I couldn't live without you. This was the only way. I know you hate me. I know I'm a terrible person. I can't make excuses for what I've done. But you must know I only did this because I love you. I love you more than I love my own life. And I've been so careful, only telling Lire what she needs to know, trying to keep you safe.'

Her hand touches my shoulder and I flinch back, but she whispers, 'It's okay, Relia. *Shh.*'

I let her pull my body towards her, into her arms, but I still plead, 'I hurt you. I'm sorry. I know you won't forgive me—'

'You have hurt me,' she admits. 'It's going to take me time to understand, to forgive you. This isn't going to be easy. But don't ever think my heart wouldn't be in the *heavens* to have you back.'

I shake my head, and she pulls back to look into my eyes. 'Relia – you've been through so much. Just to bring us back together. Even if I'm angry, and upset, I understand what you did and I am so grateful. I'm so sorry you had to do this. But it's okay. You're okay now. We're going to be okay together.'

'*No,*' I say. 'No. No. Don't show me kindness. Please. I'm begging you. I don't deserve that.'

'I have nothing else to give you, my love,' she says.

'*Dawn.*'

'Devotion is all I have ever had for you – for both the versions of you I've fallen in love with.'

I shake my head. 'You're only saying that because of where we are. You're in shock, and Amora's magic is getting to your head. I'm telling you, Dee, you aren't safe.'

'My feelings are the same as always, Relia.' She says my name like it's the last time she'll ever say it, like it's filled with magic. 'I'll need you to explain everything. In detail. And I can't say that I'm not upset, in many ways, but how could anything overshadow my relief to have you with me again?'

She runs her hands over my arms, up and down, up and down, staring at her fingers. 'And to know that the person I fell in love with, my Carlotta, the only light I've had in these terribly dark months, was my Relia all along? *You* woke me up. Not Jacob, or Lire, or anyone else. After a hundred years, I never felt okay until I met you. I have you to thank for everything.'

'But—'

'Relia, I have my entire life to be angry with you. Right now, nothing could ruin my joy.' She wipes her eyes. 'I won't let it.'

'I'm so sorry,' I whisper, leaning away from her. This is so much worse than her hating me. It only reminds me how terrible a person I am compared to her. It only reminds me how I need to push her away to protect her. She is so good that she can't see I'm a monster. 'I'm so sorry.'

She pulls back and lifts her hands to my face. She traces her fingertips along my eyebrows, my cheekbones, my nose and lips. Dabs away my tears with her sleeve. 'You know, I did wonder if you were too good to be true.' She laughs lightly. 'But I've always adored you too much to care, really.'

'*Stop.*' My voice is anguished. I want to hide, I want to be invisible – and I want her touch, her warmth, more than anything.

But she continues, 'I need time to process it, to properly consider how I feel, but for now *I love you.* I would take any version of you, in any lifetime, and love you with my entire soul. From the shallows to the depths. You are all I have ever wanted.'

I take a breath, fingers crunching as they try to grip the dirt beneath us.

She stands, leaving me there for a moment, and from her pockets she places a few pieces of triarue in the safe, closing the door. 'For our allies,' she says. 'Whoever they are.' When I don't move, she frowns, moving over to me and holding out a hand. 'Well, are you coming?'

I look up at her, her form blurry through my tears. The sun has moved, and the basement darkens in the twilight. I wipe my hands on my skirt. 'I don't know where to go,' I whisper.

'What do you mean?' She keeps her hand held out, waiting for me to take it.

'Lire won't take me back now that I've ruined my ties to you. She has nothing left to offer me, and I have nothing to offer her. So there is nothing for me. I have no one and nowhere. I may as well let myself die again. I had the second chance I wanted.' My face screws up with pain again. 'It's time for this all to end.'

Dawn looks at me like I've said the most ridiculous thing in the world. 'My love, I need you to come out of the recesses of your mind and join me in reality.' She takes my hand and pulls me up – she's too strong for me to fight it. 'I don't know how I could make it any clearer. You're staying with me. I will never, ever let you get away from me again. Is that understood?'

'But – *Dawn*. I told you. I'm not safe for you to be with. I can't stay with you.'

'We're going back to the carriage now. That's an order.'

I stare at her, searching for a secret behind her words, searching for the truth – that she hates me, she's furious, that she wishes I were dead. Because surely she can see the madness in all of this. But it's all Dawn, genuine and caring.

Her blessings are once again a curse, her charity, her ruin.

CHAPTER 17

SOMEWHERE, SOMETIME . . .

Princess Dawn had only ever loved two people, a hundred years apart. She had not thought herself capable of loving anyone but her first love, and it turned out she was right. *Relia. Carlotta.* It didn't matter.

She knew the soul she loved, and for her, it was that simple.

Their story began at a ball – one of the first both girls were allowed to attend – held in a kingdom that no longer existed. At eleven years old, Dawn was dressed in a yellow gown, a gold bow atop her head, with a bright-blue triarue pendant on her neck.

Though she was young, she was intelligent. She knew why she was there and what she had to do. She was a princess, and events such as these, where the powerful mingled, were important. And, as she was about to find out, people adored her.

Was it the charm she possessed from her blessings, or the allure of her curse – the knowledge that despite all her good qualities, they would be wasted on a potentially endless sleep – which attracted people like magnets?

Regardless, the spinning lights of the night and the people in the ornate, cold ballroom were a wonder. For a child like Dawn, it was the most fun she had ever had. It felt as if with every new person she spoke to, she was filling up with energy.

Then she spotted a pale, red-haired girl across the room. She was shifting, fiddling with her fingers, hiding behind a woman Dawn assumed was her mother.

Dawn tilted her head, perplexed. Why was this girl having such a terrible time, in such a wonderful setting? The princess excused herself from the conversation she was having, stopping by a table of drinks to pick up two glasses of water, and made her way over to the only other girl her age.

The mother nodded her head politely as Dawn stopped in front of them, offering a smile and a simple, 'Hello, Your Highness.'

'Good evening,' replied Dawn, her voice squeakier than she'd have liked. She hoped to grow out of that soon, if she were ever to be taken seriously as a leader. 'I am Princess Dawn of Bearra.'

Dawn didn't catch the woman's name or place of origin as she introduced herself; she was too busy staring at the girl as she played with a strand of hair, looking away.

'. . . and this is my daughter, Relia,' the woman said, motioning to the girl. 'My other two girls are around somewhere, probably already talking some princes' ears off! It's lovely to meet you, young princess.'

Relia. Dawn loved the name immediately, thinking it fit the girl very well. But Relia still wouldn't look up. If anything, she had retreated even further behind her mother.

'Are you not enjoying the ball, Lady Relia?' Dawn asked. 'I'm finding it quite cold myself, being from Bearra. But I think it's still very lovely.'

Relia mumbled something unintelligible, and her mother nudged her forward. The girl stared at Dawn wide-eyed, as if she'd suddenly learned to make eye contact and couldn't stop. 'I'm s-sorry, Your Highness, of course it's a l-lovely ball.'

Dawn frowned. People weren't usually so . . . difficult. Most seemed to open to her immediately, no matter how hard they appeared on the outside, like eggs cracking and spilling just at her appearance. But Relia was giving her . . . nothing. 'Your dress is beautiful,' Dawn attempted. 'The blushy pink makes your hair look incredibly vivid.'

Relia placed her hands behind her back; Dawn noticed they were shaking. 'Thank y-you. You look very nice as well.'

Dawn smiled. It was rare to find someone she just knew she had to have in her life. It was rare for anyone – but *this* was one of those times. She was determined to make Relia her friend. 'Why don't you come outside with me for some fresh air?' Dawn asked. 'I've heard there are dogs in the garden. Friendly ones we could play with.'

Relia's eyes turned up to her mother.

'Go on,' the mother said, with an amused expression. They didn't look very similar, for a mother and daughter. 'But don't wander too far.'

'I'll look after her, don't worry,' Dawn promised. She took the girl's freezing and trembling hand, and dragged her through the crowd towards the doors. People tried to stop and talk to her along the way, but she shook her head and made polite excuses.

Relia was panting by the time they were outside. 'Are you sure this is . . .? Those people all wanted to talk to you.'

'But I want to talk to you, Relia,' said Dawn. They walked slowly down the stone steps into a moonlit courtyard. Hedges shaped like animals rose above them eerily, yellow roses dotting the shrubbery. 'Tell me, why do you seem so—'

'Oh, shy?' Relia offered. Her voice was lower than Dawn's, but so quiet. 'That's what everyone says about me. Not everyone is *Princess Dawn*, you know. Things aren't so easy for the rest of us.'

Dawn stopped, her shoes flat on the manicured grass. 'What do you mean?'

Relia paled, her eyebrows knotting. 'It's only that— Well, you *know*. You're very famous. Throughout the entire world. People love you and you don't even have to do anything. For me . . . I have no blessings, and I'm not royalty. And I have . . . People call it nerves. I can't stand . . . All the people, and the sounds and lights and colours and the itchy dresses. My family says I'll grow out of my discomfort. I hope that's true.'

Dawn was quiet for a while. She truly had no idea what the girl was talking about. She'd never felt *nervous*. What need was there for such a feeling? But with Relia, it seemed it wasn't just a feeling – it was an affliction. And was it only Relia, or did everyone see Dawn like a, a . .

. *doll*, or even a deity, instead of a person? She knew she was special, but she was a girl just like Relia, wasn't she?

'Then why are you here?' Dawn asked. 'Why come to a place that is so difficult for you to stand?'

Relia laughed shortly. 'I have no choice. My adoptive parents made me – they said it's time I begin *socialising* again.'

'Adoptive?' Dawn led them around a hedge and sat on the grass. She gestured for Relia to follow.

'My real parents died when I was younger.' Relia sat and plucked a blade of grass to fiddle with. 'I don't remember them very well. They say I used to be louder, before my parents died. My new parents took me in because they were close friends of my real ones. I'm lucky, because they're very wealthy. But it means I'm subjected to things like . . . this. And my adoptive sisters are younger and irritate me to no end.'

Dawn couldn't imagine losing her parents. The thought of it alone made her feel ill. 'This is my first ball,' she said, not knowing what to say to Relia's story. Maybe she would tell Lire when she returned to Bearra – the fairy always had great wisdom to share with Dawn. In fact, losing her would be akin to losing her parents. 'I love it, and I'm sure there will be plenty more.' Relia cringed. 'Let me make you a promise. Whenever we find ourselves at an event like this together, I'll help you through it. In return, I just ask that you be my friend.'

She shook her head. Dawn's excitement fell at first, but Relia explained, 'You could be friends with anyone. Don't you know that? You should get away from me before I taint your perfection.'

Dawn narrowed her eyes and made a decision she was determined not to regret. She dug her fingers into the ground, twisting them into the dirt, then smeared as much of it down her arms as she could manage.

Relia's jaw dropped. 'Princess! What are you—'

'Tainting my perfection,' Dawn said. 'Now you don't have to worry.'

'But you can't—'

'I *like* you, Relia. I like that you're different. You were right. I don't have to do anything to be loved. And it isn't right, is it? I don't want to be loved for nothing. I don't want adoration if it's empty. But you . . . you're real.' She reached over, painting a line of dirt down Relia's wrist.

Relia's eyes darted around for a minute, her mind seeming to run faster than a galloping horse, then she stopped, let out a single disbelieving breath, and burst into laughter. Dawn beamed, laughing alongside the girl, until both of them were rolling in the grass.

Finally, Relia sat up straight, clutching her stomach. 'So, where are the dogs you promised?'

'Oh.' Dawn sucked in her lips, then said, 'There aren't any. I just thought . . . It seemed a good way to get you out here. People like dogs.'

Relia giggled again, and Dawn stored it away in her mind as her new favourite sound – it was a song that reached the depths of her soul and immediately took root there.

'So?' Dawn said. 'Are we friends, then?'

Relia smiled. 'It would be my honour to be your friend, Your Highness.'

'Then I hereby promise,' said Dawn, 'to always take care of you, if you promise not to leave my side. I don't care if you hide behind me, as long as you're always honest with me, even when no one else is.'

'I swear it,' Relia said, pushing her hair back, the tops of her ears pink with a blush. 'Every party, gathering, ball, wherever we are, I'll be a friend to you.'

Falling for Carlotta, even as she continuously pushed Dawn away, was a heartbreak the princess of Bearra had never known. How could the person to bring her the most happiness also be the person to bring her the most heartache?

But now? Now, it was all clear. Now, it was more wonderful than she ever could have hoped. Because Carlotta loved her. And because Carlotta wasn't any replacement for Relia – she *was* Relia.

The situation was terrible and dangerous and heartbreaking, yes, but Dawn was so overcome with joy that she couldn't think past her luck. Well, she could be angry at Relia some other time, couldn't she?

That's what Teddy and Maya were doing; pretending all their trust issues didn't exist for now so they could love each other through the war.

As Dawn and Relia – *Relia*, she still couldn't believe it, her giddiness only amplified by Amora's magic – travelled slowly back to the carriage, Relia told Dawn everything. While Dawn lost Relia only a year ago, Relia waited the entire century for her. That sacrifice was enough to trust her, wasn't it?

The princess felt her strong ability to restrain her emotions waver over the previous few months. But in this moment, she was completely in control. *Except* for the fact that she wanted to take Relia and kiss her fearlessly, passionately, never letting go. Still, she knew it was not the time, so she kept herself poised.

Carlotta's face, because it was, in fact, Carlotta's face and not Relia's, which was incredibly confusing, was twisted in distress as she told her story.

Dawn kept quiet, only nodding and occasionally gazing into the distance as she thought. She knew Relia well enough to hold space like this for her – one wrong move, and the girl might disappear, a candle in a breeze. Once she was sure Relia was done, she said, 'We don't need the mirror now.'

'Sorry?' Relia replied.

Dawn's excitement built, and she knew it was wrong, but she couldn't help it. Was it the magic in the air, or just her own elation? Either way she knew she was blinded, she was going too fast. *You can't trust her. You should be angry.* Pfft. 'You can just tell us who the other spies are,' Dawn said, 'and you can feed Lire false information! You'll be *our* spy now.'

Relia stopped, her voice low as she scanned for eavesdroppers. 'Dawn. You are taking my situation too lightly. I don't know why you aren't angry or afraid, but you should be. Just because you've found me out doesn't mean I'm on your side now. I still can't break my promise to Lire.'

'Whyever not?'

'If it were that easy, don't you think I'd have revealed myself by now? She has power – she'll punish me if I disobey her. She'll let me die again. Without her magic . . .'

Dawn raised her brows. How was Relia just not getting it? 'Oh, no,' she teased, 'if only we knew someone who has plenty of their own *Lire* magic.'

'I don't have enough to fight her, to keep myself alive! I don't know if I even *am* alive.'

'Not you,' said Dawn. '*Teddy.*'

Relia shook her head, continuing to walk. It was so lovely, Dawn thought, to see Relia again, even with Carlotta's face. She wasn't pretending to be someone else anymore. Relia's old mannerisms were back, the way she rambled, worried. She had been so quiet before.

Now she spoke to Dawn as they once had, a century ago. 'There's no way Teddy would help me. You might be lenient with me because you know me – because you naively want this to work out – but your friends? I'll be dead to them if they don't just kill me themselves.'

'No. They've all made mistakes as much as the rest of us. Teddy is Lire's son, and my best friend. Don't you think out of anyone, he would be the one to empathise most with your situation? I know he'd be willing to help. And if he isn't, well, I'm still his princess. He has to listen to me.'

'*Dawn.* Please. I need you to take this seriously. If you're going to survive . . . You're supposed to hate me. You're supposed to run.'

Dawn sighed. Finally it was beginning to hurt again. She felt like a bucket in a well. Thrown all the way to the bottom, in shock when she first saw Relia's reflection. Drawn back up as she realised what it meant. Relia was her air; she was nearly out. Now, as reality set in, she was being lowered back down. Further and further from her love.

But she wouldn't let that stop her trying to convince Relia that things could work out for the best. 'I refuse, Car—Relia. I refuse to abandon you. Doomed as we are already, I won't lose you again. And on that note, we need to discuss what I should call you now. It's all very confusing. I should call you Relia, shouldn't I? It just feels so strange. But it would feel wrong not to.'

Relia paced a few steps ahead, unsteady on her feet, as if still wondering if she should run away. 'You shouldn't call me anything. You should be going back to Bearra, alone, and forgetting about me.'

Dawn kept following. 'So your answer is . . .?'

Relia threw her head back and relented, 'Don't refer to me by my real name in front of others. That's too dangerous. In private, I would prefer to be myself.'

'Understood,' Dawn replied. 'We won't reveal who you are. Yet. But when we get home, we'll come up with a plan to, well, I'm not sure. Make you a life that's yours again.'

They were nearly at the carriage now, and Dawn wasn't certain of their next steps. She wasn't ready to go home yet. Yes, they had the mirror, and yes, it was their duty to hurry home, but after what she'd just discovered?

Dawn was ashamed to feel delighted when they reached the spot they'd left the carriage and found it *gone*.

Relia gasped. 'Is this— Did we come to the wrong place?'

Dawn tried to sound disappointed and shocked. '*No* . . . Someone must have stolen it.'

'It can't be stolen!' Relia's eyes darted around the mostly-deserted street. 'That was part of the enchantment!'

'The enchantment doesn't let anyone else drive it,' Dawn said. 'That doesn't mean it can't be carried away.'

'Carried away! How!'

'It isn't impossible. Maybe whoever took it has more magic than our friend at home. They somehow undid the enchantment.'

Relia's white face turned green. 'What are we supposed to do? How do we get back to Bearra? Without the carriage we might not be on time before the month is over!'

Dawn hid her grin. 'I suppose we'll have to walk for now, and hope we find some transport along the way. We can take this as an opportunity to meet more people – hopefully some of our hidden allies.'

Relia winced. 'You're thinking of your parents again, aren't you? Dawn, we've been over this too many times. I know how badly you want to see them again. If I could bring my mother and father back . . . You just can't be spending all of this time on them. You won't get the outcome you're hoping for.'

It was a fair thing to say, though Dawn had not actually thought about her parents all day. She just wanted more time with Relia. 'I'm not suggesting we never get home. I'm just saying that it isn't the end of the world if we have to go slowly.'

She bit her lip, an uncharacteristic reaction, and Dawn wondered if Relia was beginning to understand why she liked the idea of not rushing home. *Time alone.* 'Well,' Relia said, 'it's dangerous, but I'll be here to protect you. I can use my magic in front of you now, which makes a difference. So I suppose I'll stop arguing and we can go wherever you like, as long as you allow me to remain by your side. But if things become too dangerous, if something happens with Lire . . .' She blinked. 'No, that won't happen. We'll be together. That's what matters.'

'There's my girl,' Dawn said, breaking into a smile. She couldn't help the growing warmth in her chest, expanding like a sun within her. She removed the ribbon holding up her hair and let it fall, putting an arm around Relia as they began their trek.

She would be angry soon. She would feel betrayed soon. Heartbroken. Afraid. But not today. Especially not if they had only weeks left to live. Even her anger at Lire seemed dimmed. Dawn was confused – she didn't particularly know what she wanted now, or how to feel, or what to do. She didn't understand the situation she was in. She was probably still in shock.

Today, though, by some miracle, she had not only gotten the mirror she'd thrown everything away to search for, but she'd gotten the love of her life back.

In a world where no one would dare think she was anything but perfect, Dawn craved the way Relia challenged her. Not out of jealousy or disdain, but because Relia really knew her, knew that despite all her blessings, Dawn was just a girl. So she'd promised long ago to always be Relia's friend, no matter what – even though they were different, and even when it got difficult.

Dawn did not break her promises.

CHAPTER 18

By the third day of walking north, I no longer feel anxious – it's like the feeling has entirely left my body in a way I didn't know was possible. Like all the good things I feel about Dawn have filled me up, pushing out everything else.

And to be able to talk about everything, to be unabashedly honest for the first time in, possibly, my entire life? The feeling is just . . .

'Do you remember that time,' Dawn starts, watching me with round eyes from her seat at the table, 'in the Reed Manor – the old Reeds, of course – when we were fourteen? The . . . What were they called, the—'

'Oyster kebabs?' I giggle.

'How does one even put oyster on a kebab?'

'And the little pearls on the top.'

'How was I supposed to know they weren't edible!'

'Edible pearls, Dee? Really? You were wearing a pearl necklace!'

'It turned out fine in the end, anyway. It . . . came out the other end.'

I burst into laughter, clutching my stomach. 'Your parents were—' I stop myself.

She glances at me, her smile replaced by tight lips. 'It's okay,' she says. 'We'll find them. And if we don't, then when we win the war, they'll come home.'

This same dance has been swinging us in circles for days. Memories and laughs, but also heartache and struggle. We're towards the north border of Amora's Territory now, the haze of the capital entirely gone and the towns more widely spread. Soon we'll be back in the middle of the world, amongst the cities unclaimed by fairies, then, soon, Bearra.

It's already beginning to warm. It isn't such a huge loss that we don't have our things from the carriage. The landscape is flat, made of wide plains with roaming animals and the occasional stream we have to find a bridge to cross. But mostly we stick to the roads, trying to stay inconspicuous, walking through small towns and using our dwindling money for meals and board.

This afternoon, we're massaging our feet in a small restaurant in a tiny town – a community from before the territories were formed, if the old buildings and lack of commerce are anything to go by. A place that only still exists because it's a stop on the way to the capital.

Earlier, Dawn only narrowly avoided a cow pat, sidestepping and hiking up her skirt with a gasp. There are a lot of farms around here, making use of the sparse yet fertile land, and many of the towns seem to overlap with them. But there's a charm to the countryside. Quaint old houses, friendly people, fresh air. Less magic and less politics. Simple people with simple lives.

My dream.

The restaurant we're in serves us cool salads and lemonade. We're squashed in a table in a corner, Dawn's hair tied back in a way that's meant to make her stand out slightly less, though it barely works. It doesn't help that she keeps taking out the mirror and twirling it in her hands, and constantly 'accidentally' catching it on me, as she's made a habit of for days. But there are only a few others in the restaurant, elderly and not paying us any attention. There's a freedom to it all, and I wish it could last forever.

'You're allowed to be pessimistic,' I say to Dawn. 'You don't have to convince me you're okay about your parents. I know *I'm* typically the one who needs comfort, but you don't have to be the strong one all the time.'

She frowns as if the concept is unimaginable. 'I don't know how to be weak,' she says quietly. 'Life tended to be easy before – well, except for the threat of the curse – and suddenly the weight of the world was thrown on me, all at once. I don't know how to need help. Pretending things are fine is all I can think to do.'

'Don't worry,' I say, stacking my fork with salad. 'I'll teach you.'

She's about to reply when her gaze lifts, her mouth closing as she leans back. A shadow passes over the light coming through the doorway. I turn my head slowly to see a man – dizzyingly muscular and handsome – staring at us. He's wearing plain clothes, but in the same manner Dawn wears them; like someone who's pretending to be someone they aren't.

He beelines towards us, perfect posture topped with white-blonde hair. I've met a lot of powerful men and liked very few. This one inspires no hope based on my first impression. Without saying a word, he pulls out a chair at our table and takes a seat as if we're old friends.

'Can we help you?' Dawn asks, brows raised in offense.

The young man pouts. 'You don't recognise me, Princess?'

She looks him up and down, unamused. Then realisation makes her shoulders fall slightly. 'Since we have never met, no, I don't recognise you. But from what I've heard in passing, and based on your appearance and *audacity*, I can only assume you are Prince Zeus of the Ice Empire.'

At that, my racing heart almost stops entirely at once. *The Ice Empire.* Just one of our many enemies, but a serious one. Kara is angry with us, with Bearra, and she's working with them, and—

'Correct,' he says, looking a little bored. 'And don't worry, I'm not here to hurt you. Nothing like that. I've met enough terrifying women to be afraid of stepping out of line around any more. Even if this one,' he points his chin at me, 'looks as if she can see a ravaging storm in the distance. Still, I know looks can be deceiving. No, dear Princess and Princess's friend, I'm not here for any trouble.'

Then he winks at me. Winks. Winks!

I cross my arms. He may not seem very scary, but I don't know what to think of him. The fact that he's noticed me at all, unlike most people, gives me the confidence to speak harshly. 'If you're not here for trouble, why are you here? Clearly we didn't want to be found. And you seem to not want to be noticed either, which doesn't make you particularly trustworthy.'

He glances off. 'I just wanted to talk,' he says. 'Because I'm hoping we can help each other. See, I'm having some problems at home, and—'

'Stop waffling,' Dawn says, cautiously eyeing the other diners, 'and tell me what you want. We are busy.'

'This is why I had your carriage removed.' He huffs. 'Because I knew you would be this difficult. *Royals.*'

'*You*—' Dawn starts, jaw gritting with anger; she can't seem to finish her sentence out of pure disbelief.

He shrugs. 'How else was I going to talk to you?'

I grip my seat's armrests. 'You stole our carriage because it was the only way you could think to talk to us? We've just had to walk for three days!'

'Well, if I didn't, you'd have only zoomed away in it again!' He shakes his head. 'I don't always think things through . . . And really, I still wasn't sure what to say yet. I needed time. And I was watching the two of you, and honestly, it felt like you needed some time to walk and relax. I don't know what drama is going on in Princess World, but . . .'

Dawn fumes, her hair curled around her head like a lion's mane, only adding to the effect of her powerful anger. 'Well, Prince, time is not something we have. So unless you can either give us back our carriage or help us . . .'

'I already have helped you! I made sure you got out of Kara's Territory. I got you your mirror. I just want you to listen to me, to get a message to Sierra, and—'

'Excuse me?' Dawn hisses. '*You* led us to the mirror? How? Even we couldn't find it. *Kara* couldn't.'

He groans, lifting his chest to show off his size again, as if we're animals competing for dominance and not people having a civilised conversation. 'I'm royalty, Dawn. Where I come from that means power. Resources. I knew, to get you to listen to me, I'd need to get you something you wanted. Once I found out what that was, it was easy. I was already in Kara's Territory. I heard about the mirror, pulled some strings, planted the note . . . It was very convenient.'

'And now?' Dawn asks, her face red. 'What is it that *you* want?'

His shoulders lower, mouth pointed in a shameful pout. 'I don't know how much you know about Candace – the false fairy – but she is taking over my empire,' he says. 'I don't need to rule the world, Princess, I just want to keep what's rightfully mine. So if I'm going to stop Candace, I have to pick a different side than the Ice Empire, which has already decided I'm worthless. I must ally myself with the world's only other existing royalty.' He gestures at Dawn. 'I'll admit I'm disappointed. Everyone always says you're so lovely, but you're absolutely *rude.*'

Dawn goes even redder.

I pick at the seam of my sleeve, hoping that if he does decide to attack us out of nowhere, that if this is a trick, I'll be able to sense it first – as I have before. Currently his emotional state is hard to read. People who are usually uncaring but emotionally volatile are always difficult to anticipate.

'That can't be the only reason,' I say. 'Bearra isn't . . . There isn't enough benefit to you. What's the truth?'

'Fine,' he says, slumping in his chair. 'I'm also here because Sierra is with you. Everyone knows it. She's with Bearra now, with her new *pirate boyfriend.* And it hurts that she wouldn't first come to me in this war, but . . . regardless, I want to see her again. Ask for her help. She owes me.'

'You know Sierra Reed?' Dawn asks.

He blinks. 'I thought you were friends. She didn't tell you about me?'

Dawn's eyes narrow. 'I wouldn't call us friends. And, no, you have never come up before. I've only heard of you as the prince who went missing for a year. A prince from a dubious line at best, who I don't recognise, I'm not sorry to say. Any connection to Sierra Reed is news to me.'

'Oh,' he says. 'Well, that's . . . Possibly fortunate. She must still think of me, only in private.' He smiled wistfully.

My mind twists in disbelief, as if a brick wall has grown inside my head; I am unable to connect these two people. 'You and her were . . . ?'

He looks offended. 'Yes. For a little while. She can tell you the story if she so chooses. But it did not end well. And now I want to apologise for it all – though she should be the one apologising, really – but here we are. I'm desperate, alright? I need her. I need you. Strong. Female. Allies!' he nearly shouts. I duck and quickly glace around, but the other patrons remain unminding. 'I've gotten you the mirror you needed. Oh, and I led Sierra to her new crew's iron sword. You're welcome. Now let me accompany you back to Bearra so I can get what *I* want.'

Dawn thinks it over for a while. 'You can come with us. *If* you give us back our carriage and swear on your life that you're entirely against Candace and all our other enemies. If you try *anything*, and if you've told even *one* lie, you will *pay*.'

He waves a hand. 'Yes, certainly, you'll kill me, whatever. It's no matter to me. If this doesn't work, I'll have nothing to live for regardless. And I have your carriage waiting in the streets – you have no idea how difficult it was to move that thing.'

'Do not test me,' Dawn says, lifting her chin. She slams her hand on the table, making a few people in the restaurant gasp. 'I have been lied to too many times by too many people, Zeus, and I won't take it anymore. If you have any ulterior motives, you had better leave *now*.'

She doesn't meet my eyes as she says it, but I know. All this anger towards this prince is anger that's supposed to be directed at me. She's been acting as if she's fine. Maybe she thinks she is. But it's all bubbling under the surface. When is her anger at me going to finally come out? When will she feel the betrayal under the relief?

Days ago, that's what I wanted – for her to be afraid, to see me for the danger that I am and run. But now that I've had a taste of what we can be again, I'm not so willing to let it go.

'I just want my kingdom back,' Zeus says, his voice softened. 'And I want to see Sierra again. My motives aren't pure or good. But I don't plan to do anything to bring harm to Bearra. Not currently, anyway. I've already proven to you that I can help. And why not help each other while we can? We all have one enemy – Lire. Everything else is just politics.'

Dawn and I hold hands as we leave the restaurant, following Zeus back to the carriage. It's unbelievable, really, how he's just walked in like this, but he's been helping us for, what, weeks?

I hate that he's encroaching on my and Dawn's days alone, but an ally is an ally. This is what Dawn wanted. And what *I* should want, considering the more power we have on our side, the greater the chance of us both making it through this alive. But even with his *resources,* I'm not sure how much a kingdomless prince can help.

And I *need* to know the story behind Zeus and Sierra. I can't imagine Sierra ever being friends, let alone more, with a man like this. What *happened?*

He's running his fingers along the top of a fence, talking to Dawn about something I'm half-listening to – something about his parents, maybe – when I get a shiver up my spine.

'Stop!' I hiss quickly, yanking them into the shadow of a shed by their collars. My breaths come quickly as I scan the area, listening intently. They look at me in shock, and I hold up a finger to tell them to wait quietly. Something is coming. I feel it in the air. Something huge.

A flash of green passes between two houses, across the lane from us.

Zeus releases a frustrated breath. '*Candace.*'

'Here?' Dawn whispers. 'Were you followed?'

He grinds his teeth before replying, '*Fairies,* that *witch.*'

'What will she do if we're discovered?'

'I'm sure I'll be fine,' he says. 'I'll just make an excuse and have her accompany me home.'

Dawn opens her mouth as if she's about to shout, then remembers we're hiding. 'And what about *us?*'

He looks down at us. 'Oh. Well, I don't know what she might want with you, so I can't answer that.'

Candace appears in the street, looking around – clearly searching for someone. We sink deeper into the shadows. White hair falls over her mint-coloured dress, and she wears a necklace of shining emerald. Although she bears no wings, she carries herself with all the surety of a fairy – a balance of confidence, power, and delicacy. But there's a frown as her eyes move around, gazing wide and peering through windows. It seems she's come alone.

With no other option, we attempt to still ourselves. I shake with fear, but Dawn wraps her arm through mine, nodding at me slowly, and I manage to take a steady, long breath. If we die because some arrogant prince has stupidly led one of our greatest enemies right to us, if he is the reason the war is lost . . . *Fairies.*

Candace comes our way, and we're all holding our breath. Her dress swishes as she moves, magic swaying around her in waves of each colour; she makes no effort to conceal herself. Unafraid. The most powerful human in the world, if she can even be called human anymore.

She's about to walk past, we're about to get through this.

Then something drops.

With a flash of light, Dawn gasps. The mirror has slipped from its hiding place in her pocket and bounced into the sunlight.

Candace's head snaps up as we crouch back. She smiles a little when she sees us – though surprise comes first – and suddenly she's stepping in our direction with all the slow confidence of a snake. My heart falls into my stomach. I grip Dawn, but we don't run.

Even my magic wouldn't be enough against Candace. If we wait, rather than run or attack, will she be civil? Will she spare us?

Dawn looks up at Zeus, her eyes wild with anger. 'You did this to us, you—'

A dart of purple steals the breath from our lungs. Lilac wings flutter right past us, carrying Lire – *Lire?* – as she descends facing Candace. Candace yelps, shuffling back. Lire flutters forward until they're face to face.

There is *no way* we have just been saved by Lire, but there she is, a miracle.

Dawn and I share a glance, a million emotions and thoughts running through each of us. Zeus starts breathing heavily. *Now* he's worried.

Candace and Lire round a corner so we can only just see them, though we can still hear them well. Lire only seems to care about Candace. Does she know we're here? Does she know *I'm* here? *Fairies*, if she sees me with Dawn, I'm going to be in a world of trouble.

Regardless, Candace isn't betraying us to her. No, she spotted us first, and she wants us to herself.

'We should run,' Zeus says. 'Get back to the carriage now while they're distracted. We have time.'

'Hush,' Dawn whispers. 'No. We run and they'll notice. We're staying here and listening for anything useful. What direction is the carriage?'

Zeus tilts his head west.

'On my signal – and not a second before – we go. But we wait until we're clear.'

I let out a breath and try to still my shaking legs, poised to run.

'Candace,' I hear Lire say, as if the name itself is bitter in her mouth. 'It's been a while, hasn't it? Last I saw you, you were barely twenty, a young politician of the Ice Empire. And now look at you. Though I must admit this is the last place I would expect for us to meet.'

'I followed you here,' Candace says – a lie, of course. 'I thought it was time for us to discuss our little war. This little world has big politics, doesn't it? Too much power in too small a place.'

Lire growls. 'What do you *know*?'

'More than you would like, I assume. More than most. So, why are you here?'

Unable to copy Candace's lie, Lire says what I assume to be the truth. 'I've tracked down one of my assets to this place. An asset that has escaped my control.'

Bile rises in my throat. She must mean me. She found me here, somehow. She knows my secret is out, that we got the mirror. Or does she mean Dawn? Either way, this is bad. Terrible. If we don't make it back to the carriage soon . . .

'Let me guess,' Candace says smugly, 'your princess? Or is it the entire kingdom of Bearra you expect to find in this small town? Or the lost king and queen – yes, that lovely little morsel of bad news has reached me.'

'It isn't any of your business, but you might be pleased to know that the queen and king of Bearra have been taken care of. All that's left now is for me to take care of their daughter.'

Candace pauses. 'Taken care of? You don't mean . . .?'

'Dead.' Lire offers a fake pout. 'Yes, I sadly had to kill them.'

I go dizzy, tossing up a wall of magic just in time to throw back the sound of Dawn's wail, almost knocking the three of us back in the process. She stifles her cries in my shoulder, Zeus watching us helplessly. I keep the spell up, the purple magic visible, but we should be hidden enough for now.

I can't think. My heart is breaking for Dawn. I can't— I can't—

'It was about time,' Lire continues. 'They were no longer of use to me. *Decades* of having to stand at the side of that idiot queen and her husband . . . The only consolation was their daughter, who also ended up betraying me in the end, just like my sons.' Her voice turns into a low hiss. 'She'll pay. Bearra will pay. Though I would prefer to keep the girl alive, fond as I am of her – if she chooses the right side in the end.'

'Are we barbarians?' Candace says. 'Killing royals, really? Are there no rules in this fight?'

'It's my game,' Lire says. 'You can play, but in the end, I'm the one who makes the rules, and that is why *I'll* win.'

'The Ice Empire won't let you undo all our hard work, Lire. The time of fairies is over. It is time for power to be shared. Our mission is to remake our world. Soon everyone will see that and turn against you too.'

A spark of lilac builds in the distance. 'You're adorable,' says Lire.

And as her magic crashes with Candace's, the sound booming like thunder, Zeus takes my collapsed princess in his arms and we run.

CHAPTER 19

SOMEWHERE, SOMETIME …

Candace hated Lire and everything she stood for.

As they fought – fire meeting fire, Candace's rainbow of stolen magic versus Lire's river of purple – Candace felt all the rage from deep in her soul pouring out of her.

'Run, Candace!' Lire shouted, shooting a flash of physical magic at Candace as if it were an arrow from a bow. Candace ducked and missed it – it impacted the shed behind them, the wood imploding on itself before the magic fizzled out. 'You can't win this! Don't test me!'

Candace shrugged, sending back a swirl of her own magic, copying the fairy's technique. It missed, of course, but Candace wasn't here to win, not necessarily. She would take this as an opportunity to learn. So she laughed at Lire. 'You old witch, don't lie! I know you wish to be tested by me! I know you want to see the extent of my power – you're loving this!'

Lire's eyes narrowed as her magic snaked over their heads, towards a falling piece of wood from the building she just hit. She pulled it down to hit Candace, who threw up a shield with her own magic just in time. The beam slid down the rainbow.

Candace copied once more, giddy with adrenaline, throwing a heavy red brick at the fairy. Lire redirected it easily; she looked *bored*. And that was understandable. Candace felt the same, but she would not get carried away.

There was something she was picking up on: Lire liked to use the physical side of magic to fight, throwing punches of power and lifting objects into the air. However powerful Candace might be, she was not immortal. And while she didn't have an eternity to learn how to use magic, she had something the old fairies didn't: she was adaptable and new. In the last hundred years – even in the last twenty – magic evolved and spread. Lire may have always been two steps ahead, but she was stuck in the past.

Lire was gearing up for her next attempt, so Candace thought fast. There *was* something she'd been working on, waiting for a target to practise on.

She scanned her surroundings with a clarity Isla would be proud of, and noticed tools on the wall of the now-broken shed. She sent her magic towards the tools, *into* them. And enchanted them to do her bidding.

Animation was difficult magic, requiring a lot of skill and power – which was why only the best engineers made objects like enchanted coaches – but Candace had plenty of both.

Lire watched curiously as the tools began flying out of the shed, hammers whacking air, shears snapping; all of it enough to kill a regular person with such ease it was terrifying.

Lire had no fear: she was studying Candace's technique as much as Candace was studying hers.

The fairy crunched her body and flew directly up as a screwdriver attempted to dig into her side. But the tools kept coming. They began hitting their mark. Unfortunately, however, fairies were immortal for a reason. Lire did not bleed. The tools hit and slashed but all they did was annoy her. They were little more than flies.

This could have been enough for Candace to run, and she considered it for a moment, but she wasn't done yet.

Lire blasted magic out in all directions, sending the tools flying outwards, their enchantment depleted.

'*F—*' A hammer narrowly missed Candace's face. If she'd turned and ran, who knows what might have hit her?

And so it continued: colours rushing and dancing and destroying the buildings around them. Lightning. Thunder. Rainbows. Flying. Screams. There seemed to be people shouting at some point, but they scattered away when they realised what was happening.

They were no closer to a victor.

Candace began to tire of it, her arms hurting as she aimed magic uselessly, her mind fogging as her ideas had to become increasingly creative. She felt anxious, which was nice. She so rarely fought with anyone that was even a slight match for her.

Still, Candace had a mission to complete, a world to save and take for herself, and a daughter to come home to.

'Are you afraid yet, Lire?' she shouted, focusing some magic on healing a new wound on her arm that she'd only just noticed. 'Now that you can see what I can do?'

Lire sneered, stopping her attacks for a moment so she could pace menacingly, her purple dress now torn to shreds, her hair out of its perfect strawberry-blonde bun. 'I'm only more excited to kill you,' she said. 'And to destroy your entire empire. Destroy everything you love. More.'

Candace laughed, almost losing her footing on the now rough floor. 'And I think the same way of you, dear fairy. Let's not leave it too long until we do this again, hm?'

'If you think you're getting away that easily—' Lire started.

But Candace had already sent a pile of rubble in front of the fairy with enough of her magic to blind and distract her. She was finally able to turn her back, and used her magic to move – fast as light – back towards the Ice Empire.

She hadn't captured Zeus as she'd expected to. But maybe she found something even better.

If there was only one person in the world Candace could be herself with – let her guard down around – it was Isla. People always had things to say about them, questioning their relationship – *If Candace really isn't Isla's mother, where did the girl come from? What exactly is their place in the empire's leadership?* – but it was mostly jealousy.

The Ice Empire wasn't like the rest of the world. Though they were modernised, they still had a monarchy; climbing the ranks outside the connection of nobility was difficult. Still, everyone was afraid of Candace, and growing increasingly afraid of Isla. The girl had no magic of her own, but she was a force to be reckoned with. Together, they had *made* themselves powerful. Together, they would take this world.

But if there was one thing that could ruin power, it was scandal. One day she might tell Isla, and the world, where the girl truly came from. She might tell them the truth that she had found out about their world – a truth the fairies kept secret because if people knew, it would change everything. Just not yet. Candace was Isla's mother, and nothing – no rumours, no secrets, no schemes – could take that away from her.

Tonight, Isla sat in her room at their home – a small but grand castle on the outskirts of the city – braiding her hair. In the style of the empire, the hazel strands were long, even when braided.

Candace hadn't decided whether to tell her where she'd been today. Isla had a confusing relationship with the prince, and Candace's meeting with Lire was somewhat . . . embarrassing.

But Isla raised her eyebrows suspiciously, and Candace knew she wouldn't get away with lying tonight. She told Isla the full story, sitting at the edge of Isla's bed with her back hunched tiredly, while Isla sat attentively at her dressing table.

Isla replied, '*Mother*,' in an impatient and chiding tone. She used that word rarely, and always pointedly. Never *Mum*, or *Mama*, or anything of that sort. It was always Candace. And if she really meant it, *Mother*.

'I had to know what Zeus was doing,' Candace said. 'He's a threat to us. To you. And unless you plan to marry him, it will stay that way.'

Isla made a gagging noise. 'Fine, I understand. But you can send people to do such things.'

Candace waved a hand. 'You know I don't trust people. That's the only reason I have the power I have now. And with this kind of magic, I can get done in minutes what would take most people weeks. Do you realise how fast I can travel?'

'I'm aware.'

'Meanwhile, Zeus is only a boy, and yet he gets *everything*, and I – both of us – have to work harder than anyone just to get a fraction of what men like him have.'

'You don't have to explain that to me,' Isla said. Even in her room, she kept her back straight, her tone even. Candace knew she had turned the girl into a soldier, but sometimes she wondered if that wasn't always a good thing. 'I've spent my entire life competing with Zeus. You were the one who invited him to dinner, remember? A disaster of a night. And what did we find out from him? Nothing.'

'His affection for you could be his downfall,' Candace said. 'I believe that.'

'He may be an idiot, but he isn't an *idiot*. Anyway, let's not spend our evening discussing something as insignificant as him. So what if he's allying with Princess Dawn? Both of them are all but powerless. Tell me, was Lire at her full power when you fought? Or did you suspect she was holding back?'

Candace huffed, shuffling back on the bed to lean against the headboard. 'If she wanted to kill me, she would have. I think we both held back. There are too many players in this war. She said it herself: this is her game, and we're playing by her rules. Everyone has been afraid to make any serious moves and take out any serious players. Except Sierra Reed, of course, but Muse had it coming. My point is, if Lire doesn't want me dead yet, it's because she hopes I can help take out some of her enemies first.'

Isla pursed her lips. 'Maybe we should have spent our time studying *games* rather than war strategies. Elm always begged me.'

'The only difference is the stakes. You know that.'

Isla took a breath and moved onto the bed to sit beside Candace, wrapping an arm around her. 'Just a joke,' Isla mumbled. 'Lire has been very careful to keep all her allies secret. We can't attack if we have no target. We could bombard her estate near Darraport, but she'd just go somewhere else. So how do we defeat her?'

'We don't, yet,' Candace said. 'We play her game – we wait for someone else to strike first. Wait for *her* to strike first. Then we jump in once everything is set in motion and everyone's strengths and motives are clearer. The best thing we can do now is retain our focus. Keep training, keep working against the royals and concreting our power, and keep expanding the empire piece-by-piece. We don't wage war until someone else does.'

Isla glanced away, tutting. 'That seems . . . cowardly. For us.'

Candace sat up. 'Must we talk about these things every second of the day? Come on, Isla, surely we have something fun to think about. Most mothers and daughters talk about dresses and boys and—'

Isla raised her eyebrows in a way that said, *But we aren't mother and daughter, really, and even if we were, we wouldn't be like that.* Though she would never say something like that aloud.

'Please?' Candace asked, begging her heart to stay strong.

Isla shook her head. 'I'm not sure how to do that anymore. We aren't the people we once were. I'm a general and you're the most powerful human in the world. How can we even think about dresses and boys when . . .'

'We must,' Candace said sharply. 'Because if we don't, if we never stop, it won't be the war that kills us. It'll be ourselves, burning out faster than dry grass in a forest fire. It's easy to equate speed to strength, but that isn't accurate.'

'I didn't set the fire,' Isla reminded her. 'I'm just the person who has to tame it. And if you think I've been left with even a second to think about anything else while we're in a war . . . I just can't.'

Candace faltered. 'I-I know. I'm sorry.'

'When we win, then we'll talk about boys. *Except* Zeus. Never Zeus.'

'Certainly.' Candace chuckled. 'Alright, then, tell me. What's your strategy for moving deeper into Rhiannon's Territory? Can we workshop any—'

'By taking Adella's Territory first. Work our way along the border until we're surrounding Rhiannon.' The tension released from Isla; she was back in her element. 'We can start on the south-east of Rhiannon's Territory as well. It's mostly unpopulated due to the cold – which means it's already advantageous for us. Being blocked by Rhiannon has too long halted our expansion. If we move against a fairy, it must be her. But she's too strong to simply attack. I trust you can ask Kara for assistance?'

Candace took her daughter's hand and looked away, hiding her small smile of pride – and the inner feeling of growing shame at the pressure she had placed on Isla. 'Kara may not wish to move against the other fairies so directly, but I will ask. And I like your plan. Bring me an official strategy soon. You'll have to present it to the royals,' she said, now meeting Isla's eyes. 'With your leadership and your mind and your strength, I have no doubt that we'll win this war.'

Isla nodded, and just for a moment, Candace saw the little girl she remembered. The little girl *she* carved into a hero.

CHAPTER 20

When I float into Lire's dreams, the carriage rocking us through the night as I fall asleep with my head resting on Dawn's stomach, I'm welcomed by a green haze – one that reminds me of Candace.

So, the fairy is consumed by their earlier fight. The one she doesn't know I saw. Or, at least, saw the beginning of. If I'm in her dreams, Lire has clearly survived, but there's no telling if Candace did.

On the cliff's edge we always meet on, Lire is already sitting, waiting. She turns to me and smiles a perfect smile, her light hair rolling down her bare back. 'Relia, darling,' she says, patting the spot on the grass beside her and I sit cross-legged. 'Do you know why we always meet here?'

I shake my head in answer, afraid anything I say or do could give me away. We haven't spoken since Dawn found out who I was, and I don't know what Lire knows. Has she already found out, somehow? Can she sense it? Is that why she was following Dawn today?

'Because,' she says, interrupting my thoughts, 'this place is a memory.'

'You called it an ocean,' I reply. 'But that doesn't exist. Is it really a memory, or just a legend?'

'Some memories are legends, when you're as old as I am.' As if the scene is clearer while Lire observes it so intensely, I can hear waves breaking against the shore at the bottom of the cliff-face. And still, that green haze I noticed as soon as I arrived is thick in the air, circling in storms over the water. 'Don't you ever wonder what's beyond the ice at the edge of the world?' She takes a breath, like she's about to tell a story, then changes her mind. 'Have you found the princess yet?'

My breath hitches – even though I'm in a dream, where I don't really need to breathe. 'I have,' I say, following one of my rules: that it's always easiest to stay closest to the truth when lying. 'I tracked her down in Amora's Territory, but she was in an enchanted carriage, so she was travelling fast. I found her just as she was leaving. She was very happy to see me. We're on our way back to Bearra now.'

'And do you have anything to report? Where has she been? Why did she leave, and why leave a fake in her place?'

I sigh. 'I think you overestimate how much the princess deigns to tell me. I'm sorry, but these things are difficult to ask. She can be difficult to talk to. Difficult to discern the truth from.'

'She's told you *nothing*?' Lire's eyes narrow, and I wonder again, *does* she know? Is this all a test? Is she playing me, or am I playing her? My stomach knots with guilt.

I shouldn't feel any shame around betraying Lire. She's hurt people. Hurt me. Dawn. Teddy and Maya. She killed the pirates' friend, and she plans to do much worse to the rest of us.

And yet, she brought me back from the dead. I had a deal with her, I made her promises, and I think, somehow, she really does care for me. While I'm lying to her face. At what point does doing the right thing become villainous? I never know what's good or bad anymore. Everything I do seems to hurt someone.

I'm sure Lire can justify her own actions in some way. If we all think we're doing what's best, why is it that we fight?

She takes a deep breath, the green haze wisping around us as she exhales. 'I'm beginning to feel afraid,' she says. 'Things aren't as they once were. People aren't as weak as I believed. Everything is changing no matter who wins the war, and . . . And I'm not sure there's a place for me in this world anymore, even though I built it.'

I tense as Lire wraps an arm around my shoulders, but then relax – or at least attempt to – when I realise the gesture isn't threatening. It's *maternal.* And though I know how wrong it is to accept such a thing, enjoy such a thing, from *Lire . . . Fairies,* I need it.

A hundred years since I said goodbye to my family forever. More since I lost my birth mother and father. Is that why I feel such guilt around betraying the fairy who took me in and helped me, even though it was ultimately all for her own gain? Or is this exactly what she wants? Is she using her knowledge of my weaknesses and exploiting them by pretending she cares?

'But if there is a place for me,' she continues after a moment, 'then there is a place for you. And the other girls from the forest, too. You know you're my favourite, Relia – how could you not be, when you're the one who has been part of my plan the longest? The only one I watched grow up, and the one who now has the most important role of you all? Still, all of you girls are special to me. You've been hurt by this world as much as I have. And when I remake it . . . You may not like it at first, but soon you'll see. You'll see I've done what's best for us, and you'll thank me.'

I swallow. 'I'm already grateful for everything you've done for me,' I say. 'You let me see Dawn again, and I've done all I can to repay you. I'll always follow you, Lire, because you did for me what no one else cared to do.'

She cups my cheek, inspecting my face with a warm smile. 'Good girl.'

When the dream ends, I try something different. For Dawn's sake. I think about her parents. First her father, then her mother, and try to break into their dreams. Are they still out there somewhere? Was what Lire said a lie? I hope, and hope, and search.

But there's nothing. No dreams, no consciousness to discover.

They truly are gone.

✦ ◦ ˚ ☾ ☀ ☽ ˚ ◦ ✦

It's still dark when I'm abruptly woken, the carriage coming to a rocky, sudden stop, lurching as we all fall forward. My cheeks are wet with tears.

'Wha—' I start, picking myself up from the base of the carriage. I rub my eyes and push my hair out of my face.

Zeus is on the opposite bench, feet up, glancing around. Dawn is halfway out the door already, her curls a blurry flash. She must have stopped the carriage.

'Dawn?' I call, hurrying to get up but tripping over my own skirt. 'Dawn!'

I tumble out to find us on a hillside in some unknown place along the way to Bearra. The hill rises behind us, but I can't see much else. We're in a dense forest, on what may or may not be a road – it's too dark to tell, and the carriage always seems to traverse whatever landscape is quickest, simply making it work.

'What's happening?' Zeus says, his voice raspy.

I spot Dawn racing up the hill, darting between trees, her hair and dress flying behind her like wings. 'I have no idea,' I say, chasing after her. I don't wait to see if Zeus is following. 'Dawn!' I shout again, then I decide against yelling. Who knows what dangers are around, and in the middle of the night, no less?

Eventually I find her on a grassy patch, sitting with her legs crossed, watching the stars with gleaming, wet eyes.

'Dawn?' I whisper, crouching behind her. Though we're closer to the centre of the world, the night has a chill to it, and I retreat into the folds of my dress the best I can. Zeus's footsteps crunch behind us. 'Are you alright?'

She shakes her head, holding her face in her hands. I hold her for a while, waiting for her, and eventually she looks up. 'I couldn't stay in there any longer. I needed air. I need to—I need to—'

'Grieve?' I say, referring to her parents. Since we overheard Lire telling Candace she killed them, Dawn has barely reacted after waking from her faint. I wonder if my trying to meddle in their dreams somehow reawakened the emotions in Dawn. 'You know you don't have to do that alone. You know I've been through it.'

My poor, sweet, haunted princess. Her pain is my own.

She meets my eyes. 'So have I. With *you*. This is different. I'm so— I'm so angry with them, even now. How could I feel that way, when they're . . .'

'They let you down. It isn't wrong to be angry with people when they hurt you.'

'And I spent all this time looking for them. Endangered myself and you, stayed away from home, in the hopes I could make things right. There was never any point to it. She'd always have killed them.'

Zeus steps towards us and says, tentatively, 'Are you completely sure that, you know, they're dead? That the fairy wasn't lying?'

'Yes,' I say quickly and finally, knowing that idea could send Dawn spiralling.

Zeus stops, sitting on Dawn's other side. I notice him slip a hand over Dawn's. It's . . . gentle. 'I lost a cousin,' he says. 'He didn't die, he just moved away, but I never heard from him again. Loss hurts. I know it's different. But it's like Relia was trying to tell you, Dawn, you're not alone in your pain. Don't shy away from it or let it consume you. I know you're strong enough.'

She glances at the plain ring on her finger. The one containing Kara's blessing, which Maya gifted her. 'You'd think it would be easier for me,' she says. 'With the blessings I already have inside me. With this one as well. But it isn't. It still hurts.' Before we can reply, she frowns at me. 'Relia, why were you so quick to say my parents are certainly gone?'

The blood rushes from my face. 'I . . .'

Because there was one more lie I was hoping to keep. Dawn already has enough against me, enough reasons not to trust me. My magic – which only makes me *more* other, reminding us all what and who I am – can only push her away more. So, no, I didn't want to tell her about my ability to enter dreams and to feel people's emotions.

'Do you have something to do with this?' Zeus says, putting an arm in front of Dawn as if to protect her from me. *Fairies.* We already told him everything about my situation. It didn't seem worth trying to hide it. Now I wish we had. 'Are you still working with Lire?'

'No!' I shuffle back, hands raised. 'No. Of course not. But I'm not— I'm not finished with her. Yet. I don't want her knowing that my secret is out. That I'm no longer on her side. So . . .'

'Relia?' Dawn says, freshly wounded.

'I speak to her in my dreams,' I admit, my voice quiet. 'It's a special kind of magic we have. Lire's undead spies. We have these abilities to . . .' I release an anxious breath. 'It's like an empathetic connection. It's difficult to explain. But when I sleep, I can enter other people's dreams. I can influence the dream and talk to the person. We – the spirits – use this power to communicate with Lire. I just spoke to her tonight, before I woke to the carriage stopping.'

Zeus's jaw drops. 'You just spoke to the fairy? The one trying to destroy the world?'

'It isn't like— I had to! If I stopped reporting to her, she would know something suspicious was happening, and that would put us all in danger.'

Dawn brings her knees up to her chest. 'Why didn't you tell me about this?'

'Because I was ashamed,' I say, my shoulders tight. I can't look at her beautiful eyes knowing I'm the one who made them look so sad, so I stare at the stars. 'I *am* ashamed. It's something I've been able to do since before, since when I was still in the forest. Something I did to pass the time. Something I did to . . .'

'Check up on me,' Dawn says, her voice tight. 'I dreamed about you so much those hundred years. Other people said when they woke, it was as if no time had passed, but I knew. I knew, because I spent so much of that time with you.'

'We needed each other, then. I did it because I loved you. And because what else were we to do? But after, when I came to the castle, when I was Carlotta . . . I should have stopped much sooner. I'm sorry. When I realised it was wrong, I never did it to anyone again. Not except to talk to Lire.'

Dawn's face falls. 'I *know* when you stopped, because when I stopped dreaming of you, I was devastated. *Both* versions of you.'

'I'm sorry,' I repeat, a heavy stone in my gut. 'I know I did the wrong thing. Once I realised, I stopped right away. Please believe that I'm done with it.'

'But Relia, you— It was such an invasion, to do something like that, to plant yourself in my head in such a way . . .'

Zeus cuts in, brows knotted curiously. 'Tell me more about this dream ability, Relia, because I've been repeatedly having dreams about a certain blue-eyed Bearran beauty who I've never met in real life, and—'

Dawn and I hiss, 'Zeus!'

He crosses his arms. 'That's *Your Highness*, to you two. And let me tell you, in these dreams, things are *high*. Rising, if you know—'

I slap his shoulder. 'I cannot believe I was starting to think you were decent! That your stupid cocky act was just an – an act! Ugh, Zeus!'

'I never act,' he says. 'People are multifaceted, you know. Once I heard of an assassin who also creates beautiful embroidery.'

'Relia!' Dawn shouts over him, bringing the attention back. 'Zeus, shut up for one second of your life and let us talk!' She stands quickly, brushing down her dress. Even in the low light, I can see her face and the tops of her arms going red with anger. She stares daggers at me. 'You were supposed to be done with the lying. I had forgiven you. I was trying to get things back to normal with you, figure out how to save you, save the world, so we could . . . But the entire time, you were still lying to me!' She's crying again. Maybe she never stopped. But it looks so wrong on her, her face all twisted up. All because of me.

This is what I was waiting for. The anger. For her to realise what I've done. I cower, wishing the grass would swallow me up.

Zeus clears his throat. 'I'm sorry, Dawn, but if you didn't know about *this*, how did you think Relia was communicating with Lire?'

She groans, her hands on her hips as she looks out at the view from the hillside. 'I hadn't even *begun* to wrap my head around that yet. I suppose I thought she just sent messages somehow, letters—'

'Anyway, who cares?' Zeus interrupts. 'We should be using this ability for ourselves.' He glances at me, then says, 'Not for *indecent* reasons. To spy on our enemies.'

'No,' Dawn says. 'Now is not the time for scheming, and I don't want to hear any more of this. I'm not having Relia spend her time in other people's heads anymore. It isn't— It's unnatural. It's invasive. I won't have it. I won't play with such dirty tricks. I don't care what Lire plans. I refuse to stoop to that level.'

I swallow, feeling dirty all over, like I've been dipped in mud. 'I never used the ability to spy on others. I swear, it hadn't even occurred to me. It was only to see you. Only to be myself with you, Dawn, and to talk to Lire – because I had to.'

'You had no right!' she shouts. 'You didn't. Not to do any of this. All you have ever done is bring me pain, Relia! I didn't ask you to die for me! I have been in love with you for so long, and it has clouded my mind. Since we were children, we knew how things would end between us, but we were so stupid, thinking . . .'

My heart drops to my feet. I stand, take a few steps back.

'I wanted you to live a full life. You were supposed to. But instead you did this. You made me grieve for you, just to come back and hurt me all over again. I have never known peace from loving you. And you thought you had the right to enter my head, to make my world even foggier, to give me even more pain? The rest I could forgive you for. But how can I excuse something like this?'

My bottom lip wobbles as I mumble, 'I don't expect you to excuse it. I never did. And I told you, I'm sorry. Everything I did was selfish. I know that.' I take a breath, look her in the eye, and say, plainly, 'But do you know what I'm also sure of? I wouldn't change a thing if I had the chance. Because no matter how much you hate me right now, you're standing in front of me. And I would do *anything* to have just one more second with you.'

'Love is so complicated,' Zeus mumbles, shaking his head emphatically. We both glare at him, and he waves a hand, turning around.

'I'm so *angry*,' Dawn says. 'These last few months, all I have known is pain and desperation and exhaustion. All I have known, Relia, is that *Carlotta* was the only thing that made it slightly better. But now I don't know what's real.'

I crouch in front of her, hoping the moonlight shows the sincerity in my expression. 'I haven't known what's real for a long time. Relia, Carlotta, I may be both or neither. I'm not who I was before you slept. I've made mistakes, done terrible, stupid things, while all you've done is become even more honourable. But if you loved me before, any of the love you have for me now is just as real. I can't change how you feel. Yes, I intruded in your dreams. I put myself in them and carried you through nightmares. I gave you space to love me, both as myself and Carlotta, in your mind. But I never made you feel anything that wasn't true. When you told me you loved me in that dream? That was real.'

She stares at me, her eyes gleaming and wet.

'And that was when I stopped, because I knew I was being selfish. Everything I've done has been for me. Everything you have ever done has been for everyone else. I know I'm not deserving of your love. Not even your friendship. But I hope I can, one day, have your forgiveness. If not, tell me now, because I'll get as far from you as I can so I don't have to endanger you a second longer. I'll go back to the forest where I don't have to help Lire, and I'll let you save the world without me hurting you.'

I exhale slowly. To my surprise, I feel lighter having revealed my last secrets and fears. Even better than when I had to tell her who I was and why I was here. This feels right, like we're truly clearing the air. And no matter how it ends, at least I'll know things ended with honesty. At least I'll know I gave her everything she needed to make an informed choice.

Her hands shake, and she pushes her hair back, standing to face me. 'I know my love for you is real,' she whispers. 'But this is all so confusing. We're blind when we're together. We put each other on pedestals, see each other as these powerful, perfect things, when we aren't. That's the greatest danger we face. We would do anything for each other. And if I were in your position, of course I would do the same. But if we can't find a way to see each other as real people, we'll never make this work.'

I hadn't thought it possible she could feel half the love for me that I feel for her. The respect and adoration. Could it be that all our problems are mutual? I was so blinded by love that I took my own life just for a chance to see her again. That's insanity. It's certainly not healthy, not good. Not how love should be. It should be joy, not endless pain. But she would have done it too.

I exhale through my mouth and utter, 'Sometimes you snore when you sleep, and I don't like it when you tie your hair back. It doesn't look as nice. You have an annoying laugh, and one of your fingers is wonky. It's hard to look at.'

She blinks. '*Relia?*'

'You wanted to be human, I'm making you human. I'm taking you off the pedestal.'

'Relia,' she says, but she's trying to suppress a smirk.

'You're an emotional wreck, and sometimes your privilege and power make you a nightmare, because you've always been so *perfect* that you don't know how to deal with imperfection. You've spent your life so guarded that you have no idea what real problems real people face. Sometimes listening to you complain is beyond irritating. *Oh no, my bed is too big and my castle is too grand.* You think you're so much more complicated than everyone else, and your pain and your stress are so much worse, but they aren't. And your orange sandwiches are disgusting. You have the taste palette of a three-year-old.'

She gasps, but she's giggling, looking at me with pure joy in her eyes. And I feel it inside her, an elation, an excitement. 'Is that— No. You really think these things?'

'M-hm. Now it's your turn.' I wave a hand at her. 'Knock me down. See if you still love me.'

Dawn takes a minute, contemplating. 'I don't like how you look now,' she says. 'This disguise you're in. It isn't that you're unattractive, but it doesn't suit your personality. It didn't even before I knew the truth. Your skin is so dull. And you have no sense of fashion. Never did. If I never forced you out of your comfort zone, you would've spent your entire life indoors. I taught you to dance, and you're still awful at it. I'm sure I have permanent bruises on my feet from you stepping on them. And in your real body, in your real voice, you're so squeaky sometimes. When you get nervous. *Squeaky squeak*, all quiet like a mouse. And you're selfish. Just like you said.'

I half-smile in reply.

'But I'd be lying if I said I wasn't, too. Because I dragged a poor girl, who had no choice, on a dangerous mission at the worst possible time, just because I wanted to spend more time with her. I invited the girl I loved to a birthday ball, knowing about the curse, knowing it would take effect that night, and subjected her to witnessing the worst possible thing happen. And when I found out what you did, I refused to be angry, because I was so selfish I'd rather have you with me as a traitor than not have you with me at all.'

She takes a breath. 'That's who we are, Relia. We're both selfish fools who would do anything for each other, even if it means hurting each other.'

Zeus sniffles behind me, mumbling something like, 'That's beautiful.'

With a grin, I say, 'Well, I forgive you.'

She takes a moment, looks me up and down, then nods. 'I forgive you too. We can move on from this. Start again. This time, we'll do better. For each other and ourselves and everyone else.'

I nod, stepping towards her. 'I promise I will. I promise I'll do better this time.'

She comes closer, and we look at each other anew, like we're just meeting. It isn't like when we were children. Me, hiding. Her, brave. This time, instead, I decide to be the brave one. I move forward, heart racing, reach up to place my hands around her face, and pull her lips to mine.

The landscape disappears. The war disappears. Zeus next to us. Lire in our minds. Each other, even, as we're lost in the moment.

Her hands curl around my waist and she pulls me closer, making me gasp, and she laughs and moves her lips so she's in control. I falter, letting her kiss me, letting her move her arms up and down my back. I feel both our emotions, the rising heat doubled, rebounding back and forth, growing and growing.

She's smiling against me. Her hands find their way up to my hair, and I drop mine down to her waist, our lips still not parting.

It's hard to breathe. The sun is rising in the corner of my eyes.

She pulls away and whispers, catching her breath, 'They were right when they said only my soulmate's kiss could wake me. Because until this very moment, I have been so far from alive.'

I kiss her again, and if we're wrapped up in it for seconds or hours or a hundred years, I can't tell.

But finally, Zeus clears his throat, and we break apart. I flush. Was he here that whole time?

Dawn is looking at me like she's just won the war, and I'm looking at her with my mouth hanging open, my shoulders falling in exhaustion and shock and delight.

'So, are you two made up?' Zeus says, picking out dirt from under his fingernails. 'Tell me you're done with this silly little argument, because we do have places to be.'

'I'm done,' I say.

She smiles. 'Yes, I'm done.'

Soon after, we've fetched some supplies from the carriage, created a small fire – with the help of some magic – and sit around it on the hillside, looking out across the forest landscape as the sun slowly rises.

Dawn and I each say a few words about her parents. And mine. She insists on it, because I never got to say goodbye to my parents either. I never attended their funerals, never let go. And it's time for us both to start new lives.

Over tears and orange sandwiches, which Zeus eats enthusiastically, we mourn.

And when we're done, we raise glasses of orange juice to the rising sun.

'To all we've lost,' Dawn says, 'and to all we are going to gain.'

✦ ✦ ☾ ☀ ☽ ✦ ✦

When we're back in the carriage, the sun rising around us, we go back to sleep. I'm curled against Dawn, expecting a peaceful, blissfully dreamless rest.

But I'm not so lucky. I find myself in the throne room in Bearra's castle, and Elsie is on the queen's triarue seat, laughing. 'I take it she hasn't told you?' the girl says, adjusting the golden crown atop her head.

Small things about the scene are wrong as Elsie controls the dream. She hasn't spent enough time in the throne room to know the tall windows are arched, not squared. And the floor is darker than this. The sunlight should be coming from a different direction.

'Elsie,' I chide. 'What is it?'

'You've been gone so long. I'm almost offended you never tried to contact me. Lire tells me nothing. You always were her favourite.'

'What. Is. It?'

Elsie smirks. 'Lire has lost her patience. She's attacking Bearra tonight. This is all about to be over. The pretending to be weak, the serving them, the boredom. Tonight, I'm unleashing all the power I've been hiding. And you can, too. You must come back. Now. Wherever you are.' She raises a hand and lets her magic twirl around her hand, but like everything else in the dream, it isn't quite right. The magic has a thickness to it, a substance that doesn't exist in reality. 'You don't want to miss this.'

CHAPTER 21

SOMEWHERE, SOMETIME ...

Teddy ducked as Ebony swung an iron knife – blunt, but still hard enough to hurt – over his head. His magic curled around it, dispelled by the metal, as the two fought on the hill in front of the castle.

'Faster, Teddy!' she shouted, turning back to the crowd of soldiers in neat lines on the green. 'Magic can't be relied on to save you from an iron weapon. And to our Ironers, don't be afraid to get *close*. The further away you are from a Magicker, the less effect your weapons have.'

As Ebony held the knife out in her hand, Arden attempted to sneak up behind her and shoot a blast of magic to knock it from her grip. She gasped, but his magic – not nearly as strong as Teddy's – couldn't go near enough the iron to disarm Ebony. He and Teddy were sick and tiring from the iron's presence, already struggling to keep up whether or not Ebony landed hits.

It was difficult, training both the Ironers – those armed with iron weapons – and Magickers – those armed with Amora's magic – side-by-side, but they couldn't think of a better way to prepare Bearra's army for the battles ahead. The Magickers didn't have a lot of magic, of course; only what Amora could spare for them. But that was a good thing. The less magic they had, the less the iron would affect them. Still, it was useful to have.

It had been quite an even split – they'd given each soldier the choice. Teddy found that since the introduction of iron, people weren't so hungry for magic anymore. Like Arden's friends, who had refused it and made him keep all of his, they didn't like the idea of being harmed by the metal. Many remained, though, who wanted to taste power. And those became the Magickers.

The group, along with Teddy and Arden, were slowly getting accustomed to the amount of iron that had been brought to Bearra. It still made Teddy nauseous when he got close, or was around too much for too long – like today – and of course he couldn't touch it. But at least they could bear to be in the same kingdom as the rare metal. Teddy could only hope their enemies with magic wouldn't have developed such a tolerance.

Ebony rolled her eyes at Arden, as if he were an irritating younger sibling. Teddy often forgot they weren't related, even though they looked completely different; one with the arched nose and tan skin of Amora's Territory, the other with the stark black hair and soft features of Grace's.

'Don't waste your time trying to disarm someone with an iron weapon,' Ebony said to the soldiers. 'Aim for their weaknesses and get away if you must. When Arden tried to disarm me, all he did was alert me to his location, so I can now—' She threw the knife towards him, but he crouched just in time. It was obvious to Teddy that she'd missed intentionally, and it seemed that way to Arden as well. He shifted with embarrassment, as if he would've preferred she had the respect to hit him. 'Do that.'

The entire outdoor area smelled of sweat and metal and broken grass. Although the soldiers were tired from the excessive training, they didn't seem to mind that the people leading them were two pirates and the son of Lire herself. They just wanted to win the war.

The protestors at the base of the hill, however, had a different attitude. They would shout at the soldiers: 'These non-Bearrans are leading you astray!' 'They only want power for themselves!' 'They're leading you to their deaths!' 'Lire will have mercy! She was our fairy for hundreds of years – not these foreigners!'

Most of the soldiers would roll their eyes, but some, Teddy noticed more and more often, would watch, listen, and consider their words.

Their training session went on for a while. Although Teddy didn't like leaving Maya's side – though *she* certainly liked her alone time – he found it important to be here. Part of the reason Dawn left him behind and in charge, along with Maya, was that he was powerful. It pained him, but he knew he struck fear in people, especially since his identity was revealed. And having him as part of this training, being a leader, was important.

Not that Ebony needed the help. The young woman was terrifying enough as it was. It was a good thing she had strong morals, that she was on their side, or she'd be a frightening enemy. Sierra was scary, but Ebony was calculating. She watched for one's weaknesses and took her time to win.

The soldiers split off into groups for sparring practise when an uproar exploded from the protestors. Most of the soldiers ignored it, but Teddy met Ebony's eyes as they peered over the hill to see what was going on.

The protestors could get rowdy, but now there was a certain anger to them. An excitement, a spark starting at their feet, making its way towards the castle.

One was leading them – a black-haired man Teddy struggled to see properly at this distance – and he was yelling things at them. Teddy strained to listen. 'Princess Dawn has been spotted in Amora's Territory!' he yelled. 'Whoever sits on the throne is an imposter! Leading us to ruin while our real princess is gone!'

Teddy's heart skipped a beat. Surely they wouldn't do anything drastic with this information? They had no proof. They couldn't use this as a reason to storm the castle.

But that was the *problem*. They wanted a reason. They had been waiting for a reason. And now they weren't just scared or angry. They wanted revenge on the leaders who had led them down a dangerous path.

The crowd began sprinting uphill to the castle's entrance, scrabbling amongst themselves. Teddy was frozen in shock when Ebony grabbed his arm. 'Maya!' she shouted in his ear. Without waiting for him to react, she pulled him, hard, towards the castle. She was already yelling orders at the soldiers, at Arden.

But the people were close, unexpected, and large in number.

They were going to hurt Maya.

As soon as they got to her, knowing what she'd done, they were going to tear her apart.

He blinked, his next step jolting him back to reality as he ran alongside Ebony. He had to get to Maya.

Ebony sensed his idea. She shook her head at him. 'Don't hurt them. Don't prove their point.'

'They're going to hurt *her*!'

Ebony stopped him, taking out her knife. 'Listen to me right now. You use your magic against them, you lose their loyalty forever. Do not lose control now. Let me handle it.'

He gritted his jaw, loosed a breath, and nodded.

They took off again, forcing their way through the increasingly violent throngs of protestors storming the castle, and heading for the throne room where Maya would be sitting, vulnerable and oblivious, on Dawn's throne.

When they arrived, Maya had her hands up, standing on the throne. The illusion wouldn't falter – Teddy perfected it more every day – but there were other ways to tell an imposter. Dawn's features were in fear, hazel eyes wide, mouth open, lines in her forehead. But it was Maya's terror.

'I'm sorry!' she yelled. 'I'm sorry. She asked me to do this – for *you*. I didn't— I didn't want this!'

Her guards and a fiery, furious General Largon were managing to hold back the crowd, but even they were beginning to lose faith. It was clear on their questioning faces.

'It's my fault you're here, I know!' Maya said. 'I should've made a decision – I should have listened to you. Or stopped you. I don't know. I didn't know what to do!'

They were screaming obscenities at her, horrible things Teddy could never unhear. Weapons appeared in their hands. *No no no.*

Teddy let go of the illusion at once, hoping it might shock them long enough to cause a small distraction. Dawn's gold fell away to reveal Maya's silver. Her grey eyes and light-brown hair. That small face. The quiet beauty that took Teddy's breath away. He hadn't seen her in weeks, and he gasped. She stopped him dead in the middle of the crowd, his heart racing. She . . . She was . . .

Ebony pulled him again, stealing him out of his trance.

The distraction seemed to work as they squeezed past the guards. Well, Ebony glared at them, and they parted to let them pass. Teddy sprinted to Maya, took her around the waist, and helped her to the ground. His entire body felt both weak and strong as he touched her. *Her.* A devastating and powerful flash-flood of sensation.

'I'm okay,' she breathed, before he even asked. 'This, it's my fault. I didn't help them.'

Teddy took her arm. 'We need to run.'

'What? We can't— We can't just go! We have to explain to them—'

'This is not your responsibility to clean up,' he said strongly. As strong as he could to her, which wasn't much. 'These people don't want apologies. They want revenge. They want to hurt you. They want an excuse to push us to surrender. Maya, *please*, let's go.'

Someone managed to break through the crowd, and Teddy felt his magic rise in and around him, almost uncontrollable. But Ebony cut down the man first, knocking him to the ground. Non-lethally. Teddy exhaled – knowing she just saved someone's life, because he would not have spared him – and his magic simmered down.

'*Go!*' Ebony shouted.

Maya was crying. Crying through her own moon-grey eyes, pulling tides within him. They stared at each other for a long moment, the screaming and banging and wildness nothing more than a dull cheering.

'I missed you,' he said quietly.

She smiled sideways. 'Me too.'

He watched her face turn braver, straightening out again, becoming Maya again. And Maya wasn't a fearful person. The girl he knew was brave. The girl he knew wasn't helpless. These were her people as much as they were Dawn's. She'd fought for them, and she wouldn't stop now. He'd chosen to love a hurricane of a woman, and that wouldn't stop today.

They were not going to run.

Teddy helped Maya back onto the throne and she stood atop it once more, waving her arms to command the attention of the battle. 'Stop!' she bellowed. The throne room was in shadows, the sun high, the only time it wasn't streaming through the floor-to-ceiling windows on either side of the long corridor. 'If you'll all shut *up* – I can explain everything!'

They did not.

'Hey!' she yelled even louder. Some of the yelling quieted down, and Teddy used a little magic, experimentally, to amplify her voice. 'I said shut up, you morons! Shut! Up! Do you want an explanation or not?'

Finally there was a lapse of calm.

'Thank you,' Maya said impatiently. 'Really. If you thought storming the castle was a good idea, considering everything . . .' She shook her head. They started shouting back at her, and with a glare from her, they stilled. 'Well, I'm not here to insult you, and I do not enjoy speeches, so I'll make this brief.'

With the amplifying magic, even the ones still shouting couldn't drown out her voice. *Her* voice . . . Where Dawn's was clear and regal, Maya's was raspy and impatient. Teddy stopped breathing.

'There are imposters in Bearra,' she said. 'Real enemies. Spies Lire disguised to infiltrate us. Ones that cannot be unmasked, except for a mirror that only Dawn – Princess Dawn – can use. She had to leave to find it, which meant someone had to take her place, or Bearra would appear weakened. Believe me, I didn't want to do this, but someone had to. Many of you know me. You know the world I saw when I left Bearra – the new world none of you have experienced. I've betrayed you all before and saved you all before. Taking the place of the princess so she could do what she had to was not something I wished for.'

Maya looked across the room without an ounce of weakness. 'But it's something I did, because taking care of the kingdom I call home is my duty. And all of yours. I know you think surrendering to Lire will save you, but it won't. I promise you. Trust me, as one of you, as a regular person, not magical, not royal, *nothing*, who has fought the fairy myself. This war isn't about pride. We aren't afraid of giving up our land to Lire. Nor our triarue, or any of the things we love in this place. It isn't about fear. If Lire only wished for power, and promised to spare us in exchange, we would give it to her. Lire wants *destruction.*'

The protestors began to falter, considering her words as General Largon nodded proudly at Maya.

'Lire is angry because this world was once hers, but it's ours now. And that makes her scared. She doesn't just want Bearra to be remade in a way that we don't recognise. She wants the whole world. If Lire wins, there would be nowhere to escape to. Do you want to lose your free will? Do you want to spend the rest of your lives in fear? Serving a bitter fairy's ego?'

They murmured amongst themselves. Were they finally understanding?

'I know I can't ask you to join us in fighting her. It's your own decision to make. But I know I would rather fight for a chance at stopping her than live in a world without a choice at all.' She took a deep breath, shoulders falling. 'What we can't have is violence between our own people. The princess will return soon, with the mirror to reveal our enemies, and they will be dealt with. Lire's attack is coming. We have *days.* If you wish to surrender, I don't care. Do whatever you want. But do not drag us down with you. Don't destroy the castle and the people who protect you. Go home.' She waved them off, stepped down from the throne, and without waiting for a reaction, left the room.

Maya.

How had the world ever survived a day without her?

The protestors left after that. Just as Maya had suspected, all they needed was to feel heard. Teddy was glad, then, that Ebony had stopped him from obliterating them. For Maya, he would have.

She was halfway through unbuttoning his shirt, hot breaths on their chests, in their favourite spot pressed up against his bedroom wall. After today's adrenaline, they were both excited to let off some steam.

Then Amora appeared.

'Ah!' Maya yelped, launching back and staring at the rainbow-winged fairy. 'Amora! You are aware that we have a *door*?'

Amora twirled her brown hair between her fingers and sat on the edge of their bed with her legs crossed. Her frilly pink skirt shimmered as she moved. 'You know I can't use the door,' she said. 'The public is still unaware of my helping you.'

'So they'd notice you at the door,' Maya replied, flattening her hair. 'But not the flutter of rainbow wings flying through a window?'

Teddy smiled at Amora, giving her a quick hug before sitting on a chair and rebuttoning his shirt. 'We're always happy to see you, Amora. But we already had a scandal earlier today, barely avoiding a battle between our own people in the middle of the throne room. Of course our people have guessed at your involvement, considering the amount of your magic we've *happened upon* for our soldiers, but . . . This isn't good for either of us.'

'I know,' she said. 'And I'm sorry to come like this. But Lire is going to attack you so *soon,* and I had to know how you were faring. Word has already spread that your royals are gone.'

'Dawn will be back soon,' said Teddy. 'And things are bleak, of course, but we might have a real chance. *If* we can just get our people to stop wanting to surrender and start wanting to fight.'

'*Humans,*' Amora said with a sigh. 'I know I'll have to start rallying my own citizens soon. Protecting the territory and readying the people for war. How *awful* it is. I wish I could stay and help you, Teddy.'

'It's okay,' he said. But it wasn't, really. He wanted Amora here with him, protecting him, supporting him. She was the only mother he'd ever had, and the fact that she needed to stay far away from him right now was hard to come to terms with. 'I know you have a responsibility to your own territory first.'

She glanced away. 'I want you to know . . .' she started. 'I have to ask, even though I know you'll refuse. Teddy – and Maya, you too, of course, sweet girl – you could come home with me. Get out of here before Lire strikes. You'll be safer in my palace. Bearra is the biggest target of the world right now. If you just escaped—'

'Is that why you came?' Maya asked. 'To convince Teddy to run?'

'It's his mother,' Amora pleaded. 'She's— She's— You know what she is. Teddy, you don't have to face her. Neither of you should. I don't want . . .' She fell into tears, her chest heaving. Teddy ran to her and cradled her head against his chest. 'I don't want you to die. I can't let her kill you. Not after all she's already put you through.'

'Thank you,' Teddy said, his chest thick with guilt. 'But my power is enough to really help people, Amora. You know I wouldn't be the person I am today without you. It's because of you that I know love – that I have this desire to protect people. I spent so much of my life running away, but I'm not that person anymore.' He put his arms on her shoulders, the tulle scratchy beneath his fingers. She smelled of roses. 'I plan to win this fight. And if I don't . . .'

'If we don't,' Maya finished, 'at least we'll have tried.'

Amora shook her head. 'I'll give you more magic,' she said. 'For the two of you. For the soldiers. I'll . . . I'll . . .'

'You're going to go home,' Teddy said gently, 'and protect your own people. You can't risk Lire finding out you're helping us. You can't make yourself and your territory a target. As soon as my mother gets proof of your involvement, she'll come for you. I'll fight better knowing you're home.'

'Teddy's right. We've fought her before,' Maya said. 'She may be powerful, she may be wise, but she's not invincible. We'll both be stronger knowing that your corner of the world is safe.'

Amora nodded, wiping her tears. Her wings straightened. 'Okay. Okay.' She stood, pulling them both into a hug that warmed Teddy from the outside in. 'I'll see you soon. The day after Lire's attack date, I'm coming. I'm coming to celebrate your victory.'

'It's a date,' Teddy said.

She hugged him again, tight and desperate, and he didn't want to let go. How was he supposed to feel, holding the person he regarded as a mother for possibly the last time? But he did, eventually, watch her leave.

Maya took a deep breath. 'Do you ever wonder if we only cause our parents pain?'

They were supposed to have well over a week. But screams woke him from his sleep, and he bolted upright. Out the window, streaks of lilac magic crossed the sky and hit their targets with resounding crashes.

'Maya!' He shook her awake. 'She's here!'

Usually she blinked awake slowly, easing herself out of her dreams, but tonight she jumped upright. She gasped at the sounds. 'But we had time!'

'She lied.' He picked himself up out of bed and threw on his clothes, tossing Maya her own from the day. 'Or she just got bored. We have to get Ebony and the others.'

The crashes and screams only got louder, and Teddy's heart was beating all over his body in distracting thumps. He wanted to take Maya and hide under the bed, protecting her with his body, but this . . . This is what they had been training for, and they couldn't be cowards now.

Ebony swung open the door. 'She's here!'

Teddy nodded, and the three of them hurried downstairs. They were not ready for this. Not yet. They had no strategies against Lire except to *try*. Bearrans soldiers poured through the corridors – iron weapons swinging and clanging, pink magic twirling along the floor at people's feet.

There was already a girl in the castle throwing volleys of Lire's magic at the soldiers, cutting them down with ease. She was a maid; Teddy recognised her. One of Lire's spies? And if she had power like this, who knew how many others were already in the castle?

It was so sickening to see power like his, his mother's, his brother's, coming from someone else. He nearly froze.

Instead he shouted to Maya, 'Stay with Ebony!' But Maya was already shaking her head, begging him not to leave her. 'I'm sorry – I have to go and deal with that girl before she takes down the ceiling!'

'*Teddy!*' Maya called, but he was already springing to the girl, using his magic to quicken his pace, trying to fling balls of physical magic to knock her down. But it was no use. She was manic, unrelenting – pure chaos delighting in the destruction.

He hadn't the time to find a way to stop her without— Without—

She laughed wildly as a soldier tried to stop her with his feeble power, but she turned it back on him with a flash of lilac. He was on the ground, bleeding from the neck before Teddy could blink.

He had no choice. She was a child, but he was the only person here powerful enough to stop her. She had to die before she could brutalise more Bearrans.

Teddy got a look out the window, stopping suddenly. He could see the gates from here, wide open. Lire's soldiers were pummelling through, using magic to cut down the vines around the kingdom. Teddy's heart sank.

At the gates, on their knees, was at least a quarter of Bearra's population. They already surrendered. They didn't even try. Maya's speech meant nothing to them.

With tears stinging in his eyes, he let magic build in his palms, hot and prickling like burning lavender bushes – and he aimed at Lire's spy.

CHAPTER 22

The carriage takes us right up to the castle doors – barging through battles and debris, not letting us out even as we try to jump into the streets, alight with violence in the dim dawn. Instead, it delivers us straight to Arden, its magic following him home.

We stumble out, bracing ourselves, and I shiver at the orchestra of screams and slashes and spells. Arden throws up a wall of magic to stop the attackers coming at us, gleaming blue in the darkness.

I send my own magic to reinforce it, bursting from my fingers in rays of lilac light. It makes my heart thump with power, momentarily numbing my nerves.

'You have— Huh?' Arden doesn't stop too long before clearing our other side. There's already a bruise under his right eye. He looks Zeus up and down. 'And who's this?'

Zeus scoffs, but before we can answer, Levi bounds around the corner of the carriage, Wren at his side. 'I saw the carriage! The princess is back!' Then he looks at the magic still smoking around my fingertips and frowns. 'Carlotta?' Then he notices Zeus. 'Zeus? What are you doing here?' His face breaks into a grin. 'Zeus!'

The two huge young men, pale and light and muscular, crash into each other in a boyish hug. For one spectacularly masculine moment, it's as if the fighting around them isn't even happening, and they're oblivious to the world.

What?

'Levi? How'd you end up in Bearra?' Zeus asks, pushing away. His . . . cousin? The one that moved away? *Fairies.* Where Levi wears his handsome face and large size with quietness, Zeus is a star incarnate, unwaveringly confident. But their icy eyes are the same shape, and they smile with a similar turn of the upper lip. 'And why on earth haven't I heard from you in years? You bastard.'

'I'm here with—' He cuts off, reconsidering his answer. 'To help some mutual friends. And you?'

Dawn waves her arms in front of them. 'I appreciate that the two of you know each other, but please stop wasting time! We need to get inside the castle. We need to make a plan.' She's blinking back tears.

And it's clear why. All around us and below, stretching across the kingdom, runs the vibrant red of people falling to their deaths. At the front gates are others on their knees – have they already surrendered? – and Lire has soldiers, of all different types and levels of magic, *everywhere.*

The sad truth pulls at my heart: people don't care to stand on the right side of history, not when survival and power are at stake.'

But those still fighting are fighting back hard. Those with magic are attacking Lire's regular soldiers, and those with iron weapons are facing the ones with magic. They work in a strategic formation I'd never have expected from our army.

Lire's troops have more power, but it's just like I noticed during their last attack. They're unskilled. Lire has recruited large numbers, but she's recruited them hastily. These are people desperate for a taste of power, but they lack the sheer will of the Bearrans.

A warmth like hope blooms in my chest. Do we . . . Do we have a chance to survive the day?

But where's the fairy?

'What do we do?' I ask Dawn, who is watching the fighting with her mouth agape. In utter disbelief, her eyes glaze over as if she's watching from behind a window.

She turns to me as all the others turn to her, with a fear I've never seen in her. 'I . . .'

'We've been waiting weeks for you to return,' says Arden, not very politely. 'It's time for you to lead us now. If you don't, someone else will have to.'

Zeus taps her on the head. 'There's supposed to be a lot of Wisdom in there. Strength, Justice, et cetera?' He frowns. 'No?'

Dawn swats his arm away. 'You stay quiet,' she nearly growls. 'Let me think.'

I grip her arms and give the others my best *watch yourselves* glare. Zeus tries to complain, but I hiss, 'Remember why you're here.'

Wood crunches and people scream as a building falls somewhere south of us. Dawn straightens her back, holds her hands at her sides, and takes a breath, her face going flat. Her voice is even when she says, 'Arden, stay here and keep doing what you can with your magic. Levi, watch his back. I can trust the two of you to work together and hold the fort out here. Zeus and Relia, come with me. We're finding the others and getting a better scope of the battle.'

'*Relia?*' Arden says. 'Wait— Long-dead Relia *Relia?*' He narrows his eyes at me. 'Your magic . . . You . . . Spy . . .? You *are* Carlotta from the forest!'

'Oops,' says Dawn. She takes my hand. 'Yes, she was working for Lire. No, it is no longer relevant. Do you know where Teddy and Maya are?'

'And Sierra?' Zeus adds.

'We lost the others,' Levi says, while Arden is still pacing in shock. 'We were all asleep when the fighting began. We left our rooms and got split up – Ebony went to find Teddy and Maya, I know that much. I found Arden here. Lark and Wren could be anywhere. I'm sure Sierra went to protect Maya. Wait, Zeus, how do you know Sierra?'

Dawn glares at Zeus, warning him to be quiet. Clearly disappointed, he says, 'I'll tell you everything later.'

A ray of orange flies towards us; a cannonball of destructive magic. We throw up our magic at once, knocking it back towards the dark sky. It explodes like fire, loud and terrifying.

Yet that same powerful feeling fills me, instilling me with more confidence.

Ash rains on us, and Arden breathes, 'The people know Maya was a fake. Many turned on us at the start of the battle. It's only been a couple of hours, but the surrenderers haven't moved. Lire's soldiers seem to be sparing them.'

Dawn fails to hide her disappointment. 'I'll find Maya and Teddy. We'll try to think of something. Something we can do to drive these soldiers back. Something magical that Lire won't see coming. Has she . . . Has the fairy shown up?'

Arden and Levi shake their heads.

'That means the worst is still to come. But for now, we keep going. Thank you for protecting Bearra.' She pulls me towards the castle's entrance.

Zeus follows close as we push through the castle, a shield at our backs. I keep my magic at the ready. Fights have broken out all around us, metal clanging and magic shimmering. Bearran soldiers, marked by triarue gems on the shoulder plates of their armour, shout that the princess has returned.

Dawn smiles at them reassuringly as we hurry through, but all they're doing is drawing attention our way. I end up moving in front of Dawn and using magic to knock enemy swords into their own helmets when they look at us too long. When the magical ones gear up for attack, I block them with shielding magic. Spots of blood trickle along the floor as we push our way through more brawls, soldiers from both sides laying sickeningly still.

My stomach twists into knots, the sounds so unbearable my arms shake, but we press on, still searching for the others. Dawn is gripping my arm and Zeus has a steady hand on my back, and somehow, despite the extra touch, their support makes it all quieter.

We find them in the ballroom. Behind a fort of soldiers, magical shields, and stacked furniture are Teddy, Maya, Sierra, and Ebony.

Teddy abandons his spot immediately as he sees Dawn, throwing himself haphazardly towards us with his arms outstretched. 'I knew you'd come back!' He crashes into her, grinning and panting as he hugs her. An arrow flies in their direction while they're distracted, and I whisk it back with magic the way it came – just in time.

Dawn holds him tight, and when she pushes him back, she's smiling – a different smile than the one she gives me, but floodingly beautiful anyway. 'I never planned to fail.'

'You got the mirror?'

'We don't need it,' I say, pushing myself into the conversation. I decide that I'm not going to be the same person anymore. Not the Relia from a hundred years ago. Certainly not Carlotta. But a newer, braver version of me. One who speaks, who takes up space, who fights instead of cowers. One with enough will to keep living even when the worst happens, one with the power to make my own solutions without relying on others.

None of the others ever did anything epic by being silent. I'm ready to stand among them.

'We did get the mirror,' I explain. 'But it isn't going to be helpful in this fight – it's too late. If any spies are left after today, when we win, *I'll* deal with them.'

Teddy narrows his eyes. 'How did you get my mother's ma—?' His face turns defeated. 'How could we all be so stupid! Of course you were one of the spies. I suppose you're on our side now, Carlotta?'

'It's even better,' Dawn says, her eyes bright. 'Lire had this big plan, and—'

A window caves in, bringing a gust of glass and wind.

'I'll tell you later,' Dawn finishes, and the four of us move to where Sierra, Maya, and Ebony are still fighting.

Seeing Sierra and Ebony fighting together is like watching two ferocious predators – sharks or wild cats or carnivorous birds – descending on their prey. It's both untamed and entirely practised, a wild dance. No one who comes near them, magical or otherwise, stands a chance. The pair cut down enemy soldiers like they're nothing but paper. Sierra is flushed with excitement. Ebony's face is pinched with remorse.

Meanwhile Maya has no weapons except a small knife, which she grips in one hand as she fumbles against the soldiers. Some of them nearly get her but the others keep coming back to help. Knowing Maya, she was told to evacuate or hide but adamantly refused.

Despite all this fighting, we're all still behind the makeshift fort, only attacking the soldiers who get through. Compared to the rest of the kingdom, we're safe. Hiding away to scheme. The pirates are treating this like their ship – their space to protect, to defend. But they can't get to a point of strategising, because they're too overrun, and half their group is elsewhere.

'What do we do, Dawn?' Maya yells as Sierra kicks a soldier on top of her – about to *stab* her – in the chest and out of the fort.

Maya scrambles back to us, panting, bruises all down her arms. 'Hello, Carlotta. And . . .' She stares at Zeus, unimpressed.

Zeus huffs. 'No one knows who I am?'

'I recognise you!' Teddy smiles at him welcomingly. 'You're that prince. Zoop.'

He looks ready to behead someone. '*Zeus.* Of the Ice Empire.'

'Well if you're here to attack us,' says Maya, 'this is not a great time.'

Zeus steps forward dreamily, his eyes on something else, offense forgotten – Sierra. 'I'm here for her.' But she's far too busy to have noticed him.

Teddy and I focus on putting up a stronger shield of magic. Within thirty seconds we have the space completely blocked off, all the soldiers back outside – only their blood left in our haven. My heart falls for the soldiers losing their lives outside our bubble of protection. Our bubble of *privilege.*

'The shield won't last long,' Teddy says tiredly, 'but it gives us a minute to talk.'

Sierra stomps over. There isn't a single flaw in her glossy straight hair, falling long down her back, although the rest of her is cut and bruised. 'Why did you put up a shield! You're ruining my fu—' She stops dead when she sees Zeus. '*You* . . . You dare show your face here, while I'm busy fighting? Doing something noble! And you're here to . . . what? What do you want?'

He scoffs. 'Here I was thinking you might want to apologise. I planned to. I was going to ask you for *help,* of all things, but now I can remember why we avoided each other for a year!'

'You abandoned me, you imbecile!'

'Blah, blah – you turned me into a bird!'

I turn to Teddy and Maya, letting Sierra and Zeus's arguing fade into the background. 'There's a maid here,' I say. 'Elsie. About Wren's age. She's the only one of Lire's spies I know of. Has she shown up?'

Teddy's eyes darken as they look past the magical barrier – where all I can see is the blurry shapes of fighting. 'I know who you mean. Was she your friend? As soon as the battle started, she began . . . She had such strong magic, and no mercy. She kept killing people. I'm sorry.'

'She had to be put down,' I reply. The mixture of feelings I have is sickeningly confusing. My heartbeat lowers in relief that I don't have to worry about her. Then there's the heartbreak from knowing that the girl who was, somewhat, my friend, is gone. And that Teddy was the one who had to kill her. 'It's okay. I knew she would be— It was my problem. I should've dealt with her a long time ago. She was no child, Teddy. That was a monster in a girl's body.'

'And it means something,' Maya says. 'For you.'

I exhale quickly. 'That the undead can die.' But at least that means I'm *alive.*

'But we aren't going to hurt you,' Teddy says, his brown eyes warm as they meet mine. He tilts his chin towards Dawn. 'The way the princess looks at you, I'd be insane to try. As long as she trusts you, I do too. Which means one less enemy, okay?'

I nod quickly, muttering a *thank you.*

Sierra and Zeus's argument fades back in, Ebony between them trying to shut them up.

'You. Turned. Me. Into. A—'

'And you ran off the first chance you got!' she spits back.

'What else was I supposed to do! You kidnapped me!'

'I borrowed you for an important task, Zeus! And I seem to re-member you enjoying it!'

Ebony waves her arms. 'Quiet! Zeus, whoever you are, what do you want? Why are you here?'

He explains everything about Candace and losing control of his em-pire, about wanting Bearra as an ally and knowing he needs someone like Sierra to help.

'This is such a bad time,' she says, softening. 'Really. You couldn't have picked a worse moment to show up, Zeus. But if I'm being honest, I am happy to see you.'

'I'm sorry for everything,' he says.

'Me too,' she replies.

They look at each other with wide, empathetic eyes and gentle smiles. So they really were . . . *lovers*?

'Now, finally,' Dawn says. 'Can we please get back to the real problem? This fighting is getting us nowhere. We'll be destroyed if Lire shows up. So what can we do to send these soldiers back?'

A sword slashes through our barrier, so I send more magic to restrengthen it. An enemy must have stolen one of our iron weapons. It takes Teddy's help to fortify the shield enough to stop the sword.

We don't have much longer. Even if we could stay hidden in here, the people out there need us.

'I think it should be noted,' Ebony says, 'that Lire's soldiers aren't preoccupied with destruction. If anything, they're being careful. Which means Lire wants Bearra in perfect condition when she takes over.'

Though the kingdom is half falling down, she isn't wrong. It could be much worse.

'Makes sense,' Teddy says. 'She built this kingdom. To her, it *is* hers. She doesn't want it ruined.'

'So she didn't hear Dawn's lie,' I mutter.

Dawn explains for the others, 'I told Kara that I had a failsafe. That if someone like Lire did take Bearra, the entire kingdom would destroy itself with magic. An "if we can't have it, no one can".'

Teddy rubs his brow with his thumb. 'Lire likely didn't believe it. Or didn't care. It's the same for her – if she can't have Bearra—'

A crash resounds from above. Dust rains on us. Another crash, and another. The heartbeat of destruction booms through my chest.

'Someone's bashing in the ceiling to get to us,' Ebony says, looking around as if there's something she can do to stop it.

'Good,' Sierra says with dark excitement. 'We've been talking long enough. I need to kill someone before I get so bored I fall asleep.'

'We still have no plan!' Dawn says.

'If you think of one, you let me know.' Sierra glances at Ebony expectantly, and she follows her to the edge of our shield, waiting for us to lower it. Zeus gives Dawn an apologetic shrug and joins them.

'But . . .' Dawn starts, but the others made themselves clear. If she isn't going to lead, they're going to do what they want. And she doesn't have any ideas.

Maya and Teddy share a look as another crash nearly caves in the ceiling. They're ready. Plan or not. Life or death. They're not going to let Lire win. None of us are.

'Dawn?' I ask, noticing a slight imperfection in her hair, where one of her curls is out of place. I want to ask if something is wrong, but of course it is – *everything* is wrong.

Her hazel eyes dart around, and when they finally land on me, she sighs. 'The others are right,' she whispers over the roaring above. 'All we can do is keep fighting and have hope. We can't hide in here planning while everyone else is outside dying for us. I'll remain here and command, but— We have to do something.'

I nod.

Sierra calls to us, 'Carlotta! Come with me upstairs. We might need your magic.'

My heart skips a beat, first in surprise as I remember most of these people still don't know my real name – it's been so nice to be known as myself, even just for a few days – then from Sierra's request. 'But—'

'The others need to stay with the princess,' Sierra explains impatiently. 'Teddy is more powerful. He'll protect her. Your magic is more useful out there.'

I shake my head rapidly, looking to Dawn for help.

She offers me a guilty wince. 'I'm sorry, but she's right. You can take care of yourself, and Teddy can take care of me.' She lowers her voice and takes my hand. 'No more selfishness, remember? No more letting ourselves put each other before all else. Come back as soon as you're done.'

I swallow. The thought of being separated fills my veins with acid, but she isn't wrong. 'Okay,' I whisper, voice trembling. 'I'll be back soon.'

As Teddy and I lower the shield, bringing back the sight of violence and blood, the noise of it no longer dulled, it's as if I can feel everyone's panic rising. The *fear* – I didn't know there could be so much of it in one place. It scratches at my skin, begging me to feel everyone's pain.

But I can't stop to take it in. Sierra's already sprinting into the battle, not waiting for me. Everyone who gets in her way is struck down in a second. I race after her, chancing just a quick look at Dawn – *oh, Dawn* – and use my magic to take out anyone who comes for me and Sierra who she hasn't already taken care of.

We make our way upstairs, a metallic smell increasing – blood or iron? – and when we reach the top I sense danger and yank Sierra back from behind. She's about to kick me when an arrow whips past where her neck was a second before. She frowns at me for a short moment before continuing on her way, making sure to toss the enemy shooter down the stairs.

We're racing through a large, long hallway with triarue gems shattered on the stone floor, when someone shouts her name.

Arden.

He's alone, and he's limping.

The battle disappears for Sierra as she sprints and crashes into him. They grip each other for a while, her arms over his shoulders and his around her waist. They're whispering to each other, things I can't hear, words of love?

I ward off attacking soldiers with my magic, squeezing my eyes shut as I throw a couple of them down the stairs like Sierra did. Bones crack as they reach the bottom. Even the ones with magic aren't difficult to circumvent.

It helps to be Lire's favourite; I'm more skilled and powerful than any of them could hope. But the thought of hurting anyone – even an enemy – sends waves of aching to my core. Terrible, debilitating guilt.

The black-haired couple join me again as we find the room above the ballroom – where people are using maces and magic to smash through the stone. The noise isn't as bad up here without the echoes of the ballroom, but the people have a terrifying chaos in them.

I sense their emotions and there's nothing but anger, maybe even enjoyment. They like the violence and destruction. Which must be why they joined Lire.

A group of six leans over the crumbling circle on the floor, bashing it with all their will. Some have shaken off their armour because of the heat, but they don't for a second let themselves get distracted from their mission: reach the princess.

Battles rage around them. The Bearrans don't have the strength to fight both the enemies and the ceiling destroyers. They don't understand that they're going to kill Dawn.

Sierra taps her foot, arms crossed. Her long hair and height make her look regal and beautiful – yet threatening, like a snake. She wouldn't care if Bearra were burned to the ground. She just wants to fight. And sure enough, one by one, they begin to look up at her, eyes widening and hammering arms faltering.

Everyone in the world fears the Reeds.

And with Sierra beside me, I feel fearless. Blood sprays around us, but who would dare approach a warrior like her?

'You keep doing that,' she tells the demolishers, 'and I'll have to kill you.' One of them starts to move, but she cocks her head and they freeze. 'Or maybe I'll kill you anyway. It's been a slow week.'

Arden's expression is pained, but he stands beside her, sword at his side. Seeing how Sierra talks to people she dislikes, it's easy to see why she and Arden took so long to warm up to each other.

Three of Lire's soldiers move towards us while three stay behind. Foolishly thinking themselves protected, they go back to bashing the floor. Red magic dances at the feet of the ones approaching us. 'Gracians,' one of them spits. 'Why defend these people, this kingdom, when Lire wishes to make a better world for us all?'

Sierra sighs, bored. 'I'm not wasting my breath on this.' She launches at the trio. Arden follows, and they fight back-to-back, taking on the enemies one at a time. Thuds and whimpers and slashes while I stand there shocked-still. Arden swings his sword around and it turns into a knife before my eyes as he guts the soldier reaching for his throat. He's holding back his magic, just like Teddy and I have. Just like the enemy is *not* doing.

Does our power mean anything if we aren't willing to use it?

I only think to jump into the fight when someone bumps into me from behind. But then, that feeling. The knowing. *Danger.*

There's a long creak, a cracking in the floor. I'm not sure if it's happened yet or it's about to. I jump back, into the next room where the support of brick beams should hold. 'Come back!' I scream to Sierra and Arden. 'It's about to fall! Come back!'

But they don't hear me. They're too busy punching and slash-ing.

I barely have time to send my magic towards them – with no idea what I'm doing except *begging* the magic to protect them – when the floor falls with a deafening thunderclap. In that split second, Sierra's hair flies up, Arden grabs her around the waist, and I fall to my knees.

I'm thrown to the floor, gasping, and I try to look over – to see the damage in the ballroom, see if they're alive, see if those below have been hit – but before I have time to react, there's a sword flying at my face.

I jump to my feet just in time, using magic to push the weapon back. Face to face with an enemy soldier, his green eyes glinting with the thrill of violence. I falter, stepping back quickly. But he keeps coming, and I can barely see because tears are blurring my vision.

Right when he's about to swing the sword, I push out my magic in one blast. It pours out of me, so many emotions making it churn crookedly towards him, and he falls through the hole onto the floor with a nasty *crack*.

I whimper, watching for more soldiers, but they're all too busy fighting each other to take notice of a girl like me. It pays to be invisible. I run down the stairs with only one thought. *I have to get back to Dawn.* My knees burn with each thudding step. I must've fallen on them harder than I realised.

I reach the ballroom entrance, the doors blown from their hinges, more blood soaking the marble floor. But Dawn is there, looking at the debris, perfectly fine. The others are all here too, still behind the barricade, Teddy and Ebony working hard to keep the soldiers away from the princess along with a handful of Bearra's soldiers. Zeus and Maya remain next to Dawn, standing either side of her protectively.

I sigh with relief, knowing at least the fall didn't hurt them. But Sierra and Arden must be hidden in the rubble.

I'm about to sprint to Dawn but a lilac glow in the window stops me dead. The glass, smashed in, glints with the light as the fairy's wings beat, carrying her in.

Lire.

CHAPTER 23

SOMEWHERE, SOMETIME . . .

Lark knew that, in most cases, love was a complicated thing.

Sierra and Arden, for example. They started out hating each other –
though Lark was convinced they never really did – and slowly, secretly
fell. Maya and Teddy, he was learning, were much the same, even if
they still had a tension of distrust between them. Ebony and Levi were
a little more simple, a case of an unlikely partnership turning into
becoming a singular entity, but their pasts were still complicated.

Lark had thought that love at first sight, that simple pure, imme-
diate love, was only a story. A song Musans would sing, as false as
anything else they believed in.

And then he met Briar.

It was so fast, as if they knew each other immediately, as if they had
always known each other.

It started at that dinner, weeks ago, when they happened to be seated next to each other. When they had started talking and then never stopped. She liked his freckles. He liked her dreamy grey eyes. She said he was humble, but she loved how smart and kind he was. He wasn't so sure about those things, he'd replied. He loved how creative she was, the way she did everything so melodically, braiding her hair in beats of three and speaking her words like lyrics. Not like words were in Muse's Territory, not music-laced lies, but a rare honesty in everything she did. And she was so romantic, every glance through rose-coloured glasses.

One evening, she took him to her childhood home. Since Maya now lived at the castle and Prima lived with her husband, it was emptier than it once was. Lark could feel the absence in the air. But even better: Briar's parents were visiting Prima, so they had the house to themselves.

She took his hands, which sent shivers up his arm, and led him through the house. She said it was small, and logically he knew that was true, but having never had a home of his own, nor a family, the place had its own magic. It could be half the size, but her scent in the walls, her heart in the paintings, made it perfect in his eyes.

Briar brushed her long, light-brown hair over a shoulder, the strands in heavy curls. 'My parents were bookmakers,' she said. 'A hundred years ago, people from all over the world loved their work. Some books we only printed, but others were handmade, completely unique and illustrated and bound by us. But when we woke, there was no need for such things anymore.' She looked up at Lark through her eyelashes.

'We don't appreciate mastery and beauty like we used to,' Lark said.

She nodded. 'Yet maybe things worked out for the best. Maybe some things are meant to be, so we can meet the people we're supposed to meet?'

He smiled, and she tugged him down to sit beside her on her bed. It was springy, but covered in handmade cushions and blankets.

'I know that's true,' he replied softly. 'If my sister and I didn't spot the right ship passing by at just the right time, we might not be alive. And now, I only met you because a year ago, I cursed a Reed.' He laughed giddily, his chest warming as he watched the beautiful woman before him. How could this be real? How could someone so perfect choose *him*? After all this time, all the longing for someone like this to hold – how was he so lucky? 'Life has a way of gifting you the things you desire, whether you realise it or not.'

She leaned forward, hands either side of him, and when his fingertips met her waist, she kissed him.

The world was ending around Lark, and his little sister was half the destruction.

Wren whisked around with Opal's old bow, knocking down soldiers in tens from the high point she and Lark were battling from. They were at the roof of the castle – one of the safest places he'd thought to take her while letting her fight. Not that he had much say.

The battle up here was intense, and Lark was barely managing to hold his own with his sword. But looking out across Bearra, to the magic firing in all colours from all angles, to the burning houses – one of which he was sure was Briar's, if his hours of longing for her from his castle window could be relied upon – and the trampled farmland in the outskirts, Lark knew the fighting below them was so much worse.

The streets were an orange brick, but the darkness of night made it too easy to imagine that they were instead soaked with Rhiannon-red blood. Maybe they were.

Soon, there may not be a kingdom to save.

He ducked as Wren shot a soldier over his head; instantly she went back to shooting the ones around the castle's base – easily hitting them even from the rooftop. She was too good at this.

Since they'd lost Opal, it was difficult to feel true joy. Difficult to feel anything in the constant stress of war. But seeing his little sister, who just years ago had been so much weaker, so much trouble, and so hated by those around her, now thriving . . .

She may be going down a murderous path, but she was happy, and he was *so* proud of her. It didn't matter anymore that they had no parents. They had grown up despite it all, and they were strong now. Her more than him. If he died today, he knew she could take care of herself.

But if he lived today, and made it back to Briar, maybe he could get what he wanted as well.

'Fight like you mean it!' Wren shouted at him, rolling her eyes at his sloppy slashing. 'Sometimes I can't believe you're my brother.'

He laughed back humourlessly. There were plenty of things to say. *I can't believe my baby sister is a murderer,* for one. But nothing positive could come of that, so he picked up his sword and worked harder –

knocking more soldiers down so she wouldn't have to. He might have been sloppy, but he'd still been trained by Sierra and Ebony. He wasn't bad, not by any standards.

Wren was a blaze, spinning and firing, going through fallen archer's quivers to collect more arrows and firing again. When she finally ran out completely, she took her old knives out of her jacket, from when she used to copy everything Arden did, and slashed at enemies with them just as she'd been taught.

Lark scraped his knee on the gravelly rooftop as a soldier nearly got him – barely missing a stab to the stomach. Okay, it was time to get out of his head and into the fight. He stood quickly, remembering his training, and stepped back, letting the soldier come at him before jumping to the side, spinning around, and stabbing the enemy between the shoulder blades.

He exhaled as the soldier dropped, and pulled his sword back out. *Fairies*, he hated this. How he wished he were back on the ship, baking a batch of caramel cakes. He could almost smell them amidst the smoke and blood.

Another soldier came at him, but this one was pushed back and parried over the roof by Wren before Lark had a second to think.

Then he saw something he thought he was imagining. A mirage in this nightmare.

'Briar,' he breathed.

On the other side of the roof, she waded through the battle. Her hair was tied back, her eyes red, hands shaking. She had no weapons, and her dress was torn, hem stained scarlet. When she saw him, she ran to him, and it was like lighting a fire – like he'd never felt warmth before that moment.

But he had to push her back. There wasn't time to spare to be vulnerable. 'What are you doing? You're supposed to be at home— Or, or somewhere safe— Or, or—'

She sniffled, running her hands over his arms, running her eyes over his body. 'I couldn't stay home knowing what was happening. I had to come and find you. Maya as well. My parents tried to stop me, but I convinced them to stay behind and let me go. I just . . . I've been running all over the place – it's all so terrible. I couldn't . . .' She inhaled and grinned weakly. 'But I found you.'

He shook his head. 'No. No, you can't be here. I need you safe, Briar. I need—'

'I'm sorry,' she said. 'I couldn't do it. Besides, nowhere's safe anyway. And I know I'm weak. Weaker than all of you. Than everyone. I see the way people think it. All the time. But I knew what my sister would do in this situation. She already is doing it, fighting in this war, leading in this war, and I . . . It was my turn to . . .'

He held her tightly.

'What's going on?' Wren asked, punching a man who tried to come near them. 'You're supposed to be hiding!' She stabbed a soldier through the neck, blood spurting as realisation dawned on her. She sighed. 'Oh. Because of *love*.' With a cringe, she said, 'Do you two really think now is the best time?'

Lark cleared his throat. 'I have to get her home.'

'*No*.' Briar jumped in fright as an arrow fired past them. 'I'm fighting!'

'Who?' Lark shouted. 'How!'

Her eyes welled up again.

'I'm sorry,' he said, his hands on her cheeks. 'I'm so sorry. But I can't— can't worry about you out here.'

'Just let her fight!' Wren called, having picked up the bow again, bashing two soldiers over the head with it at once, then lowering it and using it to send them careening off the rooftop. A new welt had opened above her left eye, and all Lark wanted to do was take both girls and hide them away, protect them with his life.

He didn't want Briar to see this side of him – the pirate. To her, he wanted to be the romantic, the lover, a man she could respect and rely on. But this was who he'd grown to be, who he *had* to be. He knew he'd lost already, that there was no convincing Briar to leave now, and every second they wasted arguing was a second longer the battle would continue, so he nodded. 'Stay by my side.'

And she did, for a while. Getting in the way more than not, and covering herself in bruises, but she kept herself alive. Even managed a few life-saving punches that distracted soldiers long enough for Lark to knock them out.

But the soldiers kept pouring in. They were getting on top of them, driving them towards the roof's edge. If they couldn't push back soon, they were going to die. All three of them.

Lark didn't care what happened to him, he didn't care about the cuts covering his body, the finger he was certain was broken – but he couldn't live with himself if anything happened to Wren or Briar.

Five men attacked Wren at once, and with hatred for them burning in his veins, Lark screamed. He tried to run to her and help, but two soldiers jumped on him, pinning him down. Someone's hands were around his neck, and he was thrashing to get back to his sister, but he couldn't move. A dark monster reared its head in him, the same boy who stole his best friend's magic to protect his family. He bit and screamed but he wasn't strong enough. He was terrified, furious.

'Wren!'

A flash of skirts flew over to her. Briar dived onto the man on top, knocking him away long enough for Wren to blow back up like an explosion, the men flying back.

Lark's lungs ached as he tried to breathe, tried to move.

Wren was on her feet again, expertly wrestling soldiers twice her size. Briar was still on top of one of them, but she was losing. *No no no.*

Lark screamed, and will one final push of everything he had in him, he strove to escape the enemies atop him; they had no weapons, they were relying on strength alone. But they kicked his hand and threw his sword away, wrapping their hands around his neck, knees against his chest. He growled, seethed, but there was nothing more he could do.

He tried to reach towards Wren – she was protecting Briar, but if she kept protecting Briar, she was going to get herself hurt. There were *so many* enemy soldiers.

Wren was still too distracted. Briar was—

A soldier behind her had a glint of silver at her back and began swinging it up. She was so scared, eyes darting around, she hadn't noticed. There was no time for Lark to escape, to scream, to help. No more air in his lungs.

The world slowed down, everything too-clear and moving one split second at a time like flickering images. Tears poured from Lark's eyes. His heart shattered into pieces. *She was gone. She was going to be killed. Saving his sister.*

And it'd be *his* fault for falling in love.

Then another body moved into the frame. An angry face that looked just like Briar's, but older, harsher, searching desperately for her. A scream that sounded like hers too, only raspier.

Briar's mother took the blade to her own heart.

CHAPTER 24

I try to sneak forward, see if I can surprise Lire, but there's no use. Her eyes catch me immediately even though I'm on the opposite side of the ballroom. She stares at me. I think she smiles, though I can't see her well through the dust and the fighting. Whether the smile is genuine or malicious, I don't know.

But it's too late to run and hide now, so I cautiously make my way over to her, where she's standing by Dawn, speaking down to her. The princess has her fists balled, her face twisted in disgust, ready for murder. I'm with her. The fights seem to disperse around me as I walk – magic, possibly? – and when I reach Lire and Dawn, it feels somehow quieter here. Like our bubble from before, only there's no magic at play.

Is this just what it's like to be in the presence of a deity?

Last time I saw her, only days ago, she was fighting Candace. She was a little dishevelled, burned out, but now she's back, primed and prepared to take what she believes is rightfully hers. Her light hair is braided back in intricate patterns, and her dress is heavy and beautiful, layers of purple striking against each other – not something any human could fight in, but why would someone as powerful as her expect to fight?

I reach the group: Ebony and Maya to one side at the back, Dawn facing down Lire, Teddy in front of Maya, and Zeus by the window at the fairy's back, arms folded. The inner circle seems almost naked without Sierra and Arden.

Maya and Ebony look to me expectantly. *Where is Sierra?* Neither of them seem scared of the fairy. No, all of them glare at her with deep hatred. They want to tear the fairy apart. Of course they're more concerned about their friend than the presence of Lire.

The weight of Sierra and Arden's *situation* rushes back. Where are they? They're alive, aren't they? But they could be terribly injured. Hidden under all that rubble. *Fairies.* How could anyone make it through a fall like that alive?

But I can't tell the others. What good would it do now? It would only distract them, make them feel more reckless. So I tilt my chin upwards as if to say, *She's still upstairs.*

Lire forgets the group around her and flutters toward me slowly, head cocked. She is in every way a snake, a shark, a dark predator. 'My *Carlotta.* So you've chosen sides, have you? I see it in your eyes. You're with your pretty princess now. You've lost interest in me.' She waves a hand as if I mean nothing to her. 'Did you really think I wouldn't know,' she hisses, her face flat, 'that it would end this way? That you would make the foolish choice rather than fight by my side and be given everything you could ever want?'

I step towards her, the battle disappearing around me as, for the first time, I show her strength. I don't falter. I don't bend to her will, pretend to be hers. I meet her eyes. 'I think you care about us all more than you want us to believe.' My voice is uncharacteristically dark, flat and unwavering. But this has been coming a long time. I want my words to cut her as deeply as she's cut me with her years of manipulation. 'I think this hurts you. Not just your pride, your ego, but your heart. You hate seeing me against you. I wish I was sorry for betraying you, but as you claim – you knew all along.'

There's a shame within me; there always has been. I can't fight. Even with magic, I'm not particularly skilled – at anything. I'm weak, a nervous disaster who has nearly nothing to offer. I'm not wise or kind or creative. I don't have a strong sense of justice. I'm not even good at being bad.

All I've ever tried to do is what I want – what's best for me, what makes me comfortable. But the power I have now is unique. The way I can know and understand and anticipate the people around me is unmatched. And even if I can't overpower Lire, I can still sense her moves.

The fury building inside her is cold as ice. Her wings are pointed high, a beautiful, dancing lilac. A fairytale to mask a monster. Was she born this way, or did she choose this appearance the way she chose mine?

She growls at me, and I can feel it within her heart – she *is* hurt. Does she truly care for me, in her own way?

'We are your children,' I say. 'We have wanted your love, but your poison pushed us away. You already lost your eldest son, and now Teddy fights against you, too. And even though you were only close to Dawn and I because you wanted to use us, I know you grew to love us. Is that why you killed her parents? Jealousy?' Surprise flashes across her features. She's underestimated my knowledge. *Good.* 'I'm one of the few people who understands you, who has been with you for the last hundred years. You never trusted me and I never trusted you, but don't lie and tell me you never cared about me. Don't tell me you always knew I'd betray you. I may have been your last resort, because if you couldn't have Dawn or Teddy, maybe I was the next best thing. But you wished for me to love you. You wish for *anyone* to love you.'

Beneath her anger, I sense her pain, deep and dark, a cavernous void.

'But Lire, no one does, and no one ever could, and it breaks your heart.'

She scowls and tries to throw her magic at me, but I see it coming before she's even lifted her hand. I step aside, using my own magic – the same as hers – to bend it around me. We are an ocean of purple. *Her* ocean, a thing of her dreams turned into a nightmare.

'Fool,' Lire spits. 'I would have made you great. I would have made you a queen, and you throw away *everything* I offer. You could have been a fairy of your own right.' She breathes deep, simmering down her boiling rage as she seems to come to a resolution. Her voice is almost eerily calm as she says, 'Fine. I revoke you, Relia. You are no longer bound to me. So you can go back to the forest.'

Her magic seeps towards me. I shuffle back, but it's different this time. *She's killing me.* Why, despite knowing the consequence of losing her as my anchor, do I long for it? *She's setting me free.* I let the power collide with me, lilac clouding the air. It makes all thoughts of the battle fade – I've wanted this for so long. Finally, the illusion will lift, I will be myself again. Even just for a moment before I lose this body.

I meet Dawn's gaze and let her honey-tinged sunshine glow upon me, ready to return to being a spirit. But even as I squeeze my eyes shut, Lire's power only tickles my skin and pours right through me.

Lire laughs. 'Oh, *that's* interesting.'

Am I still alive? I pinch my arms. *I'm still alive.*

'What are you doing?' Dawn demands, nearly getting between us, but Lire ignores her, pulling her magic back, a tide rushing out. The room watches us curiously.

'I suppose,' says the fairy, 'I'll have to kill my failure of a protégé the old-fashioned way.'

I inhale sharply, my heart racing. 'I'm no longer tied to you,' I whisper. 'Your enchantment is *gone.*' And, I realise, it has been for a while. 'You can't control me anymore. And I'm still alive.' I clench my fists, take a breath. *Alive.*

But I'm still masked. Why?

Teddy glances between Dawn and myself. 'You kissed,' he murmurs. 'Soulmates . . .' His hair is ruffled, a patch on the side scorched. His eyes are half-lidded and gleaming, and he barely looks at his mother. 'That's what you did, isn't it? Lire's power that brought you back was like a curse. You . . . broke it before she could.'

Lire starts to spit her next retort, but I ignore the world around me. *Especially* because if this is the end for us, I want it to be as myself. It was *me* holding onto Carlotta all along. Was I too afraid to be myself again?

Well, I'm not anymore.

I find the part of me gripping onto the illusion and snap it open, letting the magic release itself. It happens slowly – I feel the changes inside and out, keeping my eyes closed – and the illusion drips away piece by piece. My body grows taller, broader, my dress tightening on me until even that changes, from starchy to silky. My face alters. The roughness of my hands and feet flakes away, leaving my familiar soft skin. I breathe through my own lungs again, a euphoric feeling, hear the beating of my own heart. I even smell like myself, like roses and earth. For the first time in a hundred years, I feel like myself again. I feel alive, and present, and—

I open my eyes and run my fingers through brilliant red hair, gaze at my white, bright skin, no longer dull and sickly. My dress is pink, hemmed with lace, like I'd have worn a hundred years ago. Oh, I'd forgotten how long my hair was. How smooth. I touch my face, run my hands over my arms.

I am who I was then, and I am Carlotta too, but I am so much better. Because now I'm new inside and out. I am Relia, evolved. I am Relia, powerful.

And although Lire's meddling has been lifted, I still have her magic within me.

Dawn is looking at me like she's just seen magic for the first time, and I'm looking at her through my real eyes, and *of course* it was true love that gave me my life back.

Lire taps her foot impatiently. 'Love might have gotten you this far, Relia,' she says. 'But you're still nothing compared to me. I gave *all* of you life. I have run this world for centuries. Without me, you'd have no land, no palaces, no society to steal. And when I rebuild this world, it will all be mine again.'

Teddy shrugs. 'The thing is, Mother, we don't care.' He paces towards Lire, still looking scruffy but determined. 'We'll let the world *end* before we give it to you. There's nothing you can say to sway us anymore. No more manipulating and lying. Do you really think we're *that* scared of you? You've already been bested by us.'

Dawn adds, 'We know you better than anyone, fairy. We will be the ones to end your reign.'

'Look outside!' Lire grabs Dawn by her hair and drags her, gasping, to the window. We all take an instinctive step forward, but no one moves against the fairy. Not yet. 'Your people are dying, princess! A quarter of your army surrendered, because they don't trust you – they trust me! If you surrender the rest of Bearra, I'll let them live.' She sneers at Teddy. 'My son says he'll let the world end before giving me what I want. He's selfish – all of them are.' She lowers her voice, speaking directly into Dawn's ear, so I can barely hear it. 'You aren't like them,' she tells her.

Dawn shakes her head. 'No, Lire.'

'You'll notice I haven't attacked you yet. It's because I want to give you a chance to make the right choice. You have a duty to these people – the people you're leading to their deaths. Why? For pride? Destroying Bearra instead of giving it to me is one thing, but letting everyone who looks up to you die? Will you do that, Princess? The Dawn I know never would. She would know that saving her people is more important.'

Zeus waves his hands. 'Don't listen to her! This fairy is *not* getting my world.' Lire doesn't even offer him a glance. And he grimaces as if to say, *Doesn't she know who I am?*

Then Maya whispers, 'Surrender.' Everyone turns to her at once. My heart freezes over, and I'm not sure I heard her correctly. 'Dawn, surrender.' Maya nods, afraid but sure. 'The people of Bearra have been calling us to give in for weeks. They don't want to die fighting a war they know they'll lose. Now it's here, and look how many have fallen.' Her eyes are red but narrowed seriously. 'They were right. *We're* killing them. I hate Lire as much as anyone. I dream about murdering her in wonderfully creative ways. We all do. But just because we would all die to stop her, it doesn't mean we can drag thousands more people into our fate.' She meets Dawn's eyes. 'Surrender before it's too late.'

Teddy is shaking his head. 'Maya, stop,' he says quietly. 'How could you even . . . *imagine* this?'

'Because I have a family out there!' Her eyes glisten with tears as she points to the window, her hand trembling. 'I want them to live, not be taken by a war because *we* made the wrong decision. I want my sister's baby to have a chance at life. We can't risk losing. There is *too much* to lose. Lire is giving us an out before it's too late.'

His expression is utterly betrayed. 'We've beat her before!'

'And that time, it was just us and her! But we still lost people. When Sierra and her friends faced Muse, *they* lost someone. At least we all had a choice. Now? Now there are thousands of people being slaughtered! I don't care about killing a fairy. I want the war outside *ended.*'

'I can't believe you,' Teddy says, turning away from her. 'I can't believe you.' He stares daggers at Lire. 'Don't you see how you only cause people pain and suffering? Aren't you supposed to be good? What happened, Mother? What made you so hateful? Why are you doing this to us?' His voice cracks. 'To *me?*'

'Don't call me *Mother,*' Lire replies, finally letting go of Dawn, who drops to the floor. 'Not when you don't mean it.'

'Please,' he says. 'Just once. Why can't you do something good? Why can't you have mercy? Why can't you ever just be happy?'

Her lip curls. 'With what? You? You are the biggest disappointment of my life. Power is the only thing that has ever given me happiness. Everything else is a means to an end.'

I want to run to him as much as I want to run to Dawn. I have never seen a boy so desperately need to be *held.* He whispers, 'I don't understand. The fairies are supposed to be pure and virtuous. The best of us, representing values we should all have. But you – the fairy of wisdom – you were always wicked. You never had a soul. You're not even a person. You're just a ball of power, churning and constantly needing to be fed lest it burns out. You think we're nothing because we're weaker than you, but at least we're human.'

She lets out a guttural, dark laugh. 'Half-human,' she says. 'For you, anyway, Teddy. What's it like, having only half a soul?'

'Stop!' Dawn screams, scrambling to her feet. 'All of this, I don't want to hear it! Shut up!'

It's as if all the noise is sucked out of the room. Everyone holds their breath.

The princess's eyes are overflowing with tears. With a weak voice, she says, 'Lire, I surrender. Maya is right.' She gestures out the window, avoiding my eyes as I try to plead with her to stop. But she's right, isn't she? Lire will kill us now, but maybe let the rest of the people live. And we promised . . . No more selfishness. 'I will not watch one more person die,' she says, 'on either side, for a fight between *us*. A fight that began before many of these people were even born.'

Teddy drops to his knees. Maya is standing with her arms crossed, shivering. Ebony is near her, frozen. Zeus is backed against the wall. I slow my breaths and nod to myself.

We lost. But maybe others will have a chance at life because of it. None of us like this end, but I can see the merit in it. I don't believe Lire will keep her promises and spare these people – but if there's a chance, it's better than letting her kill them now.

I resign myself to the end, let my shoulders fall.

Then: a flash of green in the smashed window. The sound barrier breaks, knocking me back.

Candace soars through. *Candace?* The impact hits and she slams into Lire, grabbing her around the waist and pushing her headfirst into the rubble.

Cheering and chanting erupt outside, and despite my eyes going blurry with shock, I see a silver flag flying somewhere far beyond the window. At the gates, an army has arrived.

The Ice Empire are here.

But to save us, or to destroy us?

CHAPTER 25

SOMEWHERE, SOMETIME...

General Isla of the Ice Empire was a soldier first, a daughter second, and nothing more. After years of hard work, after over a decade of dedication to expanding the empire, she was finally about to win. The richest and most powerful kingdom in the world was hers to take.

Isla pulled down on her jacket and tightened her braid. Watching out the window of her carriage, she gazed upon the castle and the city walls of Bearra; in her mind's eye she saw the sparkling of endless triarue in the woken kingdom's famed mines. Of course, marring that vision were the screams of battle, the metallic scent of blood and swords, and the blinding sparks of blazing fires at midnight.

It was a shame to see such an ancient city burned to the ground, especially considering it was about to be hers – well, the empire's. But Isla was used to battle. She had trained for this her whole life.

Fairies, if not for *her,* the empire wouldn't even be here right now. Candace wouldn't already be within the castle walls, and the sparks of purple flying out the castle windows would already be choking the entire civilization.

Isla took a deep breath in and a deep breath out, and—

Is that Zeus's carriage?

She bristled as an overly gilded carriage made its way to the castle gates. If that wicked, lazy, useless, horribly charming Prince was here, Isla was about to lose her—

That damned letter. She should have known. Someone tipped her off about this battle – someone told her to come at the right time. They'd never moved faster, relying on Candace to enchant all their carriages and practically fly them into the centre of the world.

And she and Candace had played right into the prince's hand, bringing the army he needed.

'General. Are you ready?' asked the soldier waiting to open her carriage door.

Well, whether or not Zeus was here, she was going to have to do her best. There was never a time he *hadn't* gotten in her way, and she supposed at least if he was here, she'd have someone to put down to make herself look better – and not have to feel bad about it.

The prince hadn't come with an army. As far as she could tell, he wasn't even supposed to be here. She knew he'd left the empire, of course, that he'd been travelling around doing whatever he wanted. But that was normal. Did he have the same idea as her, wanting to offer Bearra help when they needed it most in exchange for anything the empire wanted? Did he plan to take Bearra for himself?

But how could he? With what army? *Hers?*

Without giving the soldier a response, she jumped out of the carriage – nearly slamming the door in his face as she swung it open. 'I'm ready,' she said. 'Let's go.'

Ten or so of her soldiers trailed behind her. Most of them were already in the kingdom battling Lire's soldiers, just as she'd told them to. She could trust her army to do good work, leaving her to lead.

All the way from the triarue gates and up to the castle, she strode in with a straight back and steady legs. She was born for this. She did not falter. She ignored all of the fighting going on around her as she, the rightful leader of the Ice Empire, the rightful leader of this army, marched up to the castle where the princess was lying in wait for her to save them all.

Isla used her exceptional geographical skills to find the room where Lire and Candace were battling. Well, mostly she followed the scent and the glow of magic twisting through the walls. That epic, deity-like glow. Yes, many of Lire's soldiers had magic, and so did the Bearrans, to Isla's surprise. But they were weak. Isla knew true power when she could sense it.

Before long she made it through the labyrinth of crumbling castle walls, which despite their antiquity were not particularly interesting – especially considering all of the beautiful palaces across the world that Isla had seen and been invited to as a leader. She and her soldiers traipsed into the edges of the ballroom, where the fairy, Isla's mother, and a handful of Bearrans fought. One in particular, a red-haired boy, had a surprising level of Lire's magic that he used to fight her. Not one of her spies, then – was the son she'd heard rumours of real?

Such drama. Isla was a general, of course, but that was more out of necessity. She knew a position in the army would help her reach the level of power she needed, but she didn't love war. In fact, she didn't know why war was necessary. Why couldn't people just turn to the best leader that they could find, and simply follow peacefully?

Isla scanned the room and landed a hawk-like gaze upon her target, Princess Dawn. She was as beautiful as everyone said, incredibly regal in a way that Isla could never dream of being. Between her aura and her bloodline, it was clear why she was beloved. But Isla had very little admiration towards the princess. The princess of what, exactly?

All she'd done was be blessed, sleep for one hundred years, and then wake up to find herself losing a war.

Isla, on the other hand, had worked hard for the last dozen or so years to prove herself as a leader, working her way up from nothing along with Candace. It infuriated Isla that people like Dawn and people like Zeus had everything at their fingertips, including the admiration and love of thousands, just because of their royal status.

Dawn clung to a redhead girl, both of them trembling while Lire and Candace wrestled each other.

Just as Isla was about to make her way to the princess and attempt to talk, she decided instead to stand behind a line of soldiers and fade into the background.

Zeus stood by the window with his arms crossed, looking only very slightly tussled and shaken. Why did he always have to show up at the worst times? What was he going to do, ask her on a date in the middle of this battle? Or did he plan to charm the princess into marrying him?

Oh – Isla thought – *I bet he is, I bet that's exactly what he's trying to do. Wait until I tell Elm about this.*

Isla faded behind the battling, stamping on a few of Lire's soldiers' feet as she went and stood by the wall, watching. She was a strategist after all, more than anything. How else could she have gotten this far in life?

She hadn't expected Zeus to be here, and that was a problem she was now going to have to solve – especially if he thought he could take Bearra from her now. *She'd* shown up at just the right time to make sure they owed her everything, to make sure they couldn't refuse her help. And now, what was Zeus going to do, pretend it was all *his* idea? That he did all of this and just to save the empire? And of course, because he was a prince, everyone would believe him.

She cast her mind back to the dinner they'd had less than a few weeks ago at Candace's request.

✦ ◦ ⟨ ☾ ☀ ☽ ⟩ ◦ ✦

Candace set them up in the parlour. Isla expected Candace would show up as well, but all of a sudden she'd *just so happened* to have an urgent date she couldn't miss. Which meant Zeus and Isla were at opposite ends of a small table, candle-lit in the corner of one of Candace's castle's most luxuriously warm and elaborately cosy rooms.

Zeus looked her up and down; he examined every thread of her outfits when she wasn't in uniform, though they weren't very interesting. A wool dress and faux-fur with her hair loose wasn't anything special

– yet he made it seem so. 'I'm so glad we could make this happen,' he drawled. 'Regardless whether it's genuine or not. You know how I love to spend time with you.'

Isla replied, 'I'm not sure why we have to do this alone. You bother me enough already. What's all this really about?'

'Well, I adore spending time with you and Elm, but how am I ever going to take this relationship to the next level if we never get a moment to ourselves?'

'*What* relationship.'

He leaned forward, nearly tipping his glass. 'Isla, I'd do anything for you. You know that. You're the one for me. I don't care that we're on different sides. I don't care about anything else but your beautiful sparkling eyes. I need you Isla. I need you more than air. I need you more than I need to *be* the heir.'

She gave him a quizzically bored expression.

'It sounded better in my head.'

She shrugged, taking a bite of a cupcake from their shared platter of empire delicacies. 'Whether or not you truly care for me, you would betray me the moment you could if it meant taking my power back for your family.'

'You mean taking back what's mine? What *you* stole?'

'You can't steal respect. Either have it or you don't.'

'At least I have their adoration. I bet you wish you could steal some of that.' He caught the snarl on her face and changed tactics. 'Can't you see that we'd be a perfect pair? I have everything you want.'

She sat back in her chair and sipped her hot tea. Of course, they'd had this conversation many times. But Isla would never stoop so low as to give him a chance.

He knew this too, but it didn't stop him from constantly bothering her. She could never be sure if he did actually care about her at all, or if it was all just part of some ruse to bother and distract her.

Yet they had been friends for a very, very long time. Well, *friends* wasn't really the word for it. Though he certainly thought it was. He considered her and Elm his greatest friends, but only because they were the only people who didn't cater to his every whim. He was attracted to that because he thought it meant they liked him enough to be honest.

No. It only meant that they weren't afraid of his power. And unfortunately, Zeus didn't simply like women who liked him. Just as he'd fallen for Sierra Reed, he only ever wanted lovers who absolutely did not want him – and, in fact, who scared him, because it was the only time Zeus felt that people were being true.

Isla felt a little sorry for him. Sometimes she wondered if she should be kinder. If maybe this alliance was worth pursuing. Zeus wasn't a bad person per se, he was just annoying to the ends of the earth and back. Especially considering she'd literally gone to the ends of the earth to find him after Sierra Reed cursed him to turn into a bird. He'd abandoned the Reed warrior and hidden himself away, refusing to come back to the palace until Isla dragged him back. The people needed their horrible, stupid, useless prince.

She thought this quest would at least earn her some of the Empire's admiration – being the one to save the beloved man. But he wouldn't let her tell a soul because he was so embarrassed. And so it ended up being completely useless on her end. Although part of her had to admit that the reason she saved him – and the reason he'd come to her first when he broke his arm falling out of the sky after his curse was broken – was because in some twisted, awfully backwards way, she actually cared for him.

The problem with Zeus was that she never knew what was genuine and what wasn't. They were on such utterly different sides, both of them fighting for the exact same power as they had always been since they were children. Which was the reason they'd spent so much time together and Zeus even considered them friends, and probably why he had the ridiculous notion she might ever love him. Their rivalry meant that any kind of vulnerability towards him could lead to her downfall.

He would always end up on top. He would always end up untouched. Because he was a prince; he was power and charm and strength. Meanwhile, when she made the slightest mistake, everyone couldn't help but remember her for who she really was: nothing. She had no bloodline. No one knew who her parents were. No one even knew who Candace's parents were. And although they'd amassed a frightening amount of power, it could be taken away from them in an instant if the people turned on them. For it was the people's opinion that mattered most.

So although Zeus could flirt with her and irritate her and take whatever he wanted from her – not that she would ever give it willingly – she could never do the same. She could never be a child like he was. She could never be *silly* like he was. She could never run away like he had and come back unscathed, because her power had to be maintained every moment of every single day.

And that meant never *ever* giving in to Zeus's charms.

He tilted his head back. 'Okay, okay. No romance. Let's talk politics, then, if it's truly the only reason you agreed to this *date.*'

She narrowed her eyes. 'Very well.'

At least he wasn't insufferable *all* the time.

Isla zoned back into the battle, watching her mother fight. Between the two, Isla was the better fighter – but Candace didn't need much practical skill when she had magic.

Isla had no use for magic of her own. She'd never cared for it, and found that the magic around her barely affected her. It was simply a part of life – in the same way that heat was real outside the Ice Empire but never touched its snowy borders. She felt apart from that kind of power.

Still, watching the way her mother danced with magic, a rainbow flying around her as she used power of every colour, Isla couldn't help but watch in awe. She didn't need to help Candace – she was capable of winning this battle, especially with the red-haired young man helping her.

It was a gamble coming here, but the empire had already won.

Yes, Isla would have to deal with Zeus before taking this kingdom for herself. No, it wasn't going to be easy. It never was, breaking into a circle of leaders who were already tight knit. Who didn't like outsiders.

But she had risen to leadership in the Ice Empire and now she would take a role of leadership here.

General Isla of the Ice Empire would have the world at her feet.

CHAPTER 26

Dawn and I cling to each other, suddenly in the background of our own battle.

Bearra had already fallen – Dawn was ready to surrender. But it's no longer Bearra against Lire. It's Lire against the Ice Empire. They're *helping* us. Which means it's not just our people screaming anymore.

There is barely a story to tell; Lire's army so rapidly falls to the power of the Ice Empire. The fairy herself must be fighting at her full strength, but against Candace and Teddy, she can't get back on top.

I try to run into the fight to help them, but Dawn tugs me back and shakes her head. *Leave it to them. This isn't your fight now.*

Lire wipes her brow with a bloody hand. But the blood isn't hers, and it streaks through her light hair. Candace has a spectral of magic around her hands, but as Lire slumps, she looks upon her enemy with nothing but a satisfied grin.

Despite knowing she's lost, it still feels like she's ten steps ahead. Like this is what she wanted. Like even if she loses today, she'll come back and hurt us tenfold.

Lire's eyes meet mine from across the shattered ballroom. 'I blame you,' she growls, her voice unnaturally gravelly. 'When this all ends, you and your friends will be the first to die. And believe me, I don't need Bearra to win my world back. The fairies will join me – just watch – and the human race will no longer be a parasite in *my* empire.'

'Lire—' I start, but I'm cut off as she vanishes in a flash of lilac.

Her few remaining soldiers race away after her, pounding to the staircases to get out of the castle – if they're lucky enough for the empire's soldiers to spare them.

Candace, panting, straightens and smirks. Her green dress is in tatters, but she runs her hands over it, magic glittering under her fingertips, and the rips and tears repair themselves. 'Bearra,' says the false fairy, making her way to Dawn. 'I never thought I'd see it myself. A beautiful kingdom, if a little dated.' She holds out her hand to the princess for a shake, and Dawn cautiously accepts it. 'I am Candace of the Ice Empire. Princess Dawn, it is an honour to meet you. You're just as the legends describe.'

Dawn nods, her eyes still red and gleaming from tears, and her arms dotted with blood. 'As are you,' she says. 'I must admit that even a hundred years ago, I never knew much about your . . . *empire*. Yet it seems you've grown quite powerful. What brought you here today?'

'Power,' a voice says behind us, and Zeus steps up to Candace, his chest puffed out like a bird's. 'Why *attack* a kingdom that can offer you an advantage, when you can make it owe you a favour?'

'*Prince*,' says Candace. Though she keeps a straight face, I can sense the effort it takes her. Clearly, Dawn and I aren't the only people Zeus has annoyed.

'*Candace*,' he replies. 'I assume it was Isla's idea to come, though you seem very excited to be here.'

'So *you* sent her the note. What exactly is your plan here, boy? What is your allegiance to Bearra?'

I clear my throat and cut in to save him. 'Candace,' I say, my voice so much stronger now that it's my own. Still with its slight shake, its weakness, but without the meekness of Carlotta's quiet. I remember my time as a noble girl, as the daughter of a powerful family, and channel all the regal power within me. 'There is no need for you to pretend, either. The Ice Empire has no business wasting time and resources helping us for nothing in return. If you were planning to attack us, now would be the perfect time, but you haven't. So we can only assume you want something. A favour, as the prince put it. What is it you have come for?'

Candace narrows her eyes as if sizing me up. It's understandable that she can't decide if I'm important, dangerous, or both. She raises her chin. 'I don't believe in mindless killing. The way I lead, the only people who die, and the only things destroyed in battle, are those necessary. I have no desire to wipe out Bearra. We've just proven that if you want to survive, you need our help. Better us than Lire, surely? But without me here to scare her off, Lire will be back.' She turns to Dawn. 'So, Princess, what are you willing to give us in exchange for our assistance? A favour is a small price to pay.'

A young empire woman stalks over from the far wall, stepping over the rubble of the destroyed ballroom. She's in uniform, slightly flustered from the fight, her long hazel hair in a braid down her back. She attracts the attention of both Zeus and Candace; she grimaces at him and nods at her.

Though her face is hard, when she looks at Candace, her eyes are warm. This *must* be the girl at home Zeus mentioned – Isla. Candace's daughter, and a general in the Ice Empire's army. I know instantly she's one to watch – a strategist to be wary of, or an ally who could help us change the tide.

'My people will begin clearing the last of Lire's soldiers,' the young woman says. 'I'm also having a team set up a hospital for the wounded Bearrans.' She gives Zeus a pointed look, and it hits me that it's because of him that the Ice Empire came. Somehow he convinced her to save us. Of all people, the one who really saved the day was . . . Zeus? 'The *many* wounded Bearrans,' Isla adds. 'I trust we've proven ourselves indispensable allies to Bearra, and we look forward to continuing that, with your compliance.'

Dawn doesn't wait to be introduced; she walks straight up to Isla. They're about the same height, but almost opposite in appearance. One sun and the other ice. 'I would like to thank you for your work today. We can discuss an agreement, but know that this kingdom and its people are not property for sale. I will not bargain away any of Bearra.'

Isla nods stiffly. Every breath she takes, every word, every step, is measured. She is the picture of a perfect soldier. 'I'm happy to help, though you must know our assistance does not come for free.'

Candace exhales. 'I was aiming for a less harsh approach,' she says. 'But yes, let's discuss our terms.'

'No, thank you,' Dawn says. 'As I said, Bearra doesn't trade in such ways.'

'You would rather die than give anything up?' Isla says doubtfully. 'We know now that your story about Bearra having a failsafe is a lie, or you would have activated it. And don't forget that by being here we're risking our alliance with Kara.'

Against the wall, watching us carefully, are Ebony, Maya, and Teddy. Teddy still won't look at Maya, and Ebony stands between them like a shield, shifty, surely desperately wanting to know where her friends are; if they're alive. None of the other pirates have been seen in hours.

Sierra and Arden . . . If they're alive, we would have heard from them by now. They would have crawled their way out of the debris.

Zeus shakes his head at Isla, and I can see why he both loves and hates her. She asserts dominance so easily, just like her mother, without even considering the royal beside her. To a man so arrogant, that fact both irritates and excites him. 'Isla,' he says. 'General. This kingdom has been through a lot. More than you know. How about we give them some time – the night, at least – before we begin making demands of them?'

'There is not much to discuss,' Isla says, Candace standing protectively behind her, though Isla doesn't appear as though she needs it. She reminds me of a mountain, unbothered by the elements, stuck in place. 'My apologies for being unclear when I merely wanted to be polite. In return for protecting the people of Bearra, the Ice Empire requests ownership of the kingdom. The land and everything on it will become ours.'

'Right. Okay.' Maya laughs in disbelief behind us, but everyone is too shocked to pay her any attention.

'I already told you,' Dawn says darkly. The sun has finally begun to rise behind us, casting long shadows, forming silhouettes. The princess could almost be a ghost of this cursed kingdom. 'Bearra will not make such trades. Especially not one as ridiculous as that. I didn't fight to save Bearra from Lire just for it to end up in someone else's hands. At least she's the devil we know.'

'Like I said,' Zeus says quickly, 'let's leave this until tomorrow. Everyone needs time to recover, rest, think.'

'No. The answer is no,' says Dawn. 'If you're only here for such selfish reasons, you may leave immediately. If you would like to stay and save some lives, I might reconsider your worth. But Bearra cannot be bought.'

Candace and Isla share a glance. 'We'll stay for two days,' Candace says. 'If you don't give us an answer by then, we'll leave. But you'll have made an enemy of the empire.'

Zeus turns to Dawn. 'I'll have the soldiers stay and do what they can to help clean up and take care of your people.' My heart warms at his earnest offer. Is he being . . . kind? Oh no. I think he might be our *friend.*

Dawn must feel the same, because gives him a faint smile before turning harshly back to Candace and Isla. 'Enjoy your stay,' she quips, before waving off all three of them.

We slump for a while on the floor, unable to speak, with Ebony, Maya and Teddy. Bearrans – both soldiers and civilians, more than I would have expected to have survived – trickle in and out of the ballroom, getting to work fixing things. General Largon makes an appearance, battered nearly beyond recognition, but she gets to work immediately, ordering what's left of her army. They all leave us alone.

Levi finds his way in, sprinting to Ebony and picking her up in a huge hug. He presses his forehead to her chest and holds her around the stomach. They check each other all over for injuries. 'The others?' he asks, with low expectations.

'I haven't seen anyone,' Ebony replies. 'Sierra was with us for a while, but she had to leave. She never returned.'

Levi frowns. He has a bloody rag tied around his arm where there must be a large cut he's tried to wrap up himself. 'I was with Arden in the beginning, but he took off to look for Sierra.'

My gut twists into a knot. The words keep getting stuck in my mouth before I can say them. *They're gone.*

But as I'm about to try to just croak it out, I feel a tugging in the rubble. An echo. An emotion. It's almost as if I can see them, trapped under there – the exact place burns in a way that I can't *sense*, but feel all the same.

'Teddy!' I call, gesturing for the tired, auburn-haired boy to come over. I begin using magic to carefully clear the broken stone and dust away, and it comes up like a powdery smoke, purple glowing through it as it pours out of my body. The power of it is intense, a non-physical strength, an adrenaline like I've been running from a beast. 'Teddy, can you help?'

My heart races with the thought that Sierra and Arden may not be gone. Not yet. That they're buried deep, probably hurt very badly, but alive somewhere in there.

When Teddy realises what I'm doing – what I must be seeing – he hurries over and uses his magic, almost indistinguishable from mine, to help clear the stone faster. It takes a while, since shifting each part can cause another to fall, each movement a risk, a push and pull, but I soon see something dark – a splash of black hair.

We uncover more, even more careful now, until Sierra and Arden materialise. *Fairies*, I've never felt so relieved. I didn't realise how heavy the weight of their loss was, all on my shoulders alone.

Ebony and Levi race over to them, and we let our magic fade out as they dig Sierra and Arden out the rest of the way themselves. The couple are huddled together, wrapped up in each other – in a cocoon of transparent purple and blue.

Both mine and Arden's magic shifts around them, keeping the rubble away from them as they sleep.

I hold a hand to my mouth and cry.

'The fall must have knocked them out,' Levi says.

'But the magic was enough to stop them being seriously hurt,' Ebony finishes.

'You did this?' Teddy asks me, waving a hand through the cocoon-shield.

I nod, breaths coming fast in relief and pain and so, so many emotions and feelings and exhaustion that I can barely *be* anymore.

'I saw them about to fall, so I pushed my magic towards them, hoping it would protect them . . . Maybe Arden had the same idea and our magic blended, creating a shield.'

'Incredible,' Ebony says. 'How do we get them out?'

I kneel beside them and place a hand over the cocoon. It bubbles at my fingertips as I release the magic, then melts away. The couple are in bad shape beneath, bruised, bleeding, still not waking.

But Ebony feels their pulses and says, 'Their heartbeats are steady. When they wake, they should recover.' Then she wraps her arms around me, making me gasp. 'Thank you for saving them. For everything you've done to save the world. But mostly for this.'

'Oh,' I say. 'Oh. That's—'

'Truly,' Dawn says, stepping up beside me and taking my hand. 'Thank you, Relia. This is a much-needed win.'

I nod shakily, trying not to tear up.

Lark, Wren, and Briar enter the room. *Briar?* They're crying, and Lark has an unconscious woman in his arms. Briar seems the most upset, stumbling and sobbing over the woman's body as Wren does her best to pull them forward.

Maya stands abruptly, her face falling into horror as she recognises the woman, limp and unbreathing. Her weak scream barely makes it past her throat, scratchy and airless. '*Mum*— Mum!' She tries to run to her, but she falls to the floor.

Teddy's arms are around her within a second, but there's nothing to be done.

Not everyone made it through this battle.

CHAPTER 27

There's so much to be done, so much to occupy me, that the two days Candace gave us pass in a blur. Yet the pain of the kingdom's destruction simmers beneath so agonisingly that every second feels dragged out.

All we can do is nurse ourselves and try to help each other. But Dawn, unlike everyone else, has no chance to rest. She has to tell the people of Bearra that the queen and king are dead. She has to be crowned the new queen, even without the now-destroyed crown that once marked Bearran royalty. She has to oversee the rebuilding of the kingdom, and keep the Ice Empire soldiers in check.

It's all so much that I can barely think, can barely consider any of it, can barely feel my emotions or even the physical pain of my bruises from the battle, in any coherent way.

But Queen Dawn of Bearra is strong, and she presses on, still refusing to cave to Candace's demands. Refusing to even see Candace, Isla, or Zeus. Despite all Zeus has done for us. And this new deadline hangs heavy over us.

Sierra and Arden don't yet wake, but their symptoms seem to improve.

Maya and Teddy disappear, likely spending time with Maya's family and preparing for her mother's funeral.

Ebony and Levi stay with me most of the time, probably unsure what to do with Sierra and Arden asleep, and I stay with Dawn until the moments she needs to be left alone, or when she takes meetings I can't be of any help in. When Dawn and I have rare moments alone together, we don't talk, we don't kiss. We just sit together, just touching, breathing.

Lark and Wren stay out on their ship, resting and healing; they only join us at mealtimes. The chaos of the battle, and I imagine the turmoil Briar is going through, has stopped Lark from cooking – something I've learned means danger for him.

It's as if the world is covered in a grey haze, colourless. The weight of the battle hangs heavy in the air, our wrists and ankles shackled to sorrow.

Teddy finally rejoins us at breakfast, just hours before Candace's deadline. He seems worn, with his shoulders slumped more than usual and his eyes dull. And he's still, like all his usual energy has been taken from him. He doesn't eat. There must be so many levels of grief within him – losing Maya's mother, taking Elsie's life, his argument with Maya when she told Dawn to surrender, and the pain of his last encounter with Lire, who showed him so much hatred. 'Maya's family needed time alone,' he tells us quietly. 'None of them are coping well.'

Lark doesn't ask him for news about Briar – he doesn't seem to have the energy.

I hold Dawn's hand under the table. She needs to decide the fate of Bearra. The Ice Empire may be our only chance at safety. But isn't agreeing to their terms no different to surrendering? It may not be as terrible as giving up to Lire, but it still wouldn't be right.

My mind is tumbling over the decision over and over when Zeus enters the dining room. The big, light-toned man shoves open the heavy double-doors, guards panting behind him as if they couldn't hold the prince back. They seem unsure what to do, immediately apologising to Dawn, but she waves them off, head resting in her palm.

Zeus looks dishevelled; panicked, to say the least. 'There's news,' he says. 'I thought I should tell you right away, because . . .'

Dawn's face is flat. What more could surprise or hurt her now? 'Tell us.'

The young man's eyes make their way around the table, and he shuts the doors behind him. He takes a breath and says, cautiously, 'It's about Amora's Territory. And the fairy herself.'

Teddy stands. He's close to the fairy of passion, isn't he? Dawn stands too, moving to him.

'She—' Zeus starts, as if someone is going to be angry at him. But I decide that if they are, even if it's Dawn, I'll defend him. He's proven to be my friend enough times now. 'We just got word that Lire went directly to Amora's Territory when she failed here. It's like she said – she doesn't need Bearra, and she'll get the other fairies.'

'What happened?' demands Teddy, his eyebrows creased in the middle, chest rising and falling rapidly.

'The news is— It's that—'

I rise from my seat and go to stand with the prince. 'What is it?' I ask softly.

His shoulders drop. 'Lire has *taken* Amora. She must have seen that Bearra had a lot of her magic and concluded that the other fairy was working with you. No one knows what's become of Amora, but we all know Lire is more powerful. She took Amora, and she . . . She destroyed Amora's Capital. The city, the palace – all of it is gone.'

Teddy's eyes meet the table, his body shuddering. Purple magic pools at his feet. 'She did this to punish me,' he whispers, and Dawn grips his arms, watching him with concern. 'To send us a message.'

My heart breaks for him, and for the people of Amora's Territory. All that pain . . . Would Lire really do that just to spite *us*?

Of course she would.

'Did the people survive?' I ask Zeus. 'Did they make it out of the city?'

Zeus shakes his head. 'I don't know. It doesn't look like it. From what my connections told me, Lire was merciless.'

I feel as if I'm crumbling into pieces, both the heartbreak and pity towards Amora and her people shattering me, and the feeling of Teddy's grief and shock and anger swirling.

Then I hear a whimper from the other side of the table – Ebony. A girl who I never thought I'd see cry begins sobbing over her breakfast.

Levi is around her, her face pressed against his chest. Lark moves to them, taking her hand.

Of course – Ebony is from Amora's Territory. Does she have family there? A home? I thought the pirates were nomads, but they must have families somewhere. Ebony's could be in any kind of trouble. They may not have survived.

The grief in the room feels like it's going to burst through the walls, caving us in, burying us like Sierra and Arden. Or spattering out, sending debris to the furthest parts of the world. I can't take it. I want to run. My skin is crawling and my arms are shaking and my gut feels as if it's being pulled out of my body.

But I force myself to stay seated, to breathe – this isn't about me.

Dawn meets Zeus's eyes as she holds a shivering Teddy from behind. 'Go back to Candace,' she says gratingly, desperation in her gaze. Right now, she doesn't seem like a queen – but just a girl, an orphan struggling to find her way, struggling to help her friends. Lost and afraid. Cold. 'Tell her she can have whatever she wants. Just tell her she has to save us. She must stop Lire. Before anything else like that ever happens again.' I glance at her, shocked at her fast change of mind, but she shakes her head. 'We will pay the costs we must.'

Zeus's eyes have more empathy in them than I've ever seen. 'Don't forget you still have allies out there,' he says. 'I know them. I've seen them. I'm one of them. You don't have to do this if you don't want to.'

'Prince,' Dawn says tiredly. 'Our invisible allies didn't show up to win our last battle. The Ice Empire did. You are their prince. Go now and tell them the good news. We agree to Candace's terms. Bearra is yours.'

EPILOGUE

SOMEWHERE, SOMETIME ...

One week after agreeing to the Ice Empire's terms, soldiers had already moved in. They stepped through the castle, along the streets, with a polite but clear sense of ownership. An invasion had occurred, and no one could do or say anything to stop it, because there was no better outcome they could have managed. Even if they had pushed on and risked winning the battle on their own – which Relia still thought they might have done – Lire would only return.

Still, despite winning the battle and now having the protection of Candace, Relia knew the war was far from being over. Whatever Lire's big plan was, it was nowhere close to completion. Lire wanted Bearra, but what she had was time. Each colossal battle to humanity was but a moment for her, a task to be completed.

There was still no word from Amora's Territory. *That's what I do,* it was as if Lire were saying, *to the places I don't see value in.* And she had given up on Bearra, so it was only a matter of time.

The only advantage Bearra had was that they expected another attack, and now had the Ice Empire and Candace to back them when it happened.

Grief drowned the entire kingdom now. Everyone had lost someone. Many parts of the kingdom were still in stages of devastation. The people were misplaced and unsettled. An already struggling Bearra was now in the pits of mourning, and what could anyone do but move through it?

Sierra and Arden awoke, to everyone's relief, but they were weak and would be no use to the kingdom for weeks at best. Levi held Ebony through the heartache of her territory being destroyed. Teddy went back to Maya and her family, staying with them in their home. It was Lark and Wren who began to spend time with Relia. They would talk about their childhoods in Muse's Territory, and sometimes Relia would join them on the *Neptune* and they'd sit in silence or tinker about to get their minds off it all.

Nothing was the same.

Dawn was too busy being a queen to give Relia much attention, balancing both Bearra and her deal with Candace. Zeus often stood by Dawn's side protectively, as if proving to her he wasn't on the Ice Empire's side.

But every night, Dawn would meet Relia in their room. She would absently brush her fingers through Relia's hair, braiding it while they discussed anything but what was happening around them. In those moments, barely an hour alone together before they both fell fast asleep, Relia felt as if the world wasn't ending.

How could it be real? She and Dawn, together, truly, with Lire no longer tied to them. The fairy would come for them eventually, of course, but Relia had never expected there to be a reality where she would be alive and with Dawn like this.

And in those few moments she wasn't thinking about war or loss, Relia felt as if she had her happy ending after all.

One night, Relia went down to the kitchens after Dawn fell asleep, running her fingers over the countertop where she and Elsie had taunted each other so many times. She missed the girl, despite everything. Sometimes she liked to come down here, or visit their old room, in remembrance. Not just of her, but of everyone lost in this war. And of her lost relationship with Lire – cruel as it had been. There was so much to mourn.

Relia looked up with a gasp when footsteps echoed through what she thought was an empty kitchen. She tried to slip into the shadows, but it was too late. A young woman appeared, glancing around the room.

Relia cleared her throat.

'Oh!' the light-haired girl said, placing down her lantern. *Isla?* 'My apologies. Relia, isn't it? I didn't expect anyone to be here at this hour. I just . . . wanted some milk.' She shifted awkwardly, and it was the most human Relia had ever seen her. In fact, before this moment, she wasn't entirely sure Isla *was* human.

She had been staying in a guest suite of the castle with Candace for the past week; it was strange seeing them around, and Relia hoped they'd leave soon.

'It's okay,' Relia said. 'You own Bearra now, don't you? You have every right to be down here.'

'I don't own Bearra,' said Isla. 'Nor does Candace. It belongs to the empire. And only for now.'

'For now?'

'Well, I don't like to say it, but . . . our future looks a bit bleak, doesn't it?'

Relia smiled, despite the topic, at Isla's honesty. 'I've found that the only way to live in such times,' Relia said, 'is to not choose blind optimism or pure pessimism. Instead we should appreciate what we still have. Bleakness is a perspective, not a reality.'

'How wise,' Isla teased. 'I can see why your whole . . . group . . . likes you so much.'

'*Group?*'

'You and the prin— queen. And Lire's son, and the *pirates*. Zeus too, apparently. How nice it must be to have such loyal, powerful friends.'

Relia frowned. She thought of them as the *inner circle*, until she'd become part of it. 'I don't know any of them very well. Except for Dawn. At least, they don't know *me* very well. And there's more arguing than sweet, tender moments. Though I suppose they have embraced me, despite . . . all I've done.'

Isla found the milk in a jar and poured herself a glass. 'Maybe I'm jealous,' she said. 'To see a kingdom run by a team of people my age – a queen my age – it makes me wish I could do more in the empire.'

'That's one way to look at it,' Relia replied, taking some milk for herself – she felt awkward now, being down here without any intention to source food. 'But none of us asked for this. Luckily we have the empire to take away all our little problems now, though.' She smiled, and Isla smiled back.

'A funny little world we live in, isn't it?' Isla said.

Relia realised she couldn't tell what Isla was feeling – the empathetic connection that she had with most people hit a block. Was that why the girl had always seemed so emotionless, cold? Relia couldn't make any anticipations about her either. There was a temptation to sneak into her dreams, but Relia had decided already to no longer do that. What was it about Isla that made her different?

'It is a funny little world,' Relia agreed.

'Do you ever wonder,' Isla said, yawning as the deliriousness of tiredness seemed to fall upon her, 'if there might be more? Beyond the ice at the edges of the world. What's out there? Can it really, simply, end?'

Relia swallowed. What a thing to think about, and at this hour? 'That's a better question for you, General, since you live so close to it. As for me, I like our little world. I don't preoccupy myself with thoughts of what's beyond. I can't, without giving myself a headache.'

'One day,' Isla said dreamily, 'I'm going to travel beyond the ice. I'm going to find out what's out there.'

'But why?'

'I just . . .' She shook her head. 'Are you ever drawn to something, and you just *know?*'

Relia thought about Dawn, and all she'd done for her. 'I do.'

'Anyway,' Isla said, waving a hand as she sipped her milk, 'that's a matter for after I win this war.'

Relia was quickly reminded of the young woman's power, momentarily distracted by this strange display of vulnerability. Isla was a powerful, great leader. Strong and assertive, intelligent and strategic. She'd be a threat to any enemy.

But Relia could sense something more. Isla was Candace's daughter for a reason. What motive would Candace have for adopting a child, if not for some kind of gain? Relia felt she understood Candace well enough now to see that she wasn't a natural mothering type. Candace knew there was something about Isla. Not something magical, but . . . *Something.*

Relia decided it could be very beneficial to have Isla on her side. When it came to the end, when Lire and Candace's plans were out in the open and everything became clear, Isla might be a key to winning. Besides, Relia didn't want to be on the wrong side of an Ice Empire general.

'You should join us for dinner tomorrow night,' said Relia, taking Isla's empty glass and moving it to a pile of unwashed glassware. 'It'll be myself and Dawn, and any of our *group* members who show up. Zeus will likely be there. It would be good for you to meet all of us, so you can get to know Bearra and how it's run. And it's always nice to have a new friend.'

Isla's lips quirked up at the sides. 'How compelling your offer would be if I didn't know Zeus would be there. Although you're right. I appreciate the invitation, and I agree. Why shouldn't we be friends?'

'Precisely,' Relia said with a smile, and she was surprised at how genuine it was. 'It's lovely to *in*formally meet you, Isla. The future is in your hands now – I look forward to seeing where you take our little world.'

Relia sat with Dawn on a balcony of the castle, one which reminded her not-so-fondly of the balcony they climbed down in Kara's Territory. The sun was setting before them, the moon brightening above. Dawn glowed in the mixed light, her gold hair a fire and her hazel eyes like citrine. As they drank cups of steaming tea, wrapped in blankets for the cool evening, Dawn smiled.

It was the first time in well over a week that Relia had seen Dawn happy, and the sight lifted a weight off the world. Suddenly the grey around them became colour again, everything brightening and saturating.

Relia smiled back. 'Can you believe it?'

Dawn's irises expanded as she met Relia's eyes. 'Believe what, my love?'

'Us,' Relia explained. 'That we're together. That I'm . . . That I'm here, and real, and we're us.'

'It's the only thing I believe in,' Dawn replied. 'Everything else is merely part of our story. If I don't have us, I have nothing.' She cupped Relia's cheek with her hand and they both giggled, despite the serious nature of their conversation. 'My parents are gone, my kingdom belongs to someone else, my friends are too busy with their own grief to pay me any mind. You are the world I'm fighting for, Relia. Maybe you always have been. I work every moment to be the sunshine, the life force that everyone expects me to be, but my love, I am only the moon. You are the sun. You are the only reason I shine, and without you, I am nothing. This, *us*, is the best gift this war could have given me. I know it's selfish, but let me have this one flaw – I wouldn't change a thing if it meant losing you.'

Relia moved closer to Dawn, setting down her tea before it spilled. 'I wouldn't either,' she whispered, her body a whirlpool of heat. 'I would end the world a thousand times to be with you.'

Dawn kissed her gently, quickly, and said, 'Here's to being flawed.'

Relia kissed her back. 'To being selfish.'

'And . . .' Dawn kissed her again. 'To love at the end of the world.'

Acknowledgements

It was not easy to write a romance in which the characters are already in love – and yet have to fall in love again (or more?) over the course of the novel. While this has been one of the hardest books for me to write, as I found myself lost again and again, I knew exactly what I wanted for Relia and Dawn, and their pining, pedestal-ing and all-consuming love.

Like all of my main characters, Relia has so much of myself in her. She's as shy as she is fiery, always puts her own needs last, and deals with crippling anxiety. Not everyone will understand her, but I know that I, too, would go to the ends of the earth for love. Who wouldn't do some questionable things for their soulmate? Or are Relia and I just Scorpios?

So, onto the acknowledging; mostly I'd like to thank myself. I've done it again! Three books out in the world. (I'm not convinced this isn't a dream.)

My hugest gratitude goes to my editing team, because their passion for and impact on my books can't be understated. Pauline Menchavez has a beautiful understanding of prose that ensures every word and phrase comes across exactly as intended – or even better than I intended. Ellyssa Paik watches my story and timelines like a hawk, and thank goodness, because she always catches when I say it's been a three-day journey but the characters have been gone a week. And Lizzie Augustine's heart shines through her eye for detail mixed with her deep understanding of my characters.

Haylee Buswell, my designer, has made magic yet again with her beautiful work. How does she keep getting more talented?

And of course, the cover art is once again by my grandfather, Robert Ixer, who I dearly miss. Not having him here hasn't gotten any easier between the release of Cygnus Curse and now.

Finally, a note of love to the queer community. The world of Woken Kingdom may be accepting of two queens, but the world we live in is poisoned with unacceptance of a thing as beautiful and simple as love. I'm so grateful that the wonderful queer people I know have led me to writing a book that so deeply touches my own heart. Dawn and Relia's story is for everyone, but mostly for those who long to see two perfectly imperfect but wonderfully strong women have a happily ever after.

Can't wait for more Woken Kingdom? Follow Isla and Zeus in their plans for world domination in *Spellbound Empire*, coming late 2024.

Follow @PoppysVintageBooks on Instagram and TikTok for Woken Kingdom content, and sign up to the Poppy's Pages newsletter for sneak peeks at upcoming stories!

poppyspagesediting.com/newsletter-sign-up

About the author

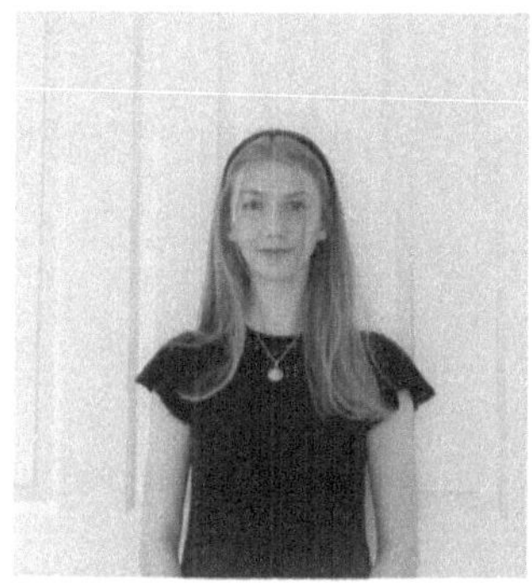

Poppy Rose Solomon's YA novels reflect the traumas and lessons she experienced as a teenager, and she loves creating 'unlikable' characters who learn to heal themselves. Evoking inspiration and escapism is the goal of her storytelling. From her home on the Sunshine Coast, she freelances as a YA editor and coach through her business Poppy's Pages, and runs the Writing YA With Poppy podcast. Woken Kingdom is her first series, with plenty more to come.